THERE WAS BLOOD ON HIS CHEEK AND IN HIS EYE . . .

Roger smiled at me, and it was not a reassuring smile. So help me, he was enjoying himself. Then his foot thrust out at me like the head of a thick snake and simply pinned my hand, gun, chest and back to the piling behind me. He bent forward with an athlete's fluidity of motion and pulled the gun out of my hand. I expected at that moment that he would shoot me and drop me off the pier, but instead he took his foot off my chest and threw the gun far out into the bay. I stood up, only inches from the end of the pier. Roger was still grinning. "You just run out of runnin' room, man," he said, advancing on me as he wound up for a final blow. . . .

DIE AGAIN, MACREADY

"*ENGAGING, OFFBEAT . . . with regular injections of brisk rough-stuff and raw, amusing dialogue, this is a solidly gritty follow-up for shamus Binney.*"

—KIRKUS REVIEWS

SIGNET MYSTERY

DIE AGAIN, MACREADY

Jack Livingston

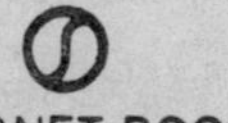

A SIGNET BOOK
NEW AMERICAN LIBRARY

PUBLISHER'S NOTE

This novel is a work of fiction. Names, characters, places, and incidents either are the product of the author's imagination or are used fictitiously, and any resemblance to actual persons, living or dead, events, or locales is entirely coincidental.

This is an authorized reprint of a hardcover edition
published by St. Martin's Press.

SIGNET TRADEMARK REG. U.S. PAT. OFF. AND FOREIGN COUNTRIES
REGISTERED TRADEMARK—MARCA REGISTRADA
HECHO EN CHICAGO, U.S.A.

SIGNET, SIGNET CLASSIC, MENTOR, PLUME, MERIDIAN AND NAL BOOKS
are published by New American Library,
1633 Broadway, New York, New York 10019

First Signet Printing, December, 1985

1 2 3 4 5 6 7 8 9

PRINTED IN THE UNITED STATES OF AMERICA

To my daughters, Laura and Juliet

When William Charles Macready (1793–1873) played Macbeth, he performed the death scene with such passion and conviction that the gallery would stand up and shout:

> "Die again, Macready!"

Old actors' tale

1

The door I was facing was the kind that talks back to you—I don't mean electronically, but with a mute rumble of its history, like a wet-eyed old man on the park bench sitting next to you. The lock had been smashed, picked, slipped, and hacked so often that a whole new piece of wood had been grafted on. Even this new piece had extra holes in it where locks had been extracted, the holes plugged up, and newer ones drilled in. It had been painted over and over again, including the aluminum numeral 3 in the center. It appeared that no paint could grip the greasy breath of the city that clung to the wood. The paint sagged and slipped. It was landlord green.

I raised my knuckles and hammered on the door just below the numeral. There wasn't any indication of what floor this room was on. This was room number 3 on *this* floor, and *this* floor was the fourth, a knee-cracking journey up the dismal stairway that angled around the shaft of a broken elevator.

I rapped again, harder this time. "Open up, Pelfrey," I said. I didn't think it would take much racket to carry through the rotting wood. "Open up! I know you're in there!"

My silences are different from others'. In the apparent absence of any sound, my other senses jump. I thought, now, that in jarring the door with my fist I had loosened exhalations of the room. A trickle of breath that was redolent of very rotten teeth had transpired from the cracks of the jamb.

The uneasiness made me shout. "C'mon, Pelfrey. Open up. It's all over now." I stood very still with my fingertips against the door and tried to feel the vibrations of anyone moving inside. Instead, I became aware of someone standing next to me. I turned and looked at him to watch him say:

"You ain't cops."

He was a young black man, about my height but so skinny that his pants ballooned around his legs. A dirty peach-colored T-shirt hung down over his waist. I held a five in front of him. "You want this?" He nodded. "Go down to the desk and get me the key for this room. Tell the manager there's a five in it for him, too.'' His black eyes measured me. When he turned to go, the light caught the neck of the pint of Gypsy Rose in his back pocket. He disappeared down the stairway.

I hammered again. ''Arnold Pelfrey,'' I called out. ''Open the door and let me in. Nobody's going to hurt you. I just want to talk to you.'' I glanced down the hall toward the stairway and several doors narrowed their gaps to a millimeter's breadth. I began to pound on the door with a rhythmic beat. ''Open the door, Pelfrey,'' I sang. ''Open up.''

They arrived with the key at last. First things first: I gave them each a five. They stood by with restrained curiosity while I put the key in the deadfall lock. The cylinders snapped open but the door sagged only slightly.

''It's bolted from the inside,'' I said. I looked at the manager whose sixty-year-old, gray, seamed face had taken on the expression of inevitability. He put his hands in the pockets of his sweater. ''What do you think?'' I asked him. He pursed his lips and shrugged. This was not a new program for him. I handed him another five and leaned against the door. My shoulder felt the soft pop of the screws on the other side as they came out of the barrel bolt. The door swung open.

The manager had been wise enough not to step inside with me and the young black man. The two of us were back out soon enough. I held a handkerchief over my face, and the lad reached for his Gypsy Rose. I stood to one side and took several deep breaths of carpet dust. ''How about it?'' I said to the kid. ''Will you sell me a drink?'' He passed the Gypsy to me.

After I'd taken a belt, I poured some over my handkerchief and put the handkerchief up over my nose. The fumes stung my eyes as I looked at Pelfrey hanging from the ancient gas pipe in the ceiling. I looked long enough to make sure that it was Pelfrey. The kid had moved to the window as if to crack it open. The words choked me, but I got them out. ''Don't touch that window. Don't touch anything, or the cops will have your ass on a griddle.'' He gave me a quick look of gratitude and retreated from the room. I came out after him and shut the door. ''What do you say?'' I asked the manager. He shrugged. He hadn't even bothered to look.

''Go down and call the cops,'' I suggested. The two of them took hold of the idea and started down the stairs, but not before I'd purchased the residue of the Gypsy Rose for another two-fifty.

I made another wine-soaked gas mask and slipped back into the room. I looked at the suspended body, but not the face. "Where is it, Arnold?" I asked him. The only answer was the roar of machinery in my head.

I was careful not to move the chair tipped over underneath the body as I reached into his back pocket. In the left, the wallet pocket, there was nothing. There were keys in his left pants pocket, but they were house keys, office keys, and car keys. No sign of a safety-deposit box or luggage-locker key. The right pants pocket held only thirty-nine cents and a crumpled dollar bill. I put it all back.

The coat on the bed had nothing in it at all. His belt was also on the bed, which explained the droop of his pants. I examined the belt for a money slit. Nothing. I stepped back and looked again. The machinery began to whine and moan.

I was getting high on the fumes from the handkerchief. I took it off my face and breathed as little as possible while my eye traveled from the upended chair to the suspended feet to the knot at the nape of the neck and the companion knot at the gas pipe. The twisted strips of bedsheet hadn't been tied around his neck with anything so fancy as a hangman's noose, but neither was it two half hitches. The knot at the straight vertical pipe pointing down from the ceiling also showed a certain intelligent experience in suspending loads.

I went over and examined the window. It hadn't been dusted in centuries. I looked at the three-drawer dresser and used my handkerchief to open each of the drawers. They were empty. The dresser had not been moved. Dust curled up from the carpet around the claw feet.

"Where is it, Arnold?" I demanded. I got down on my knees by the bed and raised the mattress far enough to slide my hand underneath and run my palm over the springs. I was in this regrettable posture when I felt a heavy hand on my shoulder. It grasped my suitcoat and raised me from the side of the bed. I turned to confront a strong but displeased countenance. The police are never far from Times Square hotels.

"What are you looking for?" asked the face.

"A quarter of a million dollars," I told it.

2

The face wrinkled with disgust, and the detective behind it said, "Jesus. You stink like a wino."

I jerked my head toward the man in the noose above us. "You like the way he smells better?" I showed him my wine-soaked gas mask.

He seemed to appreciate the idea of the mask, although there was a lack of enthusiasm in his eyes for me. His eyes, in fact, were demanding explanations—fast ones, good ones. "I'm a licensed investigator," I said. I hauled out the tickets and flashed them. "Joe Binney's my name. But before I say anything else, let me explain that I'm deaf. I'm totally deaf. I can only communicate by lip reading. I have to see you when you talk."

He didn't like it. Nobody does. For that matter, neither do I.

"It's just so we don't get mixed up," I said placatingly. "I have to see what you're saying."

There was a plainclothesman and two patrolmen with him in the room, prowling around, screwing things up. When I dared to take my eyes off the detective's face, I could see that the three subordinates had enjoyed watching their boss being handed a bomb.

He was not unaware of it. "You can talk all right, though, huh?" he asked me.

"Yessir."

"Start talking," he suggested. He looked as if he were going to read *my* lips—right down to the lungs.

"Well, it all began . . . ."

"Cut out the crap," said the nice policeman. "This guy your client?"

"Nossir."

"So?"

"So what?"

"So who's your client?" He took out a cigar and began to unwrap it. It would give him something to chew on other than me.

"William Macready," I said. The eyes bored into me over the cigar and prompted a fuller response. "Well-known star of stage, screen, and television."

"Never heard of him," said the detective. "Hey!" He glanced around the room, freezing his cohorts mid-smile. "Any of you guys ever hear of William Macready?" His grimace gave the name what is sometimes known as a special reading. The three faces were sea-bottom primitive, preternaturally blank. "Nobody ever heard of him," the detective concluded for me.

"Well," I began, "he's starred in numerous off-Broadway productions and has had prominent supporting roles in *on*-Broadway productions, not to mention innumerable television . . ."

"Are you a dick or a flack?"

"All right," I surrendered. "Let's start over and do it your way. William Macready, my client, is a working actor, well known in the business. The man on the string," I gestured aloft, "is Arnold Pelfrey, my client's bus . . . *ex*-business manager. To the best of our knowledge, Mr. Pelfrey absconded with about two-hundred and fifty thousand dollars of my client's money."

"About," said the detective. "Doesn't anybody know for sure?"

"For sure," I replied. "Two-hundred and sixty-six thousand, one-hundred and twenty-two dollars and thirty-three cents."

"Sixteen-thousand bucks difference is nothing to you guys, huh?"

"My client is painfully aware of every cent," I assured him.

But not so aware as the three faces staring hungrily at the hapless Arnold. Their expressions were a curious mixture of respect and regret. Arnold was no longer simply a poor silly bastard strung up in a flea bag but, indeed, a man worth over a quarter of a million dollars. On the other hand, he was a corpse *(regret)* and you may beat a corpse until your arms ache, yet the only answer you will obtain is an assortment of bad smells.

"I want this room searched," announced the detective. I blanched.

I had begun to speak, but there seemed to be a trapdoor closing in my throat. I pushed it open. "I may have further information on this case, sir," I said. "May I ask to whom I have the honor of speaking?"

"Shope," he said. "Matt Shope. Lieutenant Shope. O.K.?"

"And the three gentlemen with you?" I prompted.

"None of your fucking business," said Lieutenant Detective Matthew Shope.

The three policemen had begun ripping drawers out of the dresser and dismantling the bed as I followed the wake of Lieutenant Shope to the door, where he paused.

"You the one who busted in?" he asked me.

"It wasn't much of a bust," I told him. "I just leaned on it, and it practically jumped open. I got the manager's permission first. He was here when I went in."

"But the room was locked from the inside, huh?"

"At least by this entry it was, sir."

He ruminated on this. "It's the only entry," he mused. "And that window hasn't been touched in a million years." He turned around to stare at the dangling Arnold. Then he turned back to me. "This guy's got a quarter of a million dollars and he hangs himself?" The thick gray eyebrows climbed.

"It looks that way, doesn't it?"

"There's a switch, though, huh? The money isn't here."

"Apparently not."

"Apparently not," he repeated. He seemed to listen to the two words reverberate from the interior walls of his skull. His face turned crimson, and the veins jumped out on his neck. "*Brace!*" he barked. If I'd been able to hear him, I suppose I would have jumped a foot. As it was, I turned around slowly and put my hands up high on the greasy wall. The plaster dimpled under my fingers.

My wallet didn't have a quarter of a million dollars in it. *Surprise*. The lining of my coat was not reinforced with thousand-dollar bills. *Regrets*. The busy fingers prowled around my person as I memorized the relief map on the wall. There were rivers, valleys, mountains, and deep forests of mold. I was spun around by the shoulder to face Lieutenant Shope. "I told you to turn around," he roared.

"I can only understand you when I'm looking at you," I told him.

I was shoved aside then by the crew coming in from the meat wagon. Flashbulbs started popping, and when they'd stopped, poor Arnold was eased down from his gas-pipe gallows. The searchers had struck out, although every conceivable cranny in the room had been probed and eviscerated. Now they stood in the midst of the M.E.'s busy crew and stared speculatively at me. I smiled at them blankly.

I promised Shope to write a statement and bring it down to the precinct later. Then, at his bidding ("I want you the fuck out of here, Binney"), I accompanied him down to the front desk, where the manager, his gray brow unfurrowed by care, was working out a racing form.

"I'm sealing off that room," Shope told him. "I don't want anybody going near it. You understand?" The manager signaled his comprehension by a barely perceptible nod and returned to the racing form. Shope and his band of merry men departed.

"How about it?" I asked the manager. "Can you rent me the room?"

"You heard the lieutenant," the gray face said. "I can't let you screw around up there."

"You can rent me the room next to it, can't you?"

He pulled a dirty blank card out of a stack of dirty blank cards and shoved it toward me across the counter. I stared into its gray depths and saw the scowling face of Lieutenant Shope. Somehow, I did not want to offer up a sample of my handwriting.

"I am seized with periods of recurrent illiteracy," I told the manager. "Would you mind doing the writing for me?"

There was almost respect in his eyes as he looked back at me. He turned the card around and picked up the stick pen securely anchored on its chain. "Name?" he inquired.

"John Doe."

"How do you spell it?"

3

The impossible takes a little longer, but locked-room puzzles we solve immediately, sir, compliments of Joe Binney, Esq., Private Investigations at your service.

I fingered the key to room five on its slippery linoleum tag in my pants pocket. It made a nice companion to the key for room three, which I had surreptitiously retained. I strode up Broadway, my head abuzz with plans and schemes.

Over a roast beef sandwich at the Cordial, I detached the key to number three from its heavy block. After lunch, I dropped number three off at a little locksmith booth on Eighth Avenue and went up to the Woolworth's only a block or so farther uptown. Spring, spring was in the air, and the dirty newspapers blew vigorously along the gutters. Mendicants stared dreamily at the sky on which corpulent white clouds were scudding and wondered if the season had come, after all, to delouse their overcoats. The season was very close to the opening of trout season, and that alone guaranteed Woolworth's compliance with my plans.

I stood patiently in line at Woolworth's to pay for my ninety-nine cent purchase and retraced my steps down the block to pick up my keys. I sat once more in the Cordial over a bourbon and soda to refasten the old number three key to its linoleum. I was now as well prepared as I ever am, although I don't know if it's wise to confess that here and now.

The manager at the old hotel was talking to someone on the telephone, and even though I am deaf and his mouth was hidden, I had the unshakable conviction that he was calling his bookie. His gray complexion was suffused with the mildest blush of excitement. I waited patiently until he had put down the phone and lovingly folded his racing form on the counter.

"I forgot to give you back the key to number three," I told him, placing the big block on the counter. He looked at me, and his eyes, though phlegmatic, were not stupid. He took the key and put it in its proper pigeonhole. I began my trudge up the stairs to room five.

As I had expected, room number five was the twin of number three. These rooms were strangers to neither suicide nor murder, and in Arnold's fate, I saw pretty much of a toss-up between the two. True enough, the room had been locked from the inside, but I thought that perhaps I had the solution to that problem in my pocket. Proving that it could have been murder, however, did not mean that it *was* murder. The immediate picture was suicide.

Something kept me from sitting on the chair at the little crooked table by the window. It was a kitchen chair and the mate to the one on which Arnold, however temporarily, had stood. I sat on the edge of the bed, which offered the sigh and sag that suggested many other occupants having sat there before—in this hunched posture—elbows on knees.

I took on the immediate picture first and tried to reconstruct a suicide. As Lieutenant Shope had piercingly observed, thieves who have made off with a quarter of a million dollars are not usually given to doing away with themselves. *Usual*, however, is a slippery word, like *average*. As the ghost of many a policeman could assure you, there is no *average* thief, no average drunk, no average wife beater, no average swindler. Mild and meek, and butter-melting smooth, they can turn with the totally unexpected gun or knife and murder you—or commit suicide. People are no more alike than their fingerprints are.

So what had been eating Arnold?

It was spring, after all, I forced myself to recollect, although there was no sign of it in this dim and dirty room. A yellow film of exhausted cigarette smoke covered the window like the filter on a camera lens. The sky through that window was not blue, but grayish green. Still, it was spring, the season for suicides—jumpers, pill-droppers, hang-ups like Arnold, and drowners. Psychologists had said that it was the empty promise of spring that got to them all, the realization that, while things were getting better for Nature, they were not getting better for *them*. I'm sure that's part of it, but I think exhaustion is part of it too after the long months of shivering, of wet shoes, of endless colds, the flu, what have you: the season when warmth has a dollar sign attached to every degree on the thermometer. The struggle: and then the mockery of spring pointing out that the struggle indeed does naught availeth. Nothing has really changed, only a few degrees of warmth without dollar signs attached. I suppose it could put a fellow like Arnold up on the string.

But with a quarter of a million dollars under his arm?

Macready had hired Arnold Pelfrey to be his business manager for one fundamental reason only: Arnold Pelfrey was honest. I was fifty percent of the reason Macready thought so. I had run a check on Pelfrey and come up empty. The other fifty percent was pure Macready. "He rang a bell," Macready had said after talking to the small man in his worn blue suit. "All I want is a guy who is honest and isn't a nut. You know—a *Get-Rich-Quick-Wallingford*. Just somebody I can trust not to go south with the bundle or invest it in an emerald mine in Arkansas." Macready, like many actors, so I've heard, prided himself on being a judge of character.

Then what went wrong? Did Pelfrey simply steal the money, piss it away at the track, and hang himself in remorse? Where were the stubs? Did he blow it all in on a blondined whore with eyes like diamonds and a heart to match? Where were the fancy clothes, the platinum wristwatch, the *aura* that would get him the right table at a decent spot? The clothes that Arnold had been wearing in his last moment would have made the busboy at a cafeteria blanch. Had he been secretly in love—oh, this was far more dangerous—with some sweet, young, poor-but-honest, soft, yielding thing, given her the money, told her to "Go out and live!" and then sacrificed himself on the altar of true, pure, sexless love? You think it doesn't happen?

"Arnold, Goddamn it," my words drifted silently in the damp, stained room, "where is it?"

The picture of penitent suicide was a little too pat, too trite. This was where my methods parted company with those of the police. *I* had no backlog, no bulging files of unsolved crimes to diminish. *I* was not looking for an answer that would simply fit the facts, the evidence. I was looking for Mr. Macready's money, and it seemed to me, now, that I would have to look far, far past the slowly twisting Arnold.

I continued my reconstruction. Arnold was shorter than I am, but he was not a midget. I stared speculatively at the kitchen chair and gauged the height to the ceiling. This was, after all, a very old hotel, and ceilings were high. I picked up the chair and placed it beneath the gas pipe in the center of the room. Was the gas pipe here cut to the same length as the one in number three? I couldn't judge it from here. I steadied myself on the shaky back of the chair and stood on the seat. From there, I reached ceiling-ward. My fingers barely grazed the capped end of the pipe. It suggested that Arnold would not have been able to stand on the chair and hitch his bedsheet strands to the vertical pipe.

Suggested only, however, and, as the Scottish say, not proven. My chair in number five, the apparent mate to the one in number three, might have been shortened in the legs to even it. The gas pipe in number three might be an inch or so longer. Both the chair and the pipe might conspire together in number three to let Arnold succeed, where he would have failed here. The knot securing the bedsheet to the pipe had been an inside rolling hitch, and while these are usually tied around a stanchion or what have you, they can be made up on the line and then pushed up and quickly tightened with a strain on the hauling part. I'd done it when I was a boot in the Navy, but could Arnold? Did he know about such things? Could he have done it, trembling, on his tiptoes above the kitchen-chair gallows trap?

I reserved judgment, although the outcome was important to

me. If he did commit suicide, I would be looking for a package. If he didn't, I would be looking for a person or persons who had the package. I sort of preferred the first anwer. The time had come, however, to use my spare key.

I did not want to be caught surreptitiously opening my door a crack to see who might be lurking. People with ears have it easy: They put their ears against the door and listen; they can even use those cute drinking glasses to amplify the sound. As far as my ears are concerned, however, there could be a squad of policemen doing calisthenics in the hall. I slowed my breathing down and tried to relax (the thumping of one's heart gives the *illusion* of sound). When I felt that I was ready, I put my fingertips against the door and tried to "listen" for vibrations from them, safecracker style.

Except for the unmistakable trembling of Times Square traffic, there didn't seem to be any vibrations on the other side of the door. I got hold of the illicit key number three in my hand so there wouldn't be any fumbling around with the lock and quickly slipped next door.

And what was the difference? Because there *was* a difference. With my back against the rotting wood of door number three, I surveyed a room that was the virtual twin of the one I'd just come from. And yet it was different. It wasn't the curtains. They were just as dirty as those in room five. The chair, which had been uprighted by the police and placed properly next to the drop-leaf table, had a normal proportionate relationship to that table. No legs had been sawed. The gas pipe jutted down at approximately the same length. The weary dresser sagged in place, its violated drawers put back in their proper slides.

I guessed it was the redolence. After the police had dusted for prints they had thrown open the window, which the manager later wisely closed, and sealed the room shut again, driving rain being what it is. In the sealed room, the odor of death had penetrated the crumbling plaster, had seeped into the rug and the poor rag of a bedspread tossed on the disheveled, unsheeted bed. The odor informed the room—and the image of Arnold, too, like a ghost in my mind's eye, dangled mistily from his gas pipe. I was spooked.

I shook it off. I went over and got the chair, put it under the gas pipe and went through the identical routine. The results were identical. It was unlikely that Arnold had been alone in his last moment.

That left the locked-room controversy. I took out my Woolworth's purchase of a spool of six-pound monofilament fishing line and cut off an arm's length of it with my pen knife.

The barrel bolt still hung forlornly on its single screw, but I didn't have any trouble locating the screws that had burst out of the door when I pushed it. They had rolled up against the wall or had been kicked there by prowling cops. I inserted them back in their holes, pushing them in like so many thumbtacks, so that the barrel bolt was more or less replaced in its original seat. I set the bolt in the open position, and with my monofilament line tied a cunning knot around the thumb latch of the bolt. I put my fingers up against the door to feel if there was anyone outside. Satisfied with the palpable silence, I slipped quickly into the hall, leading my fishline around the jamb, and then closed the door gently. I pulled the line toward me through the crack of the jamb, and felt the bolt slide into the lock barrel. Then I gave the line a quick jerk, and the thread came out as I had planned. It hadn't broken; it had slipped the knot, as it was supposed to do—as the murderer had known it would. The murderer was someone who knew at least as much about seagoing knots as I did.

Murderer. Yes. Arnold Pelfrey had been murdered. I leaned against the door to knock the bolt loose, as it had been before. I turned my extra key in the lock, as the murderer had, and went back to room five.

4

Once upon a time, they say, there was a fellow named Heil in these parts who ran a restaurant with the homey name of Heil's Kitchen. When the character of the neighborhood became clear, they lengthened out the letter *i* in Heil and called the area Hell's Kitchen. During Prohibition, the police called the fat part of it "The Roaring Forties." Now much of the area is known by the pallid name, "The Clinton District." This district includes San Juan Hill, once the habitat of cultured blacks who later drifted up to Harlem. The little brick church of St. Benedict the Moor, however, still stands on Fifty-third Street as a memento of better days. On the south, this neighborhood is generally bordered by Fortieth Street, on the east by Eighth Avenue, and on the west, most often by Tenth Avenue, of *Slaughter On* fame, and sometimes by the Hudson River, the lordly Hudson, itself, which cruises past and smiles. The original Hell's Kitchen extended all the way from Thirtieth Street to Fifty-ninth.

It's a screwy part of the world, all right. It's an amalgam of the theater district, with its remnants of Broadway's glory, of the large old Irish families who burst out of their tenement flats, of the huge Mediterranean and Mideastern mixture that pours down Ninth Avenue, the Puerto Ricans, and even some of the blacks who have stubbornly held on. If you rub it between your fingers you can feel the fabric of the families who have stretched themselves taut to sustain the idea of a neighborhood. It is pretty tough sustaining: Eighth Avenue, never quite a grand boulevard, is now, in its lower precincts, the Minnesota Strip, where young girls fleeing the snow and boredom of the Midwest come to sample the sour gray slush of Manhattan's gutters, the boxing skills of their pimps, and the cold hands of their customers. The solid old establishments of McGirr's pool parlor, Jim Downey's Steak House, and Jimmy Ray's (Gilhooley's in an earlier avatar) now share the avenue with porno flicks and peep shows. Studded amid the sleaze are the new apartment buildings with their special branch of sleaze, cold-faced impostors to the notion of a domicile, lacking even the amenities that poverty is sometimes known to invite.

These glacial upthrustings were the harbingers to New York's favorite monopoly game—gentrification—by which working-class, family-raising folks are booted out of their neighborhoods to make room for airline stewardesses, flacks, and stock grifters. It's not all bad, of course. In the Forties on stretches between Eighth and Eleventh, some working people—mostly theater people—have turned old buildings into town houses of startling taste and distinction.

My client, Macready, was not one of these. My client, Macready, rented his digs, and I honestly believe that he would have preferred to rent his clothes. Macready did not like to buy things because buying things meant parting with money. The idea of buying a town house would have stunned him. To say that Macready is cheap is to intimate that ducks are aquatic. Yet Macready lived in a penthouse. How can this be?

I pondered this as I approached his dwelling in the twilight. It was an isolated tenement in the midst of what would have been a realtor's "package," were it not for Macready's intransigence. Barren pasture on which grew only splintered bricks and broken wine bottles extended to either side of his dwelling. In these empty lots were cavities from which teeming buildings had been uprooted and the tenants dispersed. Dispersing Macready was another matter.

The penthouse he lived in perched like a slouch hat on the roof of a five-story tenement that was part of the spawn of many thousands of such red-brick, narrow-windowed buildings in New York. The penthouse, itself, had been the afterthought of some nut who had bought the building, gotten permission from a crooked building inspector, and proceeded to erect a kind of shed on the roof, where he lived while collecting rent from the people below. It had been virtually abandoned when Macready came upon it years ago, and the new owners, agog at the opportunity to make the little shed actually pay for itself, signed what they considered to be a very sharp deal with Macready. Had such a lease been made on normal property, these gentlemen would have been stoned to death at the next conference of New York realtors. (Are there such conferences? Are there such stonings?) At any rate, the lease permitted Macready's hand, with viselike power, to close around their throats.

A pretty picture it was for them indeed, when Elephantine Projects, Inc. decided to build a package in the area. The buildings around them were all quickly evacuated and dismantled. Their own tenants on the five legitimate floors were dispersed with unseemly haste, and the unlucky realtors stood in the chambers of Elephantine Projects, Inc. with their fountain pens drawn and their tongues protruding. The wrecking ball stood ready, but Macready would not move.

Of course, all the windows in the building except his own were quickly blinded with sheet metal on which huge portentous X's were slashed in paint (a procedure now against the law, I believe), but that didn't faze Macready. A curious train of human detritus began to stream in and out of the doorway of the building, a doorway that had lost any pretense of being a civilized portal. There was no bell to it, no lock, and even the handle had been wrenched off. The door swung vacantly with every breeze and was properly shut only when the little covey of vagrants and miscreants in the hallway were up to some mischief they wanted not to be seen.

Groups of these undesirables seemed to appear in schools, like varying species of fish. One of the earliest species to appear were the black queens, black male prostitutes in netted tank tops and other, more exotic habiliment, whose voices, Macready told me, coo and twitter like birds, but whose ropelike black satin muscles betrayed any concept of femininity. They congregated on the worn stoop of the building, impeding both ingress and egress, and not infrequently imposed their invitations on passersby.

Again, Macready had not been fazed. When the landlord appeared at the penthouse door wearing a very sly look in his eye and asked Macready how he could stand living where such creatures hung out, Macready noted that it was an unlooked-for benefit. He pointed out that ordinarily he would have to range far and wide to seek out these types to study them—they *were* interesting characters—but now, what do you know? Here they were on his doorstep. When the landlord departed, it was Macready who had the sly look in his eye. The landlord had blood in his.

There seemed hardly a pervert, degenerate, or miscreant in New York who did not eventually circulate to Macready's doorstep. They had been recruited to instill dread in the tenant, but in Macready they stimulated only professional interest. He marveled at them and made copious sketches and notes. He drove the landlord a little nuts.

The landlord stopped sending good money after bad and gave up recruiting these offspring of the gutter for Macready's delectation. However, the doorway had become a habitat independent of any inducement, and the troop of vagrants continued to file in and out. They were now of an even lower order—except for those who preyed on them. Careless of excretory functions even at best, they were often incontinent, and the wine, malodorous in the bottle, was even worse when excreted and running down the stone steps.

Macready's nose was made of iron, his guts of concrete.

The penthouse Macready defended was not the kind so usually seen in the glossy movies of the thirties associated with the aura of Cole Porter and Fred Astaire. It shed no radiance on any skyline. It was a *shabby* penthouse—a mockery of a penthouse.

The nut who erected the shed had built it out of cinderblock, (concrete blocks would have come crashing down through all five floors). The shed covered most of the roof and left a space of only two feet between the cinder walls and the coping of the roof. Access to the roof could be gained only through a narrow door that opened inside the main room of the apartment. The windows were mostly "picture windows" sealed into the walls, and whose pictures consisted of disheartening stretches of parking lots, gin mills, abandoned buildings, and the windowless back of a warehouse.

Once you arrived, breathless, at Macready's front door, you realized why he had little fear of burglars. The entrance to the penthouse was the original heavy, metal-clad fire door that had been installed as an exit to the roof. Behind that door, he had a deadlock that would have broken the nerve of Willie Sutton.

The four rooms comprising the apartment were disproportionate. The main room took up most of the space, with a kitchen and bath at the back. The bedrooms were to the left as you came in, one of them being his, with an oversized bed, and the other a guest-room catchall. Boiler heat had been cut off long ago; Macready kept himself warm with a gas-fed space heater that was probably totally illegal.

Most of Macready's furniture (not the bed) was the instantly recognizable characteristic of any of the main cities of America . . . i.e., it was junk. New York, New Orleans, and San Francisco are all distinguished by their junk because these are cities that have artists living in them, and the artists furnish their rooms with junk, it being all that they can usually afford. And artists, being by definition creative, do interesting and tasteful things with junk—to the despair of Grand Rapids. The Salvation Army stores, the Volunteers of America, and other charity establishments have always been the Bloomingdale's of the creative world. However, the true mark of New York's creative decor is furnishings that are not bought at all, but found.

The curbstones of New York are a bazaar that makes the *souk* of Port Said seem empty by comparison. This bazaar operates on a premise that the worried pundits of Wall Street might do well to look into. *People throw things away*—quite good, quite usable things. *Other people pick them up and carry them home. Other* people throw *other* things away. *The people who threw things away in the first place come by and pick up the things that other people threw away.*

Now simply throwing things away, I mean casting them right out into the street, is strictly forbidden by any number of fingerwagging statutes in New York. Therefore, this whole peripatetic *souk* is carried on by twilight. Nothing is ever thrown away in front of its original dwelling. It is, so as to deceive the authorities, carried a block or so away and surreptitiously dropped. So that you may sometimes notice of an evening a man walking down the street with a couch on his back, only to see him a few minutes later sprightly retracing his steps *sans* couch. If you are an idler in the area, you will then see *another* man with the same couch on his back purposefully striding toward his dwelling. It is a magnificent barter system that makes all of its customers happy and doesn't cost a dime.

Macready's apartment was a veritable showcase of this market. I don't mean that there was a great deal of furniture, but that the furniture was being constantly upgraded. Macready's nimble eye would light on a curbstone coffee table, a chair, a settee that represented a distinct improvement in his status. So he would pick it up, carry it up the backbreaking six flights of stairs, and on his next trip out would carry down the supplanted piece and discard it. Upward Mobile Macready! Not only did it not cost him a dime, it kept him fit. He had, for instance, a huge, curved, down sofa, quite obviously the remnant of a bankrupt whorehouse, that must have cost him quite a struggle to get up the stairs.

I stepped over the vagrant sprawled on Macready's stoop, and recoiled as much from the sight of his red, swollen, pustule-covered calves as I did from the customary stench of the hallway, which he had recently reinforced. The reward of toiling up the endless series of stairs from landing to landing was that, as one ascended, the odor thinned. Still, it was spooky. The entrances to all the apartments had been nailed shut, and so far, none of the vagrants had broken into them. As I passed each door, I sensed the empty rooms with only dusty woodwork and peeling wallpaper to bear witness to the many years of memories that crowded among them. The building remained undisturbed by copper pirates because the plumbing had never graduated from the old, traditional galvanized pipe.

I arrived at Macready's massive door both breathless and nervous. Usually, the door was fastened securely. Now, however, it stood ajar. I pondered knocking before entering, but with a sudden quickening thought that there might be an emergency, I pushed it open and walked in. If I had had ears I wouldn't have been as startled as I was. Three men were sitting on the whorehouse divan, and at least two of them, to judge by the bulging veins in their necks, were screaming at Macready.

5

One of the unwelcome surprises of entering Macready's penthouse is that you emerge directly into the center of the room. The fire door is set in a curved metal protective companionway that was originally meant to jut up on the roof. I never got used to this arrangement, and once I stepped inside and closed the door, I always had to orient myself.

The big divan with its three occupants was in a left-hand corner of the room facing me as I came in. A table and four chairs of various design were placed against the right-hand wall and constituted the dining area. Elsewhere in the large room were scattered occasional chairs or easy chairs in varying states of disrepair, and near each of the chairs was a table of some sort. The table in front of the divan was a coffee table of carved imitation mahogany (the carving was a galleon in full sail) that was meant to be covered with glass. The glass was missing, so that nothing could be put on its surface with any degree of safety. Macready believed that not far in the future he would find a suitable piece of glass to complete it. Directly to my right, behind the dining area, a narrow door fitted with a Yale spring lock led to the precarious walkway on the roof.

As I'd noted when I came in, two denizens of the big soft divan—one on each end—appeared to be screaming at Macready. In the middle sat a gray-haired man in a gray suit who appeared to be silent, but who had the fateful manic smile of someone who has just received a very bad telegram. I couldn't see Macready until I closed the door. He had been standing off to the left a little behind the entranceway and had been watching the three men attentively.

He seized my arm when he saw me, like a drowning man grasping a log. Mouths closed and necks returned to normal size while Macready introduced me around. The man on the left end of the divan was Macready's agent, Norman Popper. At the other end was a television producer named Emerson Kite. The stunned man in the middle, whose face was nearly as gray as his suit, was Vincent Namier, program director for the network. Wisely, Macready introduced me merely as "a friend of mine," so that the nervous, harried eyes of the trio bounced off me quickly, registering only the brief half-pitying, half-contemptuous glance following the recognition that I was deaf.

I stared penetratingly at Macready until he applied himself to the bottom cupboard of a rescued china closet at the back end of the room and produced a bottle of bourbon, a half-gallon of vodka, tonic water, seltzer, and glasses for all. He went to the kitchen for the ice, and while he was gone the three visitors stared at me with a mixture of curiosity and hostility. I remained my cool bland self and smiled sweetly at them. Macready came back and put ice in all the glasses. The glasses did not have *Socony Vacuum* printed on their bottoms, but they were gas-station giveaways if I ever saw one.

While we were all diving for the liquor, Macready remained aloof, standing to one side of the doorway. He was the only man I'd ever known who could look as relaxed while standing as he would while sprawled in an easy chair. And now, I must say that it is going to be hard for me to describe Macready, even though he was wearing, in very few pieces, what appeared to be about a thousand dollars worth of clothes. He had on dove-gray slacks, beautifully cut, of some material that appeared to be softer than flannel. His dark brown moccasins were butter soft and were not of a kind I had ever seen in a shop window. He had on a polo shirt, black, of classic simplicity, and over this he wore a short suede jacket that was better than one I had seen at Burberry's priced at more than five-hundred dollars. Perhaps only his agent and I were aware that each garment hid a slight imperfection, and that each was the trophy of endless hours of shopping in the vast pipe-rack emporiums secreted in the Lower East Side of Manhattan. The price of his entire outfit, really, would have been closer to one-hundred dollars than a thousand.

But the man inside the clothes is harder to describe, because Macready was one of those people who seem to flash on and off like a neon sign. Relaxed and unreflecting, he was all but invisible, a hole in the air. When he spoke or reacted to something said to him, however, he became alive in a way I have seldom seen. He vibrated with energy; there was an electric charge about him that captured all attention. I suppose that people who can hear attributed a lot of this to his voice, which was said to be extremely captivating. But to me he was a silent movie, with all the lightning magnetism that those faces and bodies supplied. Voiceless, he was quite enough for me.

There was absolutely nothing about him to separate him from the ordinary except—I think the word must be *regularity*. At six feet, he was two inches taller than I am, but you never got the impression of tallness from him. He was reasonably slender, although you would never describe him as thin. He was adequately muscled, although no one would mistake him for an athlete. The only truly distinctive thing about him was that he could stand absolutely still. His eyes were blue, his hair was an undistinguished straight brown thatch trimmed by a cut-rate Puerto Rican barber. His features were simple: a straight nose, a normal masculine chin and cheeks, and, well, his mouth was a little different. There were some odd tucks to the upper lip that weren't even noticeable under a certain light. He also had an unusual shape to his mouth when he was relaxed and unthinking. One corner of his lips curved upward, and the other down.

As I followed the argument developing in this strange, scattered room, I watched Macready's face as much as I did the men on the divan because Macready had once given me a valuable piece of information: "Acting," he had said, "is reacting." So I spent most of that session watching his face and lips to try to gather what was being shouted or snarled as the three men lunged for the vodka and tonic.

The burden of Norman Popper's complaint was this: "Who took you on when you didn't have two rags to paste to your ass and you didn't even know how to cross a stage? Was it me? Norman Popper? Believe it. I *made* you."

Macready's face remained perfectly impassive. If this was reacting, it was underplaying of a very high order. Only at the phrase, "*I made you,*" did his eyes roll heavenward.

"And this is how you pay me back!" I would hardly have had to read the agent's lips. Bitterness was in every line of his face. "This is what I get for crawling on my belly like a snake to get you an audition for a part—a part that could be the break of your life. A part that could make you forever. A part that every actor in the country would give his balls for. A part that should make you as rich as Chase Manhattan. A running part, the lead in a sure-fire, can't-miss series that will not only be produced for years and years, but will pay residuals until the second coming of Christ!"

His dark eyes got lost in the spiral of time. But he took a deep breath and resumed the attack.

"After I snag you the part, after the network says they like it, your test, after it goes to the top for approval, after the budget is set, with money handed out to you like you wouldn't believe, plus guest shots, spinoffs, promotion, products, the whole ball of wax, now you're telling us you're turning down the part? Do you know what you're doing to me? You're killing me. That's what you're doing to me. Killing me."

I really did think that he was going to burst into tears at this point, but sheer rage saved him from it.

"Because listen, Mr. Hot Shot Baby Boy, it's not just the money, the bread you are taking straight out of my mouth, not to mention my wife's mouth—and how lucky you are *she's* not here! And the mouths of my kids, Bruce, Donald, and Susan," he drove home these three spikes of generation. "Oh, no. You are also killing me professionally, do you understand? You are wiping out a career I built up brick by brick, stone by stone, straw by straw." I noted Macready's fingers count the materials.

"Who's ever going to listen to me now?" Popper queried earnestly. "You think I can walk into those offices again with some other actor, some other client? You think you're the only leading man in town? You think I can give them the gold-plated pitch? Forget it! You know what you're doing to a whole generation of aspiring young thespians . . ."

"At least keep it clean," muttered Macready. I could read *him* even when he muttered.

". . . young actors who want to come up in the business the same way you're coming up. They'll come to me now to be helped, to be developed, and what can I tell them. *What can I tell them?* 'You're wasting your time with me.' That's what I'll have to tell them. I'm dead in this business! That's what I'll have to tell them. Dead in this business because I was killed by William Macready, a no-good *schmuck* who sold me down the river and laughed in my face! Dead! Dead! Dead!" He was about to smash his glass down on the coffee table, but prevision of a badly cut hand from broken glass stayed his arm, and he contented himself with placing it firmly on the surface. Even this gesture was a miscue, however, because he had placed it on the bare carving. The glass turned over and spilled vodka all over the varnished mahogany.

This got a reaction from Macready. "Look what you're doing to my coffee table,'' he cried. ''You're ruining it!'' And he ran into the kitchen, presumably to find a towel.

Popper addressed me squarely. ''Will you believe it?'' he asked me, his arms spread wide in a plea. ''Will you believe what is happening? We are talking about millions of dollars, literally millions, and this *schmuck* is worried about some piece of shit he dragged up out of the gutter that the ragpickers, no, not the garbagemen would touch. Coffee table, coffee table,'' he repeated dementedly. His mouth opened wide and emitted what Macready described later as a shriek resembling the cry Laurence Olivier had let loose off stage when he tore his eyes out in *Oedipus Rex*. Still screaming, beet red in the face, Popper got up and began to pound his small fists senselessly against the wall.

His rising to beat against the wall broke a kind of hypnotic trance in me. I had been so intent upon the faces of the three visitors—Popper's a small, brown, clenched face, the producer's a heavy, pale moon face, and Namier's a long, noble-looking face with deep seams from the edge of the nostrils to his firm square chin—that I hadn't taken in the whole impression of any of them.

When Popper stood up, I noticed that he was wearing a brown tweed suit with creases in the trousers unusually sharp for tweed. His shirt was a tasteful pale green, and his tie a faultless thick brown knit. He was rounded off at the bottom with tan pebble-grained brogans. You could say that his attire was blameless except that it was too studied—too clearly plucked from the pages of *Gentleman's Quarterly*—in other words, an *outfit*. In the brief wild glimpse I had of him as he turned away, I judged him to be in his late forties. His hair was black, but suggested a touch-up. His eyes, although they were mostly slits of fury, appeared to be black.

Kite, the producer, was the obverse of the sartorial coin, a coinage stamped on his side: *slob*. A man of about thirty-five who had gone from pudgy to fat, he presented a huge torso encased in a cotton turtleneck that clung to the creases separating his rolls of flesh. It was very good dark blue cotton, to be sure, with a hard sheen to it that suggested Sea Island. Kite's belly disappeared into the waistband of shapeless tan trousers, the top button open and held together with a necktie. He had on old tennis shoes, no socks. Next to him, on the curved arm of the divan, he had thrown down a long tan leather jacket with a good deal of fringework to it. His hornrimmed glasses were pushed up high on his balding head, and his exposed eyes were revealed as a very cold, pale blue.

I hardly had to look at Namier at all. I had taken in the gray worsted Ivy League suit when I first arrived, and it so conformed to the uniform seen in the executive echelon streaming out of the network buildings along Sixth Avenue that he was instantly recognizable—as a streetcar conductor was once linked to trolleys. His face had the familiar, haunted pensiveness that appears on the sidewalks, lobbies, and parking garages in the communications zone. His shirt was white, his tie dark, his shoes black, and his hair gray. Seen anywhere but on Sixth Avenue, he might have been mistaken for the aging bell captain of a very tasteful hotel. His eyes were dark gray, pain-filled, and brooding.

Macready came rushing back with a large rag he had found and knelt down to mop off the surface of the table, working carefully into the interstices. Then he inspected the carving minutely. "No harm done," he said cheerfully. "Nothing's turning white." Namier and Kite both stared at him. Popper's face was still turned to the wall.

Kite's belly trembled when he spoke, and the big blue quivering expanse distracted me from reading the lips between his jowls. "Bill," he said. "Look at me. Put the rag down. Forget about the coffee table and look at me. I have something to say."

Macready shifted back on his heels and gave Kite his attention. "Have I ever lied to you?" Kite began. Something in the tilt of Macready's head made him abandon that line of introduction. He dismissed it with a slice of his hand. "All right," he began anew, "but have I ever led you wrong? You've worked with me before, how many times? Five? Six? And haven't we each time done something beautiful? Shot something so perfect it couldn't be bettered in a thousand takes? You know it. I know it. There couldn't be a better team than you and me.

"That's what made the magic." He leaned forward, intensely, his belly descending between his thighs. "That's what has made this project what it is right now—the absolute primary goal of the network. When we did that test together, you and I—you know, they insisted on a test, although I told them that it was absolutely in your mitt—you know how they are. They insisted on that test, and when they got it, Jesus, you could have yelled fire in the screening room with nobody noticing. They were hushed, awed.

"What you and I did with that test, Bill, is make history. We pushed the whole ratchet of what can be done on television up by one whole notch. They never saw work on the tube like that before. Not ever. And when the scene closed, they were riveted, entranced, spellbound."

Kite was doing a little spellbinding of his own, I could see. Macready, crouching, weaved like a cobra in his basket to the flute of Emerson Kite.

"There is a tremendous future for us," he continued. "I don't mean in terms of money, success." He waved these vulgar considerations away. "But in the whole history of the medium. We can make a breakthrough. We can change the industry. We can do for television what Chaplin, Barrymore, Muni, and Tracy did for the pictures . . ."

"Tracy," Macready interrupted. "You mean Lee Tracy?"

"I mean Spencer Tracy."

"I like Lee Tracy," Macready announced. "A whole genre of acting there. Best there was." He stared off into space. "I like Pat O'Brien, too," he said vaguely.

"Sure, certainly." Kite returned to the battle. "I see what you mean. Raw energy poured on—just simply poured on like gasoline on a fire. Speed that is unbelievable. Nobody could do it today. Except you. You can do it, Bill. You can drive a scene. You know that. If you take this series, we, you and I, can make American television the authentic wing of the theater it was always meant to be."

"And which it almost became thirty years ago," said Macready.

"You think they don't know that?" Kite's jowls trembled with passion. "You think they're not dying to go back to the authentic medim they lost?"

"No, I don't," said Macready. There was a finality in his eyes that made Kite sit back on the divan. The cold blue eyes swept Macready with the hatred that grows only out of a failed lie.

"You think you can pass this up and get away with it," said Emerson Kite. "Think again. You're not Al Pacino, you know."

Macready stood up from the coffee table. "I'm every bit as good as Al Pacino," he said. "And don't you forget it.

"Furthermore," he added, "if you're so crazy about Al Pacino, why don't you hire him for the part?"

Popper had been listening, and he rushed away from the wall. "Al Pacino, Al Pacino," he said. "What's all this talk about Al Pacino? He's so much? So he wants to play Shakespeare, running around some lousy platform down in the Village with a hump on his back? What's so great about that?"

"What's so great about Al Pacino," said Macready, "is that he wouldn't touch their show with a fork."

Namier closed his eyes briefly and leaned back in the divan. When he opened them, he had decided what he wanted to say. "I have been listening and thinking," he said to Macready, who stood respectfully and attentively at his post near the door. "And I have been torn between admiration for your integrity and fear for your future." Macready remained stock still, expressionless. "You know, of course, that we will work endlessly with you and Chet Harshaw, the lead writer, to bring the script around to what you can live with. My respect for your integrity wouldn't let me do less for you. But if your integrity includes not working for television seriously at all, I think you're doing both yourself and us an injustice.

"This project could be the jewel in the crown of American television, and you know it. It could accomplish in a running series what the BBC has been able to do only in a few set-piece mini-series: 'The Search for the Nile,' 'Brideshead Revisited.' It would be better than 'Brideshead Revisited.' And it wouldn't be one shot. It would be continuing. I think you owe it to yourself and to the theater. Notice, I said theater, not industry."

He had bent forward in his intensity, but now he leaned back again and clasped his hands around his cocked knee. "I've been in the industry an awfully long time, Bill. I can look forward to a whole new era that would begin with this project. I can look back on a lot of triumphs, but also on a lot of tragedies. You know, I lived through the whole blacklist business—the Red Channels mess. I saw what can happen to people. Integrity isn't as rare in the industry as you may think. I've known a lot of people with integrity, tremendous integrity, and the talent and brains to back it up—just like you. But I also saw that when they overstepped themselves, when they got beyond their depth and clashed with the powers that be, they were lost, finished.

"I'm not just talking about television and network broadcasting. For instance, you mentioned Lee Tracy. And you're right, one of the finest actors and leading men ever to work in the American theater, the original Hildy Johnson of *The Front Page*, in 1928. You know what happened to him after he got into that drunken scrape in Mexico, don't you? He didn't work again for something like twenty years. John Gilbert got on the wrong side of Louis B. Mayer and he was sabotaged, finished. He just died off.

"There are a lot of ways to finish your career, but the most certain way is to make a direct challenge, to force the powers that be to somehow get rid of you—no matter how valuable you are. They're a different race of people from you and me. They're supposed to be hard-headed businessmen, who go by the numbers, but if you challenge their honor, their clout, they'll cut you off. And what's more, they'll chase you to the ends of the earth to see that nobody else hires you, either. And I don't mean just in their medium. I mean anywhere. The clout of a powerful person is that no one wants to be his enemy.

"I've hired young people like you before," said Namier. "I understand the structure. I don't want to see you get caught under the wheels and dragged down the road."

"Osgood Perkins," said Macready. "Osgood Perkins played Walter Burns in the original production with Lee Tracy."

Namier smiled. "That's right."

Popper said, "You two guys must have been around for the original *Hamlet*."

"No," smiled Macready. "But Richard Burbage opened in it. He owned a piece of the show."

"So young," marveled Popper, "and you know all this already?"

Macready waved him off and addressed himself to Namier. "I'm sorry if I sounded flip to you," he said with an air of conciliation. "I didn't mean to, and I promise you my final decision won't be a flip one."

At the words "won't be," I thought I saw chests heave with relief on either side of Namier. He, however, remained steady.

"When can you let us know?" he asked.

"I'll call you very soon and give you a definite date for either yes or no."

"I wish it could be now," persisted Namier.

"It just can't be, Vincent," said Macready. "But it won't be long."

The three of them got up then, and Kite appeared to be grumbling while he pushed the fringes aside and thrust himself into his jacket. Popper adjusted his trousers, his tie, and coat. He went to the corner to find a very jaunty brown fedora and searched vainly for a mirror to adjust it in. Namier, however, simply stood and awaited the others. When Macready went over to say something to Popper, Namier said to me, perhaps silently, "You're his friend; try to talk sense to him, won't you? It's terribly important to him—to all of us." I nodded, but it was a noncommital nod. Namier shrugged.

Macready opened the door, where the trio was assembled, and Popper began to lead the way out, but he backed in hurriedly. "For Christ's sake," he said. "It's pitch black out there. You want us to kill ourselves on the stairs?"

"Would you like a candle, Norman?" Macready asked him soberly.

Kite was furious. "There could be anybody on those deserted stairs," he said. "We could be mugged . . . killed . . ."

"All right," said Macready. "Don't panic." He flipped a switch at the side of the door and a powerful floodlight pierced the entire stairwell. Even at that, however, they rather shrank. It was a harsh, desolate light that revealed every ugly stain and scar that defaced the walls.

"Good night, gentlemen," said Macready. Unhappily, the three men began their descent to the street. Macready listened carefully until he was sure they had reached the outer door. Then he stepped back in and turned off the floodlight.

When he swung around to face me, his eyes were snapping with urgency.

"All right," said Macready. "Where's the money?"

6

And that, in the sequence of my memory, is the last thing I remembered for quite a while.

There was Macready's blue piercing stare, and his demand, "All right, where's the money?" and then a sweet familiar face framed in honey-gold hair staring at me with obvious concern in her deep green eyes. I stared back at that face for an unmeasurable lapse of time before I realized that the soft hand holding mine went with it. I made a great effort at recognition; it was Edna, my secretary, a visitor from the world out of which I had been absent.

Her lips moved and tears came into her eyes. I observed the tears blankly but hadn't the least idea of what the lips were saying. I didn't have the energy to read them. I glanced down at her hand, in which mine was clasped. It seemed to communicate a lot more than her lips. I moved my hand slightly, and her grasp tightened. Surprisingly, the grip did not hurt my hand. It was the only part of me that didn't hurt. She got up quickly and ran out of the room. I wondered why. In short order there was a gathering of white coats and nurses' uniforms at the door, with Edna's face peering behind them. The sight of the white-clad army bearing down on my bedside was too much for me. I fainted.

The face was there again when I awoke. The hand, soft, warm and comforting, was still clasped around mine. I moved my hand again and wondered why it didn't hurt. I stared into her eyes, and this time her face just smiled. She didn't try to say anything. No tears.

I spoke the classic formula: "Where am I?" At least I thought that I had said, "Where am I?" Her forehead wrinkled and her eyes searched mine. Now, it was plain, she couldn't understand me any more than I could understand her. Since I cannot hear my own voice I had no idea of what utterance I had put into the air. I gently detached my hand from hers—the muscles in my forearm burned and shrieked—and put it to my head. The size of my head seemed to have no relationship to my body. It was a puffy balloon. My lips were huge pads of swollen flesh. I tried again: "Where am I?" Edna's face strained with an attempt at understanding, and her lips said something I couldn't comprehend.

I took my hand away from my head and held it out where I could see it. There wasn't a mark on it. It was as innocent as a newborn babe's. That seemed somehow significant to me, although I couldn't imagine why. When I refocused my eyes to look beyond my hand, I got the answer to my question: I was in a hospital. I sniffed the air for confirmation. Definitely a hospital. I tried to raise my eyebrows in a question to Edna, but the sudden shock on her face told me that the attempt had only widened my eyes alarmingly. I quickly tried to look reassuring. It didn't quite work. She got up, very gently this time, and slowly left the room.

While she was gone I studied my hand. How had it escaped? In time, I realized it was my left hand I was staring at. I raised my good right arm, not without pain, and stared at my right hand. Like my left it was innocent of any mark at all. Two useless lily whites. They were trying to tell me something.

Behind my brain a cloud of sense had been forming, a sense of battle. All of my body told me that I had been in a battle—all except my hands. My hands told me that it hadn't been a battle at all, but a beating. I had been beaten. There hadn't been anything like a fight. I'd never struck a blow.

Behind that sense of battle there loomed a huge dark shadow, and even the flash of it made me catch my breath in the kind of terror I hadn't felt since I had been a very small child. It was ghostlike, and yet it had the vividness that frightens children in their dreams. Slowly the shadow took shape—houselike. As big as a house? Maybe. But houselike, like an old-fashioned cheap frame house, the kind I was raised in, a simple structure with a high-pitched roof that sloped down from the peak in an inverted V. The slopes of that inverted V were arms.

Forewarned, the medical crew came back, this time more cautiously. The doctor entered alone, his stethoscope dangling around his chest. He sat down by the bed and put his trained young face up next to mine. He said something with a smile that I suppose should have been comforting. I couldn't make head nor tail of it. He began to probe around then on my rib cage, which hurt like hell, but when he began to dig into my abdomen, I let out some kind of noise that made his face turn white. The young doctor stood up and heaved a huge sigh. He wrote something on a pad while talking to a nurse who had entered unseen by me. They both left, but after a while, she came back and gave me an injection that put me back to sleep.

For the third time I came around, and Edna was there again. I looked at her and drank it all in. I am not in love with Edna, but I loved her then. She had hold of my hand again; perhaps that is why I had been sleeping so peacefully. I needed somebody to hold my hand. I tried to smile, also trying not to frighten her. "Who's watching the store?" I croaked.

She understood me! She laughed. Then she started to cry. Her hand shook on my hand.

Now that I knew I was in a hospital, I was able to pose the next classic question: "What happened?" I asked her.

She began to talk excitedly, her free hand flailing the air.

I slipped my hand out of hers and grasped it, the other way around. I squeezed so that she would pay attention. "Slow down," I gasped. "Slow down. One syllable at a time. I can't read you."

The young doctor had come into the room and was trying to observe things without intruding.

"I tried to call you up that night and nobody was there," said Edna.

The doctor's eyebrows rose as he wondered how a deaf man could be called on the telephone. "It's a system we have . . . deaf people . . ." I began. But the effort of speaking exhausted me momentarily.

"It works by flashing lights instead of a bell," Edna explained to him. "And there's a little red light on his set that flashes Morse code, really a Phillips code, a kind of shorthand for Morse. It's called Code-Com."

I could see the wheels turning as the doctor made a mental note of all this, reserved information for his next deaf patient.

"When you didn't answer, I got worried," Edna said to me. "I called Mr. Macready, but he wasn't home, and his answering service didn't know anything. How did he manage to hire a snotty answering service?"

I shrugged. Somehow, it was in character with Macready.

So, Edna told me, framing her words slowly and carefully, "I took a chance on calling the Cardinal Hotel. I just wanted to know where you were."

"There aren't any phones in those rooms," I said. "Besides, I wouldn't have been able to use a phone like that."

"I know that." She grimaced impatiently. "I talked to the room clerk. He said he didn't have a Joe Binney registered there. So I told him to go up and look around the rooms where they found . . . you found . . . the dead man. Boy, was he mean. So I said that either he could go up and look or I'd call the police and have them go up and look. He didn't like that. He didn't want that."

"I'll bet." I thought about it. "He wouldn't want to make the climb, either."

"The clerk told me to call back in fifteen minutes. When I called back he said that you'd had an accident and so I said, 'Well where is he? How is he?' And he said you'd come over to the hospital here."

"They'd called an ambulance?"

"No," Edna said, "and that's what makes me so mad. They didn't want any trouble with the cops, they said. No police. So they had you brought here in a cab. They said it's the nearest hospital since Polyclinic closed down."

"They live well into the past," I observed. "Polyclinic closed down fifteen years ago."

I tried to picture the old man and the Gypsy Rose kid easing me down those four flights of stairs. Maybe that's where the real accident happened.

I said, "There's no way I could have been in that hotel. I was finished there. I had everything I wanted." Edna and the doctor stared at me patiently. "I was at Macready's place," I said. "Three guys were there arguing with him. They left and Macready turned to me and said, 'Well, where's the money?' That's the last thing I remember."

The young doctor moved closer to my bed. "There's an explanation for that, Mr. Binney," he said. "You've had a concussion and you may have partial amnesia—a loss of recent memory. It will all come back in time."

He had meant to be reassuring, but in the far reaches of my brain, I was not at all sure that I wanted everything to come back. There was a sense of terror hovering in the back of my mind, spreading its dark wings.

"I remember," I said, "that the three guys were afraid to go down the stairs in the dark. Maybe I fell down those stairs when I was leaving. Those are dangerous stairs. Then maybe I walked back to the hotel in a kind of stupor, you know, with the concussion and all."

The doctor said, "I don't think your injuries are consistent with that. However you got them, it wasn't just from falling down, even if you'd fallen off a building."

"Then how did I get to the hotel? Why did I get to the hotel? Maybe I was mugged on Macready's stairs. It could happen."

"You wouldn't have walked anywhere with those injuries, I don't think," said the doctor.

"Then I went back to the Cardinal Hotel in good shape and full consciousness," I mused. "But why?"

"Joe," Edna got my attention by squeezing my hand. "Do you really feel strong enough to talk?"

"I'm doin' it, ain't I?"

"But not for much longer," said the doctor.

"What does the word *pool* mean to you?" asked Edna.

"Pool?" I examined the word laboriously. "A game like

billiards, a place to swim, a betting plan, a lot of things together like in resources . . . ." My head began to hurt savagely.

"While you've been here," she said, "the only word we could make out that you were saying was *'pool, pool.'* You were terribly worried about a pool."

"That's crazy," I decided aloud. "I haven't been worried about any pool." But my head hurt worse. I had to shut my eyes. With my eyes closed, communication vanished. I felt the doctor's cool hand on my forehead. A little later I felt an injection. I think that then I slept for a long, long time.

7

A brick through the rose window of a church is like the shattering of memory. The colored bits of glass go flying everywhere. Patiently, the pieces are picked up from the floor and reassembled—perhaps not perfectly. It will never be quite the same.

I didn't have to pick them all up by myself, of course. Edna had already helped, and the young doctor was letting me know the extent of my injuries. Aside from the concussion, he told me, the serious injuries were visceral, contusions, lacerations, and a near rupture of my insides. I didn't ask for too many details, but it was obvious that I hadn't gotten this way from falling down stairs. More and more, however, the young doctor's conversation had drifted toward Edna.

"I have never seen such devotion," he said.

"Who, Edna? She's all right. Nice kid."

His expression said that he had sized me up as an insensitive brute—a clod. "She seems to be deeply in love with you," he said. "You should be grateful to have someone who cares that much."

I would have smiled if I could. "You're seeing a lot of things that aren't there," I contented myself with saying.

He wouldn't let it alone. "As an objective observer, I might be seeing more than you do."

"No," I contended. "What you're seeing is the surface, not that it isn't nice. Edna and I go back to some troubled times and tough spots. Sure, we love each other, but we're not in love, *capish?* We are friends, deep friends, and we love each other like friends. Why would she want to hook up with an old fart like me?"

The explanation suited him so happily that even his badge seemed to glow. I held on to him to ask, "How long do you think I ought to stay here?"

"Till the end of this week anyway," he offered. "Three or four more days. We're keeping a series of lab tests going on you. We want to be sure that nothing opens up on us."

"Thanks," I muttered to his retreating back. I suddenly felt ill at ease in a way that had nothing to do with my physical injuries. Whenever I had been in the hospital before, in the course of my gumshoe career, I had been pretty eager to leave. Now I greeted the news that I'd be leaving soon with something like dismay, fright. I had been frightened, but I still didn't know by *what*. I kept musing on the word that Edna had mentioned: *pool . . . pool*. Where was the connection?

Macready came in, finally. He'd been there before, but I had been too sick and dopey to make sense with him. This time he supplied a huge chunk of memory around which other bits and jottings of my recollection were able to gather.

It was obvious that he hated hospitals. He sat rigidly on the edge of his chair. He was wearing a suit and a tie, very unusual for him, I think, and a costume usually reserved for weddings and funerals. It was a serviceable dark blue suit of a very good cut. "You look like a funeral director," I told him. "I ain't dead yet."

"A bit on a soap," Macready explained. "I'm on my way over to ABC. Just thought I'd stop off."

"Nice to see you, anyway."

"Nice that you recognize me," said Macready.

"Oh, they told you about that, did they?"

He nodded. I said, "Look, have you got much time to spare?"

He glanced at his watch, a dull gold Baume & Mercier that he had by no means sprung for, but had won in a poker game. "About fifteen minutes," he allowed. "The call is at two o'clock."

"Can you fill me in on what happened after those three guys left? That's where my memory stops."

After he had left I was terribly, terribly tired. I fell asleep and entertained nightmares that I do not now want to describe, although I have no trouble in recalling them. They reduced me to the status of a child, and they evoked the bottomless dread that only a child can experience in dreams.

When I awoke, I pushed the button that makes the bed rise to a sitting position, and even with this effortless mobility felt a deep pain in my guts. Sitting up by myself, I realized, would be next to impossible. I concentrated on what Macready had told me, held on to it, and was able to fit other stray shards from my own memory into the scene.

Macready had turned to me, his eyes snapping, and said, "Well, where's the money?"

"I don't know," I told him. "I haven't got it."

"Did you find Pelfrey?"

"Yes, but . . ."

"Well, where is he?"

"He's dead," I told Macready. "I found him strung up in a hotel room."

"He hanged himself?"

"It looks that way, but . . ."

"And the money's gone?"

"Not a sign of it. Not a nickel."

"Jesus Christ," said Macready. "You told me the guy was clean."

"You thought he was, too," I countered. "And maybe . . ."

"Son of a bitch," said Macready. "It had to happen, didn't it. I thought I'd never get taken like all those other poor bastards. I thought they were chumps. Now I'm the chump."

"Who are you talking about?" I asked him.

"Don't you know the score?" There was a bitter, fathomless pain in his eyes. "Don't you know how many actors have been taken for a ride by their business managers?"

Macready did not smoke a great deal, but now he demanded a cigarette from me to help him explain.

"An actor gets lucky enough to make some money. So he gets a business manager to help him handle it. It's supposed to be the smart thing to do. The business manager promises him the moon. 'But,' says the business manager, 'you've got to follow my orders the same way you would a doctor's orders,' get me?

"So the first thing they do is take the guy's money away and give him an allowance, like a kid. Walk-around money. Then they give him a lot of bullshit about tax shelters and investment plans.

"But, get this, he has to stick to the budget. Those parasitical bastards feed on power. They enjoy making the guy crawl for a few bucks."

He suddenly assumed the stance and expression of a glittery-eyed, merciless zealot. " 'What's this? You want a new car? What's the matter with the one you've got? What are you, childish or something? What makes you think you can afford it? You want to break up this beautiful plan for a lousy car?' "

He relaxed for an instant and then resumed the characterization after saying, "And then they try to scare the guy to death. 'If you're just going to raid every plan we've drawn up here for a lot of irresponsible expenses, don't expect me to help you when the government comes around for the taxes.'

"Ah, yeah, the taxes." He abandoned his role. "They act as though giving the government a nickel was a crime in itself. Only suckers pay taxes. In effect, they postpone life.

And in the end, for a lot of the actors I heard of, and I even know one or two, they find out that life hasn't even been postponed—it's been stolen. All that bullshit about taxes and annuities and stocks, all the wonderful plans for your security—bullshit—pure bullshit. You find out that these guys have piled up your money and skipped. They're living in Brazil, or Sri Lanka or Timbuctoo, or some Goddamned place, lushing it up with a bunch of broads on your money.

"And what is worse," he would not let me speak, "Is that you find out that they never paid for anything you owed. The bills for everything have piled up like a snowdrift at your door. And even worse than that—they never paid any taxes at all, so the IRS is breaking down the door and wrenching out your back teeth for the gold.

"I knew what these bastards were like." He stared at a corner of the room as if visualizing them. "I knew it. I did everything to avoid it. And now I'm screwed just like every other fucking moron who went to disco down in Hollywood!"

He stared at the expression on my face. "What's the matter?" he demanded. "Are you having trouble understanding me?"

"I hope so," I replied. "I hope you've been listening to yourself. I've just told you the guy is dead, and all you can think of is money."

"You said he'd hung himself," responded Macready. "What do you want me to do, cry? He pissed my money away and couldn't stand the gaff. I got no sympathy for the Dutch act."

"I never said he hanged himself."

"You said you found him hanging in a hotel room."

"But I didn't say he hanged *himself*."

Macready stared at me for nearly five seconds. "Oh," he said.

"It was a pretty good job," I told him. "Enough to make the thing at least look problematical. They even locked the room from the inside."

"They?" said Macready. *"They?"*

"Whoever." I waved him off. "It's my professional opinion that somebody strung him up and took the money."

"Somebody followed him to this hotel and knocked him over?"

"It wasn't that simple. What was he doing in the hotel? It was pretty elaborate. A setup, I think."

Macready surveyed the refreshments he had set out for the little conference. "I could use a drink," said Macready. "How about you?" I agreed readily and he fixed a bourbon and water for the two of us. He handed me my drink and guided me over to the curved divan. He sat next to me then, but was silent for some time, staring into his drink. Finally, he said, "I must seem like a terrible prick to you, yammering about nothing but my money."

"I don't blame you," I began, but he put up a hand to forestall me.

"Let me tell you what the money means to me," said Macready. "You saw those three guys up here, leaning on me."

"Yeah," I agreed. "They were excited. They want you."

"They want me," repeated Macready. "And without the money, they'll get me. . . ."

"Is that a tragedy?" I asked him. "From what I could read, they want to make you a star."

He had been sipping his drink, but now he almost choked on it. "A star!" he exclaimed. "You've been watching 'The Late Show,' or *Forty-Second Street*. Nobody makes stars any more. I doubt that they ever did."

"Aw, c'mon," I started to protest.

He shut me up with a gesture. "Let me explain what this is all about," he said. "And why the money is important to me.

"These three guys," the sweep of his arm indicated the removed presences, "are circling around a piece of material that is now known as a 'hot property.' It's a hot property for one reason and one reason only. The Old Man, the head of the network, fell in love with it. This property comes from a book that was written about ten years ago by that asshole Namier mentioned who is now lead writer and story consultant: Chet Harshaw. The book never went anywhere when it came out, and Harshaw dribbled off a couple more novels that also never went anywhere. He was sort of bobbing around in his career like a float bulb in a toilet tank.

"But the network was in its usual panic a year ago, and everybody was looking for new material. The outline of the book popped up in front of Namier, and because Namier knew something about the Old Man, he started turning gears so that the Old Man would notice that there was a project in the works. You could never do anything as violent as actually show the outline to the Old Man. There had to be vague signs and currents in the air. But when the Old Man sniffed the wind, he knew he loved it."

Macready bummed a cigarette from me, got up to find a match, and remained standing while he smoked and explained it to me.

"Now Namier was playing a very dangerous game, because once you get the Old Man involved, either you produce or it's your ass. They got a script together, and then they sent out casting calls for the lead. They said they wanted an 'unknown,' but of course that's bullshit. Nobody is unknown, not anybody they really want."

Macready paused and looked away, as if revisualizing the situation. He drained his drink and prepared another for himself. Mine was only half gone.

He turned to face me again to continue. "Somebody put the bug up Norman's ass, and he asked me to go down for an audition—a test. He was very nervous, and I got the idea of the dimensions of the thing. So I balked. I was very uncertain. In truth, I was scared. I didn't really know if I was scared of failing to get the part, or scared of actually getting it."

I signified complete incomprehension.

"I didn't want to go on my ass with an opportunity like that," said Macready. "The actor doesn't live who doesn't believe that, given the opportunity, he couldn't knock them dead. You can't be an actor and not believe that. So I wanted to be sure that if I took a shot at it I wouldn't fail."

Macready's face twisted in remembered indecision. "On the other hand, I have never really wanted to be wired into a series. Certainly it means security, a lot of money, blah, blah, blah, but it also limits you and slows you down. I'm a little young for that. Later on, I can see it. But right now, it would hurt me. I know it."

"But you *are* young," I argued. "If what they say is true, you could come away in a few years with enough money to do anything you want."

"If what they say is *true,*" he emphasized with a forefinger pointing from his drink. "The tricky part is that they actually believe what they're saying. They believe it in spite of all their experience. They have to believe it. But that doesn't mean *I* have to believe it. All that crap about equalling the BBC falls apart the minute you look at it. The BBC doesn't have to sell a cure for acne. The networks do. Unless they sell the cure for acne, there's no network. It's that simple. Everything is secondary to selling snake oil. Don't let them kid you.

"And then there's the big success." He stretched his arms to indicate the dimensions. "Let me tell you something. They all talk about wanting a hit, a big success. But once it happens, they regard it as a threat. Why? Because it becomes bigger than they are. The whole industry has a kind of schizophrenia. When a series becomes a hit, it's the actors, the producer, the writers and the crew that have made it a hit."

"What about directors?" I asked innocently.

"Producers *are* directors," he said impatiently. "It's a hang-over from radio."

"I thought Namier was a director."

"*Program* director. It's altogether different. He picks and chooses, develops shows, and places them. He's an executive. It doesn't have anything to do with directing."

Things started falling into place for me then, because I had been puzzled by the apparent difference in status between Kite and Namier.

"So here's this hit." He noticed my glass had emptied, filled it, and took his own drink to the center of the room. "It's up in the ratings, it's making money, it's got a solid audience. It all looks great. Right? Wrong. The hit belongs only to a certain number of people. The other people are saying. 'So where's my end?' They're saying, 'Where's my name? What does this make me look like? It makes me look like a midget!'

"So the sniping starts—to bring the show down to size. People start getting snotty. Rumors are floated. Dissension starts splitting up the troupe. The lead—the so-called star, who's been carrying the show—looks around, and if he has any brains at all, he says, 'Oh, oh. This ain't going to last.' And so he follows the first law of American Enterprise: *Get the Money*!

"Now, they've been given a budget they've got to live with. But the star gets the money, right? Where does that leave everyone else? Starving. That's where. The supporting actors start saying, 'Jesus Christ. What is this, a monologue?' So they start asking for more money, which they don't get. What *they* get is written out of the script. Dumped. An accident gets written in, a death. And they don't get much work after that, either, because they've been identified with the part in the hit series—aside from the reputation as a 'troublemaker.' It's all very shitty. It all gets down to nickels and dimes. Eventually, the whole thing goes down the toilet and everybody's standing around wondering what happened. But they're relieved! It's no longer a threat. However, there's a new threat on the horizon. It attracts their attention."

I sat back. "Either you're nuts or they're nuts," I said.

"I'm not crazy," said Macready. "I'm trying to be an actor, which is probably crazy, but I'm not crazy. I live like this," he swept the room with his arm, "so I can keep my money and have a choice. To develop. To see how far I can go."

He came back to the divan and sat down next to me. "That's what the money was for," he said. "The nut. It's the 'Say no,' money, the 'Fuck you,' money. What it means to me is whether I can be myself."

"Two-hundred and fifty-thousand dollars," I observed, "is a lot of self."

Macready sat back. "Actors need a lot," he said. His face was moody. "Actors do a lot of starving, and sometimes they get frightened in a way that seldom happens to other people. They say to themselves, 'What am I doing here?' They feel like idiots. They are utterly alone. They are defenseless. I know actors who have managed to make a buck, and they buy freezer after freezer full of food. Closets are stocked. Stuff is stored up like a bomb shelter. You don't know how terrified actors can get."

"Maybe you don't know," I said slowly, "how terrified coal miners, assembly workers, and delivery men can get."

"It's different," he insisted. "Actors are alive only when they're working, when they're getting a response. When they're not working they're like ghosts—vampires who can't see themselves in a mirror. The money is all that keeps them from going nuts.

"I need the money," he said, staring into my eyes. "I need every dime of it."

He got up again and went to the center of the room, where he turned to me. "And while you're at it, I want you to get whoever killed that poor little bastard—unless the police get him first."

I fixed myself one more drink, which I promised myself would be the last one of the day. I took a sip and sat staring into space. Macready tapped my arm.

"I know what you're thinking," he said. "You're thinking, 'Who's going to pay for all this?' "

I was offended. "I wasn't thinking that at all," I said. "I was thinking about Pelfrey. It's going to take a long time to get rid of the sight of him up there."

"Then you're on?"

"Oh, sure," I answered. "I was on when I came up here."

"You already figured out what happened, right?"

"Only a small part of it." I restrained his enthusiasm. "I figured out how they worked the locked room bit."

"Tell me," Macready demanded.

"It was done with a thief's knot," I said. "I don't mean the knot of a thief, but the kind of knot that's called a thief's knot. It's a variation of the slip knot, and it's mostly used by seamen, and sometimes steeplejacks. They use it when they're working aloft and want temporary support."

He looked pretty blank at this, so I continued, "Supposing a seaman has to go aloft to free up a sheave on a block or something like that. It isn't going to be a long job, but he can't do it just hanging on to the spar. He shinnies up with a coil of line, puts a thief's knot around the top of the spar, and then either makes a bight in the line to support him, or coils part of it around his leg to hold him up. He does the job and then eases himself down with the help of the line. The line is still made fast to the top, right? How is he going to untie it without shinnying up again? He gives the hauling part a quick jerk, and the whole thing comes tumbling down, because a thief's knot remains secure as long as there's a strain on the hauling part of the line, understand?"

"Not really," said Macready. "But I believe you."

"So, whoever did this took advantage of the fact that the door was old and loose—it wouldn't work with your firedoor, for instance—and he put a thief's knot on the nub of the barrel bolt, closed the door, pulled the bolt home with the hauling part of his line, and then jerked it free. Then he locked the deadlock with an extra key that he probably got the same way I did, and there's your locked room mystery."

"So the guy who killed Pelfrey . . ." Macready began.

"Was equal parts sailor and thief with murderer thrown in for good measure," I finished. "The best shot is that he's familiar with the deck department of a ship or boat. Merchant seaman, tugman, fisherman, maybe even yachtsman."

Macready pursed his lips. "This all sounds wonderful in theory . . ."

"But you don't think it would work?" I was miffed. "I did it myself on that door in that room."

"You did?" He was impressed. "You carry all this stuff around with you? Pieces of string and so forth?"

"No," I answered, annoyed. "I don't carry my Dick Tracy Boy Detective's kit wherever I go or my Orphan Annie secret code ring. I bought a spool of fishing line . . ."

Macready was alarmed. "What's the matter?" he said. I was staring into his face and past his face at a dingy hotel room.

"I took some line," I said woodenly, "from the spool, and did the stunt."

"Yes?"

"And the spool . . . the spool . . . with my big fat fingerprints, which are on record in every agency in the country, is lying there on that lousy table, right where I left it. If the cops come back and find it, they will turn me every way but loose.

"I've got to go back and get that spool," I said.

8

And that's what I'd been muttering about in my delirium—not *pool, pool,* but *spool, spool.*

I sat in my hospital bed and contemplated the partially restored window of my memory. In the center there remained a huge space that I wasn't sure I wanted to fill. I tried to make my mind blank, so that it would all come back to me, but the result of that exercise was that I fell asleep.

They were fussing around me when I woke up, and they managed to feed me (soup). I took the requisite number of pills, endured the probing and other ministrations, and then they disappeared, leaving me alone with my thoughts.

My thoughts told me that Macready had seen me out. He switched on the powerful floodlight, protected in its wire cage, that lighted the stairwell, and walked downstairs with me. We paced along, side by side, for a block, then he went one way for his evening's fun and frolic, and I went mine.

I pursued the memory of myself walking those strange sidewalks that manage to be both riotous and desolate. There were bands of people having a hell of a good time who passed by quickly, drunks in doorways, and casualties in the gutter. Some people, evictees from the SRO hotels, strolled by in violent argument with unseen persons. They argued, pleaded, and roundly cursed the phantoms in their brains. Later, they would congregate down at the Port Authority Bus Terminal, where they would not be permitted to sleep, and they would sit soberly in the waiting room, staring at phantom rooms in phantom homes that had long since been abandoned, until their medication exhausted itself, at which time their nonobjective arguments would commence again.

Hell's Kitchen, it seemed to me, was becoming more like Hell itself.

I turned at the next block and hurried down toward the hotel. I was so fastened on the problem of recapturing my telltale spool of fishing line that I didn't have the wits to recognize the car parked on the block where no car should be. When I peered into the lobby under the curved red sign that arched over an obscene-looking cardinal, I got an electric jolt through the nerves. Lieutenant Detective Matthew Shope was leaning familiarly on the registration counter and conversing with the gray-faced clerk. A plainclothesman stood next to Shope. The clerk, thank God, was so absorbed in the conversation that he didn't notice me in the fraction of a second I took to grasp it all. I fled.

I wanted to be off the street because I did not want Shope, cruising past, to spot me and pull me over for a chat. At this point, I wanted as little to do with the NYPD as possible. I looked around for a friendly coffee pot, but everything, it seemed, was exposed to the street.

Although I did not really want a drink, the only place that seemed to fit my predicament was Ferguson's and McCloughlin's, an old Irish bar that had hung on gamely a few blocks north. The decor of the place is functional, to say the least. It is a drinking establishment, pure and simple, and like most Irish bars, does not invite inspection from the street. The clientele is a mixed bag of workingmen and the usual collection of individualists to be found in any amicable saloon that promotes conversation. I ordered a bourbon and soda and sat at a table well in the back. Since all the stools were occupied, there was nothing particularly noticeable in taking a table to myself.

I decided to stay there for a full hour, which would give Shope all the time he needed to abandon the neighborhood. Filling out that hour required two refills, but it also gave me time to assemble my brains and see where I was and where I was heading.

My relationship to both Macready and Pelfrey was a purely professional one. When Macready had decided he needed a business manager, he located Pelfrey via a grapevine, and then had wisely located me and asked me to check him out. I had gone to see Macready first, to get his story straight, and then set Edna to work on the telephone—a fairly useless device for me. When she'd made all the rudimentary checks by phone, I went down to the courthouse and looked up various rolls to see if Pelfrey's name appeared anywhere. It did not, I had Edna make an appointment with Pelfrey at his place, and went up there to see him. It was all very routine.

Pelfrey had lived in two rooms on the east side of midtown. One of the rooms was a kitchenette, the other tripled as his living room, bedroom, and office. The building was old, but not interestingly so. The furniture said tacitly that it had been there when Pelfrey arrived and would still be there when he left. It implied that the rooms were permanent, the residents were not. The only personal note in the room was a cheap, unfinished pine desk that Pelfrey had obviously and laboriously finished himself, with Minwax or something like it. It was hideous, but served the purpose of holding up a telephone, an answering device, and several stacks of papers. There was a coffee table in front of a convertible couch, and the surface of the table bore a carefully displayed fan of financial reports and newsletters. A rather elaborate home computer was much in evidence. Too big for the desk, it rested on the gate-legged dining table.

When Pelfrey let me in, he was in his shirtsleeves and his tie was loosened. He was wearing the bottom half of a nondescript blue suit and had on carpet slippers. He had obviously been working, and while he was moderately courteous, I had the feeling that I was eating into his time.

He was not at all disturbed that I was checking him out; in fact, he appreciated that it was a wise move. He handed me a *curriculum vitae,* which was a twin to the one he had given Macready. It bore the expected background of someone who wanted to set himself up as a business manager: certification as an accountant, about fifteen years' experience with an established firm, and a number of individual independent accounts he was servicing. He was firm and courteous, but not hospitable. He did not offer me a drink or a cup of coffee. I doubted that he had the makings for either in his kitchenette.

I mentioned that the CV did not state whether he was married. It flustered him just a little. I think he had practiced answering this question and thought he had it down pat. But when you cannot *hear* the answers, as I cannot, you tend to observe slight changes of complexion, small tremors, and nervous gestures just a bit more closely. His pointed, pale face, with its almost plastically smooth skin, turned just a shade whiter.

"I was recently divorced," he told me. "The decree was granted just last month, in fact." I gave him time to fill it out. "The divorce was uncontested," he offered. "But of course I have to take care of them. They have the house and everything, as they should have. It's nobody's fault and nobody should suffer."

He gestured around the apartment. "This, really, is all I need to live," he said. "My work." He smiled faintly. "I guess it's the main reason I'm divorced."

I liked him. There was something pared down and puritanical about him that appealed to the ascetic side of me. I too had once lived like this—when I was much younger, of course. I hadn't been a CPA or anything remotely resembling the altitude of a business manager. I had been a free-lance bookkeeper. Neither had I been nearly so enamored of my work. To me it had been a way for a recently deafened young man to make a threadbare living. To Pelfrey, obviously, it was a calling, a vocation, an identity more important than his marriage and children.

His calmness, his forthrightness, and his absence of a sales pitch convinced me, as it had Macready. The next morning I had Edna call Macready and tell him everything was jake.

And so it was—for about three months. Macready set up a system of weekly reports from Pelfrey, usually done over the telephone—Macready's account wasn't all that large or complicated—and that had been the last I'd seen of either of them. I submitted my routine bill for services rendered and was promptly paid. Then one morning Edna got the unexpected phone call from Macready.

He'd been trying to get hold of Pelfrey because Pelfrey had missed the last two reports. Macready had let the first one go by because he had been busy, embroiled with the preliminary negotiations over the series. But with the second omission, he was alarmed. He kept trying to reach Pelfrey by telephone and getting the answering device. He'd gone over to Pelfrey's building and rung the bell to no avail. He had called his bank and found out that, aside from a few thousand dollars in his checking account, his assets were zero. Bills that were routinely sent to Pelfrey now began to turn up at Macready's mailbox. Many of them, of course, had been opened by thieves looking for checks and thrown on the wet, filthy floor.

I searched out the janitor to Pelfrey's building and got into the apartment. It had that famous air about it of immediate departure. A glass of milk, half empty (or half full, as the optimists insist), was on the counter of the kitchenette. The milk was soured to curdling. He had been working hard when he left, and, as I had suspected, work was not done at the horrible little desk but at the gate-legged table. The table was covered with scratch-pad calculations he'd read off his machine. Pay dirt was found next to the telephone: a memo pad with the single word CARDINAL printed on it in deep, blunt penciled letters.

I zeroed in on the Cardinal Hotel finally, and a brief description of Pelfrey to the clerk got me directed to room number three on floor number four.

Life is not always so simple, of course. I don't know how many times I've looked into a skip where the apartment or office was as bare as a vulture-picked skeleton. Some skips get into a passion of anonymity and vacuum, so that not even a trace of personal dust remains. It put me in mind of the ancient joke about the Chinese immigrant who learned about capitalism. He came over and started a laundry (what else?) and set aside half of his income to invest with a stockbroker, who had promised to double his money. At the end of the first year he went down to collect his money, but was told, "I'm sorry, but the market has fluctuated." He went back to work, donating his fifty percent to investment, and was told at the end of the second year, "I'm sorry, but the market has fluctuated." This went on for the third and fourth years, and each time he was told, "I'm sorry, but the market has fluctuated." At the end of the fifth year, he went down, opened the door, and found the office empty. The desks had been removed, the telephones were disconnected from the walls, dust had settled on the floor.

He looked all about the empty room and sighed.

"Flucked again," said the Chinese fellow.

I was laughing to myself at the back table over my seventh bourbon of the day. When I raised my head, I saw that a few people at the bar were looking at me. Screw *them,* I decided. I had always liked that story. Nonetheless, my time was up.

This time there was no car occupying with suspicious flamboyance an illegal parking zone. I stared into the lobby from the edge of the window. There were no visible policemen. Even the gray desk clerk was not visible. The young man with the Gypsy Rose was there. He was leaning on the counter and idly leafing through a magazine whose contents did not seem to electrify him.

He glanced up as I came into the small lobby and recognized me instantly. "Anybody looking for me?" I asked him.

"No."

"Any cops been around lately?" I tested the ground.

" 'Bout an hour ago."

"What did they want?"

"Askin', you know, if there was any suspicious people around."

"Were there?"

"No."

"Did they go upstairs?"

"No." He suddenly grinned. "They don't like that climb, neither."

"Is that elevator ever going to get fixed?"

"The man say tomorrow," he reported solemnly.

I grunted and headed for the stairs. The bourbon had not improved my wind, and by the time I reached the fourth floor, I was breathing deeply. I went directly to room three and let myself in. I was not foolish enough to turn on the lights. I lit my little penlight and went directly to the table by the window, which could be seen by the streetlight. I played my light over the top of the table. The spool of fishing line was gone.

I cursed very softly and replayed the scenario. I had been standing at the table when I had unwound the needed length of line. I had cut off what I wanted and put the spool on the table top. Then I had made my thief's knot on the bolt and let myself out. The spool could *not* be anywhere else in the room unless someone had moved it. Yet, according to the young man downstairs, no one had been here. I sighed and began a laborious search of the room no wider than the beam of my pencil light. It was a half hour before I was satisfied that the spool was nowhere in the room. I did not have to worry about the bolt when I let myself out this time.

I did, however, have to worry about observers in the hallway. I tested the vibration of the door again, and slipped quickly to my room next door. I popped inside and put my back against the door, wondering if I should turn on the light even in here. I decided that it would be foolish not to. I ran the palm of my hand over several square feet of the unpleasant surface of the wall before I found the switch. Lighted, the room was even uglier than I had remembered. I turned impatiently away from the switch and saw my spool of fishing line—the sight of it nearly gave me a heart attack. It was dangling in mid-air, at about the level of my eyes.

The sight of it mid-air so paralyzed me that I barely took in the dark blue expanse of sweater behind it. The sweater covered a man's chest, but the chest spread out to almost the limits of my vision. It blocked out the rest of the room. I was staring, eye height, into the chest of a giant. I looked up and saw a calm obsidian face. He had been dangling the spool from his hand held level with his shoulder. His shoulder was above the top of my head.

I had a sense of waiting, but the sense was permeated with doom. I wanted that high huge face to speak, to communicate something besides terror. It refused. Even the eyes were open only slit-wide, and they looked at me with no more expression than a cat's. Instead of speaking, the giant twitched his fingers holding the fishing line so that the spool began to swing like a pendulum: a silent tick-tock, tick-tock. I looked up from it into the face that seemed to move only infinitesimally toward a smile.

I glanced back at the pendulum, and the blow of his open right hand caught me on the side of the head. I hadn't even seen it coming. It had arced up in a wide loop from his hip.

The fishing spool was dropped, apparently because his left hand grabbed my shirt and pulled me into the backhand blow that was the mate to the first. I remember my numb head rocking back and forth under a series of these forehands and backhands. But after that, it seemed that I was nothing more than a cloud full of silent explosions.

9

With the unwelcome completion of my memory came the consciousness of my machinery. The machinery noise in my head, doctors had explained to me too many times, was constant and perpetual. Consciousness of it was not. The roaring, clanking, groaning, and sometimes whistling noises that steamed away inside my skull were a memento of the wound that had deafened me. It is the only noise I am able to hear, but a noise that no one else can hear.

At this time it served to remind me that I was still alive, a functional reality I'd held in some doubt as I'd sailed through the blank skies of my hospital room. But if I was alive, it followed that I had things to do, a living to earn, etc. My trouble was that I didn't want to do anything at all. Simple attention to my bathroom requirements left me exhausted. I had graduated from the bedpan, but an orderly was needed to help me to the toilet.

Paradoxically, the better I got the more I saw of young Dr. Sartin. The paradox resolved itself when I noted that I was also seeing more and more of Edna, and that Dr. Sartin always managed to drift in whenever the scent of her perfume disrupted the sterile odor of the corridor. He was there with her now, glancing with frank admiration at the worried expression on her face.

She was saying, "We have to make plans today about what we're going to do."

The machinery banged away in my head to punctuate every silent word. "Do," I repeated dully, "about what?"

"Where you're going and all."

"Going?"

"When you leave the hospital," she augmented gently.

"And when is that?"

She turned prettily to Dr. Sartin for confirmation. "Tomorrow," he said. "Tomorrow afternoon."

"My God," I responded. They both looked at me gravely.

I could see the wheels turning in Edna's shapely skull. *"This isn't the Joe Binney of old."* Indeed it wasn't. In my battered head were stored countless scenarios of the manly man leaping from his bed of pain and rushing out into the street to exact justice. I'd even done this once or twice myself. But never before had I been quite the invalid I was now. I could not envision batting a mosquito. Defending myself against a grown man was unthinkable, against the dark giant who clouded my dreams, beyond imagination.

"What," I began uncertainly, "what did you have in mind?"

"What you need now," said the young doctor, "is not so much hospital care as nursing care for the next few weeks."

"So we thought," chimed in Edna, "that maybe what you needed was . . ."

"Wait a minute," I protested. "Back up. Who's we?"

"Dave and I," said Edna primly.

"Oh," I replied. I folded my hands and looked at them. Dr. Sartin had the courtesy to blush. Edna, of course, is shameless.

"Well," she burst in, brushing aside any opinions I might have on this new liaison, "we thought that what you needed, maybe, was to go to a nursing home."

"A nursing home!" It must have burst out of me with considerable violence, because the young doctor looked concerned. "You think I'm going to sit around on a wicker settee swapping war stories while some old bag is bringing me cookies? I'll be Goddamned if I'll do any such thing."

Although the doctor looked shocked, there was a gleam in Edna's eye that reflected a certain reassurance on her part. What I was displaying was indeed the Joe Binney of old.

"What would you suggest?" she asked from behind a sickeningly sweet smile.

"What I would suggest is. . . ." but the next words were unsaid because, unknown to the young lovers before me, the door to the room had opened, revealing the totally unprepossessing countenance of Lieutenant Detective Matthew Shope.

If there was any sympathy in his voice when he spoke, it was certainly not repeated in his expression. "Saw your name on the list of possibles from emergency," he said. "How come no complaint?"

"Would it do any good?"

"Maybe," said Shope. "Let's hear what happened."

Doctor Sartin said to him, "Mr. Binney is not in any condition for extended conferences."

"I'm not asking him to recite the Gettysburg Address," Shope told the doctor. "I just want to hear what happened in as few words as possible."

I put up my hand to avoid dissension. "In as few words as possible," I told Shope, "I don't remember."

"You *what?*" His face broke into an assortment of planes. His eyes bulged with anger.

"I don't remember," I repeated happily. "The last thing I remember is seeing my client Macready at his place. The next thing I knew, I was in the hospital."

Shope glared at me. He put a cigar in his mouth and was about to light it, when Dr. Sartin stopped him. Shope glared at Sartin. "Is this for real?" he demanded, waving his cigar at me.

Dr. Sartin said, "Mr. Binney has partial amnesia, which is very common following a concussion."

"And how long is this supposed to last?"

I thought, happily, "*As long as I Goddamned well want it to.*" Sartin replied, more diplomatically, "It's almost impossible to say. A week, a month. Possibly forever."

Shope fixed me with his frustrated stare. "All right, wise guy," he said. "What do you think happened?"

"They tell me," I began slowly, "that I was brought here in a cab. That means that some passerby rescued me from the street, possibly the driver himself."

"A good Samaritan, eh?" sneered Shope.

"Who knows? The driver got me here and left me on the doorstep."

"Anybody get the cab number?"

"No. He beat it."

"You got any idea of who might have had it in for you?"

"Nobody I can think of. I guess I was jumped and slugged. Maybe I put up a fight. I don't know. Maybe the muggers got sore and decided to work me over. Maybe they were just having fun."

"Muggers," Shope repeated. He put the cold cigar in his mouth, but then remembering that I couldn't hear, took it out so I could see what he was saying. "They didn't take anything, though, right? You had your wallet, your watch, everything."

"Maybe the cabby interrupted them."

"The cab driver," Shope said with an expression of scorn, "is going to jump out of his cab and pile into a gang of muggers kicking the hell out of a stranger? Tell me another one."

"He wouldn't have to get out of the cab," I reasoned. "All he had to do was lean on the horn and use the two-way radio."

Now Shope used my deafness to his own advantage. He glanced at Edna next to the young doctor, deliberately turned his back on them, and mouthed the word, "*Bullshit.*" I was properly shocked at this silent display of bad language.

"I tell you what I think, Binney," said the lieutenant, apparently audibly this time, since both Edna and the doctor jumped slightly. "I think you shoved your long nose too far into that hang-up at the hotel and somebody broke it off."

"Broke it off over a suicide?"

"It wasn't a suicide," Shope declared. "Down at the morgue they measured the stiff, and we worked it out. There was no way he could have done it from that chair. What's more, they found some woolen threads on his back teeth that probably mean he was gagged. There's the money, too," he added, waving the cigar. "What'd he do with it. Eat it?"

"The money," I told Shope, "is my only real concern. All I want is Mr. Macready's money."

"You're still going to chase after it?"

"As far as I can," I promised. "That's how I make my living."

I could see his belly heave with a grunt. "Some living," said Shope.

"We can't all be public servants," I told him demurely.

The comment seemed to rile him. "Somebody took a room next door to the hang-up," he said with a certain forcefulness. "Was it you?"

"Was my name on the register?"

Shope gave me a sour grimace. "John Doe," he said. "John Doe was on the register. Spelled out in block letters. Could the clerk describe him? Sure, average height, average age, average clothes, average eyes, and average hair. Any distinguishing characteristics, like eight fingers on one hand? Not that the clerk can remember. So we talked to everybody in that firetrap. Anybody hear anything? Anybody see anything? Oh, no. Not a thing, officer.

"I think we've just about had it with that rat hole," he concluded. "I think we better see about closing it down."

I remained silent under Shope's scrutiny. I'd said all I was capable of. I glanced over at the doctor, and he took the cue nicely.

"I'm afraid that's about all we can have today, sir," he said to the policeman. "You'll have to go now."

Shope looked at me with real malevolence. "If anything wakes up in your skull, Binney," he said to me, "I'm the first one to know. Get me?"

"I get you," I answered. I felt that I was speaking from under water.

He left reluctantly with many an injured backward glance at me. His threats were implicit, and despite the security of the hospital bed, they frightened me.

"What a horrible man," said Edna.

"Horrible men," I told her, "make the world go round. What Shope sees in a day's work would make a sword swallower puke."

"But David sees it every day too," she said, gesturing daintily toward the young man at her side, "and he's not like that."

"Let him wait," I advised her.

Those were my last words for a while. I slipped into sleep under the weight of all the problems and unwelcome attention.

Lipreading, no matter how expert the reader, is hard work. When one's safety and destiny are at stake, interpreting the curl of a lip can be an overwhelming burden. Lieutenant Shope overwhelmed me. I did not want, at some future date, to replay my prevarication on the unsympathetic stage of the precinct house.

The other problem that pushed me into a grateful sleep was my imminent departure from the hospital. I had a little circle of dread over how and where I would live in this helpless condition that kept spiraling back to Edna. It was possible for her, of course, to bridge the gap of communication to my apartment with the Code-Com phone. She could order meals sent up, etc. But it seemed to be a very shaky bridge.

It was even possible that Edna could move into my apartment for a while and flex the housemaid's knee. I doubted that she'd be enthusiastic about it, but she could do it. She was perfectly aware that any romantic feelings I'd had about her had faded into the mists of lost or abandoned opportunities. We were, as I'd told Doctor Sartin, good friends who had been through a lot together, but good friends only. Would she? I wondered. She was my best hope.

My apartment was large enough so that we wouldn't grind up against one another. There was a guest room, which, while not stylish, was adequate. There was even a tiny but workable television set that could keep Edna apprised of the events in "General Hospital." She could. She *could*. She could take over for just a couple of weeks while my guts got themselves back together.

The great dark form flittered like a bat in the caves of my mind. What was I asking of Edna? If he came back to get me, is it likely that he would let her go? Let her live? If she were asleep in the guest room, is it likely that she would hear him slip into the apartment? And if, with the sudden slash of light flicked on across her sleeping eyes, she awoke to the towering nightmare standing at the door, sat up in bed and shrieked, could I hear her? Indeed, I could not. And if he, with those incredibly long, incredibly strong arms, reached down across the room to seize her and tear her from the bedclothes, could I help? He would grab my arms as easily as he pinioned hers, and would I thrash and struggle helplessly in his grasp with his iron grip around my arm . . . ?

My eyes flew open as I struggled to pull my arm back from the hand that was holding it. There was a face close to mine.

"Jesus Christ," said Bill Macready. "I thought you were going to flip right out of the sack."

I struggled to get upright and finally pushed the button that raised the head of the bed. I was gulping huge drafts of air, and the heaving of my chest sent little tongues of flame licking the various organs of my insides. "Bad dream," I said to him. "Nightmare. It must be all the junk they're giving me in here."

He was observing me so carefully that he forgot to look sympathetic. He said, "Want to tell me what it was about?"

"Give me a cigarette," I demanded. After he'd lighted it, I told him, "Fear. I'm afraid. I'm four years old again. I'm afraid of the dark."

"But what happened," he asked me, "in the nightmare?"

"Ah, it was probably as much fantasy as a dream," I said.

"I'm worried about what I'm going to do when they boot me out of here tomorrow, that's all."

"Worried?" said Macready. "Why should you be worried?"

"I haven't really figured out how I'm going to survive," I answered. "I can't move around very well. I'm worried about the simple functions of living. I . . ."

"I don't know what the hell you're stewing about," he interrupted me. "Didn't they tell you? You're coming with me."

The shock of it relaxed every muscle in my body. I sank back into the pillows, saying, "I don't know how to thank . . ."

But he rode over this, telling me, "You can take the spare room. It's not the Plaza, but it's a place to flop. I'll take care of all the cooking and everything. I do anyway. No strain."

I took a deep drag on the cigarette, which had a nice anesthetizing effect on my insides. "There's something, in all honesty, you ought to be aware of," I told Macready against all my instincts of survival. "The guy that put me here isn't joking. He left me for dead. When he finds out I'm alive and comes looking for me, it could be very messy. It means that he could be looking at your place."

"My place isn't all that much of a pushover," Macready said.

"You don't know what this guy is like," I began, but then I wondered if I was whining. I stopped it. "Is Edna still around?" I asked him.

"Down by the nurses' station."

"Can you bring her in here?"

She came back with Dr. Sartin trailing behind her and Macready bringing up the rear. "You knew all along that Bill Macready was going to take me in?" I challenged her.

She shook her head. "Only after you'd fallen asleep," she said. "When we talked with him as he was coming in to see you he said he'd assumed you knew you were coming with him."

That made me feel better. I was not ready for teasing. I said to her slowly, "Edna, there's something I'd like you to do, but I'm not sure you ought to." Macready sensed a *double entendre* and smiled. Because he was standing, unseen, behind Edna, I ignored him. "I want you to get some things for me over at my apartment, but I'm not sure you should go there alone."

Dr. Sartin stepped forward instantly. "I'll be off in an hour," he said. "I'll go over with her." Macready scowled.

It wasn't much, but it was something. I told Edna where to find my toilet kit and the few clothes I'd need. Then I came to the important part. "On the floor at the right-hand side of my bed as you're facing it," I told her, "there's a loose floorboard that doesn't wiggle. It seems very solid, but it's not. It's easy to pry up from the end nearest the wall just by putting your fingernails in the crack. You won't bust a nail," I assured her. "It comes up very easily. It's oiled. Underneath that floorboard I have a revolver. It's big and it's heavy. It's also loaded and ready to fire. I want you to bring it along with the other stuff, but for Christ's sake remember it's as dangerous as an armed hand grenade. Pick it up carefully by the butt only. Don't get your hands near the trigger and, above all, don't drop it. Make sure you've got a firm hold on the handle.

"In the drawer of the night table next to my bed," I continued, "you'll find a box of cartridges. They fit that gun. Bring them along too. Also, in the drawer, you'll find an oilskin pouch. Put the gun carefully in the oilskin pouch and carry the pouch the way you would a bag of gumdrops. You got me?"

She nodded, her face pale and serious.

"When you've got the stuff together," I said, "call Macready and arrange to meet him somewhere. He'll tell you where. Give him the stuff and my extra set of keys. Let him bring it all up to his place. You stay away from it. You understand?"

Again, she nodded solemnly.

"And above all," I glanced over to include Dr. Sartin in this instruction, "while you're up in my apartment, the two of you, don't fool around. Is that clear?"

Doctor Sartin blushed a fiery red. Edna looked as if she'd been slapped. Her eyes popped, and her mouth flew open. "Well," she said, "of all the nerve! Of all the lousy . . ."

"No, no," I protested. I began to laugh, and oh, did it hurt. "I mean, don't go wandering around the place. Don't try to take anything I haven't asked you to. I've got too many gimmicks in that joint. They're meant to upset burglars, but gimmicks don't know if you're a burglar or not. They're dangerous. Understand?"

I was still holding my sore belly, laughing, when they trooped out of the room.

10

Macready had hired an ambulance. The hospital orderlies wheeled me out in a wheelchair, and the ambulance attendants lugged me up the dark, smelly staircase to the penthouse. By the time they'd got me through the heavy, metal-clad door, the two of them looked as if they'd finished first and second in the Boston Marathon.

Macready's spare room was a shock. He'd gone out and rented a hospital bed that could be adjusted electrically. He'd added an adjustable bed table and other sick-room accoutrements. The two attendants helped me get into the high bed and stood there, panting. Macready paid them off and gave them, as far as I could tell by the expressions on their red, perspiring faces, a sizable tip. When they'd left, I began to remonstrate. "You shouldn't have gone to all this trouble . . ."

Macready cut me off. "There's no use doing things half-assed. If you have to recuperate, then recuperate. Get some R and R. Is there anything you need right now?"

"Just one thing," I told him. "Did you get the suitcase from Edna?"

"It's under the bed."

"I can't bend over too well," I said. "Could you reach under and get me the oilskin pouch?"

He'd been listening while I instructed Edna. He raised the pouch out of the suitcase exactly as if he were lifting a bag of gumdrops, with the top of the pouch bunched in his fist. I carefully took the gun out and eased the hammer on to safety. It made me breathe easier. Macready, too, relaxed the tense muscles in his face.

"Could you hear anything," I asked him, "when I snicked the hammer?"

"I wasn't listening," he said, "but I think so."

"That's the reason I keep it cocked at home," I told him. "The little snick can be a giveaway. It's stupid to leave a gun around like a loaded bomb, but you have to think of the reason for having it there in the first place."

"You going to leave it on safety around here?" He was trying hard not to seem anxious that this should be so.

"Anybody who sleeps with a cocked gun under his pillow is asking to get his head blown off in the middle of the night," I told Macready. "The purpose of this gun is to shoot carefully selected targets: not myself or you."

"I was hoping you'd say that," he admitted.

There was something a little off center about Macready's reaction to the gun, a kind of studied indifference. The gun, after all, is a big, professional-looking bastard, a single-action Colt Python .357 magnum with its ventilated rib and ramp sight extending over a four-inch barrel. Fully loaded, it was a three-pound handful of explosive firepower. In the home defense category, it was a monster. But the point of home defense is to *stop* an assailant, and stop him quickly.

Macready was standing perfectly, inimitably still as I wiped the gun off with a rag from the bottom of the pouch and slipped it under my pillow. He showed not the slightest curiosity. All men—that I've run into, anyway—are fascinated one way or another by weapons. It seems to go with the masculine territory.

But here was Macready, not so much cool as reacting with a *studied* cool. After I'd put the thing under my pillow, he said without any expression showing on his face, "Do you really think you'll need it?"

"If that guy shows up here, believe me, I'll need it."

"You'll be sure it's him?"

"No way I could mistake him."

"I'm going to fix us something to eat," said Macready. "Relax a while."

Well, I tried. I stared out the steel-framed window, one of the two in the apartment that actually opened. My view was south, toward one of the few indeterminate skylines in Manhattan. I wasn't close enough to the window to look down and see a few of the gin mills, where, I assumed, some life must be going on. The walls of the room, made of plasterboard, were painted a rather sickly peach color that had not improved with age. Only King Kong, I told myself, could climb the walls of the building to present himself at my window. Unfortunately, my antagonist put me exactly in mind of King Kong, and so I quite deliberately drove the thought out of my mind. Nerves can be controlled.

I thought instead about Macready. If his reaction to the revolver was uncharacteristic of men in general, his sudden concern with my well-being was uncharacteristic of anything I had experienced previously with my client. Macready was a notorious tightwad—not a confidence-man type of nickel bender like Never-Meet-A-Tab-If-You-Can-Beat-A-Tab O'Neill, a charming acquaintance of my younger days, whose life was full of fun and frolic, but a real, genuine cheapskate.

And yet, the very modern hospital bed in which I was resting had not been offered to him free, I was sure, nor had all the other hospital equipment bunched around the bed. The people who supply such things, I have been told, also rent oxygen tanks, and have been known to pluck the oxygen mask from the face of an expiring invalid should the rental payment be so much as one day late. Can this be true? Was it O'Neill who had told me that? Had it been, indeed, O'Neill who had done the plucking? No matter. Macready had paid a stiff rental on the equipment here. I had, with my own eyes, seen him pay the ambulance attendants and, furthermore, tip them nicely. The whole thing constituted a bend in Macready's character around which I could not see.

I had been sniffing the air for flavorsome aromas after Macready had promised dinner, but nothing identifiable had been forthcoming—only the sort of stealthy humidity that is given off by plasterboard dampened through seeping walls. The source of this miasma was revealed when Macready brought in two plates of chicken pot pie: one for each of us. He put mine on the bed table and scattered some utensils next to it. Then he pulled up a chair preparatory to eating from his lap. I looked at the product of the frozen-food industry on the table before me and worried about my bruised insides. The white gravy, running over the shriveled peas and carrots that hid the random slivers of chicken meat, did have the look of badly soaked plaster gone to ruin. "Microwave?" I asked pertly.

"Nah," said Macready. Remembering my deficiency, he cleared his mouth before speaking again. "Toss it in the oven, wait a while, and what the hell."

"Um," I commented. Nonetheless, I was hungry. It had been a venturesome day for an invalid. I stuck my fork through the crust and ate my dinner like a little man. Midway in grinding up one of the twigs of chicken muscle, a happy inspiration overtook me. "This stuff is pretty expensive," I suggested, holding up a specimen of it on my fork.

His eyes widened with doubt. "Cheapest they had in the place," he said.

"No," I said, constructing my base. "I mean that frozen food, all frozen food, is expensive."

"Convenience," explained Macready, cleaning his plate. "All convenience is expensive."

"Ulcers are not convenient," I indicated shyly. "And they are very expensive."

He gestured at his plate. There was a half-smile on his face. "You think this stuff will give you ulcers?"

"You'd be lucky to stop with ulcers," I assured him. I nodded at the remnants on my plate. "That white gravy gets into the bloodstream. Six months of this crap and you'll wind up looking like one of George Segal's statues."

He sat back and laughed. "All right, wise guy," said Macready, "you live alone. What do you cook?"

"Ham hocks and sauerkraut," I told him happily. "Boiled beef with horseradish sauce. Broiled calves' liver smothered in onions. Red beans and rice—the real kind. Broiled fish once a week, striped bass, but mostly the really fresh fish of the day, whatever it is. Vegetable stew, with good stew meat . . ."

He waved me off. "That's housewife's cooking," said Macready. "The stuff you buy could be cheaper, but I haven't got the time."

"Sure you have," I insisted. "You just don't know how to use it right. I'll show you how to do it all. But only on one condition."

"Conditions now?"

"That you let me pay for the food, and also," I gestured around the room, "for all this hospital junk."

"Aha," exclaimed Macready. "So that's what you were leading up to. You're worried about the money."

"Also, believe me, about the food," I answered seriously.

Macready stood up and took the offending plates into the kitchen, where, I hoped, he would sterilize them. When he came back, he leaned against the doorjamb and said accusatorily, "You think that I'm such a rat bastard that I can't put up a sick friend for a few weeks and buy groceries?"

"I'm not going to send a bulletin to the *National Enquirer* about this,'' I asserted, ''but I've had the distinct impression that you're a careful man with a buck.''

''Have you ever had to wait for your money?''

''Never,'' I consoled him. ''That's not what I mean. Careful is not crooked. But still,'' I paused for a little while and looked at him, ''it *is* careful.''

''There's only one thing I'm careful about,'' Macready said very soberly, ''and that is work. I want to be able to do the work I want to do.''

''You *are* doing the work you want to do.''

''You saw what went on the last time you were here.'' He gestured toward the big living room. ''I'm a commodity, a product to be exploited.''

I put my hand up. ''My father,'' I said, ''was a commodity who was exploited. He was a longshoreman on the docks in Boston. He carried loads from A to B. He was a two-legged mule. The best year he lived I don't think he made seven-thousand dollars.''

''It's different,'' said Macready. He put his hands behind his back and began to pace up and down in the best Admiral Nelson quarterdeck manner.

''Whoa,'' I called out. ''I can't understand you when you're running around. Stand still where I can see you.''

''The difference between what I do and what your father did,'' said Macready, ''is that your father had a connection, an allegiance to a number of things that I don't have. When you say, 'longshoreman who went from A to B,' you're talking about a man who was secure in his job and in his life—his identity. He knew who he was and what he was. Actors don't have this.''

''Acting,'' I said, ''unless I'm mistaken, is a job, a profession, like anything else.''

''No,'' Macready told me. ''No. It's not like anything else.'' He began to pace again, but then remembered himself. ''Acting,'' he said, ''is the art of impersonation.'' He put his hand up to abort my impatient twitch at the threat of a lecture. ''That's a simple-minded statement,'' he admitted. ''But you have to establish the fact before you can think about actors.

''The trick is that actors do not impersonate people. They impersonate ideas, figments of other peoples' imaginations. Bits and pieces of real people get put in, of course. But the impersonation is made up like a mosaic with bits of human flesh. The mosaic is bigger than life, more memorable than life. It is not the impersonation of life. You don't render things true to life, you render them true to the idea."

I did, undeniably, ungovernably, twitch. Macready took some cigarettes from his shirt pocket and offered me one. I took it. This was no time to quit smoking in my estimation.

"I'm not going to lecture you on acting," said Macready, at which I heaved a sigh of relief, "but you have to understand what it means to be an impersonator—an actor. You have to understand how the rest of the world looks at an actor. They think you're a freak, a faggot, a sex-maniac, a drunk, a pervert, a congenital liar, a coward, and a sort of world-class cheat who doesn't really work for a living."

I had taken a deep lungful of smoke that had the effect of making me dizzy. When I had put together all his defamatory attributions, all I could exclaim was, "Aw, c'mon."

"So actors," he continued, "in this country anyway, get defensive. They get paranoid. They get a little crazy. A lot of actors take on the emotional coloration of the world around them, and they begin to feel contempt, even hatred, for themselves. To defend themselves against this, they develop very strong egos. If they can't develop the ego they tear themselves apart. Sometimes they do anyway, and then the strongest ego is the most powerful engine of destruction.

"The main defense that actors have against the public attitude is in going back to their one true church, the theater, where they are among their own kind. Where everybody, supposedly, speaks the same language.

"And he can scale it back even further. He can limit his church. He can come back to the stage, where, you'd think, everybody is singing the same psalm, the same number in the book.

"That's theater," he said, driving the word home with a forefinger that seemed to go right through the wall, "but the other side is showbiz.

"Showbiz," he looked to the ceiling for inspiration, making it difficult for me to read him, "is a kind of freak slapped up together in equal parts of ego and money. The theater owners, with their stop clauses, as final as a firing squad, are money—pure money. And with them, you know where you're at. Make the draw and you stay alive. Get empty and you die.

"But with the producers, and now the directors, you're getting into ego: power struggles, the desire to control, not control yourself, which is what actors have to do, but to control others, somebody else, events, contol events—fate.

"Daly, Frohman, Belasco started this," he said. "Before them directing and producing were something that actors did in their spare time. The actor-managers were hated a lot because they were sons of bitches. The play was mounted to show them off in their best light, and there wasn't any question of anybody else getting a chance to shine. It was dog eat dog. You got out there in front and you fought for your life. And if you were *too* good, the actor-manager would throw your ass out in the alley. But direction was pure theater. Production was pure theater. It was still the church.

"Then we got the conceptualizing geniuses: producers and directors who believed that their ideas were more important than the play or the performance. Their goal was power, and power is what they got. The only important thing about them is that they're dangerous. They're dangerous because they will do anything in the world to preserve that power. They fight to preserve it because it is terribly, terribly fragile. It's an illusion of power. It's not the ability that puts a show up on the boards.

"These are the people that actors have to defend themselves against. They think actors are children. Why? Because they themselves have seen how easy it is to get along without having actually to *perform*. So they look at actors, who are struggling, who are exposing themselves—naked—and they feel contempt. They're divorced from all that.

"These are the people I'm defending myself against with money," said Macready, "because money is the only defense you've got."

I stared at him. "I want to be independent," said Macready. "I've earned it and I want it. It all boils down to what they used to say. 'All that's needed is two planks and a passion.' That's all you need. Two planks and a passion to make a performance."

"Or a crucifixion," I reminded him.

But those were the last words I remember of this particular conversation, because I had fallen asleep.

11

That was the first of many harangues on the subject of acting, but as the subject began to exhaust itself, it was inevitable that he should ask me, finally, "How did all that happen—with your ears?"

We had pushed ourselves back from the table, stunned with the sheer number of calories bubbling up from the liver and onions and mashed potatoes, and were sipping the coffee I had brewed. I was dressed for the first time since I'd been there, and had abandoned the pajamas for slacks and my old Navy sweater. I was feeling comfortable for the first time—even human.

"Korea," I told him. "I was in underwater demolition. I put a shaped charge on the shaft of a North Korean gunboat. It had a delay fuse that didn't delay. Practically turned my skull inside out."

"You look younger than that," he said.

"It must have been nearly one of the last actions of the war. I was nineteen."

"Where'd you learn lip reading?"

"Navy hospital."

"That where you learned the detective business?"

"No. That's where I learned bookkeeping: correspondence course. I started off as a free-lance bookkeeper so I wouldn't have to talk to anybody. The detective dodge came later, after I'd chased down a few skips and swindlers for my bookkeeping clients."

"I hope it's not offensive to you," said Macready, "if I say I think you do it very well."

"You're not offending me," I assured him, "but you're probably overestimating my talent. I pick up an average of fifty percent of the spoken words. The rest is guesswork. Very educated guesswork, but still guesswork."

"Did it take long?"

"It took me about a year before I could function with any confidence at all. After that, it was experience and practice. But

I worked very hard that first year, most of it in the hospital in Philly. Even now, though, I still hit a lot of clinkers. There are some people I can't read at all.

"You, though," I smiled, "you come through as clear as a bell. There are times when I can almost hear you."

Macready got a very odd smile on his face. "It's very funny," he said.

"Comical?"

"No. Funny strange. You had to learn a new way of hearing in the hospital. I had to learn a new way to talk."

I wasn't sure that I'd read him correctly—it was a strange thing for him to be saying. "A new way to talk?" I repeated uncertainly.

"Yeah." He pointed to his upper lip. "I caught a frag in the mouth in Nam. I spent about a year in and out of hospitals putting it back together."

"Where?" I asked him. "Not in Philly Naval. That would be too much."

"Nah," he smiled. "Army General, Fort Benning."

Broaching the subject, I suppose, opened the gate to a lot of memories for both of us. "I'm going to take a major step in convalescence," I told Macready. "I happen to know that you've got a jug of Old Fitzgerald in your cabinet, and I'm going to ask you to buy me a drink."

"I'll have one with you," said Macready. He got some ice from the kitchen and brought in a pitcher of water. The first taste of my drink was like coming back to the old homestead after a long and dusty trip.

"It doesn't show, but I suppose you know that," I told him.

"It doesn't show because I was one of the luckiest sons of bitches in the world to draw one of the best plastic surgeons in the world. He rebuilt my whole upper lip. What he did was a miracle."

"Maybe it was because he knew you were an actor."

"He couldn't have known," Macready smiled, "because I hadn't even thought of acting then. I hadn't thought of anything in the world except chasing ass. He just did it because he was good."

"How come you had to learn how to talk again? Did it screw up the muscles?"

"It wasn't only that," said Macready. "All my teeth were gone. Also, I think, I was a little nuts."

I sat back and absorbed some of my drink. "Yeah," I said. "I understand some of that. I know about it."

"If I'd been brought back right away, it wouldn't have been so tough," said Macready. "But I was a prisoner."

"A prisoner!"

"Yeah. We were in a fire fight, and when I got hit I was stunned. I got up to run, but I was really unconscious and I was sort of running in circles. The other guys in the squad saw me get up and they thought I was O.K., you know? That I'd make it back. But I ended up running in the wrong direction. When I came to, I realized I was surrounded by VCs."

Macready took a sip of his drink and let it trickle down as a salute to reminiscence. "I don't know why they didn't just grease me. Either they had some special orders or just wanted me for a pet. They were a loose-assed outfit that scrounged around out in the boonies. They weren't really bad natured, except that I never knew from one minute to the next if somebody was going to waste me just for convenience. Sometimes one of them would pretend he was going to kill me, just for a joke. They'd laugh like hell. It got so I kept my eyes fastened on the guns, you know, so if one was raised up, I'd try to slide out of the way. Then it got so I couldn't look at the guns at all. I just wouldn't look."

"How long did this go on?" I asked him.

"I found out later that it must have been about six weeks. Personally, I lost all my sense of time. A lot of the time I was half nuts or unconscious. I guess they were holding me to take back to the base camp for interrogation, but it would have been useless. I couldn't talk. All I could do was make a kind of *wah wah* sound.

"They bandaged up the hole in my face and put some gunk on it, and part of the lip grew back while the other part sort of dangled, like a flap. I couldn't eat much, not that there was very much around to eat. My gums got infected, and the rest of my teeth dropped out. Toward the end, I was pretty much of a skeleton and with a high fever all the time. They knew I was never going to make it back to the base camp. They decided to shoot me. It wasn't meanness of their part. It was sort of like putting an old sick dog away."

Still holding his drink, Macready got up and stretched and walked around in a tight circle, as if proving his freedom. He sat down again, took another sip, and said, "They had me tethered to a tree. It wasn't really very dramatic. I was just tied up to a tree like a sick dog, and I knew that sometime during the day somebody would have to come up to the tree and put a bullet in me or cut my head off or something. I just waited.

"So I waited. I didn't look around at anybody. I didn't want to know what was happening, and I didn't want to attract attention. I hadn't even realized that they'd stolen out of camp until I heard the noise of a fire fight, maybe a hundred yards away. I flattened myself on the ground out of instinct, pure instinct, and I could hear the bullets whisper and splat. And then the noise stopped and a whole twenty-four-hour day must have passed before I heard footsteps coming back. I could tell by the sound of the boots that they weren't VCs."

I reached for the Old Fitzgerald, popped a couple of ice cubes into my glass, and rebuilt my drink. If ever there was a moment for my sore guts to find out if they could stand up to alcohol, this was it. Macready, however, did not replenish his glass. He seemed far away.

"It was a long time at the hospital before they could even think about surgery," he recalled. "They had to clear up the infections and put some weight on me because it would be a long procedure. It turned out to be a lot of procedures. I forget how many. Also, they had to let my gums get back to normal size. Finally they did; the gums shriveled right down to bone. All I've really got in here," he pointed to his mouth, "are upper and lower ridges of bone."

"The army gave you teeth like that?" I couldn't help admiring them. They were classic movie actors' teeth. They fitted his face perfectly and had no appearance of falseness about them at all.

"Shit, no," said Macready. "I paid for these out of the money I've earned and you wouldn't believe what they cost. No," he pursed his acquired lips, "I have no bitch at all about the Army, but they couldn't afford china like this. What they did was build me a new set of teeth that were okay for life, but not for acting. They were good enough," he added, "for me to start learning to talk again.

"And that's when my life started over," he said, "when I had to learn to talk again. You have to understand, I was nuttier in the hospital than I was in the bush."

"I understand all right," I told him. "I was crazier than a shithouse rat in Philly."

"Yeah, well. I spent some time with the shrink, but what the shrink never discovered was that they didn't really have to shoot me out in the boonies. Something died out there tied up to the tree. There were the dog tags, but that's all that there was left.

"And when we started speech therapy, working my way back from the *wah wah* sounds, I knew it wasn't me. It wasn't my voice, and it wasn't my speech anymore. You know, the way you talk, the way you sound to yourself . . ." He stopped, suddenly stricken. "But you can't . . . you don't . . . do you?"

"No," I answered, "it's true. I don't hear myself. I really never know what I'm saying. It's just vibrations going out into the air. There's no real feedback."

"*Feedback.*" Macready seized the word. "That's what I mean. What was getting fed back to me wasn't me. The whole personal sound and feeling of my own voice was gone. It was somebody else making those screwy sounds that you have to make when you're learning how to talk. It was somebody else saying those nutty sentences that have nothing to do with life or with logic . . . just a long collection of sounds . . . a tale told by an idiot." He sat up very straight and said, "Goddamn it, I think I will have another drink." He reached for the bottle.

After he'd fixed his drink and tasted it, he demanded of me, "When you were in the hospital, did you read a lot?"

"Like a machine," I responded. "All the time. Anything and everything."

"That's it," he said excitedly. "Anything and everything. I would have read the marks on toilet paper.

"I got into the donations, you know? Stuff that people send in to be nice. Of course, most of it was shit, *Reader's Digest* outlines of bullshit novels, *How To Build Your Own Lawn Furniture*—you know—but somebody sent in a collection of magazines I'd never heard of called *The Partisan Review*. It was the whole set, going all the way back to the forties or even earlier, I think.

"It was the craziest Goddamned stuff you ever saw in your life. I thought the short stories were shit. They had poems, but I couldn't understand them. The rest was either politics about years gone by or criticism of stuff I'd never heard of.

"But one day when I was thumbing through them, I came across a photograph that kind of floored me. There hadn't been any photographs in this bunch of magazines. It was a picture of three people who were obviously on a stage and obviously rehearsing something. The caption said that it was André Gide,

Madeline Reynaud, and Jean Louis Barrault in a rehearsal of Gide's adaptation of *The Trial*. I'd never heard of any of them or of anything called *The Trial*.

"What the photograph showed was the three of them discussing something about the show. But the one I couldn't take my eyes off was Jean Louis Barrault. Gide was standing there with a topcoat thrown over his shoulders, dressed for the street. Madeline Reynaud was stylishly dressed, and she was deep in conversation with Gide. But Barrault was in costume. He was in a beat-up, dusty business suit and he looked *in place* on the stage, there, as if he had just grown up through the boards like a plant in a garden. And the thing that got me, fascinated me so that I couldn't put it down, was that Barrault was half into his character and half out of it. In other words, he was listening to the conversation about the play, but he was listening from the other side. He was caught halfway between himself and the character. It was the most mysterious thing I'd ever seen. He was two people at once. The Goddamned photograph spoke to me. I tore it out of the magazine and kept it. I don't usually do things like that.

"It had a kind of magic, you know? Like the old myths have, where a girl turns into a tree or a man turns into a stag. He was halfway between changing.

"And it came to me that acting is changing. You change into someone else, and then you change back. I was looking at the whole thing in transition.

"I got excited and started to bug my speech therapist about it. 'Who is this guy?' She got interested, and after a while she found out there was a revival of a picture he was in down in New Orleans, and she put me on a bus to go down and see it. It was *The Children of Paradise*, and it nailed me. It not only starred Jean Louis Barrault, it was about acting itself. She gave me a book about the character Barrault had been playing, *The Great Deburau*. You know the story about him."

"No," I said, "I don't."

Macready took a swig of his drink and stood up. While I don't know how he did it, I was suddenly conscious of his playing a scene.

"Paris, the eighteen-forties," he said. "A distinguished-looking man comes in to see a doctor.

" 'What is your problem, sir?' asks the doctor.

" 'I am weary of life,' says the distinguished man. 'Life has no meaning for me any more. I am sick of living.'

" 'You need some happiness, some cheer,' says the doctor. 'I have a prescription for you. Go at once, this evening to the *Funambules* and see The Great Deburau. He will illuminate your life. He will make you laugh till you cry. He will charge your life with happiness and beauty.'

"The distinguished man steps back and looks sadly at the doctor. 'I am Deburau,' he says."

A smile had spread across my chops until I thought it would split my face. "That's beautiful," I said. I kept repeating, "That's beautiful," because I had been, there was no other word for it, enchanted. Macready, with a few economical gestures and lightning changes of his posture and his face, had created in front of me a small, kindly French doctor and a tall, deep, exhausted tragic figure.

He sat down, appreciating my appreciation. "Gotcha, huh?" he asked me. I nodded happily.

"Yeah," he said, "well, when she saw I was interested, and interested is a very mild word for what I felt, she started working on a different tack. My ordinary speech improved rapidly after that, but she started teaching me breath control, projection—how to talk out of your belly—all kinds of things she wasn't paid to do.

"The hospital was anxious to discharge me, but she screwed around and screwed around keeping me on until she thought I had a chance to look and talk like a normal human being. Also, she knew a guy who was running a little theater in New Orleans, and she arranged for me to go down there and be a dogsbody when I was discharged.

"But during that time I came across something else in the library. It was three volumes. I read it all and that's where I got my name."

"Your name?"

"Yeah. Macready isn't the name I was born with. It's the name of an actor who's been dead over a hundred years. William Charles Macready his full name was. He was mostly billed as Charles Macready, so I took the first name, William. He was a very great actor, and I wanted to be a very great actor, so I took what I could of his name.

"The old name, the one I was born with," he said looking distantly over my shoulder, "I left tied to the tree."

12

My convalescence at Macready's almost ended in gunfire.

It's embarrassing to recall it even now; explaining it to Lieutenant Shope, who was seated in my office, with Edna looking on, was excruciating.

This was only my second day back at the office. My first day back had been very strange, as if the office were some place I had never been before nor had much desire to be. My absence had broken the skein of familiarity with the shabbiness. Rejoining the ugliness of the furniture, the dusty blinds, the soot piled on the windowsill, the cracked paint, and the glaring, revealing light had been, on the first day, exactly like meeting an unpleasant cousin at a family reunion.

By the second day I was rehabilitated. The overhead light did nothing for Shope's complexion. His skin was city gray enlivened by the red threads of broken capillaries that found their main junction in his nose. His eyes were a pale, frigid blue. "I only accidentally saw the squeal," he was saying. *Squeal* . . . complaint . . . there had been a complaint, then. "And the address rang a little bell. Macready's place. You were camped there, right?"

"Mr. Macready," I said, "gave me the use of his spare room so I could recuperate."

"Tell me about it," Shope urged me. He took out a cigar and turned to Edna, asking, I supposed, if she minded his smoking. This was an unusual gesture in Shope, and one that was fraught with danger. Edna signaled her assent without speaking. Her eyes were fastened on me.

"It was a misunderstanding, pure and simple," I began slowly.

"No, it wasn't," Shope contradicted me. "The boy saw what you were doing."

"He *thought* he saw . . . through a dirty window."

"Tell me about it," he repeated.

"I was cleaning my gun, and . . ."

"No," he interrupted. "You weren't cleaning your gun, unless you clean guns in your sleep."

"How serious is this?" I asked him directly.

"You have a license to carry a gun," Shope replied. "We have to figure out whether to continue the permit. If you want to give me some kind of fairy tale about cleaning your gun, you're not going to keep the permit."

"Before I tell you," I began again, "I want you to think about my record. This is absolutely the first time . . ."

"People only get killed for a first time," said Shope. "People never get killed a second time."

"Nobody was killed," I insisted. "Look, I need a break. There were extenuating circumstances."

"Tell me about it."

"All right. I've had my marbles rattled. You know that. Some people beat me up and damn near killed me. I still don't know who they are, nor could I identify them if I had to."

The small blue eyes bored into me. "I thought I said something about fairy tales," he said.

"It's the truth!" I slapped my hand on the desk for emphasis.

"Let it roll," said Shope.

"So I'm apprehensive."

"You're apprehensive you'll be mugged by the same people twice?"

"It wasn't really a mugging," I said. "I thought we'd sort of agreed on that."

"First I've heard of any agreement."

"Well, you sort of convinced me up there in the hospital."

Shope caricatured the razor slit of a smile.

"I've become convinced," I continued, "that the beating had something to do with the death of Arnold Pelfrey."

"The murder of Arnold Pelfrey."

"Yes," I agreed. "When you told me he was murdered, it got me to thinking."

"Thinking what?"

"Thinking that those guys had left me for dead. That they wanted me dead. That somehow I'd seen something up there that they didn't want me to see."

"And what would that be?"

"I honestly don't know," I told him with all the sincerity I could muster. "I haven't seen anything you guys didn't see. On the other hand, these guys aren't going to go around knocking over policemen. Too much heat. But they can grind me out, all right." I said this with what I hoped sounded like bitterness. "I get beat up, and I'm the guilty suspect."

"You're breaking my heart," said Shope.

"So I was apprehensive—all right, scared. I was afraid they'd come back and finish the job. That's why I had the gun." I stared at him with deadly seriousness. "And that's why I want to keep the gun. Without the gun I'm a dead man. I'm beat up and I'm sick. I couldn't wrestle a kitten right now."

"But you'd shoot a kitten?"

"*No,*" I said violently. "That's all over. I'm ashamed of what happened. It makes me sick."

"That makes two of us," said Shope.

"I was asleep," I admitted. "Macready and Sally were chasing each other around the furniture, but of course I can't hear and . . ."

"Sally," said Shope. "Tell me about Sally."

"Sally Hennigan," I told Shope, "is a very dear, close friend of Mr. Macready's."

"Macready likes girls, eh?" asked Shope.

"What's he supposed to like," I queried reasonably, "turkeys?"

But under that gray tissue of skin I saw the answer in Shope's mind. Nobody, really, was supposed to like anything. Nobody was supposed to live like Macready. People were supposed to be *normal,* schoolbook normal. Macready was an insult to the idea of normality. "Get on with it," he said through the blue smoke of his cigar.

"Sally visits Mr. Macready quite frequently," I resumed. She had, in fact, been there three times before, and a sudden shocking picture of her pink naked body sped through my mind. "They're not engaged or anything, but I guess she's what you'd call his steady girlfriend."

"So he gets it on with her," Shope said impatiently.

"Yes," I agreed. "They have what is called, I think, a normal sexual relationship." I didn't look at Edna, who was looking at me—I could *feel* that. "Miss Hennigan is what you would call on the West Coast, I guess, a starlet."

"And what do we call them back here on the East Coast?" Shope inquired.

I admit that the word *whore* raced unbidden through my mind, but it was not uttered. "She's a sort of actress," I said lamely. "You know, she gets walk-ons occasionally and hangs around."

"But she's not what you'd call successful."

"Not in acting, anyway."

"O.K. So let's go back to where he's chasing her around the room."

"I was in my room, in bed, dozing."

"I was told you had the light on."

"I was reading," I replied, "and I started to doze." I did not want to tell Shope that I *usually* sleep with a night light, like a six-year-old. I do it because I'm deaf and while I'm impervious to noise, the slightest shadow across my eyelids will wake me up. That was none of Shope's business.

Neither was my dozing off the sweet sleep of an untroubled mind. Two images had been flickering through my mind all day: the naked image of Sally on my flexible bed, and the obsidian face I had first seen in the hotel room.

Sally had been up there before, and I had not needed ears to feel the thumpings and vibrations occasioned by her lovemaking with Macready. On the night before the event with the gun, however, she had been up there with me alone.

That evening she had shown up for dinner, which, unfortunately for her, had been ham hocks and sauerkraut. When Macready announced that he had promised to go to see a show, she pleaded sauerkraut tummy and lagged behind. Macready opined that he would be coming back very late indeed, since he was slated to attend a party with the cast, and could he drop her off somewhere? No, he couldn't. She'd go home herself, she said, after she felt a little better. She was indisposed to move.

Her total recovery was coincident with my finishing the dinner dishes. She announced gaily that she was going to take a shower and feel "all better." She began shedding garments on her way to the bathroom, and was wearing nothing more than diaphanous panties when she reached the door—which she left open. Her emergence was signaled by a quick spurt of pink bouncing flesh from the bathroom to Macready's bedroom. She emerged from there wearing one of Macready's shirts. I was being confronted, I recognized, with a terminal case of the cutes.

It was also at this point that I realized I was still wearing pajamas—it being one of those days I'd felt too lousy to change. My flimsy costume made me conspicuous, and I was happy she pointed to the curved end of the couch and said, "Sit down and let's talk." Sitting down made me less conspicuous. She sat at the other end, which had the instinct of maidenliness to it, but in the surrounding arc presented her distinctly to view. The shirt she had chosen was a big blousy affair, and she had begun the buttons far, far down. "Honestly, Joe," she said, reaching artfully for a cigarette on the coffee table, "what do you guys do all day?"

"Do?" I had spotted a newspaper on the far corner of the table and pulled it back across my lap. "Do," I repeated stupidly. "Well, nothing much. Bill is usually working, rehearsing, learning lines, making phone calls."

"And you? What do you do with yourself all day, poor thing?"

"Cook," I said. "Clean up a little, you know, pick up things around the house. I ran the vacuum cleaner yesterday."

"But what about talking? Don't men ever talk?"

"Oh, sure, we talk."

"And what do you two men talk about?"

Suddenly I saw why she was limited to walk-ons and cattle calls. She had struck a tomboy, Tom Sawyer attitude with her clasped hands dropped between her knees and her face thrust out in what was supposed to signify uninstructed innocence. It was a parody of innocence.

"Bill does most of the talking," I admitted.

"About his career?"

"In a way, yes," I answered. "A lot about his career."

She slid off her end of the couch and moved across the floor to my end, where, from her knees, she gazed up into my face. "And what does Bill say about his career?" Her brown eyes, upon which I had rigidly fixed my gaze, were luminous.

"Oh, you know," I began weakly, "about how he got started in acting. He likes to talk a lot about the history of acting, you know, how the theater developed and changed and . . ."

"That's not career, silly." She put her hand up against my cheek. It was rather like having a raccoon touch you. "What does he say about his career?"

"I'm not sure what you mean," I answered guardedly, although indeed I was.

"What's he going to do?" She emphasized the last word with a tap on my cheek.

"Do?" I feigned ignorance. "He's going to go on acting."

She smiled knowledgeably. "It's not very nice," she said, "my being here like this and talking about nothing in the world but Bill Macready. You're important too. Every bit as important.

After what you've been through, getting beat up and everything." Her eyes acquired a misty look to them. "Did they hurt you terribly, poor thing?"

"They got to me pretty good." I could feel the gravel shifting in my chest.

"Bill said they broke you all up inside—in the tummy?" She lifted my pajama jacket. "Oh," she said, "you've still got bruises there." She began to stroke my midriff. "There," she said, "does that make it all better?"

I took her small cold hand very gently and moved it away from my straining flesh. "Excuse me," I said, and got up, pivoting swiftly to head for the bathroom. In there I doused my face with cold water and stared at it in the bathroom mirror. I remained there looking at the reflection for quite a while.

When I came back she had vanished from the living room and the shirt was a linen puddle on the floor. Finally I discovered her on my hospital bed without any clothes at all. She had the little pushbutton console in her hand. She smiled up at me. "Don't you like me at all?" she asked.

"Sure," I answered miserably.

"Do you like me better like this?" she asked. She pushed the buttons that lowered both the head and the foot of the bed, leaving her blonde-bedecked pelvis in high prominence at the middle. Her body flowed with invertebrate ease backward over the two slopes. She looked at me and grinned. "Like this?" she asked, and raised her gorgeous legs with choreographic precision straight above her pelvis, where she split them into a V. After a pause, she peeked out at me again and asked, "Or like this?" She pushed the button raising the head of the bed so that her entire beautiful body was displayed, arms and legs outstretched on a slanting field of white.

"I'm tired," I announced. "You can play with that thing all night if you want to. I'll sleep on the couch."

She scrambled off the bed with a grim little snarl on her sunny face. The snarl turned into a sneer and she said, "What is it with you? Have you got it on with Bill?"

"I don't like hitting a wet deck," I told her. I snatched up a spare blanket and went in to curl up on the scimitar couch. Through slitted eyes I watched her assemble her clothes, get dressed, and leave. I assume that she slammed the door.

Shope brought me back to reality by touching my shoulder.

"Are you trying to remember what you were reading?" he asked me.

"No . . . no." I jerked up in my chair. "I'm trying to reconstruct things exactly." I turned the gears of my mind to order the events of the day that followed that evening with Sally—the disastrous day.

"It's hard for me to separate," I told Shope, "between the dozing and being awake."

"Let's take it from the top," Shope suggested. "What time did Sally get there?"

"About seven in the evening," I recounted. "We'd finished dinner."

It had taken Sally about ten seconds that evening—the following evening—to realize that I hadn't told Macready anything about her gyrations the night before. What was there to tell? The routine clicked back into place.

Because I had been fairly withdrawn and morose all day, Macready was not surprised when I pleaded fatigue and retired to my room—I was beginning to think of it as my cave, my lair. There was more on my mind, however, than fatigue or even Miss Prettyparts as I propped myself up in bed and switched on the lamp of my night table. There was the irreducible fact that I had identified my assailant. The huge dark face hung just behind my forehead, like a cloud settling along my optic nerve.

It would be nice to think that I had identified him through tireless detective work, but it happened, like so much of my life, through sheerest luck. I had been snipping out theater reviews for Macready, who had offered me this task as a kind of occupational therapy. Macready had years ago decided that he would keep and catalogue reviews of each and every play reviewed by the *New York Times*, *News*, and *Post*. Like any decent normal man, he had fallen hopelessly behind in this enterprise and had permitted heaps of entertainment sections of these newspapers to collect in the true Collyer brothers' style. Would I mind, he'd wondered, snipping out these reviews, taping them on a sheet of paper, entering the dateline, and filing them alphabetically? It was precisely the kind of lazy, utterly mindless task I had been looking for. *Snip, tape, write, file; snip tape, write, file*. The golden hours dissolved before me harmlessly.

I had worked my way up to papers that were only one year old. While I was separating out the reviews from unimportant items such as wars, massacres, dissolutions of hegemonies, and the exploration of outer space, I came across the head and shoulders cut of the man who had beaten me in the hotel. The shoulders were important because they sloped down from the neck in an unarguable statement of deadly power.

"*Basketball star Roger Grim,*" read the legend, "*released today from prison.*" The short following item that had been jumped from page one observed that Roger Grim, who had been convicted of conspiracy in a point-shaving scandal, had now served his sentence minus allowance for good time. The item was short because remarks from Roger Grim had not been forthcoming. Standing before the prison gate and glaring down at the reporter, Roger Grim had been "unavailable for comment." Then he had been whisked away, according to the reporter, "in a long, black Cadillac limousine."

"What time did the fun and games begin?" Shope asked rudely.

"I don't run a clock on them," I answered irritably. "I went to bed before eight o'clock and started to read."

But it wasn't really reading. Prison had not made Mr. Grim's face pretty. There was a granitic hatred in the visage that had stared down at the photographer, and it was indistinguishable from the face that had looked down at me. The face instilled in me a curious mixture of shock and relief. The shock came from the reality of the identity: It was a face, now, that I was going to have to hunt down and make my settlement with. The relief came from the fact that he was no longer a phantom, a powerful ghost, a bogeyman. He was an identifiable human being. It was also a relief to know that I had not been taken by some cheap hoodlum living in the woodwork of a rotting hotel, but by a rogue athlete whose strength of arm and speed of hand would be too much for anyone but a top-ranking professional boxer.

"So what happened then?" asked Shope.

"Sally hadn't eaten any dinner, so Macready called up the deli to have some sandwiches sent up."

Bogeyman! It's easy to say that the photograph in the paper dispelled it, but the face haunted me as I drifted in and out of sleep between the paragraphs on the magazine page.

"And they were delivered?"

"Yeah, they were delivered. Macready had flipped on the hall light in the stairway so the delivery boy wouldn't be too scared to come up."

But scared or not when he arrived, the delivery boy had gotten himself disoriented. I don't think it was so much from the desolate aspect of Macready's hallway: A local delivery boy would have seen many approaching, if not equaling it. I think it was the scene in the penthouse that turned his brains around. I think that Sally had been running around with little or nothing on, and probably had made only the slightest effort to cover herself. I think that the kid was confronted with a scene right out of *Playboy*, and it made the old eyes bulge. When Macready had taken the sandwiches from him and invited him inside while he dug up the money, the kid had had a chance to feast his eyes on Sally. After Macready had paid him and gone with Sally into the kitchen to unwrap the feast, the kid had not left by the door he entered, but by the narrow one that opens on the roof and locks automatically.

Once out on the roof he must have wandered the narrow walkway looking either for a stairway down or another door to let him back in. And so he circled the penthouse on the outside until he came to the window that looked in on my curious room. And what was he to make of a man dozing exhaustedly in a hospital bed while a fun couple were chasing each other half naked through the rest of the rooms? Possibly he knocked on the window. I wouldn't know. Possibly, because I did not seem to awaken to his knock, he thought I was not dozing, but dead. *Something* woke me. It might have been the movement of his head against the lights of Manhattan that shone dimly into the room—the faintest flickering of a shadow.

At any rate, I did awaken, shook my head and looked up—to see a black face through a dirty window staring unblinkingly at me, staring through a window that was previously totally uninhabited.

Several thousand volts of electricity went through me. I reached under the pillow, pulled out the Colt, and took aim at his head.

13

"I sat up all night," I said, glancing away from Shope's face. "And in the morning I packed up my stuff and moved out. You don't have to tell me. I could have been anybody out there, Macready, his girl friend, a face—that's all, a face.

"I'm living back home now, and the gun is back under the floorboards where I'd have to be thoroughly awake to reach it. Look," I added, aggrieved, "the window was dirty and more or less inaccessible. I'd never seen a face out there before. Macready never went out there. It's only a little runway around the house. It was a mistake, a terrible one, but a mistake nonetheless. And, after all, I must have had some kind of subconscious doubt, didn't I? I hesitated, didn't I? I didn't shoot him, did I?"

"He split the second he saw the gun," said Shope.

"But I didn't shoot him," I insisted. "That's the important thing, isn't it?"

"No," said Shope. "The important thing is that he was gone before you got the gun cocked. What you had there was a cannon."

"It's a defense gun," I said, "a stopper. A lot of policemen carry them now."

"Yeah," Shope agreed. He stood up and stretched and examined his cigar. "It's gotten to be a fad. Now all the hotshots on the other side have got them too, so we're right back where we started. It's like those Teflon-coated bullets, you know? The police wanted them because they go through steel plate. Wonderful. They also go through bulletproof vests, vests that policemen are wearing. It's gotten to be a Goddamned arms race."

Abruptly, he changed the subject. "We ran a scam on your client and came up empty," he said. "How come?"

"How come," I countered, "is that Macready never did anything wrong."

"That's not what I mean," said Shope. "What I mean is that this guy Macready never did anything at all. Never drove a car, never was in the service, doesn't own a credit card. Every line we put out runs right into the sand. The guy's a well-known actor, but he doesn't exist except for Social Security."

"Well, for one thing," I offered, "William Macready is his stage name."

"Then what's his real name?"

"I don't know," and at Shope's piercing indignant stare I was forced to add, "I really, truly, and honestly don't know."

"Can't you find out?"

"I don't think so," I answered and put up my hands to fend off what I expected to be a torrent of abuse. "Let me explain.

"Macready is something of a nut. He *was* in the service, and he had a hard time of it in Vietnam."

Shope looked wise. He knew all about Vietnam veterans.

"While he was in the Army hospital he got interested in acting. He read the autobiography of William Charles Macready, a famous actor of the 1800s and took that name from that time on—just dropping the middle name, Charles. It was all done in total ignorance. He didn't even know that there was already a famous living actor named George Macready. He simply became William Macready. He didn't make a legal change or anything. He just *became* William Macready. He took out a Social Security card in that name when he got his first job down in New Orleans."

"And he refused to tell you his real name?"

"I never asked him. Why should I? He pays his bills under the name Macready."

"We'll find it if we have to."

"Okay. You can fly down and nose around Army General in Fort Benning and maybe find somebody there who can identify him. But the question is: Why should you? What has he done?"

Shope had permitted his cigar to expire. He relighted it and looked at me. "You lived with the guy for two weeks, right?" I nodded. "Now let me ask you something. Has he got any funny pictures up there?"

I stared at Shope.

"I mean did you see any indications that this guy Macready is making porno movies?"

"Porno movies!" I couldn't believe I'd read him right. "Are you crazy? This man is one of the best-known young actors in the country. He's being pursued to star in a TV series that will make millions of dollars for him. Read his reviews. He's talented. He's an actor, for Christ's sake, not a stud."

"Actor . . . actor. . . ." Shope waved the cigar. "What's the difference?"

"What's the difference between a lieutenant detective and a night watchman in a supermarket?"

He reflected on this before he said, "We went up and tossed Pelfrey's apartment after we figured out what happened. You ever been there?"

"Yes," I said. "I was up there when I was checking out Pelfrey for the work with Macready."

"You see any funny pictures up there?"

"No," I answered. Life was getting curiouser.

"We think Pelfrey was a chicken hawk," said Shope. "We found a ton of pictures in the blanket compartment of the couch."

"Ah." I let the news settle in. "When I was there, Mr. Pelfrey was also there, and he did not invite me to open his couch." I paused. "Was he active? Dry Dock country?"

"Jesus Christ," Shope replied in exasperation. "How can you keep track of this shit?" A sudden rigidity in his shoulders suggested that he had just remembered Edna's presence. "Some of the shrinks say these guys look at the pictures and then they don't have to cruise. Do you believe it?"

Edna got my attention by punching me in the shoulder. "What's chicken hawks?" she asked.

"Men who pick up boys for sexual pleasure," I told her. "Young boys. It's a great big grown-up subculture."

"That's disgusting," said Edna.

"See your chaplain," I advised her and turned my attention to Shope. "You think Macready and Pelfrey were mixed up in some kind of porno ring together?"

"It didn't pop for me until the kid you aimed at described what was going on up at Macready's place," Shope admitted. "And incidentally, the kid didn't put in the complaint, his boss did after the kid told him about it."

"I'm glad to hear it," I said, omitting to add that I had given the kid twenty-five dollars to keep his mouth shut. No matter. It's hard to keep your mouth shut when you've had a gun trained on you.

"But the delivery boy told us that this broad was running around half naked and Macready—I assumed it was Macready—was wearing nothing but his jockey shorts."

"Perfectly normal after-dinner socializing," I commented. "Look, Lieutenant, Macready likes girls and Sally likes boys, but I never saw anything in either of them that made me think they would even look at pornography, much less perform in it. I know that Macready doesn't need it and wouldn't risk it. I doubt that Sally would.

"As for Pelfrey," I shrugged helplessly, "*somebody* buys those Goddamned pictures and goes to those movies. Apparently, he was one of them."

Shope got up and went over to the doorframe, where he rested his back and considered it all. "Where does this leave you now?" he asked me.

"I am still retained to find the money my client lost through his financial manager," I told him. "That's the package I'm looking for. All in the world I want is to get hold of it and return it to him. It didn't disappear into thin air. . . ."

"Or a porno movie?"

"If it did, that's that," I answered. "But I'm being paid to find out."

"And when you find out?"

"I'll tell you everything I decently can."

"Decently?"

"Everything that doesn't touch client confidentiality."

He took his time regarding me over the tip of his cigar. When he'd made his decision, he said, "All right. I don't want you killed, but I don't want you killing anybody, either. If you were a street cop you wouldn't get off this easy, but if you were a street cop we'd put you at a desk where people couldn't jump you. If you turn out to be a gun-crazy kid, it won't just be your permit, it will be your license, and I'm not kidding.

"You come across anything—anything," he gestured with his cigar, "you call me and call me fast. Understand?"

I nodded solemnly.

He shook his head. "Chicken hawks," he said. "That's all I need." Then he was gone, although the odor of his cigar lingered powerfully.

I turned to Edna then, who had been watching me. She said, "I never thought you'd pull a gun on a grocery boy."

"Think what you like," I replied graciously. "I saw the picture in the paper of the man who worked me over and it made me jump. When I saw a black face in a dirty window, I thought it was him come back to get me.

"I couldn't tell Shope that because it opens too many avenues of inquiry—where this all happened and why. As far as Shope knows, I'm still in the dark as to who beat me up."

"What are you going to do?"

"I'm going to go out and find him and bring him in," I said. "But, please, ma'am," I added, smiling weakly, "not today."

"There's something else I have to ask you," Edna began tentatively.

"It's my day in the barrel," I responded expansively, "ask away."

"This thing about porno movies and chicken hawks . . ."

"Are you now asking if I was part of a porno ring while I was recuperating up at Macready's?"

She had the virtue to blush. "No, but could Macready be in it? Or that girl, Sally?"

"Macready would have to be a lot crazier than I think he is."

"But could he have been in the past?"

"Something tells me no," I answered her. "Macready really is in love with acting. He took the name of a great classical actor for exactly that reason. He kind of reconstructed himself when he came out of the hospital, and I don't think that being a circus performer was what he was trying to construct.

"As for Sally," I reflected on the golden figure undulating the length of my mechanical bed, "I suppose that Sally would be capable of anything, but I also think that porn would be too much of a comedown for her. She lives in a different world—I think."

"Then why does Lieutenant Shope . . ."

"He's looking for some kind of a link that makes sense," I cut her off. "And I don't blame him. But just because Pelfrey had a taste for chicken doesn't mean that Macready had anything to do with it."

"Chicken hawks," said Edna. Her lips seemed not to like the taste of the words. "They prey on children?"

"Oh, Jesus, Edna." I sighed. "The kinks are endless. They prey on children, children prey on them. . . ."

"Children prey on grown men?" The green eyes flashed indignantly.

"Let me give you a cautionary tale." I staved her off. "There's a little town upstate that lives in a kind of time-warp—or appears to live that way. It has frame houses with gingerbread on them, people washing their cars in the driveway, malted milk shops with high-school kids congregating. It's all off the cover of the

Saturday Evening Post thirty years ago. On the surface it's all *Andy Hardy* and *Happy Days*."

I found a pack of Luckies in the drawer and lighted one. "Like most little towns," I continued, "the big thing for everybody is the high-school football team. They're the town heroes. They're hand picked and hand raised by the school and the church. Basically, the kids on the football team get more attention than anybody else.

"Okay. The kids are supposed to look good and keep happy, right? Only these kids were looking too good and too happy. They were blossoming out in beautiful jackets and sixty-dollar designer jeans. They always had money down at the malt shop and money to put in their cars or maybe even to buy a motorcycle. Nobody knew where the money was coming from, and the apparent fact is that everybody was afraid to ask. The parents didn't ask; the school didn't ask; the church didn't ask; and the town fathers sure as hell didn't ask. But an enterprising newspaper reporter did ask, and what is more, his paper printed the story.

"What all these upstanding young athletes were doing was breezing into New York City on their time off and making themselves available to the chicken hawks in Dry Dock country. The chicken hawks were not the stereotype of the slimy degenerate, but were tired, well-dressed New York businessmen—executives—movers and shakers. They paid these kids and paid them well. There was no hustle, no pressure, no extortion. It was all a straightforward business deal. These kids learned that they had a commodity that was in demand among some of the most successful men in our country, and they went out and sold it."

I waved away Edna's interrupting. "Now, the question is: Were these slick, smart New York executives corrupting the youth of the nation? And the answer is *no*, they weren't, because there wasn't anything there to corrupt. These kids were thunderstruck to find out that there was any real odium connected to being a whore. They didn't even realize that being a whore was supposed to be inferior to what their parents, their school, their church, or their city fathers were. How can this be?

"Well, the kids were interviewed, and it turned out that the only value they carried away from the heartland of America was a very simple one: *Get The Money*. Everything else was meaningless. Money was status, power, recognition, and luxury. Nobody, at least in their town, had ever recognized anything else.

Nobody had told the kids about virtue; nobody even told them anything about being a man.''

''All *right*,'' said Edna, with a sharp downward slash of her hand, ''but there's younger kids, little kids, too, aren't there?''

''Yes,'' I admitted, ''and of both sexes, too, apparently. And here is where I bow out of the analysis game, because here we are deep in the heart of Krafft-Ebing country. As far as I know, there are two kinds of people who go after chicken: those who think it's cute and wildly sophisticated enough to get a thrill out of it, and those who are genuinely stunted and can't perform any other way. Some of them, apparently, are obsessed by it.

''My trouble is that I don't give a shit what causes it. I think it should stop. If you try to see the world from the point of view of a ten-year-old boy standing naked in a hotel room while some fifty-year-old, gray-haired drunk in a Brooks Brothers' suit is slobbering over him . . .''

''Stop,'' said Edna. ''I'm sorry I asked.''

''So was Pelfrey a chicken hawk? Was he divorced for that reason? Did he wind up on the pipe for that reason? These are things I'll have to find out, although, remember, having funny pictures under your sofa and screwing children are not one and the same thing.

''Was there some kind of unholy alliance between Pelfrey and Macready? That's something else I'm going to have to find out. Talking to Macready himself is kind of like staring into a spotlight. You get dazzled. I'm going to have to talk to some people who know him and work with him.

''Finally, is Joe Binney going to find a seven-foot ex-basketball player, and is he going to haul him down to the station, just like that? Tune in tomorrow, folks. Same time, same hospital.''

I smiled at Edna. ''That, however,'' I said to her shyly, ''is not on today's program. Today we are just going to put a toe in the water. I want to talk to somebody who knows something about Macready professionally, and somebody who can make sense. My finely honed instincts tell me that that person is Vincent Namier, the only sane person I ever met in Macready's penthouse.

''I want you, my girl,'' I pointed at her lovely chest, ''to call up Mr. Namier at the network and ask him if he'll see me for a few minutes this afternoon. If he wants to know what it's about, tell him it's about William Macready. I think he'll listen.

''And after I swim my way through the deep rugs of the

network, my dear,'' I told her, ''I'm going to come back here, pick you up, and take you out to a very nice dinner to wash out the foul taste of our conversation. What do you say to that?''

''That's awfully nice,'' she began, ''but . . .''

''But? You're turning down candlelight and wine?''

''I'm seeing David this evening,'' she said with a very demure look in her eyes.

''David?''

''Dr. Sartin. Don't you remember?''

''So Dr. Kildare's making time?''

''Watch your lip,'' said Edna.

14

All right, I'm an auk. Not a *great* auk, maybe, but definitely an auk, a megatherium, or a mastodon. I belong to that extinct race of New York inhabitants who can remember when people lived on Sixth Avenue: people with children, husbands, wives, and crazy uncles. Many of them lived in red brick walk-up tenements and of an afternoon would take their children up to Central Park to play. This was before the great march of the glassfronts.

Preparatory to the great march, all the small buildings had to be torn down and the people scattered. Walls were sheared off, and the rooms invited inspection from the street. It was shocking because it was so homely. Walls were covered with shades of acid and arsenical greens undreamt of by Peter Blume or Giorgio de Chirico, purples undeveloped by Salvador Dali, all done in landlord enamels. Bathtubs hovered serenely in midair, supported apparently by nothing but their tubing. Pictures torn from magazines and catalogues were taped to the walls—beloved pictures that tied the corners of the rooms together. Some toys, abandoned or forgotten, crouched on the floor awaiting the never-to-occur return. Items of furniture were left: a dresser whose mirror reflected only the sky, an overstuffed easy chair covered in a certain diseased shade of mauve mohair, gaping defunct refrigerators.

So the people have gone. Central Park is a racetrack of joggers and muggers in pursuit of joggers, and any children seen up there today are purse-snatchers. Where did the people go? Some, they say, were scattered so far as Queens, where they are reported to live in yurts, heat themselves with dried yak dung, and subsist on the fermented milk of wild mares. Can this be true?

No matter. What we have on Sixth Avenue now are tourists, who are the projections of people, and executives—many, many of them network executives—who are the shadows of people. The gray suits, blue shirts, and sober ties seem to be tattooed on their skin—the attaché cases a growth from their hands. They all have an abstract, uneasy expression from which their eyes peer out warily as if from slits in a castle wall. They are fearful of being broached.

The buildings, too, look fearful. I know that they're meant to soar, but my impression is that they're tensed up on tiptoe, like a man about to scream. That is only my impression, of course. Doubtless, the people who work in them find the buildings friendly, lovable, and inspiring of hope and security. Can this be true?

It's curious how they avoid good taste inside. It isn't that they're in *bad* taste. It's the absence of taste that gets you, as if taste (read human values) were irrelevant. It's a curious attitude in outfits that make their living off human values, human susceptibility. They have abandoned the human scale along with the values. Plazas and vistas extend until dies the eye, as *Time* magazine might have put it. Elevators whose numbers soar beyond half a century are embedded in granite walls, as if on entering one passengers had the promise of the immediate judgment one expects on entering the tomb: a flight to heaven . . . a drop to hell.

Namier was up in the heavens, amid the archangels. Because of my hearing loss, I am excessively prompt. Appearing on the strike of the appointed hour helps me to identify myself. However, I realized that waiting for the proper elevator to take me on the long journey up was going to make me a few moments late. I kept inspecting my watch as the elevator paused interminably on floor after floor up past the express stop. No one noticed my nervousness. Each of the passengers was either just as nervous or was frozen in the glaceéd rigor that denotes chronic and excessive use of tranquilizing nostrums.

I was three minutes late in announcing myself to the receptionist in the waiting-well and, after she'd made the phone call, took one of the deep leather chairs she had indicated. The chair was comfortable, but the area was not. A horrifying amount of expense had gone into the decor, but the walls enclosed a series of subtle wars. The shadings of gray and ochre on the wall coverings meant that the company did not intend to retreat into pastels, but, on the other hand, did not want to yell out a "statement." The two paintings, well hung and well lighted, were expensive, but they were also reproachful. They had been chosen so as not to clash with the decor and so had the sullen look of someone who has been "put in his place." Neither was a Dali or de Chirico, either of whom would have destroyed the area. One was a Kenneth Noland, whose cool circles, like the iris of an unfriendly eye, receded into the wall. The other was a semicircular Frank Stella composed in bands of color that impressed me as a rainbow that had been struck by lightning. Overwhelmed by their surroundings, the paintings muttered from the walls.

I was staring back determinedly into Noland's unfriendly eye, when someone tapped me on the shoulder and I looked up to see the first amiable thing I'd found in the building. This was Namier's secretary, obviously, and she had the kind of old-fangled pretty face that has been pointedly ignored by the fashion magazines. It was a squarish face with a soft mouth and a rather fleshy nose, all supported by a blunt, dimpled chin. She was smiling, and her brown eyes were crinkled at the corners. Her dark brown hair was glossy and shoulder length in a coiffeur that had the distinction of being simply a decent, businesslike way for a lady to arrange her hair.

"Mr. Binney?" she asked me as I hastened to my feet. "Mr. Namier has been detained at a meeting, but he asked me to bring you into the office. Will you come with me?"

While she was opening the big door into the corridor, I got a look at the whole girl and was mightily pleased with what I saw. Her figure announced a healthy, buxom woman well into her thirties who had spent much of that time seated at a desk. She was by no means fat, but there was an ample supply of hip and bosom with a proportionate amount of connecting flesh along the flanks. Unlike the receptionist, whose dress seemed to have been rocket-expressed from Milan, this lady's costume was the time-honored two-piece blue business suit over a plain white blouse. Well-turned calves descended below the hemline and terminated in no-nonsense dark blue pumps. It was impossible not to like her. Encased in all this day-to-day, the-hell-with-it, thrown-on ensemble was an impression of vigor, competence, and poise. Her being spoke out for itself; the walls might dominate Noland and Stella, but they did not dominate her.

We had quite a way to go down the corridor, and halfway there, I realized that Namier must have a corner office. The office I was invited to wait in, however, was not his but his secretary's, a much smaller room directly in front of it. Nevertheless, there was a couch, on which she placed me and bent over to ask, "Would you like something while you're waiting? A drink? Coffee?"

I glanced at my watch. "It's after four o'clock," I noticed aloud. "Somewhere there's a yardarm with the sun slipping over it."

"What would you like?"

"A bourbon and soda would be wonderful, if you have it."

"We have it." She opened the door to the main office and disappeared within. The couch, obviously, was strategically placed so as not to reveal any significant part of the office from its seat, but I got up and moved over to see what I could see. I sighed heavily. Hollywood was right. It was the perfect Hollywood version of a major network executive's office . . . which had been copied from an earlier Holywood version, . . . in a series of mirrors. Through the windows behind the long, low desk I could see the glittering skyline of Manhattan, but from close up, I realized, one could look *down* on Manhattan. On the window ledge there was a bronze winged sculpture that gave out emanations of Samothrace. I retreated to my once-luxurious couch, which now seemed shabby by comparison.

The lady returned, shut the door behind her, and handed me a drink in a beautiful crystal glass. "This really is wonderful," I told her. "What is your name?"

"Betty Middleton," she announced. "I should have told you when I asked you in."

"This is marvelous bourbon," I informed her, tasting the silken fire that burns with no other flame.

She smiled back with very nice white, even teeth. "It's something a little special that Mr. Namier puts by," she said.

I saluted her with the gleaming crystal, "Mr. Namier," I said, "is a gentleman, a scholar, and a man of taste, and not just in bourbon."

She shifted slightly, and her smile became a bit fixed. "Taste?" she repeated. "Not just in bourbon?"

"That winged bronze on the ledge behind his desk," I asked her, "isn't that a Nakian? If he went out and bought that, he has taste, except that taste is a poor word for it."

Her smile relaxed again. "I'd like to thank you in his behalf," she said, "but he didn't buy it. The company did."

"But he requested it?"

She leaned her hips against the desk and put her hands together. The lips tightened up a bit. "You don't really ask for those things; they're assigned."

"They go with the territory?"

Her fingers cut a square in the air. "On the chart," she said.

"Tell me something, though," I pursued. "Does Mr. Namier like it?"

"Oh, yes," she replied. "He likes it very much."

"Of itself?"

"Of itself," she assured me. She had understood what I meant. "Will you have another one of those?" She gestured toward my glass.

"Only if you'll have one with me," I answered, feeling the fumes reach into my cranium. "Would you have one with me?"

"That would be very naughty," she said.

"And are you going to be naughty?"

"No," said Miss Middleton.

"Then I'll just nurse this along till Mr. Namier arrives."

She said, "If you're comfortable, will you excuse me while I clear up a few things on my desk?"

"Certainly."

She went to her desk and plunged into a spasm of efficiency, dispensing, in five minutes, with more items than poor Edna could have handled in a day. I tried to catch her system so that I could pass a little something on to Edna, but, like all fine arts, it was inimitable. Letters got zipped out of her typewriter in less time, it seemed to me, than it would take to read them. Memos were scanned with machinelike rapidity and key words were underlined, with notations made in the margins. Bills were scanned, checked off, and set in one of two piles, one presumably for payment and the other for questioning. It was all done with a degree of smoothness and dispatch that made the idea of an automated office puerile and tacky. It would be hard to design a machine like Betty Middleton.

I sipped away at my bourbon, blissfully oblivious, until the telephone rang. Of course, I can't hear a telephone, but there is a certain tension in people's attitudes when the phone rings that makes it unmistakable. She picked it up and answered, it seemed, pleasantly enough, but then her expression became grimmer. She glanced quickly at me, and then turned around so that I could not see what she was saying. While I was deprived of the opportunity to read her lips, I could still read her back, and the bobbing emphases of her head. Her shoulders tightened the fabric of the small suit jacket and her head nodded sharply to make certain points, so sharply that she might have been driving pegs with her forehead. She put the receiver back and sat perfectly still for a few seconds. When she turned around to look at me her face was composed in a cheerful smile that had only a hint of strain to it.

"Mr. Namier," she said, "has been so hopelessly delayed that he thinks it would be better if we joined him, rather than his coming back here. He asked me to bring you over to the restaurant." She paused and looked at me searchingly. "Do you mind?"

I had expected that we'd be going down to one of the restaurants in the building, or even one of the glossier spots nearby. Instead, she hailed a cab, and we were suddenly caught in the toils of crosstown traffic headed west. She did not try to talk to me in the cab, for which I was grateful. She sank back in the seat, her face relaxed into a pensive, almost forlorn expression. I held my tongue.

The cab turned south on Eleventh Avenue, went down a few blocks, and swung in a U turn to discharge us in front of the Landmark Tavern. Miss Middleton had the money ready in her hand to pay the driver before I could even reach for my wallet.

When we got inside, I saw that the place was decorated as an old-fashioned saloon, with a long expanse of mahogany for a bar and a period-perfect mirror with authentic appointments surrounding it. The help all seemed to be of the "tonight a singing waiter, tomorrow a star," persuasion: young, healthy, and, for the most part, vacuous men. Namier had been waiting alone at a side table near the window and stood up when he saw us come in. Standing at the table, he looked much older and frailer than I remembered him as being up at Macready's. He looked of an age close to retirement. The deep lines of fatigue in his face accentuated the gothic curves descending from his nostrils.

He greeted me very warmly, shaking my hand, and kissed

Miss Middleton on the cheek with a fatherly peck. He had the remaining half of a double martini in front of him, and he swigged it down before ordering drinks for all of us. I stuck to bourbon, of course, but Miss Middleton ordered a martini, albeit a single one, and looked a bit troubled when Namier ordered himself another double Tanqueray, straight up.

"I'm sorry to have put you to all this trouble, Mr. Binney," he began.

"Please call me Joe, and rest assured it's no trouble at all. I've always wanted to come to this place and never managed. Although," I observed, "it's one hell of a place for a conference."

"Conference!" His chest heaved with what I interpreted to be a short bark of laughter. "It wasn't a conference. It was a raid."

I searched him inquiringly. "A personnel raid," he explained. "We need some people. Another network has got them. I'm here on a thief's errand."

"But I thought," Betty began.

"Thought what, my dear?"

"That you were meeting him at the Slate."

"We drifted down here for a little more privacy."

"You say you want somebody from another network?" I asked to keep the ball rolling.

"I didn't say *want*. I said *need,*" Namier corrected me. "There's a difference. With wanting someone you simply trail your kimono. When you need them, you *get* them." He snapped his nondrinking hand shut as if catching a fly.

"And did you get them?" I asked.

"Oh, yes," Mr. Namier assured me. "Oh, yes, indeed."

"And what did you need them for?" I pursued.

"*For?*" His face went so completely blank that I was able to see sharply just how much he had been drinking that afternoon. "For? Hell, Joe, you certainly know what for. For 'Tycoon.' "

Now it was my turn to look blank.

" 'Tycoon,' " he repeated. " 'Tycoon.' Don't tell me Macready never mentioned it to you."

"No," I answered honestly, "he never did."

"My God," said Namier, and drained his glass.

He was so eager to order another round that, unable to catch the waiter's attention, he got up and went to the bar to place his order. I looked at Betty. "What's the big deal about 'Tycoon?' " I asked her.

"That's the series Macready is slated for. He honestly never mentioned it?" She seemed almost as dismayed as Namier.

Indeed, Macready had mentioned it, although not by name and not in terms I thought it politic to impart at this moment. I did manage to say, "Oh, well, I know that there's a series brewing and Bill is thinking very seriously about it. I just didn't know the name of it."

She pursed her lips. "That's a black mark against it right there," she said. "The name is supposed to be irresistible, like 'Dallas' or 'Roots.' "

I smiled defensively. "I don't find those names all that irresistible," I told her.

"Millions do," she said unsmiling and pointedly.

There was an awkard pause while I churned my brain for something not stupid to say. I concluded lamely. "You can't judge things by my opinion. The only things I ever watch are ballgames and boxing." By that time, Namier had mercifully returned, closely followed by a waiter with a tray of drinks. The first hearty sip of the martini seemed to calm him sufficiently so that he could continue.

He gave me a somber look. "I hope you're not saying that Bill isn't even considering the role," he said. His hand was so tight on the stem of the glass that I was afraid he might snap it.

"There's been a misunderstanding," I advised him. "Bill talked a great deal about the series, about television. He just never mentioned it by name. I mean, he talked all around it, but never about the substance."

"A mistake," said the executive. "He should be eating it, drinking it, and living it. Above all, he should be talking about it. By name: 'Tycoon' . . . 'Tycoon.' Everything goes to build up the groundswell. And it's all to his own advantage. He's in this with all of us, you know."

I forebore to point out that Mr. Macready was *not* in this with all of them, and was doing his level best to stay the hell out. But to grease things a little, I offered, "He may have been talking about it without my understanding him. I'm not one-hundred percent, you know."

Namier said, "You're awfully good, though. I can't imagine how you get as much as you do."

"It's the mathematical horse trick," I said, "as much as anything." They looked puzzled, and I explained. "There was a horse called 'Clever Hans,' who could add, subtract, multiply, divide, and so on. He answered all the problems by tapping out the number with his hoof. Two times four was eight taps, twelve from fifteen was three taps, the square root of eighty-one was nine taps. You get the idea. The owner was watched like a hawk for possible signals. Nobody found any. Then some brightwig realized that *everybody* was giving the signal. They would all tense up while Clever Hans was tapping out his series, and when he reached the correct number they would all exhale or relax *en masse*. That was enough for Clever Hans. He'd stop and wait for his carrot. To quite some extent, that's what I do. I watch for reactions, and wait for my carrot."

"Clever Hans," said Betty.

"But not infallible. I may have missed a whole frame of reference with Bill. Is this 'Tycoon' thing more than the name implies?"

"Much, much more," Namier said. His features took on a religious expression that made his face look more gothic than ever. " 'Tycoon' goes to the soul of America," he said. "To the spirit that made America what it is today, and against the background of this spirit, the petty problems that entangle us today are seen as mere transitory phases, ephemera to be brushed aside in the march to our destiny.

"And that's why Bill should be steeping himself in the role this very minute, absorbing every bit of business he can. He's going to represent the genius of America, the embodiment of the driving force of Henry Ford, John D. Rockefeller, Dale Carnegie. . . ."

"Andrew," Betty reminded him.

"Of course. Andrew Carnegie and all the others who represent the engineering and organizational genius of America all concentrated into one character, the tycoon, who will be followed from early manhood to ripe old age.

"He's going to represent America the way Laurence Olivier represented England in *Henry the Fifth*."

I sat back, replete with the sense of having gotten the *word*. "That's quite a responsibility to lay on an actor," I ventured. I did not mention my concern for the writer who was being asked to match Shakespeare line for line.

"Yes, it is," Namier agreed with an air of portentousness. "And that's why Bill is getting every available scrap of help we can offer him. That's why I'm on a flying-squad mission like this one today, to get the best possible team around him. That's why Garson is preparing to build an incredible complex of sets inside the biggest studio in New York, sets that cover a time span of nearly a hundred years. An incredible investment . . ."

"Garson?"

"Cy Garson, of Garson and Gross Productions. Surely you've heard of Garson and Gross Productions." I nodded the necessary vague agreement. "Garson saw the test, and, of course, he saw that Bill could carry it, could carry the show. Garson said it was the most exciting test since Brando did *The Godfather*. So Garson came in."

"And today," I asked, "on this flying-squad mission, you're getting supporting actors?"

"No, no," Namier contradicted me. "The rest of the casting isn't really of much concern. That can all be done by the book. No, I was helping to put together a marketing team—a little more complicated than casting."

"And more important?"

"Certainly. That's how the money comes back." He paused over this mundane consideration and sipped his martini. "But you made the appointment to see me," he said, recovering with a smile. "And I've been monopolizing things with my problems. How can I help you?" He leaned forward and tried to muster an attitude of professionalism behind the alcoholic fog that was gathering in his eyes. He was suddenly becoming very drunk.

"Bill Macready's business manager died very suddenly," I told him. "And though it looks like a suicide, the police are beginning to think it was murder. Did you ever have any dealings with him? His name was Arnold Pelfrey."

"Arnold Pelfrey?" Namier shook his head. "Never heard of him. I didn't even know Bill had a business manager. You say he died suddenly?'"

"He was found hanged in a hotel room."

"Terrible. A terrible thing for Bill. Actors are so sensitive."

"Tough on Arnold, too," I noted.

He was oblivious to the thrust. To Namier, people like Arnold were *born* dead. "Are you aiding the police in this?" he asked me.

"Indirectly," I answered. "Directly, I'm doing it for my client, Bill Macready."

"Really!" He was taken aback. "Bill is paying you to solve this? That's very unusual. Has he given you any reason for this? For his interest, I mean?"

"He feels responsible, up to a point," I said. "He feels that it may be somehow connected with him."

"But why?"

I did not want to tell Namier that the *why* was securely wrapped in a quarter of a million dollars that had disappeared. If they knew that Macready was virtually broke, he wouldn't stand a chance. "Pelfrey was supposed to meet Bill for an appointment," I lied. "Somehow, he got intercepted on the way, or else he just stopped off and hung himself. Bill would like to know why."

"Remarkable," said Namier. "A remarkable sense of responsibility."

Namier was becoming difficult to read. I had the feeling that he was holding himself upright by sheer force of will. His eyes were glazed now, and his lips were loose and moist with spittle at the corners. I realized that I would have to move quickly if I was going to get any information in this session. "I think it's remarkable, too," I told him. "And I keep wondering if there was anything beyond the client-manager association. Do you have any ideas?" Namier shook his head slowly. "Is there anything in Bill's past," I pursued gingerly, "you've heard of that could lay him open to any kind of pressure from . . . from, well, what we call the underworld?"

"How do you mean his past?" asked Namier blankly.

"Acting is an economically risky outfit, apparently," I said. "Do you think that Bill ever had to do anything a little off-color just to stay alive financially? Anything that would have gotten him mixed with the wrong kind of people?"

"Not that I know of," said Namier, letting his mind drift down through a gallon of martinis. "His professional life is pretty much of an open book. He came up very fast out of nowhere, and he seems to have got hot and stayed hot—very unusual. He seems to have been able to work all the time. I don't see where he'd need anything else. But you never know," Namier mused. "You never know, do you? I'll have to think about it and look around."

He was wavering, now, in a rather broad arc where he sat. He took out his wallet and handed me a card. "Anything you hear," he said, "I'd like to be the first to know. It could be very important to me, and important to you, too, if you know what I mean." He was holding the card out toward me, but his eyes, pointed slightly over my left shoulder, were unfocused. Betty noticed my puzzlement over the card and reached for it. The raised lettering on the card said, DIAMOND ENTERPRISES, and had Namier's name and a telephone number at the lower right-hand corner. She handed the card back to Namier.

"Mr. Binney already has your number," she said. "Anyway, I'll give him one of your regular cards." She helped him to put the card back in his wallet and the wallet back in his pocket. "I think we'd better go," she said.

"No!" objected Namier, almost violently. "I mean—I'll go, you just put me in a cab. But I want Mr. Binney to have dinner here, if he will, on me. And I want you to have it with him. That's an order. Just have them put it on our account."

Betty's face was the mask of resignation bought with experience. "All right," she said. She smiled at him. "Let's get a cab." A sharp gesture from her free hand told me to stay where I was and not to interfere.

15

Coming back into the restaurant, she appeared to be spent; her shoulders slumped. The outfit that had looked brisk and businesslike had lost its snap and clung more closely to her body. The first thing she really saw when she arrived at the table was the martini I'd ordered her. She gave me a look of frank gratitude. "Thank you," she said. "I wanted that."

I helped her to get seated and sat down myself. Nodding toward the doorway, I asked, "Is he really as bombed as he seems to be?"

"More exhaustion than anything else," said Betty. "He works very hard, and when he's on something like this, he works like a demon."

"Don't get sore if I say this," I offered tentatively, "but sitting around in hyped-up restaurants belting double martinis doesn't fit the average idea of work."

"The average person doesn't know what he's talking about," said Betty. "Let the average person drink three or four sharpshooters under the table and then close a deal with them, a deal that stands up however you look at it, and then the average person will know something about work.'' She closed defiantly by swigging down her own martini. I signaled for another and ordered another for myself.

''If I'm going to have this one too,'' she said, ''we'd better order some food. I'm not the hard-drinking type.''

She was no trencherwoman, either. She ordered only a cold soup and a plain salad with a little of the house dressing. I ordered a sirloin, medium rare. I was starved. The rolls and butter appeared with heartening promptness, but she didn't touch them.

''You mind if I ask how long you've been with Mr. Namier?'' I asked her. I had had to wait until I swallowed a generous chunk of buttered roll before inquiring.

''Six or seven years,'' she replied, watching the crumbs disappear from my lips.

''And before that?''

''Oh, I've always worked for the network,'' she said. ''It's what I'd always wanted.'' She glanced to one side, as if inspecting some area that charted the whole history of what she had always wanted, but she was silent.

''Come on,'' I prompted, smiling. ''I can't be a detective unless you tell me something.''

She took it in good humor. ''I had the usual after-college crisis,'' she said. ''Should I learn to type or not? Should I learn shorthand? Would I write my doom in the Pittman system? I wanted to get into television: writer, producer, something rich and famous. The only jobs open were in the typing pool. I went from being a lousy typist to being a good one. Those entrance jobs are all pretty well closed now. Now it's all word processing.''

''From a typing pool,'' I suggested, ''the way to the top must look like staring out of a well.''

''Not necessarily,'' said Betty. ''The networks are a little different. Mr. Namier, for instance, started as an usher for radio shows out on the coast. Careers that started in the mail room are famous. One producer started as a doorman. The main idea is to somehow get into the business. You don't just walk in at the top.''

She contemplated what she had told me and sipped at her martini. ''From the outside,'' she offered, ''it all seems terribly rigid and structured. And that, in fact, is the image they want to present: the illusion that they really know what they're doing. I think they picked it up from the big agencies, like J. Walter Thompson, many, many years ago while it was still all radio. And they inherited the same defects the agencies have—outward calm, rigidity, and hysteria on the inside. They're like a teakettle full of boiling water. Inside, some bubbles are shooting up from the bottom, and other bubbles are going down and exploding."

"The ones at the top explode too," I objected.

"That's called retiring," answered Betty, smiling.

"Let's get back to the script," I said, grabbing another roll out from under her bitter gaze. "Here you are in the typing pool, with your degree from . . . where?"

"Bard."

". . . in your hand. And then what?"

"Then it was typing scripts on different colored sheets of paper: you know, a different color for each revision."

"They let you type scripts right off the bat?"

"They would let an orangutan type scripts," said Betty. "Business and legal correspondence are something else. No typos or strikeovers allowed up there."

"So," I asked, "what happened?"

"The more scripts I read and typed—not all the typists really read what they're working on, you know—the more I was convinced that I was meant for television. All the while I was typing these scripts, my head was shouting, 'No, no! That's not the way to do it!' It made me slow and inaccurate, but they didn't seem to care. To them it seemed that a script was a physical object you could weigh, count, or measure, like a box of doughnuts. After typing scripts all day, I went home and wrote my own."

I asked, out of politeness, the necessarily doomed question. "Any luck?"

"It wasn't really a matter of luck. I was pigheaded, and wrote scripts out of my own philosophy—my philosophy, not theirs."

"That's unusual," I ventured. "How were you different?"

She leaned back, pursed her lips, and stared in the general direction of the empty street outside our window. "*How* I was different isn't really important," she said, with a slight nod of her head to emphasize the word *how*. "We work . . ." she smiled suddenly. "Funny saying *we* work. I used to say *they* work . . . within very narrow limits, with very rigid borders. There can be slight variations, but these variations have to be tested somewhere else before we can risk the kind of money it takes to produce a show—even a pilot."

"A pilot?"

"My God," she said. "You must know what a pilot is. The first introductory production of a possible series."

I was properly abashed.

Her face assumed a puzzled, even haunted expression as she looked out again through the window, as if attempting to locate herself on the empty street. "When we produce something you might call 'new,' " she said to me, turning back, "something like 'All In The Family,' or 'Sanford and Son,' or a mini-series, like the one we're talking about now, 'Tycoon,' it's usually been developed somewhere else, and that somewhere else is usually Britain. They've got the time and money to experiment. We don't. We have to produce in the here and now, and we absolutely have to earn money.

"I came into this business with a lot of schoolgirl ideas in my head. I thought I saw the possibility of tight little cabaret-type scripts, and I worked away at this style—if you want to call it that—without really paying attention to what they wanted, what they needed. I was writing things that were tight, logical, constricted, economical, and sharp. What those scripts really were," she smiled sadly at the memory, "was unproducible—unsalable. They would have gotten me an *A* back at Bard, but they were useless to the network.

"I stayed pigheaded for quite a while, and I sent the scripts in cold. They got sent right back to me—courtesy of my own postage and self-addressed envelope."

"This was while you were working there as a typist?" I asked her. She nodded.

I shook my head. "Couldn't you put any English on the ball from the inside?"

"At the time, I thought that that would be a very good way to get myself fired," she said, musing. "I'm not sure even now that I wasn't right about that." She smiled at me. "What we want from a typist," she asserted, "is typing."

"Finally, I did get my courage up and decided, 'what the hell,' " she said. "I wrote a script that I thought was very good. I'd made friends with Mr. Namier's secretary, after a long and careful campaign. Secretaries," she announced with a wide and satisfied smile, "are very, very powerful. I got her to read the script, and she took it to Mr. Namier.

"Mr. Namier *did* like the script. He took me out to a long, long lunch and treated me like an oncoming genius. I blurted out all the crazy ideas I'd stored up in school and that I'd been incubating in the ratty little room I had—and he was very sweet. He was funny and he was nice. And he bought the script. But even Vincent, Mr. Namier, as much as he liked it, couldn't get it produced. He bought it, at the minimum fee, but it just stayed in the files. Finally, because his secretary was getting married—for the third time—and was leaving, he offered me the job as his secretary. He'd done all he could in trying to promote the script, and all that failed. I'd done everything I could in writing it, and all that failed. It was make or break time, you see. So when I accepted his offer, I promised myself I'd be the best secretary that he or any other network executive ever had. I stopped writing. Stopped thinking about writing.

"Just like that?" I asked her gently.

"Just like that."

"The next question," I ventured, rotating my glass self-consciously, "is the old standby. And then?"

"And then is what you already know. What you see is what you get."

I remained silent and looked at her. She stirred uneasily. Finally, she said impatiently, "You're wondering: 'Well, is she married? Divorced? Kids?' "

I nodded.

"Well, I'm not married and I don't have any kids. I am, in the wonderful old vernacular, a bachelorette."

I smiled.

"Neither do I have a companion," she continued, "of either sex or neither sex."

"I'll cut it out," I said.

"The expression on your face," said Betty, "tells me that you're wondering: 'Why is she so defensive?' "

"It occurred to me," I admitted.

"It occurs to me, too," she reflected. "Bachelor, bachelorette. You're a bachelor, aren't you? Do you feel guilty about it?"

I considered this. "As a matter of fact," I said, "I do. But then I'm a very old-fashioned, union-suit kind of person."

"So why aren't you married?"

"No guts."

"Did you ever ask anybody?"

I thought briefly of City, up at the recording studio. "Yeah; I tried."

"And?"

"I got turned down."

"So you put your marbles away and went home."

"I don't exactly run around the streets asking women to marry me," I confessed irritably. "I also have the feeling that now it's just a little bit too late. I'm all settled in. I really am a bachelor. A guilty bachelor, but a bachelor."

"What do you think you're missing?"

"Kids—responsibility. You're not really a man unless you're supporting a couple of kids. It goes with the union suit and the handlebar moustache."

"Yes," she agreed dolefully, settling back in her chair. "It's all true. You're not really a woman, either, unless you've had some runny-nosed brat stuck under your arm. And, like you, it's a little late for me to pick up the challenge." She laughed suddenly. "If married people could hear us now, they'd think we were crazy," she said. "Married people are bailing out as fast as they can. Married people are trying to be us."

I smiled back. "Married people think that being single is all penthouses and *Private Lives:* witty dialogue between Amanda and—what was the character's name? Cyril, Basil, something like that?"

"Ellyot," she supplied. "The trouble with married people is that they don't know that Noel Coward isn't writing our dialogue."

"And we don't live in penthouses."

"But your client, the actor, Macready," she said brightly "he lives in a penthouse, doesn't he?"

"If you want to call it that," I answered. "It's more like a chicken shack perched on a ruin."

"A penthouse is a penthouse," insisted Betty. "It has windows, doesn't it? Where you can look down on all the little people?"

"You can't really look down on anything from there," I replied. "Maybe a couple of gin mills and a liquor store. The rest is warehouse brick walls and a nowhere skyline. You don't see much in the way of people."

"It is," she emphasized the point, "a bachelor penthouse. Mr. Macready, now, does he feel guilty?"

"For living in a penthouse?"

"For being a bachelor."

"Not that he confided in me," I said.

"Then does he try to make it the Noel Coward scene? Martinis in real martini glasses? The silver-plated shaker? Dressing gowns? Songs on the piano?"

"Jesus Christ, no." I said feelingly. "In the first place, he hardly drinks anything at all: about one-twentieth of what I drink. He doesn't have a piano. No dressing gowns that I ever saw. Either he's dressed or in his underwear."

"That doesn't sound like a real bachelor's penthouse." She pouted. "Does he have sophisticated ladies like Amanda come up there for all the witty dialogue?"

"Sophisticated, no." I answered. "Witty, no. Ladies, no. Women, yes."

"Ah! Women—in plural?"

"In singular," I retreated. "My mistake. Very singular."

"Very singular," she repeated. "Does that mean the one and only? Serious?"

"I don't think so." I pondered. "Not serious. No. In fact, if that's serious, then Groucho Marx is Schopenhauer."

"But he does like the ladies."

"Yes." I reflected. "I would say that he likes them exactly the way I like bean soup."

"And do you like bean soup?"

"Very much."

She absorbed this information with a controlled smile and stared past my ear out the window. Then she said slowly, "So he likes the ladies. Anything else? Gambling? Coke? Uh—unsuitable companions?"

This made me sit back in my chair and regard her steadily for a few seconds. "I guess Mr. Namier wasn't as drunk as I thought he was," I told her. "I'm old enough to know there's no such thing as a free lunch, or dinner, or cocktails with beautiful women. Tell Mr. Namier for me that he puts on a great drunk act."

"Am I supposed to blush?" asked Betty. "Of course he asked me to find out what I could. He'd be criminally negligent if he didn't."

"What made either of you think I'd tell you anything?"

She actually laughed then. "Stop looking so embattled," she said. "You weren't lured here to be pumped. That was the furthest thing from anyone's mind until you brought up the subject with your asking *us* if we knew anything about Macready's background. Didn't you think alarm bells would go off?"

"Ah, hell," I said.

"And why on earth should you ask us, instead of asking Macready himself?"

"Because I don't want him to lie to me," I said promptly.

"And are you sure he would lie? Your own client?"

"Oh, yes," I answered. "Just as I would lie to him. We've sort of become friends, and friends always lie to each other."

"To protect themselves? That doesn't seem right." Her face was troubled.

"No . . . no. To protect the other guy. If you've made a friend, you can only hurt him by revealing really bad or dangerous things about yourself. You've shifted the load over on to him. Friendship grows by people keeping their mouths shut and denying everything . . . by keeping the load on their own shoulders."

"But suppose," said Betty, "supposing we'd said, 'Oh, God, yes. We happen to know that he's committed all kinds of hideous crimes.' "

"You wouldn't say anything like that." I smiled. "Because you wouldn't consider hiring him if you knew all that."

"Then what were you expecting?"

"A hint. A suspicion. A direction."

"And what would you do then?"

"Defend him."

"Ah," said Betty. She took a long pull at the martini and remained still for a while. "That makes you a very good friend to have, all right. What has he ever done to earn it?"

"I like the cut of his jib," I answered. "And I owe him a little because he thought he owed me a little, when he didn't, really."

"Owed?" asked Betty. "Money?"

"Money owed is payable with money paid," I said. "No, not money."

"What then?"

"I got worked over, and I was laid up pretty bad. He took responsibility for me. I don't mean the hospital bills. I mean for me."

"Is that so unusual?"

"In my line of work it is. In my line of work most people are ashamed of having hired you. They don't really want to be associated with you—or even the idea of a private detective."

"That doesn't fit with all the glamorous things I've read. Parker Tyler, for instance . . ."

"Yeah," I said. "I read that. 'Somebody has to walk down that dark alley, and by God, it's Sam Spade.' "

"Well, it's true, isn't it?"

"It's true of a lot of people, and not all of them are private detectives. Public detectives do it all the time. They'd turn in their button if they couldn't. Saloonkeepers do it. Janitors do it. The fact is, some individuals do and other individuals don't."

This seemed to satisfy her. She nursed the dregs of her martini. "And you and Mr. Namier," I pursued, "have a lot on your desks, not to mention your minds. Why did you grant me the time? What were you expecting from me? I mean, before I started asking suspicious questions?"

"Oh," she said. "Everybody knows that you're thick with Macready, and that you stayed up at his place. Anybody who has any interest in him will be willing to talk with you."

"To get information?" I was dismayed.

"No. To influence you, and him through you. You're suddenly important."

"I'm not flattered," I said as much to myself as to her. "But I'm glad."

"Are you going to see other people?"

"Oh, yes. Certainly."

"And ask the same questions you asked us?"

"A little more skillfully, I hope. I don't want to alarm anybody."

"Who do you have in mind?"

"His agent, Norman Popper, for starters. Emerson Kite, the producer. And maybe one more name I just heard today—Garson. Garson must have a lot riding on this, too."

"Yes," agreed Betty. "He does. But seeing Garson isn't all that easy. He's very, very big. Anyone else?"

"Yes," I said. "One more person, even bigger than Garson. Bigger than anybody. The biggest you can imagine."

"And who's that?"

"Roger Grim."

She shrugged. "Never heard of him."

Our drinks were exhausted, and by tacit consent I signaled for the check, which Betty signed after adding the tip. Outside the restaurant we stood together rather uncertainly, awaiting a cab. "I suppose you live uptown?" I asked her.

"Yes. And you?"

"Downtown. But it doesn't seem fair that you should have to pay for your cab, too."

"Then why don't you ride up with me?" she said. "It's not a penthouse, and I don't have a piano, but I do have a nice martini pitcher and even a leftover dressing gown. Paisley, in fact."

I looked at her face by streetlight and put my hand very gently on her shoulder. "How about the bean soup?" I asked her.

"Oh, yes," she said brightly. "There's plenty of that."

16

I don't suppose I was really awake until I was out in the street, not much past the light of dawn, feebly trying to flag down a cab headed south. Betty's vaunted martini pitcher had been put to frequent use, and the awful result was that even this soft gray light of a cool spring morning hurt my eyes so that I averted them except to glance up now and then for sight of a cab.

When I had awakened, I had crept softly from Betty's side, adorned myself with the Paisley dressing gown and staggered into the bathroom. She had laid out a new guest toothbrush, intact in its pristine plastic box, and a set of throwaway razors. But staring back into the red eyes and brutalized features, I did not trust myself for anything more than splashing cold water on my face. The clash of my complexion with the Paisley, which did not quite close over my chest, was frightful. I threw on my clothes, let myself out into the corridor and took the elevator down. The soft bump at the bottom almost undid me.

By the time the cab dumped me in front of the furniture store over which I live, I was at least thoroughly awake. I paid the driver, who regarded me suspiciously, there being no visible signs of any residence or even any business open in the offing. He waited until I had let myself in the little side door, and then, satisfied, pulled away. The lights flashing on as I opened the door to my apartment stabbed at my eyes. I fumbled for the switch and turned them off. The morning light filtering in was enough for my purpose, which was to make a pot of coffee as quickly as possible.

After coffee and a shower, I worked away with brush and razor, got dressed, and went down for a lengthy, peaceable breakfast buttressed by the *New York Times*. I took a subway up to the office and arrived just as Edna was fumbling with the lock, an occasion that flustered her. Edna likes to be there a few minutes earlier than I am, which gives her that edge of moral superiority without which no right-thinking girl can exist.

"You look terrible," she said in an effort to recapture lost glory.

"Slap me up some coffee," I mumbled, heading for my desk in the back. "And lay off me for a while."

I went through the previous day's mail, which was discouragingly devoid of anything resembling faith, hope, or charity. I had been expecting, in my foolish way, a number of checks that were long, insupportably, overdue. No doubt, they were all stuck in somebody's computer. I decided to dictate a series of stiff notes for Edna to send out, and back them up with a series of nasty phone calls, relayed, of course, by Edna.

The morning mail, delivered by Edna with a mug of coffee (my sixth), brought not one more whit of promise. Even more discouraging was the letter from the New York State Department of Probation in reply to my query on the whereabouts of Roger Grim. Roger Grim, they informed me, had completed his sentence without benefit of parole, and thus was lost to the inquiring eye of the Probation Department. They had no information on his whereabouts.

This blank news made Mr. Grim loom even larger, if possible, in my prospective view. It gave him a kind of moral stature that added to his already intimidating physical stature. I doubted that he had lost out on parole through any behavior on his part. I would think that the parole board would have jumped to get rid of him. He must have stayed cool and turned them off, simply to serve his time and be done with them once and for all. It gave him a kind of superiority and control I didn't like to see. I don't suppose the parole board liked it either. It's an attitude that takes the play away from them—a negation of their powers.

I called Edna in and dictated the four stiff notes. "Give those letters three days to be delivered," I told her, "and then I want you to call up each one of these sons-of-bitches and tell them if I don't have a check on my desk next week I'm going to come down and start breaking legs."

She smiled. "What are you smiling at?" I demanded. "Do you think I'm kidding? I'll go down to their nice, carpeted offices and make a stink—a public stink—a scene."

She gave me a different, kindlier smile. "Leave it to me," she said.

"Leave it to you? You're going to break legs? You're going to make a scene?"

"I'm going to call the woman in Accounts Payable in each of these outfits," she said primly, "and find out what the hang-up is. Some places make a policy of not paying. Some are just greedy and inefficient. You might only have to break one leg."

"All right," I agreed grudgingly, "but next week I want some checks on this desk." I thumped it for emphasis.

"Don't threaten *me,*" said Edna with a very cold expression.

I was penitent. "I'm sorry," I said. "I apologize. But think of it as a means of paying your salary, O.K.?

"Now," I changed the subject, "what I want you to do is make an appointment for me to see Norman Popper, Bill Macready's agent, as soon as possible."

Since I didn't have the number, I waited patiently while Edna thumbed through the Manhattan phone book. She appeared to strike zero, looked up another number, and made a call. Then she dialed another number, and by the expression on her face I knew she had struck a vein. She chatted a while, made a few jottings on a pad, hung up, and gave me the sheet. "Three o'clock," she said. "Here's the address." I recognized it as one of the big buildings a few blocks north of Times Square.

"What were all the calls about?" I asked her.

"Popper isn't listed in the Manhattan directory," she said. "So I called somebody I know, and she gave me the number of the Representatives Association, and they gave me Popper's number, which is listed, incidentally, under the name Mendelsohn Theatrical Agency, or MTA."

"You astound me," I said frankly. "Other people screw around all day on a thing like that. Let me take you to a nice cheap dinner tonight."

She smiled. "I have a date tonight."

"Doctor Kildare?"

She nodded happily. "Look out for that stethoscope," I warned her. "He can always tell when your heart is beating madly." Her smile spread into one of those awful, secret, self-satisfied grins. "If you leave me for a mere doctor," I threatened her, "I'll never forgive you."

Edna said, "We could have called Bill."

"What?"

"You could have gotten the number from Bill Macready."

"No, no," I objected. "I don't want him to know I'm snooping around. He'll know sooner or later, of course, but I don't want to alert him to it."

Edna looked dubious at this, but finally accepted it and asked, "What else is on the agenda?"

"As long as you've got the phone book out," I said, "I want you to look up the addresses of the National Maritime Union, the Seafarer's International and the tugmen's union. I'm going to go out and see if they've got a Roger Grim listed anywhere. He could have grabbed a ship to Mombasa for all I know."

Edna pursed her lips at this string of requests. "Are you really sure he's a seaman?" she asked me.

"No, I'm not," I admitted petulantly. "I'm going by two sets of instincts: his and mine. I think he used a thief's knot to get out of there, which probably indicates some time spent on a deck somewhere. But what sells me on the idea is that he used a running bowline to hang the guy. That's a knot that would be used almost by instinct for a seaman in a hurry. A lubber would use a double half-hitch, which is just two overhand knots, or a slip knot, or something like that. Then, too, he used an inside rolling hitch to suspend the line from the pipe."

"Couldn't he have learned those as a Boy Scout or Sea Scout when he was a kid?"

"But not to use instinctively," I countered. "He's too young to have built up much experience on a deck, where the habits would be lifelong. To me it means he's working somewhere on a deck right now.

"And there's something else." I stilled her interruption with a gesture as I remembered the huge dark form that had confronted me in the hotel room. "When I saw him, I remember that he was wearing a dark blue wool Navy or Coast Guard sweater, you know, like the one I've got myself. And when I looked up at him there was a dark slant at the top of his forehead that makes me think it was a watch cap. And there was the smell, too, about him that's sort of coming back to me, unless I'm imagining it, a smell of the waterfront, diesel oil, coffee and—and, well, fish."

Edna looked veiled.

"All right!" I expostulated. "What else have I got to go on? Can you think of anything?" She shook her head, startled. "So get me those addresses and let me get the hell out of here."

But Roger Grim had not signed on for any trips to Mombasa or anywhere else, it appeared. "Do you know how bad it is?" the desk man at the NMU shipping hall asked me. "Do you know that we're asking the Navy—the *Navy*—to hire ten-thousand merchant seamen? Can you think of anything crazier than that?"

"No," I answered seriously. I had come down to the NMU first because the NMU had had checkerboard crews back in prehistoric times and seemed the likeliest union for a black man to join. The atmosphere in the hiring hall was funereal. Some of the men played cards and others talked—endlessly, it seemed. There was about them a sense of life being over. I had flashed the official-looking check I had made out with my check-writing machine to ROGER GRIM for $500.00, signed by E.C. Budlington of Budlington, Bosworth, Crickstart and Evans, a law firm that exists only in my frontal lobes and the spurious piece of paper I waved under the hiring agent's nose. "I don't know why he's got it coming," I told the man at the desk. "I only know that they asked me to find him and deliver it."

But the rolls turned up no Roger Grim: age, late twenties; race, black; height, six feet eleven.

"Six feet eleven!" exclaimed the agent.

"Yeah," I said. "You'd know him if you'd seen him."

"Not in this hall," said the agent.

Checking the rolls of the SIU took me out to Brooklyn by subway on what used to be the old Fourth Avenue line. This outfit had a more suspicious, more militant air. When I got in, however, the big blackboard behind the shipping desk was just as empty as the NMU's.

The shipping agent had funny hands. He had to work them like the old mechanical claws they used to have in penny arcades: the claws that would, for a nickel, pick you up a wristwatch, a fountain pen, or a nickel-plated pistol-type cigarette lighter. What you got for your nickel, of course, was gumdrops, and inedible at that. He noticed me looking at his hands. He held them up and smiled. "Mementos," he said, "organizing. Most guys lose their teeth. I lost my hands." I looked at him and waved my check. "Bullshit," he said. "How much does he owe you?"

"He doesn't owe me a dime," I said honestly. "But I want to

see him. You'd know him. You don't have to look him up. Just tell me. Does a guy come in here who's black, in his late twenties, and is very, very tall? I mean six feet eleven?"

"No." He said it involuntarily. "Six feet eleven! Jesus! He'd never fit in a bunk. A guy that size wouldn't be sailing. It would be agony for him."

I thought about the time my quarry had fitted himself into a prison bunk and shuddered.

The tugmen's union was less forthcoming, but I read the expression in the agent's eyes, and it told me that Mr. Grim was not a familiar figure.

There was a chance, I thought, that he might have signed on with one of the non-union or company union outfits—some of the company-controlled oil tankers, for instance. I'd have to make a list, I thought, and have Edna call.

I got back on the subway, which shot me up to Times Square where I had a couple of hot dogs for lunch. It still left me time to kill before my appointment with Popper. I looked up the name of the agency on the building directory well ahead of time, as per custom. The building itself was one of the Broadway beehives. It hummed with conversations, deals, aspirations, outrage. It was a relic of the age when theater and show business were nearly one and the same thing: the excitement and the sweat of the stage. It was one of those pivots, I recognized, that in the past had been the hub of worldwide theatrical enterprise, whose spokes swept not only through all of America but out through the world: Australia, South Africa, wherever there was a platform and an audience.

And Mendelsohn Theatrical Agency, MTA, reflected it. I don't think the furniture had been changed in fifty years—if then. There was a golden oak railing, stout enough, I decided, to keep back the most excited aspirant. Within this railing sat a gray-haired lady who operated as receptionist, telephone operator, secretary, and, perhaps, nurse. Her eyes, when they looked at me, took my measure and told me that nothing was beyond her. A boy and a girl sat on the banquette couches that were bolted to the wall. Each of them had something to read, although neither was reading. I announced myself to the gray-haired lady. "Joe Binney to see Mr. Popper," and retired to one of the benches. I noticed, however, that the two youngsters at the sound of my voice had dropped any pretense of reading and were staring at me with frank curiosity. It is my deaf-man's voice, of course, a voice that I have never heard, but whose effect I have seen reflected in a discouraging number of faces. In a theatrical agency, the haven of cultured tones, it must sound like a lion's roar—or perhaps a mouse's squeak. I gave them my best dummy smile, and their eyes popped directly back to the reading material. I picked up a *Gentleman's Quarterly* and watched them covertly over the top of it. When I saw them both begin to rise, I glanced back at the reception desk across the railing, and, sure enough, the iron-clad old lady was gesturing to me and saying: "Mr. Binney, Mr. Popper will see you now." I crossed the office, smiling a real smile, while the two youngsters watched me with expressions of outrage mixed with awe. They had not tumbled, I thought (hoped), to the fact that I am deaf. Possibly they were wondering just where a voice like mine would fit into stage, screen, or television. Let them ponder.

The furniture in Popper's office matched the decor out front, and the outfit he was wearing stepped from the pages of the magazine I had hastily dropped. This time it was a thick tweed suit of powder blue. The shirt was cream with very wide, if muted, maroon stripes, set off by a maroon heavy silk tie and a matching silk handkerchief that flowed from the pocket. His shoes were thick black bluchers that must have added a good inch to his height. He had a nice, welcoming, relaxed smile on his face as he stretched out his hand to greet me. It was a more controlled and happier Norman Popper than I had seen up at Bill's dwelling. He drew me over to a chair near his desk, but I remained standing, transfixed by what appeared to be an acre of old photographs covering nearly every square inch of his walls. When I turned to look at him again his smile had widened to nearly a laugh of pure enjoyment. "We go back quite a ways around here," he said.

They did indeed. There were signed portraits of actors I had heard of only dimly, and others that were a distinct surprise. One portrait of a strikingly handsome matinee idol wearing a fireman's cap was signed, "Regards to 'Fix.' Sydney." A small typewritten label underneath identified the idol as Sydney Greenstreet in *The Still Alarm.*

"Sydney Greenstreet!" I stared. "The 'Fat Man.' "

"Not always a fat man," Popper assured me. "He was a real heartthrob in his day. What an actor! A man who could do anything, everything." The photographs went on and on: actors I had barely heard of in plays I had never heard of. Beyond them were many photographs of vaudevillians: dancers, jugglers, acrobats, animal acts, magicians, ukelele players, banjo players, comedians, dramatic acts—the whole wall buzzed and sang and hummed and tapped, and cried "Regards to Fix!"

"Fix," I said, looking at Popper. "That can't possibly be you."

"Christ, no!" he exclaimed alarmed. "Do I look that old?" He passed his hand rapidly over a haircut that had the unmistakable gloss of Grecian Formula. "No, no," he repeated. "Fix—that was Mr. Mendelsohn, the man who hired me for an office boy." He smiled sadly. "Even that dates me, all right," he said. "Who the hell has office boys anymore?

"Mr. Mendelsohn inherited the agency from his father," Popper explained, as if stamping out any notion of his age. "That's how far back it all goes. Back into ancient history. Tom shows. You wouldn't believe, although Tom shows were touring later than you think: into the thirties, even."

"Tom shows?" I *am* ignorant.

"*Uncle Tom's Cabin,*" said Popper. "You never heard of it?" He looked concerned.

"Of course I heard of it," I said, blushing. "But I thought all that ended with the Civil War."

"My goodness, no," said Popper. "It opened before the Civil War in places like Barnum's Museum, but believe me, it was still touring in places in the 1930s. Now Mr. Mendelsohn's father—that's another story. He nearly did go all the way back to the Civil War. A lot of the tours he booked—a lot of them—were partly by stagecoach. A lot of them by ship, some of them sailing ships, would you believe it? Lecture tours he booked out to California by sailing ship around the Horn. There wasn't even a Canal. A steamship couldn't carry enough coal to make it all that way. But when his son, Felix, took it over, of course, they all had trains. Trains everywhere. Except to Australia, of course," he added hastily.

"Felix," I repeated, scenting, perhaps, the mildest of send-ups. "Felix Mendelsohn?"

"After the composer, of course," said Popper, "whom old Mr. Mendelsohn. . . I never saw the old Mr. Mendelsohn. . . ." he interjected. "Dead for years, of course. Dead for years before I was an office boy. Loved, loved the composer Mendelssohn, and named his boy, who he wanted to become a great violinist—a Paganini. Even booked his boy on a tour. In velvet knickers.

Some bastard stole the photograph right off my walls! Booked him for a tour. The Infant Paganini! It never paid for the train fare. Who can tell? So Felix went to work in the business."

"Felix," I ruminated. "So then . . . Fix?"

"No—yes? Maybe part." The blue tweed shrugged. "But what really would happen is that something would go wrong. Something was always going wrong. Hell, everything went wrong. You think this is easy, this business? Everything is still going wrong, otherwise why are you here, eh?" It was my turn to shrug.

"Mr. Mendelsohn would get a telegram, a telephone call. He would be sitting at this desk, right here. Do you think I would change the desk? Are you crazy? The telephone, maybe, but not the desk. He would be sitting right here. And he would read the telegram with his eyes bulging out, like the words would be tearing out his eyeballs. Or he would be listening to the earpiece on the phone, and again, believe it, his eyeballs would bulge out like he was reading the words he was hearing over the phone. And then he would jump up—straight up, right out of his chair. Not the same chair, this one," he apologized. "All the patches came loose finally. He'd jump straight up and he'd yell, 'All right! All right!' And then he'd snap his fingers. And believe me, what a snap. He had fingers like saplings with big calluses from being the Infant Paganini. And he'd snap those fingers like a firecracker going off, and he'd yell, 'I'll *fix* it!'

"And he always did," concluded Mr. Popper. "He always fixed it one way or another. Stranded actors, stranded troupes, train wrecks, shipwrecks, and thieves! Thieves! Thieves! My God, the thieves! They would steal not only money. Oh, money wasn't all of it. Entire wardrobes. Trunks and trunks full of clothes, expensive costumes. . . . Blizzards!" he ejaculated suddenly. "Let me tell you about blizzards. . . ." but then he stopped. "No," he said. He smiled. "No blizzards today. Another day, perhaps."

"And you?" I asked him shyly. "How did you come into all this?"

Popper shrugged. "Relatives," he said. "What else? From my mother's side. A cousin." Popper turned and stared moodily out the window that looked over Broadway and then turned back. "We were financial geniuses, the Poppers," he said. "We managed to stay poor right through World War II. Everybody else it was defense contracts, defense work. Overtime, double time, triple time. The war made a lot of money. But not for us. At fourteen, in the middle of the war, I had to leave school. I was still in knickers. It wasn't even legal, leaving school that early. Did anybody give a shit? The school board? Forget it. I was office boy for my mother's cousin. Twelve dollars a week. Office boy for the Infant Paganini.

"It was an education—like being thrown into a cageful of lions is an education, believe me. In the high school I never went to, they had a track team. You think they could run like me? Forget it. Never. I was greased lightning. Listen, my friend, you want to be an athlete, be an office boy on Broadway. So I got my twelve dollars a week, which I took home to my mother. I got tips now and then, which I kept. It was only fair." He appealed to me. "Wasn't it? Don't you think it was fair? My father found out from the tips—in the pockets of my knickers. *'Where did you get this money?'* He thought I stole it. He wasn't mad about the stealing—only about the keeping. From then on I left my tips at the office.

"So Mr. Mendelsohn worked me hard, but he worked me fair. And he taught me. He was going through a terrible time. Everything was changing. You know, they talk about vaudeville dying like it was shot through the head, but vaudeville took a long time to die. Even after the war, they were still booking acts here and there. But what really hurt was that the Legit was dying too. You don't know how many shows were going out on the road, actors here, actors there, company after company. Every city that thought of itself as a city had a house to be booked. And you knew that there were a certain number of people in that city would come to see the show. But now," he put his palms up, "who can figure?

"The old theater, the great, great troupes, the Lunts, Cornell, Maurice Evans, Ethel Barrymore . . . That is gone, all gone, my friend. The great tours are gone. And Broadway," he gestured toward the window, "is following down the drain." Suddenly he pounded his fist into his palm. "The *schmucks*," he said. "So beautiful it was."

He remained staring out the dusty window for a few moments, into nothing, and when he turned back to me, there was a small, sad, resigned smile on his face. "So," he said. "You didn't come here for a lesson in history. What did you want to see me about?"

"About Bill, naturally," I answered. "Nothing specific, but just some general information about him."

"You've got some questions about Bill, and you're his friend?" The black eyebrows went up. "So why don't you ask him?"

"For the same reason that people go to shrinks," I said. "Bill can't see all around himself. I have to know more about him than he knows himself—than he consciously knows, I mean."

"And why is this?" asked Popper. "What is the big concern?"

"His business manager, Arnold Pelfrey," I began.

"He hanged himself. Yes, yes. I heard. A terrible thing."

"The police don't think that he hanged himself anymore," I said. "They think that somebody did it for him."

Popper's dark eyes widened perceptibly. "That is a terrible thing you are saying."

"The police are saying it," I emphasized. "And, naturally, Bill is concerned."

"Concerned how?" There was suddenly the still air of caution around Mr. Popper.

I told a lie to avoid any mention of Macready's missing nut. "Bill thinks that Pelfrey was on his way over to see him and got stopped off. If all this had anything to do with Bill personally, he and I want to know about it."

"I see, I see," said Popper, putting a thumbnail to his teeth. His eyes did not express what he saw, if anything. "So what do you want from me?"

"Just a quick rundown on how you see his career with you, and how you see his career as it stands right not."

"Career . . . career," the agent muttered. "They call them careers, as if there was some plan, some intelligence behind what they do. Career. Do they listen?" His mouth tightened, and his eyes flashed contempt. He put his arms out expansively. "Actors are like children," he said. "They live for the moment, for the glory, the billing, the name in lights, the glamour. Do they plan careers, for instance, like a business executive? A business man, so careful, so cautious? Will they listen? No."

I held my peace.

"I saw him first in one of those, what they call, boutiques. A garage, a loft, I can't remember. My wife told me to go, so I went. When your wife says go, you go. Right? If you've got any brains, you do. So, I'm sitting there on a wooden bench with possibly splinters in it, and I'm thinking more about the splinters than I am about what's going on up on the stage. It was some play nobody ever heard of by Wedekind or maybe Hauptman. Why should anybody put on such things?

"Now, young Mr. Macready had almost nothing to do. The ushers had more to do than he did. And for me, what the ushers were saying was more interesting than the dialogue. No matter. So he was there, up on this orange crate of a stage. Did he have special lighting? No. Did he even take advantage of what lighting there was? No. Did he know anything about what he was doing? Obviously not. But he was upstaging the lead. He was upstaging the lead without doing anything. He was just there.

"Now, look. Any actor with any experience knows what to do when he's being upstaged. He turns it to his advantage. He makes it backfire. But that's only the normal upstaging with some silly kind of business like picking your nose or scratching your balls. Macready wasn't doing anything like that. He was still—like a statue—but what a statue! You couldn't take your eyes off him. You know why? Well, the lead, he was into his part. Acting! Acting! Acting!" The agent gestured with a violent demonstration. "And you knew exactly what he, the lead, was going to do next. It was all logical. It was all of a piece. I suppose in its way it was right, you know? The right thing to do. What the director told him to do. All in the script. But with Macready, just standing there, you didn't know what *that* son-of-a-bitch was going to do. You didn't know if he was going to jump on the lead's back and stab him. If he was going to run amok in the audience. If he was suddenly going to climb up a rope—anything! You *wondered,*" he pointed to his temple, "what that young man, so still, upstage, was going to do.

"All right. My wife was right. Not for the first time, let me tell you. I tried to find his name on the program, a piece of paper. Who could tell one from another? I went backstage, if you want to call it that. And he's standing up. There wasn't even a place to sit down, cold creaming to take off his makeup. I gave him my card and I said, 'I'll be across the street having a cup of coffee if you'd like to talk for a little bit.'

"So when he came into the cafeteria, he recognized me, but I didn't recognize him. That's a good sign, you know? He was somebody completely different. And I told him the usual spiel. '*Maybe* there is something I can do for you. You want to come around to my office tomorrow?' He was cool, very cool. Cold. A little crazy. Good.

"Those kids out there on the bench," he waved toward the

door, "you think I don't know they're there? Them, too. There is something—not like Macready—but there's something. Maybe I can help them. Maybe not. Who knows? They'll be mad as hell when they come in here. Up on their high horse. That's good. You know? Show me something about how they look when they're alive.

"So I was able to get him placed: here, there. Off-off Broadway; off Broadway. And Broadway. A few roles. Nothing big on Broadway. He isn't a rocket. Not everybody sees it. Not everybody knows what they're looking at. And television. I got him some eating money. Soaps for scale. Did he want a running part on soaps? We had it in our mitt. No. Bits, yes. Running part, no. He'd rather do Wedekind, Hauptman, Buchner, Brieux—all nothing from nowhere. I wouldn't even ask people to come down to see him. Who can sit through it?

"And pictures," Popper gazed out his window ruminatively. "Yes, my friend. I got him pictures. Four of them. Three here, one on the Coast. He actually went out to the Coast." The agent smirked. "It was a concession, you understand. He did the world a favor by going to Hollywood to make a picture. Nice of him. No? It's wonderful that he should be willing to do such things."

"But all this time," I asked carefully, "ever since you took him on. He's been working?"

"Oh, yes!" I could not, of course, hear the raised volume of Popper's voice, but his expression made it obvious. "Has he been working? Yes. Has he been working in what he should be working in? No. A big fat no. You want to talk career? Hah!"

"His earnings," I persevered. "Would you say he's been making a living? Enough to put something by? Money in the bank?"

"Did I mention pictures?" Popper asked me. "Four of them, yes? That money went in the bank, my friend. Broadway shows? Yes. That money goes in the bank. TV? Oh, yes. And that money goes in the bank.

"For off-off Broadway he gets a minimum of about two ninety a week. If the gross goes up he gets over four hundred. Can anybody live on that? He can—Macready can. Can he live on unemployment? You've seen it. Yes. Macready can live on unemployment.

"But is this a career?" Popper asked me. "Always a difficult question," he answered himself judiciously. "What is a living to one actor is a chauffeur's salary to another. Has he made enough to stay alive? Yes. Has he made enough so that those two youngsters sitting out there would think he was wealthy? Yes. Has he made enough so that he can talk smart to network executives? No, my friend. Oh, no. Not in a million years."

"Ah." It was my turn to ruminate. "That's what gets me. How crazy they are to get him. Is that normal? O.K. So he's good. They say he's good. You say he's good. He says he's good. When I was staying up there, he even *showed* me he was good. All right. He's good. But is he *that* good? Is anybody that good? They keep talking about this test he did. . . ."

"Let me tell you about that, my friend," said Popper, cutting me off. "Because I was asking just exactly the same questions you are asking. Can he be that good? Who knows?

"Can you guess how many asses I kissed to get a xerox of the scene they wanted to test? Of the synopsis of the series? You will never know. If I wouldn't tell my wife, would I tell you? Forget it. But I got ahead of time the scene they wanted to test, and a step outline of the show and the series: the projected series. Who can tell if it will bomb, the pilot? And I called him over and showed it to him. Listen, it was like I was showing him the crown jewels in his pocket. So he's reading it all. You know, lying on the couch there, not even sitting up, but lying down on the couch. And he puts it all down, all the stuff I got him, and he sits up and he says: 'What toilet did you pull this out of, Norman?' Do you wonder that I haven't had a stroke? It's my wife. She feeds me like a racehorse. I'll never have a stroke. Let the other ones, the high livers, have the strokes. Not me. Not with my wife.

"Yes. So I stayed very cool. 'You've seen a lot of toilets with the crown jewels in them?' I ask him. 'You know what this could mean to your career?' Career again." He rolled his eyes. "To make a long story short, I ask him, 'Will you do it? Will you do the test?' He says to me, 'I might. It might be a hoot.' A hoot! A network. Millions of dollars backed up in the pipe. A concept! So he took it home with him—to the woodshed. And he did the test. And you know the rest."

"I know the rest," I said. "But how and why? That's what I don't know."

"Aha!" said Popper. "How and why? That's what I asked *him*. 'What did you do?' I asked him. 'You've got these people coming in their pants.'

"Would you believe it? The little shit? He told me, 'There

was no way I was going to do this crap straight. No way. There was no way to do it straight. So I made another part,' he says. 'I made a part of a not overly bright actor who sees this role as his big chance and he goes in and wows them.'

"What do you think of that? *He wasn't even playing the part*!" The beautifully suited agent jumped up and down a little with this pronouncement. "No! He was playing the part of somebody who was playing the part! How do you like it, eh? How do you like that kind of bullshit? And he got away with it. They're crazy about it. And now he says, after he's jerked off an entire network, after he's got decent, honest, hardworking family men climbing the walls to put this thing on the rails, he says maybe he won't do it after all! Maybe he won't do it." The dark eyes smoldered. "Does he know what he's saying? Does he know how many mortgages, alimony payments, children's educations, insurance policies, careers . . . careers . . . careers . . . he's playing with? Who is he, he shouldn't do it? Who the hell is he? The little shit?"

He paused for a moment, and, gradually, a slow, soft smile stole over his face. "The little shit," he repeated, smiling. "He aced the network. Everybody. They didn't know what they were looking at. Can you imagine it?" His eyes clouded over with dreaminess as he imagined it.

"Just two questions," I said, breaking into the reverie. "The first one is: When you saw Bill working in that boutique or whatever, how was he making a living?"

"Who knows how they live?" replied Popper. "They live like fireflies, off the morning dew. They bus tables in cafeterias, wait on tables, tend bars, push racks in the garment district, steal, lie, swindle, peddle . . . who knows?" He pondered this for an instant. "Maybe he had a pension?" His eyebrows climbed. "He was in the war, you know," said Popper with a pious expression. "A veteran."

"No," I told him. "No pension. They stuck him back together in the hospital, and that was it. But, when you first took him on, did he ever mention anything like film?"

"Film?" The agent was astonished. "What would he know about film? I'm the one who got him his first picture. Me." He jabbed his chest with an outstretched thumb. "He didn't know what the front end of a camera looked like."

"I don't mean Hollywood," I pursued. "Any kind of film at all. Modeling clothes for ads—anything at all."

"Never," Popper assured me. "Anyway, that was all over, the little local ads they used to put in the movies, by the time Bill got started. Television killed all that. No. William Macready did not have one single foot of film to his credit when I met him, nor . . ." he put up a hand to forestall me, ". . . did he ever mention anything like that to me. Never."

"All right." I surrendered the notion. "Now the next thing is: Can you think of anybody who doesn't want Bill to have this role?"

"Every actor in New York," said Popper. "No. No. I'm joking. But, what a question! You were up there at Bill's with all of us, in that pigeon coop you saw how all of us were begging and pleading with him. How should anybody not want it?"

"Things are not always what they seem," I said as smoothly as I knew how. "Think about it for a minute. Don't leave anybody out. Think about each person involved, even Garson."

"Garson?" His face opened in surprise. "What do you know about Garson?"

"Only that he must be very deeply involved. This is going to represent a big investment for him."

A pitying smile overcame the agent's features. "A big investment," he repeated, "for Garson?" He made a downward motion with his hand. "A lot you know about it. Forget it with Garson." He sought counsel in the ceiling. "Let me see," he mused. "Is there anybody could be hurt?" He pursed his lips. "Only one, maybe. And it's not such a strong case you should take it seriously. There's only one man might not like Bill getting the role: the producer . . . director, Emerson Kite."

I did not ask the obvious question. I waited patiently while he put it together. "Directors," said Popper, "like to have a pretty firm hand in the casting, and not always for purely professional reasons. I mean not always to make a better show. Kite worked very hard to get himself in line for this gold mine—this series. Suddenly, he's got the star handed to him—take it or leave it. 'The Old Man wants him.' Some directors would walk out, you know? They wouldn't take it. Bill has worked with Kite before. Are they crazy about each other? You saw up there. Are they in love? An item? No. They don't even trust each other. All that gets washed away, of course, when they start to work. They're professionals.

"But we could look a little further," he continued. "All this time Kite has been angling to get the show, did he make promises? Did he say to some actor, 'You do this for me, baby, and you're into 'Tycoon' like a bandit?' Did he make promises that now he can't keep? A serious thing for a director. No show runs forever. Kite will have to go on doing other shows. He's got a reputation to keep up.

"It all comes down to clout," Popper concluded. "Kite wasn't even consulted about this. I mean they said, 'The Old Man wants this actor, so you work with this actor, and if you don't like it, we'll replace you.' No director likes that. How does it make him look?"

"Emerson Kite." It was my turn to look dubious. "Not much, but a start. Who knows?" I seized his hand so suddenly and warmly that he jumped. "Thank you very much, Mr. Popper . . ."

"Norman, Norman," he protested. "For Christ's sake."

"Norman," I said. "I've enjoyed talking to you and I've learned a lot. I've got just one more favor to ask."

"So ask me."

"Could your secretary out there make a phone call for me? I want to see if I have any messages at the office."

He took me by the arm out the door and said a few words to the gray-haired guardian. He beckoned then to the young man on the bench, whose eyes had been drinking in the camaraderie between me and Popper. With a ferocious sneer, he forged his way into the office ahead of Popper, who winked at me and closed the door behind them. I gave my number to the secretary, who called and busily began jotting on a pad. When she put the receiver down, she handed me the message:

> Very important that you meet me this afternoon. Same time, same station.
>
> Beanie

The secretary's face was as hard and expressionless as the oak railing that fended off a voracious world. All the same, I was glad it wasn't Edna who'd handed me the message.

17

I'd been running so many errands that I'd neglected to notice what a beautiful spring day it was—even on Broadway. Broadway was filled with the gawkers from out of town and the inmates, who gawked at nothing but seemed to walk through a tunnel that closed them off from the world. I decided that, even though I am a certified inmate, I would gawk at the blue sky on occasion as I walked the westward blocks to the Landmark. Even walking slowly, I realized, would get me there a half hour or so before the "same time, same station" appointment. I looked forward to a leisurely drink at their fine old-fashioned bar.

Indeed, I had already stepped up to the bar and was about to order before I noticed that Betty was already there, at the same table we'd shared before. She hadn't noticed me when I came in because she was talking animatedly to a man seated across from her whose back was turned to me. At first I thought it was Namier, but there was something in the youthful set of the shoulders, and then, of course, the blond hair, which had looked silvery under the lights, that dismissed the idea of Namier. It was a young man, and a vigorous one.

I didn't want to intrude, but on the other hand, I was totally, irrationally, as mad as hell. Some tiny portion of my so-called intelligence told me that this was a business meeting. There was certainly nothing romantic in Betty's expression, and the young man's gestures, though vigorous, were not amorous. Nonetheless, I couldn't help myself. I walked over to the table and stood there until Betty noticed me.

"Joe!" she said. "How nice. Sit down." There wasn't any hint of real surprise in her face. I pulled out a chair and sat down, getting my first look at the young man, who hadn't bothered to look up at me. Betty nodded toward him and introduced us. His name was Conrad Medellin, and he was exquisite. His face had a good deep healthy tan that set off his cornflower-blue eyes. His blond hair was repeated in long thick lashes and curled yellow hair on the backs of his hands. His teeth were of astounding brilliance and regularity. He was beautifully dressed in a light blue shirt, a dark, figured tie, and a suit that was navy blue of a light material that seemed molded to his athletic shoulders. I hated him. I felt like a bum, a fool. We did not shake hands. His blue eyes snapped over me with the acceptance of the introduction and then dismissed me. I felt like a waiter in the establishment who had pushed his luck.

He leaned toward Betty as he handed her a thick envelope of the kind that contains contracts, leases, or summonses. I guessed it was a contract. I could not see what he was saying, but Betty was very attentive. She nodded and put the envelope in her capacious purse. The business seemed to be concluded, then, because he stood up, said goodbye to Betty, and gave me a brief tight smile of farewell. On the way out he picked a dark cashmere topcoat off the peg and shrugged himself into it. It appeared to be about eight-hundred dollars' worth of topcoat and seemed to have nothing at all to do with keeping one warm.

We couldn't take our eyes off him. We waited and watched him flag a cab, which really seemed to appear magically at the snap of his fingers. Then I said, only breathing the expression, "Wow."

"Some production, huh?" said Betty. I had the uncomfortable feeling she was laughing at me.

"What's he made out of," I asked her. "Ice cream?"

"There's ice in it somewhere," she answered, smiling. She seemed completely relaxed, so relaxed that I realized that whatever romance we had begun had not been threatened. The sad truth was that Betty looked just a bit shabby next to that Adonis. I couldn't believe that he'd made a pitch for her. It was a shameful, unworthy thought on my part, but, nonetheless, I was grateful. I looked into her face again and smiled. Suddenly I felt an intense wave of affection for her. Like me, she had put in a day's humdrum work, and like me, she was the kind of mortal on whom it showed. She wasn't wearing a business suit today, but something softer, something that expressed more vulnerability than efficiency. It was a light green dress of some soft jerseylike material, with a white collar that stood up and framed her face. It had white cuffs, too, that ended the sleeves well above the wrists. She put her hand over mine. "Were you jealous?" she asked, smiling.

"So jealous that I'm going to take a drink," I said. I signaled the waiter, noticing, incidentally, that there were only coffee cups on the table, and that his was nearly untouched. "What are you having?"

"A martini," she answered. "But one, and only one." I said nothing, because I've heard that vow before. I gave my order, and the drinks were served promptly. "Don't tell me," I said after my first sip of bourbon and soda. "Let me guess. Mr. Medellin is not my competition. He's Bill Macready's competition. Right? For the part in 'Tycoon?' "

Her eyes widened in surprise. "You think he's an actor? Is that what you think?"

"A very successful one."

She laughed. "You don't know very much about actors, then. Nobody would hire an actor who looked like that—like a stuffed doll. Actors don't look like that unless they're made up to look like that. And they don't wear the equivalent of makeup out in the street."

"Well, he certainly looks like a tycoon," I defended myself.

"Not that I've ever met."

"And you've met plenty of tycoons, I suppose?"

"Scads of them," she said, smiling securely. Then she asked me, "You really don't know what he is?"

"A tennis player?" I stabbed desperately.

"A lawyer."

"Impossible," I refuted her. "No briefcase."

"Lawyers like Mr. Medellin don't carry briefcases," said Betty. "They have other people to carry their briefcases. That, in fact, is why we met here. He'd had a meeting with Mr. Namier in the studio building up the street. Then he called his office to have the papers delivered down here, and Mr. Namier had another meeting back at the network building. So I was dispatched to pick up the papers after he'd signed them here. Mr. Medellin," she continued with a moue of mock seriousness, "was very annoyed because some poor old man from his office took all of thirty minutes to get up to this restaurant."

"Then it has nothing to do with you personally—his being a lawyer, I mean."

"Do I look as though I could afford a lawyer like that?"

"I'm surprised he can afford himself," I said. I paused for another swig. "So what's in the envelope he handed you?"

Betty smiled primly through the slight expression of shock on her face. "Even if I knew," she said, "I couldn't tell you."

"Couldn't we peek?"

She said, discomfited, "I keep forgetting that you're a detective."

"Because of my cunning disguise."

"You have many cunning disguises," said Betty, grinning. "I like the one you were wearing last night."

Self-consciousness caused me to drop down the rest of my bourbon. It was, after all, the first one of the day. "Polish that off," I pointed to Betty's martini, "and I'll get you another."

"No can do," said Betty.

"Then come down to my place. I've got a martini pitcher just as good as yours, and a whole barrel of etchings I want to show you."

"No bean soup tonight," said Betty with businesslike finality. "I've got to take these papers back for Mr. Namier to sign, and then we're going to work together far into the night. That's why it's just one martini, and actually, I shouldn't even have had that."

I studied my empty glass. "Are you going to be jealous of Mr. Namier now?" she asked sweetly.

I sighed. "Can you sit here for a few minutes while I have another?" She nodded, and I signaled the waiter for one—mine.

When I was served, I said to her gruffly, injured, "You said in your message that it was important for me to see you—not that seeing you anywhere isn't important—but I came steaming down here all prepared . . ."

"All prepared?" said Betty, smiling widely. "Really?"

"Well," I said, flustered, "for something a little more . . ."

"All right," said Betty. "I do have something to tell you. Something I didn't think would get across on one of those 'While You Were Out' pads. . . ."

"Which are suitable only for bartenders," I added.

"Yes. Anyway, you now have an appointment to see Mr. Garson." She sat back, and her attitude was more or less, 'You now have a royal pass to play with a splinter of the True Cross.'

"An appointment?" I asked stupidly. "When?"

"Tomorrow morning at nine," said Betty. "I hope you're impressed."

"Where?" I asked her.

"The Sherry-Netherland. . . . You mean you're not impressed?"

"I don't know," I said. "Tomorrow morning? Nine? It's a little early."

"Early!" Her face expressed outrage. "Some detective you are. Nine o'clock is too early?"

"No. . . no." I corrected her. "I mean it's early in the game. I don't know enough. I'm not really prepared. I didn't want to see him this soon."

"When you see Mr. Garson," said Betty, "is when he wants it. Not when you want it." She sat back and pouted. "You don't seem to appreciate . . ."

"I didn't think it was going to be an audience with the Pope," I said.

"An audience with the Pope can be arranged," said Betty. "But with Cy Garson, you need channels. And I got you the channels. And you ought to be grateful . . . you bastard," she concluded.

"I guess I don't really understand," I began.

"I'll say you don't," she asserted. "You don't understand at all. You don't just walk in on Cy Garson and start asking questions. You work hard to get his general acknowledgment that you're alive. Then, if he feels like it, you're admitted into his general area, let us say, the same city he happens to be in at the time.

"As a special favor to you, I begged, pleaded, and implored Mr. Namier to call Garson and get you an appointment. Any time. Any place. Finally, to shut me up and get some peace, he agreed and put through a call to Garson. Luckily for everyone, it turned out that Mr. Garson will be in New York to look at the big studio he's going to use in 'Tycoon.' He'll be at his regular New York center, which is a suite in the Sherry-Netherland.

"I hope you realize," she added, full of injured dignity, "what this cost Mr. Namier."

"I'll be happy to pay him for the call," I said, getting sick of it.

"Pay him!" exclaimed Betty. "How could you possibly do that? What that means—his calling Garson—is that now he owes Garson a favor. That's the way it's done—like little boys trading jackknives or marbles. Are you in a position to do Mr. Garson a favor?" She sat back, satisfied, with her chin firmed up something like Winston Churchill's.

"All right," I said, putting my palms together in a prayerful steeple. "I'm grateful. At nine sharp tomorrow morning, I show up at the Sherry-Netherland, and Mr. Garson will be sitting in a big chair in the lobby reading a newspaper and smoking a cigar, right?''

Betty rummaged around in her purse for a few seconds and pulled out a pink ''While You Were Out'' slip. ''You will be at the Sherry-Netherland promptly at nine,'' she said. ''And you will ask the desk clerk to call this number and announce you. Then someone will be sent down to look you over and check you out. And you will, I hope, be presentable enough to be taken up to the suite.

''When you arrive there,'' she continued, ''do not expect to burst in on Mr. Garson and dazzle him with your wit and gaiety. His words to Mr. Namier were, 'Get him up there at nine in the morning, and somehow, I'll fit him in.' ''

''What kind of favor does he want back for all this largesse?'' I asked irritably. ''A piece of the network?''

''Never mind that,'' she went on imperturbably. ''You will be seated in a large, comfortable waiting room. All the morning newspapers will be there. There will be coffee. There will be things to eat. There will be liquor. Lay off the liquor. There will be beautiful girls. Lay off the beautiful girls.''

''O.K.'' I agreed. ''I stick to coffee and Danish. Anything else?''

''Some time along the day, Mr. Garson will fit you in,'' she said. ''Don't think you're going to be lost in the shuffle. Nobody gets lost in the shuffle. He made a promise and he'll keep a promise. That's a promise.''

I sat back and laughed. ''You don't know what you've just been describing,'' I told her.

''I don't?''

''You've been describing almost exactly a meeting with a Mafia don in the back room of a sanitized restaurant.'' Her jaw dropped a little. ''Don't worry about it,'' I told her. ''I'll handle myself all right.'' I laughed again. Betty was a bit shocked, a bit impressed, and a bit amused.

She looked at her watch. ''I've got to get back,'' she told me. ''Right now. Hurry. Get me a cab.'' She stood up and took her light tan cloth coat from the back of the chair. Standing, she kissed me quickly on the cheek. ''Get me a cab,'' she said. ''Hurry. And don't forget. Nine o'clock.''

After I'd put Betty in the cab, I went back to the bar to have another drink and settle the bill. I sat at the bar to reassess my position, or to make what John Foster Dulles used to call "an agonizing reappraisal."

I had strolled down to the appointment signed "Beanie" with the simple, straightforward intention of getting laid again. Not terribly admirable, I admit, but, please agree, an entirely human impulse. However, the few moments I'd spent with her, having got rid of the blonde god, had shaken me. Getting laid had become secondary. There had been about her, in her soft green dress, the look in her eyes, and the relaxed features of her pretty face, a youthfulness and vulnerability that hadn't been there on the previous evening, a gentleness that belied all the rigorous, businesslike instructions she had been giving me. She was establishing, tacitly, and without false or alarming gestures, the bridge that spans the gulf between a coupling and an affair. I was not sure that I wanted to enter anything so demanding—not only for my sake, but for hers as well. There seemed to be very little I could offer Betty beyond mere physicality. And even that—even my physical future—was in some doubt.

For, accustomed as I am to self-deception, I could not delude myself that there was not going to be a reckoning between myself and my tall black opponent. Nor could I pretend that the timid stabs I had made today in locating him were in any way a sign of my eagerness for that confrontation. I would continue to go through the moves—more or less formalities—but I knew in my bones that the search would degenerate, as somehow it always does, to legwork and eyesight. Somewhere on some waterfront was Roger Grim, and there I would find him, if, indeed, he hadn't got word of my survival and come looking for me. If that was the case, then the romantic future of Betty Middleton and Joe Binney was very limited.

Neither was I overjoyed with my performance in getting a grip on the relationship—if there was such a relationship—between Bill Macready and Arnold Pelfrey. I was being very tentative and feeling guilty even about that. In trying to feel out some of Bill's past, I had been truthful in one thing while questioning both Namier and Popper: There was no way I could question Bill directly. There was no way I could ask him: "Hey, you ever perform in a circus? Hey, Bill. You ever screw a nine-year-old boy? Hey, Bill, you been putting money into chicken flicks? Snuff films?" You cannot ask such questions of your friends. His friendship was important to me: fragile . . . fragile. It is hard to detect when you don't want to find out what it is you are supposed to detect.

I had finished my drink without even noticing that I had been drinking it: a very bad sign, they tell me. I would add it to my list. I felt empty and directionless. I did not want to go directly home to my apartment, despite the wall full of books, so many of them still unread. Neither did I simply want to hang around this amiable bar and tie one on. There was too much to be done, too much alertness required, for me to be gliding around the streets of Manhattan in a quasi-stupor. I glanced at my watch and realized that if I hurried I could still get to my office without all the sign-in, sign-out routine and fumbling with elevator keys that is now *de rigueur* after sundown in New York. Edna would not be there, but I had a deep itch to see if one of the delinquent checks had arrived.

But Edna *was* there. At least I hoped it was Edna. A light shone over the transom, and we are very careful not to leave lights on. I put my key in the lock as soundlessly as I knew how and swung the door open with my arm, standing well back in the hallway. Indeed, it was Edna, bless her, but there was also a young man, facing her, whom I did not immediately recognize. Since there was no sign of concern on Edna's face, I was not alarmed. In fact, the only alarming thing about Edna's face was that it was dreamy—or sappy, if you want to look at it in a curmudgeonly way. The young man, I finally realized, was Dr. David Sartin.

I'd never seen him in street clothes before, and, for that matter, had never looked at him from a fully erect position. He and Edna were standing quite close, though not close enough for an embrace. They seemed to be trembling on the brink of one. I sensed that my intrusion, if it can be called an intrusion in my own office, was not wholly welcome. "Well," I said stupidly. "Well, well, well."

"So well, what?" snapped Edna, moving back from the brink. She had the courtesy to blush.

"So, well, nothing," I answered, moving back to my desk. "I just came back to see if any of those checks had turned up."

"No," said Edna. "No checks."

"You won't be so flippant about it," I warned her, "when your pay envelope turns up empty." She found this unworthy of comment and merely sniffed at me. However, she rolled her eyes at Dr. Sartin with a "Do you see what I have to put up with?"

expression. "Check or no check," I continued implacably, "I'm glad you're here because I won't be in tomorrow morning. I've got an appointment that just might take all day."

"So?" she queried nastily. I think she was nettled because I was staring at Dr. Sartin. Although he did not flinch under the inspection, he did seem to shrink somewhat. I had before me not the young Dr. Kildare or Ben Casey of the white-coated authoritative manner, but a youth in rather ill-fitting clothes who was entirely unsure of his position. So far as I could discern, he and Edna had been doing nothing wrong. There was certainly no smell of sex in the air, and if there had been, I would have ignored it. "Live and let screw," I always say. But Dr. Sartin was acting like the ghost of Hamlet's father just at cock-crow. To put them more at ease, I moderated my demeanor, sinking softly into my chair behind the desk and saying as gently as I could, "If you don't mind, Edna, just a few notes for tomorrow while I'm gone."

She did not exactly flounce over to her notebook, but clearly she was eager to be off. Who could blame her?

"Tomorrow," I said, "I want you to call the Coast Guard to see if a Roger Grim has taken out seaman's papers of any kind." She pothooked busily. Dr. Sartin stared with disapprobation. "Then, I want you to look up all the oil companies who run their own tanker fleets—most of them are non-union or company union—and see if they've got a Roger Grim working for them." Dr. Sartin looked even more dour. "Finally," I said, "I want you to get me the home address of Arnold Pelfrey. I don't mean that shoebox he was living in over on the East Side, but what his actual home used to be. If he had a wife and kids, he must have kept them somewhere. I want to go out and talk to his wife."

"How lovely for her," murmured Edna.

Young Dr. Sartin brightened at this show of defiance; me, it depressed. "I'm looking forward to it," I told her. "Order me a new box of thumbscrews while you're at it."

I looked up then and stared at Dr. Sartin. I suppose I was challenging him. It was not a nice thing for me to do, but, I consoled myself, he started it. Divested of his white uniform, his badge, his stethoscope, the finger-snapping obedience of hot and cold running nurses, he appeared to be a mere shell of himself, an uncertain youth like any other. He was wearing a blue plaid sports coat that was too big for him, and tan slacks of an indeterminate material that were too small. He looked *poor*.

There is a kind of ill-dressed professional who looks merely eccentric, but this was not the case with Dr. Sartin. He simply looked young, defenseless, and poor. I began to appreciate the armor with which hospitals enclose their house officers. I supposed that underneath that too-often-laundered white shirt and bright blue tie, his heart was fluttering with uncertainty. He was off his turf, and was finding himself in a world where there is no real authority, no discipline at all, no future and no past worth speaking of. It was a world in which both everything and nothing happens, where people go neither forward nor back, where there are no careers, no hopes that extend beyond the end of the week. I suddenly felt sorry for him and wished him well. "That is all, my girl," I said to Edna.

She dropped her notebook like a burning coal and linked arms with the doctor. They turned and were halfway out the door when I gave them the benediction: "Go forth and multiply."

Well, this was the second leavetaking I had endured today, and it did make me feel like a lonely old bastard. I reached down into the lower drawer my desk and, in the time-honored fashion of private detectives everywhere, poured myself a belt of straight bourbon. I sipped it for a while, and said to myself, "This will never do." I poured the remainder of the drink very carefully back into the bottle—a trick my father had taught me.

So I went home. I went by subway simply because I wanted people around me: working people, thugs, mercenaries, what have you. I walked the few blocks from the subway to my little side door, endured the sudden shock of the blazing lights, and went into the kitchen to fix myself a thick ham sandwich on pumpernickel, and also a proper drink of Old Granddad and soda. I ate the sandwich in the kitchen standing up and took the drink over to the easy chair in the big front room. My books surrounded me. The small step ladder invited me to reach to the ceiling for something old and familiar, which I kept up there for precisely the reason I would seldom want it. There was a weighty tome I'd been *meaning* dutifully to read resting at chest height on my shelves. There was also a new book on Thomas Kuhn I'd bought, which I wanted very much to read, lying seductively on the end table. However I knew that if I started the book on Kuhn, I'd be up very late, and I wanted to be so bright as ever in the morning.

I reached for the weighty tome. I was only a few pages into it when I fell asleep.

18

The lobby of the Sherry-Netherland is beautifully appointed and serves gracefully, as if it had absorbed some of the *noblesse oblige* from A La Vielle Russie, the home of storied antiques that nestles in the side of the hotel. Like all good hotels, it seems to make itself courteously to home for anyone with decent manners and reasonable attire. I handed the slip Betty had given me to a young man at the desk and asked him to call and announce me. I explained that I was deaf and couldn't make the call myself, but it turned out that I wouldn't have gotten through anyway.

Because ordinary paging systems are useless to me, I kept my attention more or less fixed on the young desk clerk who had made the call. A sudden alertness in his eyes made me turn to greet an approaching young man, who was also looking to the desk clerk for a clue. The young man was clad informally but expensively with a very good sports jacket and slacks whose provenance was unmistakably Rodeo Drive. The jacket covered a light green sports shirt, very open at the throat, and the slacks terminated in Guccis. The easy casualness of his clothes made me feel acutely what all persons of uncertain finances feel when they put on their best clothes—overdressed. Nonetheless, he was extremely courteous, and even solicitous. "Mr. Binney?" he said. "I hope you weren't kept waiting."

"Not at all," I answered and followed him to the elevator. After we'd ascended, we stepped directly across the hallway and through the double doors of the big reception room to the suite. It was furnished in a more or less eclectic gathering of antiques, but whether they were real or hotel reproductions I couldn't guess at the moment. There were tea tables with coffee urns on them and a dessert cart with pastries far removed from the plastic-wrapped Danish that is shoved across a lunch counter. The young man asked me if I'd like some coffee, but since I was already snapping with caffeine, the legacy of an early rising, I declined. "Drink?" he asked, gesturing toward the well-stocked bar in the corner. I declined this also, with a smile. "Well," he said uncertainly, "make yourself comfortable." He retired to a small desk at the other end of the room and busied himself with checking off a list. I sank into a down-filled wing chair that faced a door I was certain led to the main office. Young men and very attractive young women kept issuing from it and returning with pieces of paper in their hands. They all glanced at me curiously as they hurried on.

So I was surprised by the man standing suddenly next to me, half screened by the wings of the deep chair. He had a shrewd, vigorous middle-aged face, well tanned and punctuated with sharp black eyes. His black hair was a well-trimmed helmet of very tight curls. He was staring at me intently and asking, "Who are you?" I stood up. His authority was indisputable. "I'm Joe Binney," I said. "Mr. Namier called you about me and . . ."

"Oh, yeah." Recognition dawned in his eyes. "You're the heat." He smiled.

"Not heat," I said firmly. "I'm a private investigator and . . ."

He said suddenly, sharply, "There's something the matter with you. What is it?" He was regarding me warily, as if I might explode.

"I'm deaf," I told him. "Didn't Mr. Namier mention it? I read lips."

"No kidding!" he exclaimed. The expression on his face seemed to turn my misfortune into a talent. I almost expected him to say, *"That's wonderful!"* Instead, he seized my hand and shook it, with his left hand on my triceps. "I'm Cy Garson," he said. "What can I do for you?"

It was an extremely polished performance. His eyes penetrated mine, and he fairly radiated dynamism. There was no doubt that if he decided to do something for you, he could and would do it. He was a tower of power, as they say. He, too, was wearing a sports jacket, a dark one of very expensive material, slacks, and open sports shirt, and very pricey moccasins. But somehow, as expensive as the outfit was, he managed to make it look cheap and irrelevant. It was the man inside who was important, not the clothes. His height lacked an inch of mine.

I began saying, "My client is . . ." but one of the attractive young women came up and whispered something in his ear. He listened patiently, nodded once, and then dismissed her so that she seemed to vanish magically. He looked at me again and said, "Look, I've got a snakepit of money men waiting for me in that room, and I've got to see them now." He pondered this while I admired him for not saying merely to me, "Why don't you get lost?" Mr. Garson, apparently, was a man of his word. He thought hard for a few seconds and then said decisively, "Tell you what. You'll go nuts sitting out here and cracking your knuckles. Why don't you come in with me and sort of sit in a corner. O.K.? If a lull comes up while they get their heads together, I'll fit you in and we'll talk. If you stay out here, I might never get to you at all."

I said, "Thank you very much. That will be fine with me." We went into the main office through the wide doors I'd been watching mistakenly while Garson had surprised me from the other direction. He had more surprises in store for me, because once we had passed through the wide doors into the room—which he had just likened to a snakepit—his dynamism vanished. I had somehow formed the idea that he would make an entrance, charging into the room—man of the hour, and all that—scattering bankers like so many guinea hens. Such was not the case. As we stepped across the threshold, with me slightly behind him, all of his vigor seemed to disappear. He relaxed perceptibly, as if he'd been issued a sharp instruction. His shoulders sagged. His gait took on the ease of a scholar's stroll. His face muscles softened into a peaceful, almost dreamlike expression of which I could see only a corner from my position. When we were inside, and the doors closed behind us, he waved idly, almost effeminately, to the group of men poised on their chairs. He went then to a settee fronted with a large coffee table on which stacks of papers had been piled. There was no desk in the room.

I found myself a chair, not quite in a corner, as he had suggested, but off to the right of his settee, where I could see him with reasonable facility, and also watch the men in front of him. They'd watched me come in with him, of course, and I could see the cogitations clicking away inside their heads, and finally read the universal conclusion in their eyes. They had marked me down as a bodyguard. I was dismayed. I had hoped to be, if not "one of us," at least included in the general train of communication. Bodyguards are not so included. I decided then to take advantage of my nonentity, my invisibility. I closed up my face.

The bankers, the money men, were seated in occasional chairs placed in a shallow semicircle some distance from the settee. They, too, had their coffee tables and end tables, and each had a coffee cup that was surreptitiously filled by another young man outfitted on Rodeo Drive. Unlike the sleek lawyer, Medellin, I'd met and hated as he was sitting across from Betty, these men all had briefcases—large, authoritative ones—that were filled with important-looking papers and computer printouts. The briefcases were all laid down on the thick oriental rugs spread over the carpeting, and propped open next to their chairs. *Their* garb was certainly not from Rodeo Drive. It was all a great deal more like the clothes I was wearing, and by no means superior in quality. The difference was, of course, that while I was "dressed up," these men were simply dressed for daily business. It was their uniform. Again, I felt aced. There were four of them. They were young, smart, eager, and impressive. Garson, on his settee, looked tired and beaten down, almost like a wilted rose. He began idly dismantling the piles of paper in front of him, until he had spread them out individually. Then he arranged them according to some plan to which only he was privy. The young money men strained in their chairs to see what he was doing. When he had satisfied himself, he turned slightly toward the young man on his right, who was closest to me. "Lonny," he addressed him (I found out later that the young man's name was Lonsdale Opendyke), "I look at the vigorish on your presentation, and all I can say is that that kind of vigorish used to get people put in jail."

I looked expectantly at Lonsdale Opendyke for a spirited defense of his figures, but a very strange thing was happening. I had understood Mr. Garson with crystal clarity, but Mr. Opendyke appeared to be totally uncomprehending. He moved tensely to the edge of his chair. It was evident that he knew Mr. Garson had addressed him, but really hadn't heard what he said. Had he been inattentive? I could hardly believe it. These young men had the air of ferrets about them, and I didn't think they were dozing off. Young Opendyke said, "I beg your pardon?"

"You beg my pardon for what?" asked Mr. Garson reasonably.

"I'm sorry," said the young man, who was now blushing and twisting in his chair, "but I didn't hear you." Mr. Garson smiled at him. The other sharp young men were twisting and turning too. They, it appeared, had ears no better than young Opendyke's. Mr. Garson began to repeat, in substance, what he had said in his first remark. It was evident that the young man on his right still caught only part of it. "Vigorish?" he asked. The eyeballs had begun a migration right out of the old sockets.

"Another word for interest," said Mr. Garson. "A different word that used to be used in different circumstances. I don't think there's any difference now that anybody would notice."

"I'm . . . ah . . . I'm terribly sorry," the young man said, reddening even more and moving forward until he was supported only by the very edge of the chair. "But I still don't think I really understand. Are you objecting to the . . . ah . . . the rates?" The other three were also on the edges of their chairs, and it was clear that they would have been enjoying Mr. Opendyke's dilemma if only they'd been able to hear what was going on.

"Yes, I'm objecting to them," said Mr. Garson. He seemed about to go to sleep.

There was a lengthy pause while the young banker tried to convince himself that he had heard *something*. He then decided what it was he'd heard, and answered, "Those rates were calculated very carefully, sir, on our computers."

"Your computers," said Mr. Garson, with his eyes still half closed, and his voice apparently no louder, "have decided for some reason or other that I was pauperized overnight." He held up the offending prospectus limply, as if it were a small dead animal that had been left next to his plate. "I've got computers, too." he said. "Every Boy Scout has got computers. I handed you my computer data on my collateral. What did you do with it? Use it for toilet paper?" There was no animosity on his face, only a weary, wondering expression.

The young man sat poised, rigid, in his banker's gray (yes, really banker's), trying to make sense out of the slight, breezelike emanations he was apparently getting from Mr. Garson. Finally, he said, "I'm sure, sir, that it was taken into consideration and reflected . . ."

"Reflected my ass," said Mr. Garson, wearily. "You people act as if the New York Studios didn't exist."

The bulging eyes and very nearly wagging ears had caught the significance of *New York* and *Studios*. He leaped to the fray, very nearly off his chair. "But, sir," he said, "we did take them into consideration. It's only, only . . ."

"Only what?" asked Mr. Garson. "That they're in need of repair?"

Mr. Opendyke's face lighted up like a Christmas tree. "Yes, sir," he said. His expression seemed to congratulate Mr. Garson, who recoiled with a look of disgust. "Yes, sir. It is exactly what is shown in the prospectus. That they are, indeed, in need of repair. That was all gone over very carefully."

"What was gone over very carefully, Lonny," said Mr. Garson, with a fatherly air, although it was still obvious that his voice was little more than a hummingbird's vibration, "was the method of screwing you out of your commission. The real estate that those studios stand on is alone sufficient collateral for the money I want." Opendyke sat, sifting and stunned. "What happened," Garson's lips framed the deadly words, "is this. They gave you a piece of paper that nobody could sell. When I look at it, I'm supposed to be outraged. I rush to the telephone and call up Seychel, who is vice president with the clout for all this, right? I protest. Seychel says," and Garson's face mimicked nicely the expression of a snake who has just swallowed a rabbit, "Jeez, Cy. Don't be like that. Come on down here and we'll fix it up for you.' I go down there and he knocks off the point or the fractions that I need, and I make the loan.

"Who gets the commission?" he asked suddenly sitting up with his eyes popping open. "You? Never! Seychel gets the commission, the bonus, what have you. That's why Seychel is vice president, and why *you,*" he wagged a forefinger at the young man, "never will be, Lonny, unless you wise up."

It seemed that Garson had spoken loudly enough this time to be heard by all. The other bank representatives brightened at the spectacle of their colleague getting the shaft. And then, thoughtfully, they began to search their own briefcases, and, indeed, Mr. Garson's statement of collateral.

Garson sank back on the settee again. "Seychel needs a lesson," he mused. He glanced over to Opendyke. "I'm not going to call him," he announced. "If you want to, you can call him. Tell him what I said. And tell him that I'm making the deal with other people—in this room, here, now, today. I'm not going any place with my hat in my hand. I don't have to."

He turned then to the other three, leaving Mr. Opendyke with the appearance of a man on a limb that was being excised by a chain saw. "You fellows don't have to look so happy," he said from his near recumbency. "You haven't got too much to show me." It was clear from their expressions that none of them had really heard him. They surged forward in their chairs, paper in hand, with the glad and beaming air of men who do not really know what they are doing. "There's nothing very attractive in the terms that any of you are offering,'' he said, it seemed with just enough volume for the bad news to sink in.

''Let's get everything out in the street.'' He gestured wanly. ''The studio is ample collateral for the money I'm asking. The money will be applied to both the refurbishing of the studio and the production of a major television series. This is what we're talking about, agreed? It's as solid as a diamond. There isn't the whisper of a risk anywhere.

''Now, I could go to one bank, one company, and finance the complete thing in about ten minutes and walk away with a bag full of money. Instead, I've split it up into four separate issues because I don't like the idea of having just one major outfit with their hand in my pants. This is a break for you gentlemen, because each of you will get a commission on the loan—providing you make the loan. And in order to make the loan, you're going to have to sweeten it a little—shave a point or fraction here and there, *capish*?

''You can work this out yourselves or huddle with the home office. There's plenty of telephones. But I want a deal, and I want it before we break for lunch.'' I got the idea that his voice had risen to audibility because all four had caught on to what he was saying. Lonsdale Opendyke mustered all his courage and spoke forth: ''Mr. Garson,'' he said, ''if you insist on leaving me out, you'll still be looking for twenty-five percent of the package you've put into your requirement.''

Garson leaned back with an almost dreamy smile of dismissal. ''From the white hats,'' he said. I don't think any of them really heard him. ''I'll pick it up from the white hats.''

I wasn't even sure I'd read him correctly myself. I'd read about ''White Knights,'' corporations who ride to the rescue of companies being gobbled up in a merger, but that didn't seem applicable here. What he meant, clearly, was that he would pick up the other twenty-five percent from sources outside this suave suite in the Sherry-Netherland. Three young men dispersed to various telephones, two of them out in the reception room, and one in the corner of the office. Young Opendyke disconsolately gathered his papers together and prepared to depart. Garson watched him in utter silence and did not seem to invite comment or farewell. The young man left, stroking his chin thoughtfully. The remaining bank representative in the corner put down his telephone, snatched up his briefcase, and hurried out, apparently to zip over to a nearby office. Garson and I were left alone.

Garson turned to me. "This is your moment," he said. "What did you want to see me about?" So many images, thoughts, and reflections were hurrying through my mind that I had, for the instant, forgotten what I wanted to see him about. "C'mon, snap into it," he urged me. "When those guys come back, your day is over."

I came alive. "My client is the actor William Macready," I began.

"Macready told you to see me?" His eyes popped.

"No. He doesn't even know I'm here. But his business manager was murdered—the police believe he was, anyway—and Mr. Macready has asked me to investigate."

"Doesn't he trust the cops?"

"He wants to find out why his business manager was murdered. He wants to make sure it had nothing to do with him—with Macready—personally."

"What an ego!" Garson stood up and stretched luxuriously. "Actors!" he snorted. "They're all alike. Somebody gets hit with a bus, and the actor is sure it was meant for him. Paranoia, they call it. It's institutional with actors." He paused to reflect. "Why would Macready think it had anything to do with him?" he demanded.

"He believed that Pelfrey—Arnold Pelfrey was the business manager's name—was on his way over to see him, Macready, when it happened."

"How did it happen?"

"He was hanged from an old gas pipe in a flea bag near Times Square. It was made to look like a suicide, but the police doped it out."

"They did, eh? They sure of it?"

"If not, they're going to a lot of trouble for nothing."

Garson asked the next question very carefully. "How did my name come into this?"

"It hasn't," I assured him. "I'm interviewing everybody who has any connection with Mr. Macready at all, simply to find out what I can."

"You must have some kind of angle," he protested. "Otherwise you're just wasting your time, as well as mine—and Macready's money."

I asked him directly, "Can you think of anybody who, for any reason, wants to scare Mr. Macready away from doing the 'Tycoon' series?"

"Jesus," said Garson. "I hope not!" He began pacing the thick rugs, rolling his shoulders to loosen them, and stretching his arms.

"Has anybody shown any sign of it?" I pursued. "Whether you think it's paranoia or not?" He gave me a sharp, threatening look over his shoulder. We are not to play games with Mr. Garson. "Does anybody stand to lose with Macready going into 'Tycoon'?"

"Who can tell?" he said, having stopped and turned to face me. His arms went out as if to embrace the entire business. "Is there anything crazier than this racket? There could be some clown living in a garret who thinks he should have this part. There could be anybody."

I asked him directly. "What about you, Mr. Garson? Are you happy with having Bill Macready for the lead?"

He stared at me. His face was masklike. Then suddenly it split into a grin. "You've got guts," he said. "I'll give you that. Where are you from?"

"Boston, originally," I answered. "You?"

"A little town in Michigan you never heard of," he replied.

"I never heard the answer to my question, either."

"A Boston harp," said Garson. "I should have guessed. The accent doesn't come through all that much."

"Nothing comes through all that much when you can't hear it yourself," I said.

"And you're touchy about it?"

"Yes," I said. "I'm touchy about it."

"I never knew a harp who wasn't touchy about something," he muttered. But then he assumed a serious expression. "All right," he said. "Do I have any reservations about Bill Macready taking the lead in 'Tycoon'? The answer at this moment is 'no.' If you had asked me a few weeks ago . . ." He paused. "And that's before the guy, Pelfrey, got hung, right?" I nodded solemnly. "I could have thought of maybe a dozen reasons why Macready shouldn't have it. But now that he does have it, now that everything's in place, there's no reason in the world I would want him out. As a matter of fact, his being out of it, recasting the lead, replacing him, would screw up everything—scheduling—everything. Does that answer your question?"

I nodded an assent as he came closer. His face was suddenly very close to mine. "It's in my interest that Macready gets and keeps the part," he said. "As a matter of fact, it's worth a good deal of money to me. I like to be informed. You understand? Information is money to me. As a matter of fact, what I've learned from you this morning is worth money, and your share of that is five hundred. That suit you?" He held up his hand before I could reply. "And anything else you come up with that isn't bullshit is worth another five hundred. O.K.?" He still wouldn't let me speak. "And if you want to talk about a retainer or a contract, maybe that can be arranged, too. O.K.?" I opened my mouth again, but before I could speak, he said, "You're refusing. I can see it. The honest harp." He took a scrap of paper from the coffee table and sat down on the settee to write out a number. "Think it over and call me here," he said. "But money or no money, if anything breaks, let me know. O.K.? I just want the news. I don't want your cherry."

The big doors had swung open, and the three young men had come back. They were smiling. God knows where Opendyke was. Garson looked at them coming in and then swung to me. "I guess this is it," he said.

"Thank you very much for your time," I told him. "I'll keep in touch."

On the elevator ride down, I thought about what I had observed and learned. A great deal, I reflected, went into the making of American entertainment. After I'd left the gracious lobby, I turned the corner of Fifty-ninth Street to look through the dazzling window of A la Vielle Russie. Easter had come and gone, but they were interested in Russian Easter, and so they had still, displayed in small velvet couches, some Russian Easter eggs by Fabergé.

19

I turned away from the fabulous, intricate jewels that managed to contain a universe in a crusted shell, and considered the much more mundane subject of lunch. It was not that lunch would necessarily have to be mundane; within the reach of a ten-minute walk were ten or twenty restaurants that could lay out a Lucullan spread—but for a price. Instead, I took the subway down to the neighborhood near my office and went to one of the old-fashioned restaurants there for a lengthy, extremely heavy lunch of the kind that is supposed to reduce your life expectancy by ten percent. The Hungarians who ate the goulash I was at this moment washing down with a stein of beer, I thought, must have lived very short lives, if very happy ones. I topped it off with another stein of beer and a cigar, which I finished on my walk back to the office.

At my arrival there, my stomach was full of lead, my brains full of beer foam, and my lungs full of rich, blue smoke. I worried not. I had an absolute *need* of heaviness, of subsidence, a weightiness that would keep me in upright orientation while I examined the screwiness I had witnessed up at the hotel.

I unlocked the door and felt a brief flash of goulash-supported outrage at the fact that Edna, my listening post on the world, was not at her desk. It was after two o'clock, and while I may extend lunches at my leisure, the same does not apply to my secretary, at least unless I know about it. The little answering device we'd bought at Edna's behest had its flag up, but, of course it was totally useless to me without Edna. I went into my office and dropped, with a burgher's belch, into my chair behind the desk. With my head propped on my hands, I was just beginning to frame some choice phraseology to rebuke Edna, when she hurried in and stared at me, surprised.

"A fine thing," I began. "Here I am out chasing all over town at work, while you . . ."

But she stopped me by delving into her purse and throwing upon my desk a plain white envelope. "Open it," she commanded.

I obeyed her instantly and found, to my delight, a check for a large sum of money that had been owed to me for over three months. "You're a genius and I love you," I said. "How'd you do it?"

Edna kept me in perspiring suspense while she hung up her coat, settled her purse, and poured herself a cup of coffee, which she placed on the corner of my desk before sitting down. "I called the girl . . . lady . . . woman in accounts payable," she told me, "and I got the usual: 'It's in the computer, you know we're having a lot of trouble breaking in the new computer system, blah, blah, blah.' " Edna sipped the black coffee demurely. "I kept my voice very sweet. I mean not nasty, sickly sweet, but real sweet and friendly. And I told her, 'Now let's be all up front and reasonable, shall we? Our outfit specializes in collecting bad debts. It's what we do, mostly. We're a detective agency and we do all kinds of nasty things, many of which involve government agencies. We call up all kinds of people in federal, state, city, and county agencies and make a lot of inquiries. We wouldn't want to stir up anything about our own clients, for heaven's sake. So why don't you just check around and see if that computer can't spit up something in the next few minutes?'

"She says, 'I'll get back to you.' and I told her, 'You won't have to, because I'll be right here hanging on.' She came back in about three minutes and she says, 'What do you know? You called just at the right time. The check has been made out.' So I asked her, 'But has it been signed?' There was another three minutes and then she said, 'Yes. It's been signed and it's going out in the mail tomorrow morning.' So I said," and this called for another swig of coffee, " 'please do not put that check in the mail. I repeat. Do not put that check in the mail. Please send it to us now by messenger. In fact, we will send the messenger over to get it from you.' And she said, . . ." Edna took a deep breath, which added a few inches of loveliness to the landscape. " 'It is against our company policy to deliver checks by messenger.' So I said, 'All right, dear, forget the messenger. I'll come over there and get it myself.' So she said, 'I'm not sure that Mr. . . .' but I never heard the name because I hung up the phone and was putting my coat on."

"Astounding," I said.

"Yeah, well, I took a crosstown bus to get over there, which took forever, and when I got there she was out to lunch. So I had to wait around for an hour in their lousy accounting department with a lot of people munching sandwiches at their desk and staring at me. So when she got back, I told her who I was, and she said, 'Oh, yeah,' like I was Miss Bubonic Plague of 1932.

"When she went over to another desk to get the check, she had to leaf through a whole stack of checks to find it. And so I knew she hadn't even looked before. She'd known it was there, all right. There were two stacks: one signed and one not signed. But the checks were all made out.

"I asked her to put the check in an envelope for me, so it wouldn't crumple in my purse, you know, and she looked kind of sad. And so I said, 'What's the matter, honey?' And she said, 'Well, you saw it all. I get sick of it. Those checks just sit on the desk for weeks—months maybe—until somebody raises the roof.

Before computers, things used to go fairly regular. You know, there were accounting principles and things like that. I get sick of it. There's new principles now. Don't pay unless you're threatened. Even then, sometimes . . .' "

Edna smiled at me. "I'd hate it if you made me do that, lie like that. That lady didn't like it either. She's no crook."

"Inside the fat of many corporations," I told her, "is a vicious, simple-minded crook struggling to get out. You'll never have to do things like that," I reassured her, "because we're not big enough. Our debts are functional. If we stiff the phone company, our business line is cut off. If we stall the rent, we get thrown out. They're dying to get rid of us anyway. If we get cute with Con Edison, we pursue our craft by candlelight."

Edna shifted her legs uncomfortably—uncomfortable for her, but not for me. She pinched her lips tight before saying, "If we were big then, would you be like that?"

"You've got the cart before the horse," I corrected her. "Those people got big *because* they are like that. They insist on payment any time within the next thirty seconds, but they won't part with a nickel of payment themselves unless they're confronted with a Thompson submachine gun."

I sat back and wondered if what I had told Edna was true. There is something about her pretty, trusting young face that invites thinking aloud, ventilating one's opinions, and these opinions are sometime bombastic . . . ridiculous. I said to her, "I'm glad you brought it up, anyhow, because this morning I was treated to the damndest exhibition I've ever seen. I want to tell you about it to get it straight in my own head." Edna reached for her pad, but I advised her, "You don't have to write anything down. Just listen. First, get some coffee."

After she'd got coffee for us both, she made herself comfortable while I was saying, "It was all kind of through-the-looking-glass this morning. This guy, Garson, is going to produce the 'Tycoon' series that Bill is supposed to star in." I clutched the top of my head. "Everybody in this business turns out to be a producer," I complained, "But Garson is the nuts and bolts of the thing. The actual physical production will be his responsibility. He's going to do it all in a big old studio he owns here in New York. He came East to look at the studio and base the financing for the production on the value of the property. So far, so good.

"Now, instead of trotting down to the bank with the deed to

the studio in one hand and his hat in the other, the way you or I would do it, Garson makes a completely different play. He calls up a number of institutions and tells them he wants a loan for what is a relatively small amount of money in this business. Each institution sends a junior loan officer down to see Garson at his staging area in the Sherry-Netherland. Garson has kept the amount of each loan below the big-league figure that would automatically bring in the senior officers. When I was there, he had four of these junior representatives lined up. I have no idea how many more sets of them he was going to see during the day. There are a lot of institutions in New York.

"The difference between people like Garson and people like you and me is that Garson recognizes that the banks can't exist without doing business. They have to make loans, investments; they have to turn over money. All we think about when we go down for a loan is how much *we* need the money. Garson is thinking about how much *they* need the money. Particularly, he's thinking about who gets what, I mean within the institution itself. If the loan is a huge lump sum, the boys at the top get the commission and the bonus. But if the loan is kept under the limit, then these hot young men on the way up get the commission and bonus. Garson has reasoned that the young men struggling toward the top are more eager to do business and more willing to come across with the money. Furthermore, he can bully them in a way that he couldn't pull with the senior officers, who would drop a hat over him.

"Garson did something very interesting up there today. He picked out one of the young men and threw him to the lions. A sacrifice. He turned on a young man—Lonsdale Opendyke, the guy's name is—and practically destroyed him in front of the other representatives. Now, this briefly took their minds off their business while they were enjoying the spectacle, and it also served as a warning. They got themselves in the position of thinking that they were, somehow, going to accommodate this guy so it wouldn't happen to them. The other trick he pulled is an old one. He lowered his voice so that hardly anyone could hear him, and nobody was really sure what was going on except me, because I am deaf and can read lips. What could they do? Could they go back to their office and tell their boss they couldn't do business because they couldn't hear the guy? What any one of them should have done, was stand up and say, 'Call me back, Mr. Garson, when your laryngitis has cleared up.' But no one was willing to do that. Each one of them wanted to 'succeed.' " I hooked my fingers in quotation marks. "Each one of them wanted to come home with a piece of the bacon.

"So the minute those guys walked into the suite and saw the mirror images of themselves there, they should have turned around and walked out. It was a setup, a pigeon shoot. The minute they had trouble hearing what Garson was saying, they should have called it off, because a person who uses this device is either a crook or a sadist. But they stayed.

"They stayed because Garson was playing around a central defect of big money business: competition—the internal struggle within the business itself for each of the officers to succeed, survive. There are companies that have been all but destroyed by this struggle because their demands for success in order to survive turned their people into crooks or fools. One outfit set up sales quotas for its sales staff: 'Meet it or you're out,' they said. The salesmen met it by writing phantom contracts. They wrote up sales that didn't exist, picked up their commission, and blew. The company found itself twenty-million dollars in the hole. Another company with the same system wound up eighty-million dollars in the hole.

"So Garson is playing these youngsters off against one another, and off against their own officers. For all I know, he's performing the same trained-seal act with a new set of finance officers right now, and may go on doing it all day. The question is: Why?"

"But," Edna replied, wrinkling her brow, "didn't you just answer that? To get a better deal?"

"To get a *different* deal, I think. He could have gone to just one outfit and made the deal with just one senior officer, who can shave points just as well as a junior can. Instead, he spent a lot of time, craft, and energy splitting the deal among a lot of institutions." I put my hand up at her unspoken question. "There's nothing wrong with that," I assured her. "The banks themselves, and certainly any insurance company, always break up a big loan or policy and lay off pieces of it all over town to share the risk. But *they* like to do the piecing out," I emphasized, "so that they have ultimate control and so they know what's going on. By piecing it out himself, Garson has ultimate control, and he's the only one who knows what's going on.

"I could be very wrong," I told her. "Garson is very well

known in the business. But I think it's a scam. I think he's overloading the property."

"Wouldn't they know?" asked Edna. "Couldn't they tell?"

"They could if they dug into it, of course," I answered. "They were sitting there with computer printouts and surveys till hell wouldn't hold it, but there's a curious thing about all that data. It has a numbing effect. Underneath all that data, you just know, instinctively, that there's something buried in there that could queer the deal. And they want very much to make the deal, do you see? I think a lot of business is done on the basis of willful ignorance, because if everybody knew everything, nobody could do anything. One man at the top might run a real analysis of all the collateral and tell Garson, 'It's no deal.' But these young men aren't about to. For one thing, Garson implied that he was cozy with all their bosses, and they wouldn't want to challenge that kind of relationship.

"Now, each of the representatives there was probably not authorized to approve more than five-hundred thousand—a relatively small loan on that kind of property and that kind of potential. The fourth man had been fed to the lions, so the three of them, even if they had come clean with each other, which they probably hadn't, were lending only a total of a million and a half—still a relatively small sum for the base that Garson is presenting. But I think there'll be another group of anxious junior executives up there, and another, and finally it's going to get jacked up to nine or ten million, which is a lot of money, no matter what kind of property you're talking about, particularly when you're talking about straight real estate, because the buildings he has, apparently, have to be rehabilitated."

"You think Garson is going to sting them?" she asked me directly.

"Not necessarily. But I think it depends on what happens to the 'Tycoon' series. If it goes—and everybody seems to expect that it will go—all well and good. But if it comes up a clinker, I think that Garson is just going to toss the dilapidated studio into the ring and say, 'There's your collateral, boys,' and all the outfits that loaned him money are going to have to jump into the pit and fight over what they can pull out."

"They won't sue him?"

"Certainly they'll sue him, as kind of a knee-jerk reflex, but they'll have to look at what they're suing: a separate corporation that's only a splinter of Garson's enterprises. There's nothing more in the kitty than what Garson gave them a peek at. If they sue him, all they'll get is the studio, which he probably won't want then, anyway."

"You've got a lump in your salve," said Edna. (It was an expression I had taught her, along with numerous others.) "Garson has to fix up the studio to make the series. That means they'll be suing over improved property. They'll be getting back their money's worth. Maybe even more."

"That's what they believe," I countered. "But I think that Garson has got more moves than a Filipino dance band. I think he'll fix up a tiny corner of the studio for certain scenes—this is an epic, you know—and shoot most of the stuff on other stages that are already improved. In the end, if the series doesn't click, they'll still be getting back junk. And he keeps his ten million to play with."

Edna sat back and beamed at me. "You figured it all out," she said. "Let me ask you a question that's probably going to make you mad." She braced herself. "If you're so smart," she said, "why ain't you rich?"

The question made me so mad I used bad language. "Everybody knows what these assholes are doing," I said. "But not everybody has the stomach to emulate them. It's not a question of brains. It's a question of self-respect. A lot of the people in this world have self-respect," I told her, "and most of those people are pushing wheelbarrows.

"*Now* you may take notes," I told her shocked face, to straighten her up. "Tomorrow I want you to go out and get me all the information you can about Cyrus Garson, his companies, and his career. Look in both the financial sources and the showbiz sources, not excluding the *Guide to Periodical Literature*. There might be something about him in the fan mags. Xerox everything you can lay your hands on, and stack it right here on my desk.

"At the same time," I commanded mercilessly, "I want you to make me an appointment with the producer-director-director-producer, Emerson Kite. You can locate him through . . . through, uh . . ."

"Beanie?" suggested Edna, brightly.

"Betty Middleton," I corrected her sternly.

"And what are you going to be doing during all this activity," Edna asked sweetly. "Bowling for dollars?"

"Where I'll be tomorrow depends on what you tell me next,"

I said. "You were supposed to pry the name of Roger Grim out of the Coast Guard . . ..

Edna shook her head, indicating failure. "They said they'd get back to us. . . ."

"The same thing they tell drowning sailors," I commented bitterly. "What about the oil-company fleets?"

"Nothing."

"All right, then. This afternoon I want you to call every yacht club and boatyard. This is a very long shot, but it's worth it. Tomorrow morning, I'm going down to the fish piers and stooge around. There's no use in calling any unions down there. I'll have to look personally."

"What a shame," said Edna.

"The other thing you were supposed to do while your nails were drying was to find the fixed abode of Arnold Pelfrey's family. I hope I don't have to wait for the Coast Guard to tell me that."

"Arnold Pelfrey's family lives in Port Chester," said Edna. "Wait." She got up and went to her desk in the anteroom, giving me a heart-seizing look at her magnificent posterior. *Ah, what avails the anatomy chart?* I thought of Dr. Sartin. How could you call one of those a *gluteus maximus?* She returned in all innocence with a piece of paper. "Here's the address and phone number."

"Call up Mrs. Pelfrey and tell her I want to see her tomorrow," I told Edna. She pulled the phone over and made the call. From the sappy expression on her face, I discerned that she was talking to a child and not an adult.

"Tomorrow afternoon at four," said Edna. She pushed the slip of paper over to me, and I put it carefully in my wallet.

"That wasn't Mrs. Pelfrey you talked to, was it," I stated.

"No. I guess it was her son. He said she'd be home by four."

"How old is the kid? Does he know what he's talking about?"

"Ten, twelve, something like that. He sounded fairly responsible. Should I call back and check?"

"No," I answered. "She might turn us off. This way, she's stuck with it." I thought about the trip. "I could take a train up and a cab from the station," I mused. "But I guess I'll drive, which means I'll have to leave here about two and give myself some time to find the house. That means I'll have to finish up on the piers around noon, come back and get cleaned up and . . ." I suddenly remembered something, "Unless there's other business. Have you checked that gismo on the phone?"

Edna looked stricken. "I forgot all about it," she confessed. When she came back from her desk she said, "Nothing special. Miss Middleton would like to know if you could meet her in the network lobby at five-thirty."

"Yes, I can," I said happily.

"You didn't even ask what for." Edna looked severe.

"Did she mention what it was for?"

"No."

I smiled and leaned back. "So mind your own business," I said to Edna, who had the grace to smile back slightly. "Furthermore," I added, "there is a perfectly legitimate reason for me to see Betty tonight."

Like what?'

"Like finding out what the hell a jargon term like 'white hats' means in the TV racket."

20

Betty smiled at me with what looked like approval as I emerged from the shower, and I beamed back at her, for she made a very pretty sight propped up against the pillows in my bed. Her smile was a pink scimitar above the rim of the dark coffee mug I'd provided her with, and below the mug her sumptuous white and pink body bloomed. She watched in apparent contentment as I got dressed: old, comfortable slacks; old, heavy, businesslike brogans; and a soft gray shirt. Her eyes widened, however, when I strapped on the holster that fitted down just about where my left elbow falls against the ribs. She watched me take the Smith & Wesson .38 out of its drawer and load it with bullets from another drawer. I took six more bullets from the box, put them in a small manila envelope, and set them aside.

"You really wear that thing every day to the office, just like that?" she asked me. She set the mug down on the nightstand.

"I'm not going to the office today," I told her. "I'm going hunting." For the first time since I'd awakened in the hospital, I felt good, put back together. My muscles did not scream every time I moved, and my insides no longer felt as if they were going to fall out. All of the tiny aches and pains and twinges had fled. True enough, I was not in good shape. Had I been cast in the puritan mold, I would have started exercising much earlier than this despite the pain. But I had been, I recognized now, demoralized. Something had happened to me to restore the old morale, however. I smiled at Betty.

"I'm trying to put things together," said Betty, sitting up very straight. "I'm trying to fit all the millions of miles of private eye films I've seen with what I'm seeing now. You don't look like any of them, and yet you look like all of them." I laughed selfconsciously. "What do you mean, hunting?" she asked me. She swung her legs over so that she was sitting on the side of the bed looking up at me.

"I've been screwing around pretending to locate a suspect," I told her. "Killing time because I wasn't ready physically or psychologically to find him and bring him in. The party's over."

Betty stood up, put her arms around me, gun and all, pressed her whole body against mine, and kissed me fully and lingeringly on the lips. She backed away, then, so I could see her say, "That was an irresistible impulse." She smiled again, and then vanished into the bathroom.

I had another mug of coffee waiting for her on the kitchen table when she came in, dressed in the clothes she had worn last night. It was still very early in the morning, and we had mutually agreed that we didn't want any breakfast. Betty would have hers uptown, after she'd gone home to change her clothes for work, and I intended to have mine down on South Street as part of my legwork. We looked at each other across the table. "We should do this more often," I said.

"Often and often, and again and again," she agreed.

She had wanted to see me last evening, ostensibly to find out what I'd learned from my interview with Garson. I'd described the bare bones of my morning at the Sherry-Netherland, leaving out the analysis I'd given to Edna. It is not my mission to carry business information from one source to another. Rather, when it *is* my business, I get paid for it. The jargon I'd been trying to identify had stumped Betty as well as me. *"White hats?"* She rolled the expression around her eyes. We had been sitting in the bar section of a little restaurant on Fifty-fourth and Madison. She sipped at her martini and said, "Well, of course, it means the good cowboys, the good guys. But you already know that."

I nodded. "His expression, somehow, did not go along with that definition," I said. We both thought about it again, and both came up empty. "The hell with it," I decided. "He probably just meant some place where he'd always done business and was always able to pick up money."

"Then why bother with the banks?" Betty asked reasonably.

"Too much money," I answered. But, also, I realized that if Garson was going to sacrifice twenty-five percent of every group that came in, there would be a sizable amount to pick up: about two million, five-hundred thousand. My mind wasn't used to circling figures like these, and the whole subject suddenly made me tired. "Screw it," I said. "It'll all come out in the wash. You want to eat here?"

Indeed, she did not. She agreed to another drink, and then, to my delight, agreed to dinner in my apartment, prepared by my own lily whites. Her delight evaporated at the product of those same lily whites, however: stuffed peppers I'd prepared earlier in the week and set aside for the final shot in the oven, all done with a very rich sauce from a secret recipe. "My God!" she cried. "I can't eat that. It'll put ten pounds on me."

"If Joe Binney puts ten pounds on you," I assured her, "then Joe Binney will take ten pounds off you."

"In bed, you mean?" Her expression was half dubious, half mischievous.

"In bed," I confirmed. "If everybody got laid every day then everybody would be as thin as a rail, no matter what he ate."

"Good for the skin, too," Betty reflected. "Well," she said, sighing, as she timidly attacked the beautifully stuffed pepper, "here's to health and beauty."

We retired early.

Now, seated across from me in the morning light, she was saying, "Does he have a gun? This man you're looking for?"

"He doesn't need one," I replied. "The last time I met him he put me in the hospital without anything in his hands but muscle." She remained silent. "The gun isn't necessarily just for him," I expanded, "although I'll certainly need it to bring him in. . . ." And with that, an important thought occurred to me. "Excuse me," I said. I got up and went into the bedroom, where I took a pair of handcuffs from the drawer. I put them in the reinforced back pocket of my slacks. When I returned, Betty asked what that had been all about and I told her that I'd forgotten something, and it wasn't important.

"You said the gun wasn't just for him," she reminded me.

"Yeah, well, I'm going to start looking down around the fish piers off South Street. In my own backyard, you might say. And it isn't too bright to be asking a lot of questions around there unless you're heeled."

"South Street?" Her face was full of disbelief. "It's practically an amusement park."

"They have other amusements, too," I told her. "Like putting people into fifty-gallon drums of concrete." Betty made the sort of mouth that expresses, *You're putting me on*. "All I know," I shrugged, "is that whenever the Waterfront Commission wants any information out of there, the silence is absolute, perfect. If they subpoena a guy, he says, 'Put me in jail. What can I do? To talk is to die.' And, apparently, it means to die very badly."

"That's where you're going today," said Betty.

"Yes."

"To ask questions."

"Yes."

"You do a lot of this?"

"Yes."

She finished her coffee. "I'm going to go home and change," she said.

"Don't change too much," I asked her.

I put on a light blue windbreaker, blousy enough to hide the gun, but not cumbersome enough to get in my way. I zipped it up regretfully, knowing that a zipper was the last thing in the world one wanted to fool with in an emergency. On the other hand, wandering around the fish piers in a business suit would have been impractical for my purposes to the point of insanity. We did not say anything to each other after I set the switches and locked the door to my apartment. I flagged a cab for Betty rather quickly, and she gave me a cold kiss on the cheek before getting in. When she sank back against the seat cushions, her face was stern.

Perhaps it was a reflection of my own as I turned to make the long but always pleasant walk down to South Street. The Lower East Side seems to constitute a through-slice of the world—almost geologic—where one can see all the layers of class, race, and nations. I passed Hasidic Jews, Chinese, Puerto Ricans, college students, lawyers, politicians, businessmen, indicted felons, clergymen, the whole vast parade of whatever racial, legal, or moral coloring constitute Manhattan. I swung left on Fulton Street and strode through the narrow channel of gaudy businesses and hustling office workers. The office workers were at this moment hurrying to work. Down at the fish piers, where I was headed, the working people would just be getting off—a topsy-turvy world.

When I reached South Street, under the shadow of the Brooklyn Bridge, I turned north, reversing my direction, and headed toward a coffee joint that perched on the division between the Disneyland version of the historic area and the workaday section that was still making the history. The place was in the next block, where the fish wholesalers bought the early morning catch and parceled it out to the purveyors and restauranteurs. I planted myself near the big window overlooking the street and the wharves beyond, and ordered scrambled eggs and coffee. I was hoping that the eggs would be scrambled with a light and grease-free hand, but I was not rewarded. I could eat them as long as I did not look at them. I unfolded my morning *Times* and divided my attention between the paper and the street beyond. I polished off the eggs quickly and killed the taste with hot black strong coffee, which was very good. I ordered another cup and kept looking.

Did I really expect to see him—tall as one of the masts of the ships tied up at the South Street piers? It was a good thing, I reflected, that he was unmistakably tall, because the brief glimpse I'd had of him in the nightmare flash of the hotel room could be illusory, misleading. I constructed in my mind the template of the man I was looking for: a very tall black man walking with an athlete's gait, wearing a dark blue Coast Guard sweater and, possibly, a watch cap. He should, I thought, stand out like a beacon, a black beacon. I had no particular desire to see that face again, with its catlike delight in trapping its prey, but it was that face I had to find.

Almost all the people who streamed past the window were white men, average sized, wearing open lumberjackets and cheap tweed caps with the peak creased from handling. These were the people who did the sorting and packing of the fish in the bins full of chipped ice. They worked in the stalls that opened on the street and were shut by rolling steel doors that came slamming down when the morning's work was done.

Three of them had come in to order breakfast and were sitting on stools away from the window. I finished my coffee, went over to the cash register, and paid my bill. After I'd gone back to put a tip under my plate, I walked up to the three, who were just being served. They were aware of my approaching them, and all three stared fixedly ahead. Intrusions are not borne with good grace in this section. I picked the one nearest me, a small, worn-down looking man of about fifty whose white complexion bespoke working all night and sleeping all day. "Excuse me," I said to him. He remained staring fixedly ahead, the peak of his cap obscuring the upper half of his face. I nudged his shoulder and repeated, in what I judged to be a louder tone of voice, "Excuse me. I'm looking for somebody around here."

This got the attention of all three of them. All three faces swung toward me with expressions compounded of hostility and alarm. Maybe my voice frightened them a little. To my regret, it often does. "I'm looking for a guy named Roger Grim. Works on one of the boats. You know him?" The three faces recoiled from the idea of knowing anybody named Roger Grim. "He's a black man," I persisted, "very tall. You couldn't miss him." I extended my hand toward the ceiling to indicate his improbable height. "You've probably seen him off one of the boats." The three faces closed up as finally as one of the steel shutter doors. "I need him for something," I told the faces. "You'd be doing him a favor."

The face nearest me said, "We don't know nobody," dismissing me and turning back to the counter to confront a greasy pile of home fries, an anemic slice of ham and two fried eggs, sunny-side up. The other faces turned, too, as if they had been pulled by the same string. After I had made a few more inquiries with similar results, they turned again to watch me leave. Looking back from outside, I saw the heads cluster together and bob animatedly.

The sidewalks of the next block were wet and silvery with the fish scales being swept and washed into the gutter from each of the stalls. The only people left in the stalls now were the cleanup men (or woman in one case) and the owners or executives who came down to check out the take. The noise of the hose in the first stall did not bother me, of course, but it apparently bothered the popeyed youth who was handling it. Finally, twisting the nozzle to reduce it to a trickle, he said, "What? A nigger? There ain't any niggers around here." He twisted it on again and dismissed me from his uncluttered mind.

The rest of the stalls involved the same dreary, time-consuming routine that is known as legwork. There would be the long, uncomprehending pause, then another long, uncomprehending pause while the hose operator hoped that I would just go away, and then finally, the shutting down of the hose, the blankly hostile confrontation and the absolute denial that such a person as Roger Grim existed on the face of this earth.

At the end of the two hours it took me to thread my way through the stalls, my clothes had absorbed much of the fine spray of the hoses and my shoes were covered with the silvery slime of fish scales. Except for two instances, I had seen only dull white faces as blank and unreflective as pieces of wax. Two faces illuminated by thoughtful expression had been those of owners or operators I had managed to catch on the way out. These men, both middle aged and both dressed in business suits with briefcases dangling from their hands, had at least shown suspicion, irritation, and then alarm. *"No. I've never seen anybody like that around here. Who are you? What do you want? What are you doing down here?"* I don't know if they had trains to catch, but I had never seen people so eager to depart their surroundings.

The hour was early for drinking, even for me, although I am less than fastidious about these things. Nonetheless, the next logical step was the big old-fashioned saloon a few blocks away. The two hours of blank stares, mumbled denials, and poorly concealed hostility had put me in the mood for something more comforting than coffee. The fine mist penetrating my clothes had left me with a feeling not so much of chill as clamminess. I stepped through the ornate old-fashioned entrance to the bar and was about to order a bourbon when I remembered that I had an appointment with a housewife-widow that afternoon. I ordered a double vodka with a Seven-Up chaser, put it inside me, and ordered another. I paid for them with a ten-dollar bill on this workingman's bar, and received less change than I'd expected.

There were about a dozen patrons visible in the big beveled mirror behind the bar, and they were a troubling assortment. None of them was a longshoreman, a breed I recognize as easily as my own face in the mirror. Three of them I put down as truck drivers, drivers who had made their runs early in the morning and were finishing off their day like any other working stiff, with a drink and a discussion of baseball scores. A close group of six I figured for men off the construction crews who were building the Disneyland version of the feisty old port. They wore the solid, well-cared-for shoes of their trade and had the tanned, bright-eyed faces that go with working in the open air.

It was the final three, the ones most difficult to see from my angle of the mirror at the end of the bar, who troubled me most. I had seen only their backs as I had passed them sitting together near the entrance. They had, no doubt, seen me come in, but none of our eyes had met in the mirror. I stepped back from the bar to get a better look at them in the mirror and realized what was bothering me. They were dressed like me.

I got a much better look at one of them as he came down the bar to go to the can. Like me, he was wearing a windcheater and old, durable slacks. I couldn't see his shoes. His shirt was simply an old blue shirt that was open at the collar, very much like mine. Now, these are quite normal, everyday clothes for a man to wear except for one thing—they don't serve any function in the working world. They are the costume of a man at his leisure. They are worn after work, or on weekends, and are the uniform of the retired or semiretired. Otherwise they are worn by operators, like myself, or persons who drift around the world of the workingman without actually working. The clothes are too good for work, too casual for business.

Our eyes did not quite meet in the mirror as he traveled back from the men's room, but I saw him check his stride very slightly as he approached my back, and his eyebrows jump very slightly in surprise. I took down the greater part of my second vodka double to hide my dismay. I had very stupidly unzipped my jacket part way to let out some of the clamminess, and had very possibly exposed a small clue to my artillery. I finished my drink and flagged the bartender for another. It seemed to me that if I was going to make my move, the time was now.

After the bartender had poured the drink, I asked him my standard question concerning Roger Grim, accompanied by the standard description. I got the standard answer, nothing. Leaving my drink behind me on the bar, I moved down to the three truck drivers and repeated my questions. They did not seem so fearfully hostile as the others had been, but their responses were automatic. No: they had not seen anyone like Roger Grim, and the tacit assumption was that they wouldn't tell me if they had. The construction crew, who took up the center of the bar, had a different attitude. They were not really part of the world down here. Their connection, linked to the job, was temporary, and when this job was finished they would move on to another in another part of town. This area did not constitute their life. So, they actually got interested in what I was saying, particularly after I described the enormous height and build of the man I was looking for. One of them finally made the vital connection. "This guy, Roger Grim, he's a basketball player, right? He was going to turn pro and something happened."

"That's right," I admitted.

"So what do you want him for?"

"Something that could be to his advantage," I lied. "Some people want to talk to him. Have you seen him anywhere around? We heard he was working somewhere around here."

But no, no one in that group had seen him, although they assured me that they certainly would have remembered if they had. During this discussion, I saw one of the three men at the end look sharply at me and depart quickly, fluidly, out the big, open glass doors.

That left two of the three who had made the electricity at the bar, the different element that set up the current. They were not only dressed as I was, they were about the same age and size. When I stepped up to them, the darker one glanced inadvertently at my left side. So, I concluded dismally, I was right; they knew I was carrying. Whether this was good or bad, I couldn't tell as yet, but my instincts told me it was bad. I began my spiel to the dark one, but he put up his hand and said, "We heard you the first time. The answer is, No, and the question is, Who the hell are you?"

"A bill chaser," I admitted cheerfully.

"This guy owes money?"

"Would I tell you if he did?" I smiled. "As a matter of fact, no. Some people hired me to locate him, that's all."

The light-haired one put his face up near mine suddenly, and demanded, "You're deaf, ain't you?"

"Yes, I am," I agreed.

He gave his partner a triumphant look. "I thought so," he said. His face took on the mixture of contempt and wariness prepared to deal with a despised but unknown quantity.

They swiveled away from me, and I had nowhere to go but back to my drink at the other end of the bar. The others ignored me as I passed behind them. Legwork is dispiriting, asking the same fruitless questions over and over again, with negative answers already written in the faces in front of you. It assails you again and again with the "What am I doing here?" feeling: out of place, out of time, and finally out of mind. I leaned against the bar and felt the comforting pressure of the holster against my side. The immediate feeling is one of security, but as I sipped my vodka, I thought that in this instance I might have things wrong-way to. I thought about the man who had so quickly departed. He was obviously off to report something, but what, and to whom? If he was reporting that someone was looking for Roger Grim, then I had struck pay dirt, and it behooved me to stick around and see what happened. But if he had simply passed the word that there was a man at the bar with a gun, a lone man who was obviously not a policeman (policemen come in pairs and they are never deaf), then the smart thing for me was to leave. No guns in the world are so valuable as those that are stolen. They can be traced back only to the legitimate, injured owner. The man who carries a gun is a lucrative target. It was something to think about.

The vodka seemed to have taken on an added charge as I sipped it. It brought the famous fire to my belly. I looked into the bottom of the double shot glass to inspect my quandary. The intelligent thing for me to do was leave. On the other hand, I had come here for information. I took another sip of the drink and looked in the mirror. The third party had returned, and the three of them were huddled together in the remote posture of unconcern. Beyond them, however, discernible through the big plate glass window were two more figures. Their backs were turned, and their hands were shoved in their pockets. They were wearing lumberjackets and watchcaps and shrugged their shoulders as if they were chilled, although it was fairly warm outside. They were waiting; they were waiting for something.

Taking the final sip of vodka, I decided my tactics. I put the heavy glass down, stepped back, and looked up as if studying the prices on the menu above the bar. Then I turned slowly and ambled toward the men's room. I deliberately took some time trying to find it, looking this way and that, and backing away from the ladies' room. I felt I had given them time enough. I stepped into the men's room and up to the urinal, which faced the door, and was additionally lighted by a high small window to my left.

The light was important because it illuminated the large round chromium faceplate that surrounded the flushing valve. I kept my eyes fixed on the faceplate while I assumed the traditional stance in front of the urinal. It gave me a wildly refracted view of the doorway behind me as I stood with my hands in the expected position in front of my fly. The door opened. I gave it a count of one, and swung away from the urinal to face two men who suddenly recoiled with surprise as the door swung shut behind them. The foremost had a sap in his raised right hand. I swung my weight on the ball of my right foot and hit him flush in the mouth with a left hook. The man behind him dodged around to get at me and made a target of his throat, which I stabbed with the stiffened fingers of my right hand. His mouth opened troutwise, and he staggered back as the man with the sap was organizing himself and coming back. I hit him coming in with a well-balanced right hand that drove him back against the door. While he was in this disarray, I kicked him in the balls. The other man was trying to kick me from his position to one side, but I doubled into a crouch, coming in low, and blocked the kick with my right arm just above his knee. Then I drove my left hand, with all my pivoted weight behind it, into his solar plexus.

I pulled the two of them away from the door and pushed them up against the abbreviated door of the crapper booth. I adjusted my clothing, waited until my breathing was reasonably normal, and went back into the barroom. I did not stop for my change. On the way past the three worthies at the end, I smiled pleasantly and nodded. I didn't have to turn to see them make for the men's room toward the back end of the bar. I could see their reflections disappear in the big window. The moment I was out, however, I rounded the corner and trotted up to the next block, where I hailed a cab to get me the hell out of there. There is such a thing as trying your luck.

My first thought on jumping in the cab had been to head back to my apartment, but I glanced at my watch and realized that I still had plenty of time to make my afternoon appointment upstate. I gave the driver the address of my office. Among other things, the trip would give me time to think and to settle down. But as I sank back in the seat, my first thought was that I was terribly happy. It is an undoubted shame that a man should have to crack two heads on a shithouse floor to feel that he is truly and well recovered, but that was the case with me. It was my first triumph since I had discovered Arnold in his awkward position. It was a triumph, I told myself, not only of brawn, which meant that I was fully physically recovered, but of brains, of craft, and, not least, of nerves.

I had judged, correctly, that by meandering innocently into the can I had offered them an opportunity that couldn't be ignored. They had no doubt rapped on the big window to bring in their two plug uglies who had hurried back to the men's room. It was the kind of setup thought to be almost infallible. The mark is standing in front of the urinal, absorbed in matters of micturition, exposed, and holding his joint in his hand. He is most vulnerably naked, distracted, and caught in an activity of almost childish helplessness. That is the scenario. But I had kept my pants buttoned, as it were, and made use of the chromium mirror. So I had caught *them*. It instilled confidence, which I sorely needed. I basked in it.

Edna, God bless her, had not gone to lunch when I arrived. Her jaw dropped when I came in the door though. "What's the matter?" I asked her.

She had just put down the telephone, and she answered, "You startled me. Scared me. I wasn't expecting you—anybody dressed like you." Her hand remained, forgotten, on the telephone as she stared at me. Her eyes narrowed. "What have you been up to?" she asked.

"Me?" I donned the expression of blithe innocence. "What makes you think I've been up to something?"

"You look exactly like a nine-year-old boy," she said, and then added thoughtfully, "and your hand is swollen up like a balloon."

I raised up my mitt, surprised, and looked at it. True enough, it was extremely puffy. "Jesus Christ," I said, "I hope I haven't broken it. I can't afford that now."

Edna was all practicality. She announced that she was going to get some ice from the coffee shop downstairs and disappeared immediately. I didn't stop her, because I thought it was a very good idea. I hadn't noticed any pain in my hand—the dangerous effect of adrenaline in the system that masks bodily injury in an emergency. Even now, although I couldn't close my hand into a fist, there didn't seem to be much pain. I held the puffy member out in front of me and carefully waggled my thumb and each finger in turn. They were all there and operating. I hadn't broken anything, just jammed it. Nonetheless, I was happy that Edna had thought of the ice. I wanted all parts of Joe Binney fully functioning.

She came back with a polyethylene bag of ice and told me to put my hand on the edge of the desk, and then placed the bag on top of it, all in the best tradition of the *Girl Scout Manual*. "Keep that bag on there," she ordered me and went back to the chair behind her desk. "Now," said Edna, with painful self-satisfaction. "What happened?"

"I was asking questions about Roger Grim in a saloon down by the fish piers and I got jumped in the men's room."

"These were friends of his?" Edna, too, can be excited by the chase.

"I don't believe it, no," I answered thoughtfully. "I think there were two things leading up to it. One, they don't like anybody asking any kind of questions down around here. Two, they cottoned on to the gun I was carrying, and I looked like an easy score: deaf, stupid, amiable. They just set me up to heist the gun."

"But they didn't," Edna said, smiling.

"No," I told her. "Foxy Joe Binney has been over that route before."

Edna's wide smile settled down to a reminiscent grin. "I haven't seen you look this happy in a long, long time," she said.

"Yeah," I agreed. "I'm all put together now." I paused for a moment before saying, "I don't mean to be personal, but who were you talking to on the phone when I came in?"

"Another accounts payable lady. I'll be picking up another check tomorrow afternoon." I beamed my appreciation and asked if there had been any other calls. No, she told me, but she had called Emerson Kite and made an appointment for ten o'clock tomorrow morning. I gave voice to an ugly expletive. I had forgotten all about Emerson Kite.

"But you told me to call him," Edna protested with a certain amount of outrage in her expression.

"Yeah," I answered, grudgingly, "but I've got the feeling I'm hot now. I wanted to charge out tomorrow morning and keep on looking. An appointment kind of screws it up." I considered the schedule. "What I'll do is go straight out after I see him. Get in half a day, anyway."

"Straight out where?" asked Edna.

"I thought maybe Sheepshead Bay," I answered. "They've still got a few commercial fishing boats out there along with the sports fishermen. Maybe it's the kind of place he'd want to hole up in."

"Are you going to carry the gun out there, too?"

I took the ice bag off my hand and tried to flex it. "If my hand is working I will," I said. "I'm no good with my left hand, even just pulling the gun.

"I'll tell you this," I assured her. "I don't want to go *without* a gun. Decking some stiff in the crapper is not the same thing as going up against Roger Grim."

21

My car is a clapped-out old Buick that I keep in a cinder-covered lot one block from where I live. It is a terrible and exasperating expense, not only when standing still and rusting away for a monthly fee, but also when on the road, where it uses gasoline as the Niagara uses water. I use it so little that the battery is often reluctant. This time, in the two o'clock sunshine, however, it started handily and, being charged up from the long drive to Port Chester, would start again in the morning. I don't often use the car in the city, but I wanted next morning to take it first to Kite's place on Central Park South, and then out to Sheepshead Bay. Being quick off the mark from Kite's was my only hope of catching the tag ends of commercial fishing in the wilds of Brooklyn. I wasn't truly expecting to find much in Sheepshead Bay, but it was a motion I had to go through before extending my search to outer Long Island, Greenport, and Montauk.

Neither was I expecting any great revelations in Port Chester. I knew very little about the town, having seen it only from a train window. I remembered the enormous roll of Lifesavers in front of the factory that made that perdurable candy. The rest of the view from the train window was the impression of a workingman's town: old, weatherbeaten houses and corner saloons. Tracks go usually through the least desirable section of town; however, I suspected that Port Chester had something more to offer.

Driving up, my right hand rested on the steering wheel, looking much better than it had when I left the office. Edna had insisted on putting the ice bag in the pocket of my jacket and I had rested my hand against it on the cab ride to my apartment. Now that the puffing had lessened, the hand showed signs of discoloration, but it was by no means going to turn into an Easter egg. I lifted it off the wheel and bent it, observing, happily, that I could now close a fist and grasp things, such as a gun. I promised myself to soak it again when I got back home.

Not that I was carrying a gun to see a widow in Port Chester. Paranoia has its limits. I'd taken off the holster when I got back to my apartment, emptied the gun, as per ritual, carefully checking the chamber, and put the gun and bullets back in their separate drawers. Then I'd put on one of my regular workaday business suits—I was not trying to impress *her*—and appeared in the mirror as my ordinary down-at-the-heels, slobbish self.

I took the Dewey up and headed for the New England Throughway. At the turnoff that cried RYE—PORT CHESTER, I made the correct fork and began to pay more attention to signs. When I pulled into Port Chester, I went into the nearest gas station with the slip of paper bearing the address of Mrs. Pelfrey. Three gas stations later found me in an old, well-ordered section of town that seemed to have been established some time before the second World War. The houses were not sumptuous, but they had a solid, durable look about them that is the despair of postwar tract housing.

I had given myself enough time to reconnoiter and search out the house ahead of time. It was, like other houses on the tree-shaded street, built on a slight rise that required stone steps to reach the entrance walk. It was a two-storey brick house, not overly large, but with a comfortable air of respectability and permanence. The steeply sloping lawn was well tended, and the ascending driveway presented a new Chevrolet Malibu at its summit. I drove past, went down to an artery, and located a lunchroom, where I had coffee and a session with the local paper. I was content. The car in the driveway meant that Mrs. Pelfrey was home.

It was still there when I came back at the appointed hour. I mounted the stone steps, went up the walk, and pressed the bell. She had been waiting for me—obviously. The door opened so quickly that I was taken aback. "Mrs. Pelfrey," I said carefully, "My name is Joe Binney. I made an appointment for this afternoon. . . ."

"You made an appointment with my son, Carl," the woman said quickly. The expression on her face told me that this line had been rehearsed. "Unfortunately, he's not here." She could not resist adding, "He's at band practice." She began to close the door.

"Mrs. Pelfrey," I said sharply. She stepped back at the unknown quantity of my voice. "I'm the man who found your husband."

The door paused in her hand. "Am I supposed to thank you?" she said. "What do you want?"

"I want to make sure he was actually murdered," I lied rapidly. "This could be extremely important to you and your children." It was a fairly surreal conversation for a doorstep, but I saw that it was necessary to shock her. She had a strong, striking face, with dark brown eyes so deeply set in the sockets that they seemed to burn from the depths of her skull. Her jawline was firm and taut, and when she spoke, she revealed large, square, regular teeth. Her hair was black, in a pageboy bob, and beginning to be shot with gray. "Of course he was murdered," she said. "The police have been here, and they told me . . ." She could not repress an involuntary shudder. " . . . they told me all about everything."

"The insurance company may not see eye to eye with the police." I told her. "There's no real proof he was murdered. I know. I was there. If the insurance people want to contest it, and it seems likely that they will, you could be tied up for years."

"What do you *want?*" she demanded. Her whole taut, trim body in the blue corduroy jumper seemed to be thrown into the word.

"I'm a private investigator trying to find out if Mr. Pelfrey really was murdered, and if so, by whom," I told her. "If I succeed, then you won't have any trouble with the insurance. It is very much in your interest to talk to me."

Her looks plainly said, "*I doubt that,*" but a glance to the side also suggested that she did not want the neighbors to witness a vociferous argument at her front door. "All right," she snapped. "Come in."

I followed her into the front room, and, with her back to me, she apparently said something, because her right hand waved out in a gesture. I remained standing a few steps inside the door. She turned and glanced at me sharply. "I said you may sit over there." She indicated an occasional chair covered in needlepoint in the corner of the room. Dutifully, I went to it and sat down. There was a mate to this chair placed in the opposite corner. She sat in that and smoothed the blue corduroy over her knees. No lamps were lit, and the corner was shaded. I saw her face move in the shadow but couldn't make out what she was saying. The shadow gave her strong face a fanatical cast, like those deeply articulated Germanic faces that haunt the edges of quattrocento canvases. I put my hand up in a gesture of supplication and said, "Really, ma'am, if you sit so far away, I can't . . ."

She moved her head toward me so that it caught some of the light. I made out her saying, "I can tell by your voice that you have a terrible cold. I don't need any of your germs, thank you."

I smiled with all the pleasantness I could muster. "Oh, that," I said. "My voice . . . well. My voice sounds strange because I'm deaf, not because I have a cold. I can't hear my own voice, and . . ."

"You're deaf!" The thin lips framed the word like an accusation.

"Well," I said with an uncertain attempt at reassurance, "it's not catching." I smiled comfortingly. "But I understand what people are saying by reading their lips." I smiled again. "If I can't see, I can't hear. So if we're going to make any sense in this interview and not waste our time, you'll have to move a little closer. All right?"

Possibly she was spooked by the idea. It takes some people that way, the idea that you can read their lips somehow suggests to them that you can read their minds . . . their souls. I cannot prove that they are totally wrong. I see a lot of things that are missed in ordinary conversation. She got up stiffly and moved to the settee in the center of the room. It was the most uncomfortable piece of furniture I have ever seen. The wooden back to it was framed by two curving members that appeared to be pythons attempting to swallow one another at the center. The back was softened only by a few cushions. The seat was a thin pad that featured huge brass nailheads along the edge of the upholstery. She sat exactly in the center of this article. She did not lean either forward or backward. "The insurance company sent you," she charged.

"No," I contradicted her quickly. "I have been employed by a client of your husband's—ex-husband's," I amended, perhaps cruelly. "My client is interested because he suspects that Mr. Pelfrey's death may be connected with him, and he wants to make sure that no threat to himself is involved."

"How could it be connected?"

"Mr. Pelfrey had been missing, but was supposed to see my client just before he died," I told her. "I was asked to seek out Mr. Pelfrey, and that's how I found him—in the hotel." She flinched at the unspoken image.

"Ma'am," I tried to make my voice as gentle as I knew how, "I haven't come here to hurt you in any way. If Mr. Pelfrey was murdered, then my client wants to know about it because it could be a threat to his own life. My best chance to protect my client is to find out who, if anyone, killed Mr. Pelfrey, and why. If I can solve that and turn it over to the police, then the threat to my client is removed."

"The police," she said, "the lieutenant who was here, said they were doing everything—everything possible . . ."

"Of course they are," I agreed. "But you have to think about what's possible for them, and how important this case is compared to others they're working on." I stopped her interruption with a gesture. "The police are very good," I assured her, "and they have tremendous resources. But those resources are spread out among millions of people. Very often the police are directed by how much the public or the newspapers want a certain case solved. This drains their resources. They certainly won't be thinking," I sat back, "about your problems with the insurance company."

She considered this carefully. "It was my impression," she said, "that the insurance company would take the word of the police and the inquest."

"They're not bound by that," I told her. "There have been a number of cases where responsible men committed suicide in a way that appeared to be an accident or murder. This makes an enormous difference in the double indemnity clause, and insurance companies will go a long ways to fight it." I added, "I'm sure there was a double indemnity, wasn't there?" She nodded.

"So the insurance company will be looking very carefully into the possibility that Mr. Pelfrey had a motive for suicide," I said cautiously. "The fact that he was recently divorced may have a lot of bearing on that." She gathered herself in, almost imperceptibly. "And there are other things," I proceeded.

She did interrupt this time. "I thought I had settled all that with the lieutenant: Lieutenant. . ."

"Shope?"

"Yes," she said, "He . . ." But her hands, which had gone white with the twisting in her lap, seemed to be strangling her own words. She broke off to say suddenly, "Would you like a cup of tea?"

"Oh, yes," I agreed, smiling. "I'd like one very much." She escaped from the settee, on whose center she had appeared to be pinioned.

Left to myself, I surveyed the room and extended what I saw to the house beyond. It seemed to me a six- or seven-room house, all told, much smaller inside than the generous outside aspect hinted at. I saw it as three rooms downstairs, large front room, in which I was sitting, dining room, which I could glimpse through the archway, showing the dark presence of an old heavy dining room set, and the promise of a bright commodious kitchen beyond. Upstairs, I calculated, there would be three or four bedrooms: one large, and the rest quite small. It was a solid, self-enclosed house of a no-nonsense design, meant to warm, feed, and shelter a family.

In the living room, I looked for the big easy chair that usually designated the master of the household. In this class of house, it was often a Barcalounger, placed within comfortable viewing distance of the television set. There was no such article in sight, although there was a large color set up against the far wall from the settee. I suspected that the two boys, whose photographs were on the mantle over the marbelized gas-fed fireplace, watched TV from the carpeted floor. I also looked for some kind of desk or secretary on which Arnold could have done his accounts. There was no hint of one in this room. Possibly, he did it all on the dining-room table. Aside from two end tables at either end of the settee, the only level surface was the plain cheap coffee table in front of it. There was no sign of a dog. It was an amazingly comfortless room, eclectically barren.

She came back into the room bearing a teacup and saucer in each hand. She set one for herself on the coffee table and extended the other one to me—I hadn't had time to rise—at arm's length, as if still afraid of some contamination or attack. The tea bag dropped its limp string over the rim of the cup, and a drylooking slice of lemon decorated the saucer. "Cream," she said suddenly, as I looked up to thank her. "Do you want cream and sugar?"

I tried to gentle her with a smile. "This is fine."

I squeezed my teabag and watched a dark cloud dissolve in the cup. "Mrs. Pelfrey," I began, "as a private investigator right now, it's my business to outdistance, to outguess the police and the insurance company. If I'm successful, it's a benefit to my client, because he'll know where he stands, and it will be a benefit to you, too. But in order to do this successfully, I have to know a little bit more about Mr. Pelfrey. I have to know this so I can look for various associates who might have wanted to do him harm. Can you think of anyone who might have wanted to murder him?''

There was a terrible flash in her eyes, and then she said, ''No.''

I began again. ''In order to do my job,'' I said, ''I have to have a complete picture of the man. Coming into this house what I see is a steady, hardworking man who was a good provider . . .''

There was another flash. ''This house was bought by my father,'' said Mrs. Pelfrey. ''He gave it to us.''

I absorbed this and tried again. ''But obviously,'' I said, ''Mr. Pelfrey did work steadily . . .''

''All this furniture,'' she swept the room with a crooked arm, ''all came from my family.''

''But he did work?'' I tried to insist on it.

''All his life,'' she said. She swigged her tea. ''He was a very hard worker. I'll give him that. He worked very hard. Day and night.''

''Could you tell me a little about it?'' I have to be very careful when I try to speak very softly because, I've learned, sometimes nothing at all comes out.

''Even in high school,'' she said ''he worked hard at his studies. He was studious, serious, careful. He was very careful. We both graduated the same year, and we got married. My father wanted me to go to college, but I wanted to get married and he was very disappointed. Arnold got a job with the Lifesaver factory, in the office part, and he went to night school to learn accounting. For a long, long time he went to night school, like forever, it seemed.

''We had a lot of plans,'' she continued, the tea forgotten on the table in front of her. ''Buy a house, then start a baby. Only it worked the other way around. It doesn't cost anything to start a baby. We were living in an apartment up over a store. Not very nice. But there was no way we could see to afford a house, not on his salary. Those salaries just exactly keep you alive. If you save a few dollars, it goes for an emergency. We lived for the future, when Arnold would have his accounting degree. But the baby was now. Finally, my father stepped in."

"Stepped in?" I inquired. "Arnold didn't go to him for a loan?"

"Oh, no. Never. Arnold had a terror of borrowing money, even buying anything on credit. No. My father wanted to lend Arnold the money to buy this house—on very, very easy terms. But Arnold said no. Finally, my father made a present of it.

"When we first came into this house," she said, her deep eyes staring far beyond me, "it was like walking into an empty castle—it seemed so big, so empty. Carl was only a tiny baby then. We didn't have any furniture at all because our apartment was a furnished apartment—with what furniture!" She shuddered. "But Arnold wouldn't even buy furniture on credit. He didn't want to be tied to payments, he said. And so the furniture," she swept the room again, "that all came from my family. Different parts of my family. Odds and ends."

"What about Arnold's family," I asked her. "Didn't they help out at all?"

"The Pelfreys were dirt-poor," she replied. "Always had been, always will be. Arnold was the roaring success of that family. That's why he worked so hard—to get himself up out of it.

"Arnold changed when he got his degree in accounting and then went on to get certified, a CPA. I didn't see the change right away because I'd seen so little of him anyway: at work all day, at school at night, and then studying, studying. So I had to keep the babies, there were two of them by the time he was certified, I had to keep them quiet and out of the way. But Arnold had put all of his hope, all of his faith in winning that degree—that certification. He thought that everything was going to open up for him, that he was going to be an—an *executive*." She emphasized the word with a blow on her knee. "Like he was going to be taken up to some kind of heaven at the Lifesaver.

"He came home from work one night and his face was terrible. He frightened the children and I sent them upstairs. He was crying and he couldn't stop crying. They'd given a promotion, at the Lifesaver, to somebody else, somebody, he said, who wasn't really qualified for anything. Some kind of a salesman who had got some contracts, who knew some people. I don't know what all.

" 'Like a child,' Arnold kept saying. 'A child. They treated me like some kind of a child. Like I didn't have any real business being there at all. Like I didn't belong with them: never . . . never . . . never belong with them.' " Her angular face took on some of the desperation.

"He started working at night, then, at home, in there," she nodded toward the archway, "on the dining-room table, where he'd always studied. He did the income tax for people, and he started doing the books for some small businesses. Our life didn't really change much. I never saw any of the money he earned. It was all invested. We never wanted for anything, but I never had anything, either. You understand." I nodded. "And then, about two years ago, I decided to get a divorce."

I worked at letting my voice out gently. "What were the grounds?"

"Incompatibility." I could see the syllables being spat out like so many machine-gun bullets.

"Meaning what?" I persisted. "You were sick of being alone?"

"The divorce was uncontested," she replied. Her face closed up.

I tried another tack. "When Lieutenant Shope was here," I asked her, "did he inquire into the specifics of the divorce?"

"He inquired into a lot of things that were none of his business."

I took my plunge. "And did he show you any pictures? Photographs?"

Her eyes seemed to move forward in her head so that they filled the deep sockets. "You know about them too!" Her hands clutched one another. "Does everybody know about them?"

"Nobody who doesn't have to," I said as soothingly as I could. "But tell me about them. You knew about the pictures, didn't you?"

She sank back, finally, against the unyielding cushions. "Yes," she said. "Oh, yes. I knew about them."

I remained absolutely, perfectly still.

"He had been working day and night," she said from her relaxed position, smoothing the blue corduroy over her knees. "Days at his job with the Lifesaver, and nights on all the jobs he was picking up—in there." She nodded toward the sanctuary in the dining room. "I don't know when he ate. Almost never with us. I'd clean off the table after dinner, and he'd start to work. He was as skinny as a stick, and his face was always white. So he got sick. He got a kidney infection and they took him to the hospital for some tests on the Blue Cross. It was only for three days, but on the second day, they called from the Lifesaver and wanted to know if he had some papers in his briefcase. Well, his briefcase, you know, it was like a valise. He always kept it locked, but I found the key. I only opened it to look for the papers they were talking about. I took out a big manila envelope to look into it, and there were these pictures.

"They were big glossy photographs—color photographs. They showed children doing things I didn't even know that grown-ups did. They showed children, boys, mostly, doing things to men and men doing things to boys. And there were little young naked girls, and grown naked women, and terrible, terrible things I didn't even know existed in this world." Her eyes seemed to see all the bright images again. "It took me hours," she said, with unconscious revelation, "to realize what I was seeing, and to realize that these pictures belonged to Arnold—that he was carrying them around.

"I tore them into a million pieces," she said. "And then I burned them. The terrible thing was that I couldn't figure out how to burn them. That's just a radiant heater in the fireplace. You can't burn anything there. I took them in the backyard, finally, and pretended I was just burning leaves and trash—even though that's against the law. I put them in a garbage can with some newspapers and some leaves I found, and I burned them. They were hard to burn.

"When Arnold came home from the hospital the next day, he saw that the briefcase had been opened. I left it open on purpose. He looked through it, and then he looked at me and I looked at him. Neither one of us said anything. We just looked at each other. Later that day, I told him I wanted a divorce. And he didn't say anything. He just nodded, like I'd told him we were going to have stew for dinner."

"The settlement," I asked. "Was it satisfactory?"

"Oh, yes," said Mrs. Pelfrey. She sighed. "There were no problems. He left me everything. The investments he made were a lot more than I expected. They take care of the alimony with something left over. I bought the car," she nodded toward the driveway, "for cash. And the television set," she smiled a very slight smile. "The boys can watch it now without bothering Arnold."

"The investments," I pursued. "Were they all accounted for? Legitimate?"

"They certainly were. Why would you ask a thing like that?"

"The pictures might have been one of two things," I said carefully. "You assumed that Arnold had them for his own enjoyment, but there is a very real suspicon that they might have been one of the investments, that Arnold was financing them and profiting from them."

"Profiting?"

"It's a very lucrative market," I said, "and one of the few things in the field that's illegal. It might be that Arnold had built up a large amount of money from retailing this kind of thing and put it into a hidden account."

"It would have to be hidden all right," she answered spiritedly. "The money he left was all perfectly legal."

"And yet he had funds to go off on his own," I said. "Has it occurred to you, or did you see any signs, that he might have had money somewhere, a fairly large account, that was completely separate from his declared income?"

She stared at me. "Are you saying," she asked, "that Arnold might have had this business on the side, making money, putting money away, his own money that we didn't know anything about, so he could just step out of here whenever he wanted to?"

"It's a possibility I've kept in mind," I admitted.

She sat bolt upright away from the cushions. "The son of a bitch," she said. "Oh, the dirty, filthy son of a bitch!"

22

Morning found me in an ill humor as I wove my way through the traffic up to Kite's apartment. I was irritated by the accidental squeezing of my timetable, which made my planned excursion to Sheepshead Bay almost quixotic in the hope of any results. The interview with Kite also threw me off balance in the way I wanted to present myself. I did not want to go up to Central Park South in a jacket and slacks, a costume that might prevent me from getting through the door, and I did not want to navigate the sidewalks of Sheepshead Bay in a business suit. But the Kite interview came first, and so I was clad in a business suit again, although this time I had my .38 Smith & Wesson snugged at my side.

Kite's apartment was in one of the very few old buildings left standing on Central Park South. It was a narrow building of six or eight storeys that appeared to be crushed between the monoliths on either side of it. Each storey of the building above the marqueed lobby was fronted with large solid windows that gazed out over Central Park and the ranks of horse-drawn cabs strung out along the street. As I understood it, the building had been erected as a series of studios for well-to-do artists in New York. The great windows had been installed to provide the north light. They were something more than "picture windows."

Surprisingly, there was no doorman. I had expected to be announced, and hoped devoutly that Kite was not the sort who would insist on identification through the speaker. I pressed the button under his name on 6-A and put my hand nervously on the big brass handle of the door to sense the vibration of the answering buzzer. He knew, after all, that I was coming, and it was exactly ten o'clock. When I felt the slight tingling in my palm, I pushed the door open, got in the elevator at the end of the narrow entry hall, and went up to 6-A, where I pushed another doorbell.

For Emerson Kite, this hour appeared to represent the first hideous blush of dawn. Even though the light in the room was filtered through closed blinds, his eyes were blinking with aversion. He strained to recognize me, and then said, "Jesus Christ. You. I forgot all about you. Come in. Come in." He moved his huge bulk back from the door to let me pass.

Kite closed the door and moved uncertainly around the big room in the murky light, resembling, in the thick white terrycloth robe, a drunken polar bear. He searched among the various tables scattered in the depths of the room, dug into the pockets of his robe, and then turned to me helplessly, saying "Have you got a cigarette? . . . I . . ." I went over and gave him a Lucky. He regarded it with suspicion and began, "Don't you have? . . ." amending lamely, "I usually smoke filters." He lighted it anyway, inhaled deeply, and produced a cough that shook the fleshy pads of his cheeks and sent ripples of flesh coursing under his robe. It woke him up. He took another drag and gratefully blew the smoke upward. His eyes brightened under the tousled hair. "Coffee!" The word had probably been barked out; he had the attitude of a man who has just cried

"Eureka!" "I'll get us some coffee. You take it black?" I nodded.

I watched the huge white haunches diminish as he plodded the length of the room to disappear through the far doorway in search of coffee. The room was large by any standard, so large that the grand piano with its lid raised on the point of utterance at the other end seemed no larger than a piece of occasional furniture. There were three groups of couches in the room, and a big old-fashioned bookshelf along the wall which supported a Bang and Olufsen hi-fi system. The other wall was accented with an old art-deco sideboard, and further down the wall, a huge secretary of the same design. The rest of the room was punctuated by a few twinnings of easy chairs and a greater number of occasional chairs. The carpeted floor was broken up by a scattering of oriental rugs. It took me a while to absorb it all and connect it to the fact that the room had once been the studio of an artist, where light, space, and perspective had been demanded.

I was startled at how quickly he came back with the coffee, and I must have showed it because he said, "Automatic. A timer. Wonderful. I set it every night like saying my prayers." Then he smiled sheepishly. "Please? Have you got another cigarette? There isn't a cigarette anywhere in this godforsaken hole."

Like Bill Macready, he enunciated his words clearly, so that even in the dim light he was easy to read. His big, pink face seemed to gather in the light and glow slightly. I felt so grateful for the advantage that I began, "It's awfully nice for you to see me like this . . ."

"Glad to do it," said Kite. "I've heard that you're very close friends with Bill Macready, and needless to say at this moment, I'm very interested in that particular career."

We sat in two easy chairs and put our coffee on a small table between us. Despite the informality of his bathrobe, under which, I discerned, he was completely naked, Kite assumed the manner of a boardroom meeting. I put my cigarettes on the table and took one for myself. "Of course," I said, "it's Bill that I've come to see you about."

"As an emissary?" His eyes widened.

"No, no," I reassured him. "I'm investigating the death of his business manager and how it affects Bill."

"How it affects Bill?" Kite repeated. "How should it affect him? The man committed suicide, which is regrettable, but . . ."

"The police believe he was murdered."

"And they suspect Bill?" His face opened with astonishment.

"Oh, no," I disabused him. "Certainly not. Nothing like that."

"Then why? . . ."

"Bill wants to be certain that it had nothing to do with him, the man's being murdered, I mean. He's retained me to find out and make sure that there's no implied threat to him."

Kite picked up his coffee and sipped it, watching me shrewdly over the rim. "That seems very far-fetched to me," he said. "But then Macready has always been a very . . . uh . . . cautious sort of man." He put the coffee down and added, "I also don't see what help I could be. I'd never even heard of this business manager—what was his name?"

"Arnold Pelfrey."

The big pink face shook in the negative. "No," he said. "Never heard of him."

"What we're looking for is any possible link with the past. Can you think of anything in Bill's past that could link him to a thing like this?"

His eyes were now watching me very shrewdly indeed. Kite said, "Certainly Bill Macready would be a better expert on his own past than I could be."

I shook my head. "No, no," I told him. "We're looking for scuttlebutt: gossip, rumors about Bill's past that Bill may know nothing about. Tales get circulated, some of them pretty wild, perhaps. Have you heard anything?"

"Let me think," said Kite. He leaned back and folded his hands over his stomach in Buddha-like repose. Finally, he said, "If there were anything at all, it would have to do with women. Bill Macready has cut quite a swath through the ladies, and I think he has left some broken hearts and dashed expectations behind him. But, again, this would be very, very far-fetched. I can't see that it would have anything to do with his business manager."

"All right." I accepted it. "Then the only other line of inquiry I can follow is this: Could someone have been warning him off the new series? Is there anyone who doesn't want to see him take the part?"

Kite threw back his head and laughed. "If that was a motive for murder," he said, "the studios would be littered with corpses.

If you want a direct answer," he said, still smiling, "I, for one, certainly did not want him to take the part."

"But you," I interjected, surprised, "that night at Bill's place, you were persuading him."

"That was after the fact," said Kite. "That was after the Old Man had bought the complete package, of which Bill had become an integral part. It was a *fait accompli*. But before that, believe me, I didn't want him."

I asked him why.

"Let me get some more coffee," said Kite, heaving his bulk out of the chair. "I won't be a second." I lighted one of my cigarettes and sat back. As I watched the blue smoke dissolve above me in the dim air, I became aware of another scent, a perfume that was redolent of something not long past. I turned around uneasily in my chair and saw Sally standing about five feet behind me and staring nearsightedly in my direction. She was wearing lemon silk pajamas, and as she approached, still squinting, the perfume became stronger and unmistakably hers. I stood up, as my mother had trained me to do, when a lady enters the room, and Sally stepped back a pace.

"Oh," she said. "It's you. I didn't recognize . . . I don't have my eyes in."

"Good morning," I said. We looked at each other.

"You're all better, I see," said Sally.

"Yes," I replied. "I'm all better."

"How's Bill?"

"All right, I guess. I've been busy and haven't seen him for a while. What about you?"

"What about me what?"

"Haven't you seen him recently?"

"You never can get hold of him," she complained. "I'm surprised he ever even gets a job with that snotty answering service of his."

"I've been told about them," I sympathized, "and my opinion is that Macready's answering service is a bag lady in a phone booth on Times Square." She laughed. It was very pleasant to see. "Seriously, though," I asked her, "doesn't he return your calls?"

"Can I have one of your cigarettes?" she asked me. After I'd lighted one for her, she said, "He might have answered and I might have missed it. I'm not all that easy to reach, either."

Kite, who had apparently noticed Sally's appearance, returned with three mugs of coffee on a small tray. He offered one to Sally, and, with his back turned, said something to her that was lost on me. I couldn't see her response, because Kite's enormous back blocked her out completely. She went to a nearby chair with her coffee and sat down demurely. Kite settled himself again in the easy chair. "Now," he said to me, "about my not wanting to hire Bill . . ."

Sally started forward in her chair. "Not wanting to hire Bill!" she exclaimed.

"Shut up, Sally," said Kite. She sat back again with her brown eyes very round as Kite resumed. "Bill has worked for me on a number of shows—four or five, anyway—and he has always been the complete professional. I have no quarrel whatsoever with that. That's purely aside from his talent, which is tremendous; I cheerfully admit *that*." He made his point with a pudgy forefinger. "Bill, right now, is one of the best actors in the country, and in time, if all goes well, he may become that very rare thing, the *best* actor in the country."

Sally sat forward again. Her face expressed disbelief. "Bill?" she said. "Come on."

Kite waved her back majestically. "The difficulty with all this is that he can break up a show—he can stop it. And I'm not talking about Broadway, now, I'm talking about your straightforward TV production. Bill could stop the show in its tracks. I don't mean he does it by farting around camera, by outrageous overacting or deadly underplaying: He simply brings an intensity to the screen that is different from what went before. When this happens, the show has gone out of control. It's not what the director, the producer, has in mind.

"And it's not just his talent." Kite heaved his weight around in the chair in squirming discontent. "He is always very buddy-buddy with the crew. They're in love with him. So what happens? He gets lighted like Tiffany's window, and the camera crawls into his pants. Again, this makes a break with what has gone before. The viewer tends to think that something has gone wrong with his set."

"If I were to boil this down," I submitted to Kite, "what you're saying is that Bill is outstanding."

"But we don't *want* him to be outstanding." Kite spread his arms out to implore my comprehension. "Don't you see? What Bill is demonstrating is a performance. We're looking for a product."

Sally shot forward to help. "What Emmy means," she explained, "is that Bill isn't commercial."

Kite sank back in his chair and stared at the ceiling. It was apparent that he had groaned. He sat up and said, "Sally, will you for Christ's sake shut up?

"When I said that *the* best actor in the country is a very rare thing," Kite continued, "I was thinking, of course, of John Barrymore. He was incontestably the best actor of his time, possibly in the entire world. There was absolutely nothing that he couldn't do. People like to romanticize about his so-called genius, which he undoubtedly had, but what he had most of was an absolutely incredible mastery of technique.

"But there is one lamentable fact about John Barrymore. Except in a few instances, he really didn't make very much money for the production companies or the studios. Did you know that he had to put up a lot of the money himself to take his *Hamlet* to England? Did you know that Warner Brothers gave him the best contract anybody ever had for five pictures and never really got their money back? The fact is that John Barrymore made his audiences—at least in the movies, because, of course, I'd never seen him on the stage; I missed even *My Dear Children*—he made them uncomfortable. He upset them because they got into deep water, into emotions and perceptions they couldn't handle. It's not what they came to the movies for.

"Have you ever seen any of his pictures?" Kite asked me. I shook my head. "His silent pictures?" Kite persisted. I shook my head again, a bit more shamefacedly. "Well," he said, "you ought at least to see *Beau Brummel* and *Dr. Jekyll and Mr. Hyde*. What Barrymore did in *Beau Brummel* was a miracle. And one of the reasons the miracle came off was because Barrymore knew exactly what he was doing!" Kite's fist slammed down on his fat knee to emphasize his last six words. "He was raised in a family not all that far removed from the world of Prinny and of Brighton. He had absorbed it from his grandmother, who raised him till he was—what—fifteen? So he was no stranger to the manners of eighteenth—nineteenth *fin de siècle*.

"In *Dr. Jekyll and Mr. Hyde,* everyone oohs and ahs because Barrymore made the change on camera without benefit of makeup. That was an enormous technical triumph. But what everyone overlooks is the more difficult acting in the picture, and that happens when he is playing the saintly Dr. Jekyll.

"Look," said Kite, demonstrating for me with his hands around an imaginary throat, "if you're strangling somebody on camera, people are going to look at you, and they're going to be interested in what you're doing. How not? But if you're simply walking down a hospital corridor being *nice,*" he grimaced the word, "oh, oh, That calls for acting. So what Barrymore presented in the role of Dr. Jekyll was the paradigm of the Victorian Christian gentleman. And he was able to do this because he knew what this paradigm was. It was a triumph of acting. Portraying a really good man is the most difficult thing an actor can do. There aren't many models for it."

Sally reached out a silk-clad leg and nudged my ankle. "He can go on like this all day," she said.

"All right." Kite put his hands up in acquiescence. "As Barrymore himself used to say, 'Let us return to the libretto.'

"When I got word that they wanted Bill because of his test, I said to myself, 'Oh, God. I know what happened. He's burned up the screen and they're hypnotized. And if I have to do "Tycoon" with him, the only thing on the screen is going to be Macready.'

"So they persuaded me to come down and see the test. And I admit, now, that I was astounded. It wasn't Bill at all. He didn't do what I'd expected. He was everything he had to be for the role, but not a bit more. He was perfect, utterly perfect. I hardly recognized him. It was as if some other, very competent actor, had tried out for the role. It was a very strange feeling, as if I were seeing Bill through a series of mirrors."

I smiled a secret, self-satisfied smile, recalling my conversation with Popper. "So," I said, "finally, you were happy with the casting?"

"God, no," said Kite. "I was terrified. There's a popular misconception among the public, extending through the industry, that actors are somehow stupid. That has never been my experience. I do not think that actors are any more stupid than any other professionals: doctors, lawyers, producers. They are different, but the difference is not a matter of intelligence quotient. I saw what Bill was doing. He was winning the part—the way Napoleon or the Duke of Wellington might win a campaign. But I said to myself, 'Once he has got the part, what will he do?' You realize, of course, that if Bill gets the part, Popper will make commitments that will tie up the networks, the studios, for years. There is an enormous investment . . ."

"I saw Popper recently," I interrupted. "He didn't mention anything about that."

"He wouldn't," said Kite. He smiled suddenly, his big face splitting. "What was he wearing? Blue, brown, gray, tan, black?"

"Blue, as a matter of fact." I couldn't help smiling too. "Why do you ask?"

"He's color blind," said Kite. "His wife buys all his clothes." I laughed. It explained a lot.

"So," Kite continued. "Here we are tied up with enormous amounts of money based on a test constructed by a very sharp, very intelligent actor. My question is: What if he reverts? What if he gets bored and starts really performing? What if he goes back to himself and begins to burn holes in the screen? These are problems that *I* have to live with. I can't even discuss them with the people upstairs. If Bill turns around on me, then it will be *my* failure, an enormous failure, a failure that could drive me out of the business, because they'll all say that I had everything going for me: all the money, the best actors, the best everything. And if it bombs, there'll be no way to explain it. If I try to tell them what I've told you, they'll say," and the fat folds of his face emulated a sneer, " 'And you couldn't bring him down?' They'll never understand that you can't bring that kind of acting down. They'll just assume that I let him walk all over me. And that means I'm dead. This whole thing is a terrible, terrible risk for me."

"I don't want to sound offensive," I said. "But seeing you in this layout," I nodded toward the far reaches of the vast room, "doesn't look to me as if you're in a very risky business. It looks very, very comfortable to me."

"This apartment?" Kite looked surprised. "My God, this isn't mine. I'm not even subleasing it. It's been loaned to me by a friend who writes music. He's out on the Coast scoring a movie." He dismissed the big room with a wave of his hand. "I wouldn't have it even if I could afford it," he said. "The Goddamned pile is falling down around the tenants' ears. Even the intercom at the door doesn't work." He was puzzled, then, because I smiled happily.

"Very well," I said. "Bill poses a risk for you. Is he a risk for anyone else?"

Kite replied that he was a risk for everybody, and I pointed out that everybody was the same as nobody. And so Kite said,

"Well, I suppose that the man who's in the riskiest position, purely through his own machinations, is Norman."

"Bill's agent?" I was genuinely surprised.

"Oh, yes," said Kite. "Norman will have taken all those commitments he's picked up for Bill and parlayed them into a thousand other deals. He will have made commitments, promises, investments, all riding on the success of this show. He is very far out on a limb."

"With no protection?"

"I'm sure he has a sizable insurance policy on Bill, on Bill's life, that is. But that's no help to him if the show goes down the tubes—unless he strangles Bill with his bare hands, as well he might."

I picked another cigarette out of the pack, lighted it, and sat back to consider the picture that Kite had drawn. He helped me by concluding, "So you see, far from anyone wanting to hinder Bill in taking the part, it is pretty well essential to everyone that he does take it and deliver what his test has promised. I, personally, am in a terribly exposed position. I really have to have reassurance that Bill is dealing in good faith. I have to know what he's thinking." I could not help glancing at Sally at this revelation, but her brown eyes stared serenely into space. "Norman is doing a bit of financial spacewalking on the strength of Bill's promise. Vincent's job is a seat directly under the sword of Damocles being dangled by the Old Man, and even Cy Garson could get hurt very badly if Bill becomes mercurial."

"Mercurial?" I wasn't sure I'd read the word correctly.

"Squirting out from under everyone's fingers. It's very attractive to see in a stage character, but absolutely maddening to deal with in real life."

"Real life," I repeated absently. "That reminds me. Sally says she hasn't been able to get hold of Bill in the last few days, and I haven't had any reason to try. Do you know where he is?"

"If experience is any guide," said Kite, "he is shacked up somewhere with some beautiful but foolish woman who is this moment making golden plans, all of which will come to naught."

"Sally," I asked, "would you see if you can get him on the phone right now? Just as a check? Tell him I just want to know how he's doing."

Sally brought the phone over to the little table and leaned forward to dial. Ever generous, she presented both Kite and me with a gorgeous view of her naked thorax inside the silk pajama top. When she had put back the phone and straightened up, both our faces clouded with the disappointment of small boys watching the dismantling of a circus tent. Sally seemed unaware of our interest. She said, "The bag lady again. 'Mr. Macready will return your call.' But she didn't say when."

"I wouldn't worry about it if I were you," Kite said with a reassuring expression on his mobile face. "He does a lot of this, very, very often."

I didn't like it, however, and while I was saying goodbye to Kite and Sally, with whom I left my cigarettes, I decided to stop in at Bill's place that evening after my stint at Sheepshead Bay.

23

When I got the first glimpse of those long legs at Sheepshead Bay, I began to shake, and was grateful that I had a few moments to collect myself. It was a shock, seeing them, because my motive in going out there had been the forlorn one of simply following through, doing a complete job of things. I hadn't really expected to find him there. It was an unlikely area for a black man to be, because, not far from there, a carful of black men had been mobbed, and one of them killed, by a gang of disaffected white neighborhood youths only recently. Nonetheless, those legs announced his presence.

I had pulled in off the Belt Parkway and angled my car, along with the others, diagonally at the center strip along the waterftont. I couldn't see any evidence of commercial fishing and walked back the way I had driven to the sportsfishing charter-boat piers. Only a few boats were tied up there, and four of the people who manned them were knotted together talking on one pier. Because they were used to dealing with the public, they answered my questions courteously and patiently. Yes, there was still some commercial fishing going on down here, but they didn't know anything about it. No, they didn't know anyone named Roger Grim, who was an extremely tall, athletic, young black man. They suggested that I inquire in some of the restaurants strung out along the wharves.

These restaurants specialized, quite naturally, in seafood, and had to resist the temptation to order my favorite kind of lunch efore my work was done. To aid my resistance, I went into the ar section and had a drink. The bartender was more suspicious ian the charter-boat men had been, but the results were the ame. No: Never heard of him. No: Never saw anybody like iat.

Once I had passed the string of restaurants, the street became emi-residential, with a gathering of neat little houses in excel-nt repair. A construction crew was laying in a new sewer line front of the houses, and two black men were working with iem, but neither was of the eminence of Roger Grim. Beyond ie houses was an apartment complex, a yacht club, and a few ot dog or knish joints, into which I went with my inquiries. hey were not suspicious, but neither were they of any help to ie. I had come to the end of the road on the waterfront of heepshead Bay. Beyond this point, the road curved back into ie Belt Parkway. Off to my right, a desolate field separated the reet from the curving shoreline. At the water-edge of the field, could see two rickety piers jutting out into the bay. It struck me iat these must be the commercial fishing piers, but there was no oat in sight. In the field itself, there was a wire-enclosed asketball court where two white youngsters were shooting bas-ets. Between that and the street, an old man sat on a park bench eading a newspaper. I pondered the value of walking down to ie piers, but there seemed to be absolutely no point to it. I egan to think about lunch and turned back the way I had come.

That's when I saw him. It seems strange to me that the legs iould have identified him so clearly. I don't recall that I had ven seen his legs in that fetid hotel room—only the big face anging in the air above that incredible expanse of chest, and the ietronomic spool of fishing line. But those legs, I thought, ould belong to no one else. They grew like tree trunks out of ie pavement, to which they were fixed by a pair of sea boots iat seemed hardly bigger than galoshes climbing up the long, iick calves. The legs ended up higher in the air than any legs ad a right to do. He was bent over the engine of a car. The ood was raised, and he was bent nearly double to reach down nd work in the interior. I stepped backward as he stood up, olding a small grayish patch of material. I recognized him. He irew the stuff disgustedly on the ground and bent again to lose imself under the hood of the huge old car.

Walking quickly helped me to stop shaking and to even off the great gulps of air that were pounding into my chest. I went along the sidewalk several cars down from where he was working on the middle strip, crossed the street to get up on the strip, and then headed back toward his car. I had my gun out, although not exposed to casual view, by the time I reach his car. I came up on the other side of it and pointed my gun under the hood, where he was working.

He was so intent on fixing the car that it took him a while to recognize what was happening. I couldn't see his face, of course, but he must have looked up to see the gun pointing at him under the hood. He straightened himself out very carefully.

We looked at each other over the angle of the upraised hood. "If you fuck around, Roger," I said, "I'll kill you right here and right now." The gun was still hidden from common view under the hood of the car, but both of us knew where it was pointing.

His face was utterly impassive. I wasn't even sure he had recognized me. He said, "What you want, man?"

The truth was that at that moment I didn't know what I wanted. I knew that he had sensed it, and I stepped backward slightly to get a better aim at him. I couldn't very well march him to the police station holding a gun on him. I had no idea who his friends might be in this area. I certainly wasn't going to get into a car with him, gun or no gun. I said, "I've got to talk to you and get some answers."

"Go ahead and talk," said Roger Grim.

"Not here, asshole," I said. "We'll go over to the piers, there." I nodded toward the field and the piers beyond. "You first; and remember, no moves. I'd be happy to see you dead, talk or no talk." When he began to move those long arms, I said, "Forget the car. Leave the hood up. Just step back, turn around, and start walking. If you even fart, I'll kill you."

I don't know what kind of picture we made to the casual observer as we crossed that long, long field. Roger walked well ahead of me at a carefully measured pace, and I followed, gun in hand, but concealed by my coat pocket. If he had stopped suddenly, I would have shot him. He did not stop. The two kids in the basketball cage were into one-on-one, and the old man on the bench had finished his paper and fallen asleep. Roger picked out a footpath through the burdock that covered the field, and the trip, while lengthy, was not difficult. When we reached the

:arest pier, he stopped. I said, "Turn around, slowly." He did. Now," I said, "be very careful and step back on to the pier. If e sit down out here, we'll be out of sight. And that's the way I ant it." Roger, reaching back with his booted foot, stepped :ry carefully on to the dead black planks of the pier. I came ter him, with extreme caution. "We'll sit down here," I said, :sturing toward two pilings on either side of the pier. "We'll sit own here and talk." He sat immediately, with his back against piling. I sat down on the other side against an opposite piling. 'e were hidden from view, but Roger's piling was just a bit ioreside of mine. I didn't think it mattered at the moment.

"Now, Roger," I said to him—I had put my pistol at the Port rms position, diagonally flat against my chest so that he couldn't ick out and grab the barrell—"I'd like to hear what that was all bout up at the Cardinal Hotel."

He said, "You deaf, ain't you." It seemed to be a flat atement. "You can't hear."

"That's right, Roger," I answered. "I read lips. I read your ps very well. I can't hear my gun go off, of course, but neither ill anybody else from where we are right now." He seemed to nile slightly. "Now tell me what happened at the Cardinal."

"I got into this room by mistake," said Roger. "And it :emed like you was coming in to knock me over. I just defend- ig myself, that's all. Then I was scared that maybe I hurt you me, and I took off. That's all that happened."

"I tell you what, Roger," I said. "You're an athlete, and you now about bone chips. But maybe you've never seen chips of one flying up in the air when a man is shot in the knee. If I on't get my answers right away, that's exactly what you're oing to see. I've got plenty of bullets in my pocket, and when ve put this load into your knees and elbows, you're not going be able to stop me from reloading. Do you understand? Do ou read me?"

"You like one of them kinky kneecappers?" Roger asked me.

"I'm as kinky as I have to be," I told him. "You want to flop hen you walk from here on in, that's your business."

I wanted to give him a chance to think about the bone chips nd the pain before automatic bravado set in, however, so I hanged the subject radically. I asked him, "What's the matter ith your car?"

"Damn fool I lent it to put gasohol in it. Filled it up. Gummed p the gas filter."

The civilized question had caused, automatically, a civilize response. That was good. That meant he could think rationally this moment and think about what a bullet could do to him Athletes know something about pain that ordinary people don know until they are much older. Athletes can be realists about i "You'll have to blow out the gas line or she'll clog up all ove again," I told him. I looked openly into his face. It was massive but it was also intelligent and sensitive. The malevolence, whic had been my earlier picture, was not there as he thought abo his car.

"Yeah. I know I will." Then the malevolence began to cree back across his face. "That what you bring me down here to te me?"

"You know why I brought you down here," I answered. "Eithe I get answers, or you get hurt."

"You think that little thing up against your chest make yo God," said Roger. "When I'm ready, I'm going to take it awa and you're going to eat it."

I took the gun away from my chest, pointed it in the directio of Roger's head, and pulled the trigger.

He went over on his right side and clutched the left side of hi face. When he took his hand away, he saw the blood on it Looking up at me, he said, "You shot me." He was as amaze as he was hurt.

"I didn't shoot you," I said. "I shot the piling next to you head. You've got a splinter in your cheek. Pull it out."

He explored his cheek again and touched the two-inch splinte sticking into his face. He gritted his teeth and pulled it out "Any funny moves or funny answers, Roger, and the next roun will go into you," I told him. "Sit up and look at me." He sa up, but moved cautiously further from the piling, as if it ha been the piling that had assaulted him. "Now, once again, wha was all that at the hotel?"

"They said you been screwing around up there. They said t dump you.'

"They is a big world, Roger. Who is they?"

"Oh, man, don't be really crazy. You think I'm sitting o somebody's knee? I don't know nobody. I do what I'm told."

"You get radio messages through the fillings in your teeth, d you?" I asked him. The gun twitched up against my chest.

"They left a message in the hotel," he said impatiently "with George."

"George is the old guy? The desk clerk?"

Roger nodded.

"I don't believe you," I said. "There's no way anybody would trust him with a thing like that. Information may go out of George, but he's no pipeline. Think again, Roger, and think fast, because I'm getting fucking sick of this."

He touched the trickle of blood that was now beginning to dry before it dripped off his chin, and looked hard at me. I looked hard right back. "They sent the kid over to my place," he said.

I interrupted. "The Gypsy Rose kid?"

"Huh?" He thought about it. "Yeah. Winey. The kid that drinks all the wine. They sent him over because I don't have a phone. Don't want one. Never heard nothing good over a phone. And the kid said I should go out and call Irish Larry."

"Irish Larry Feltzheimer," I said.

"Yeah. You know him?"

"I've heard of him. Never saw him, except for a photograph. I know he was mixed up in gunrunning."

"He's mixed up in a lot," said Roger. "So when I went down and called him—it was a pay phone, you know—he told me what to do. He said I should dump you."

"Kill me?"

"If I had to."

"And did you have to?"

"I don't know," said Roger Grim. "When you get to beatin' on somebody, it feels pretty good, you know? When I hit you that shot down there," he inclined his head slightly, and his eyes sought out the lower quadrant of my abdomen, "I thought, 'By God, that's done it. That bust his spleen all right.' " A faint smile of reminiscence stole over his face.

I asked him gently, "Has it always felt that good, Roger? All your life?"

"Oh," he shrugged, almost modestly, it seemed. "I was always the enforcer, even in the playground, in high school, because I was so strong. A lot of big men," he commented, "there's a lot of 'em, but they ain't all strong, I mean strong like me. A lot of 'em ain't just naturally strong—just tall—and some lose their strength, or ruin it, you know. Even the clap," he mused, "you can catch the clap and lose your strength. You know that? It gets into the joints, where the muscles come into the bones. I never had the clap," he asserted. "I always stayed strong."

"But did you always enjoy beating on people?"

"No," he said soberly. He turned his head slightly to look out over the peaceful bay. "When I was playing, it was just an assignment, like anything else. Sure, I was proud of myself that I could do it, you know. But it's only lately that I get the jive."

"Do you like that?" I asked him.

"Like, don't like, what's the difference? I do what the man says."

"Why do you do it? You've got a job, haven't you? That's all that anybody else has got, and a lot of them don't have that."

"Are you really stupid?" he asked me earnestly. "Or are you playing games with me just because you got the piece in your hand? Who do you think got me the job? Where do you think I'm going to get another?

"*This,*" he said, nodding his head toward the bay, "is what they meant when they said they were going to take care of me after I took the fall. 'Take the fall, Rog,' they said. 'How bad can it be? Take the fall and we'll take care of you.' " He smiled a bitter smile, and his eyes smoldered. "So I'm took care of. And this is how I'm took care of. On a fishboat. I'm still supposed to be an enforcer, but they won't take me right in among 'em, because I look too different. So I'm like a janitor, just cleaning up here and there for them."

"So you cleaned up Arnold for them."

"Who?"

"Arnold Pelfrey, the man on the string."

He looked at me a long, long time before he answered, so long that I became uncomfortable, even though I was holding the gun. "The little guy up in the hotel," he said. "Yeah. I did him."

"Did you enjoy that, too?" I asked him.

"Got away slick, didn't I?" said Roger with a slight grin. "But when I found the spool on the table, I knew you dug it. You had to go, man."

He conjured the scene up for me. "That Pelfrey was a wiry little bastard," he said. "Fought like hell, and I couldn't hit him 'cause they didn't want any marks. Had to catch him, shove my watch cap in his mouth and hold him under my arm. Got his arms tied with his belt so he couldn't scratch, and I still had trouble measuring him up and all. Had to hold him between my legs while I tied the bowline, then hold him up to it with one hand, practically. Got him, though, huh? Slick."

"What did you do with the bundle?" I asked him.

"Bundle? What bundle?"

"C'mon, Roger."

He smiled a very wide smile, then, the blood on his cheek forgotten. "Oh, yeah," he said. "There was a bundle. They wanted the bundle. It was about just so big, in a heavy kind of envelope, you know, fastened up with string and all. About this big, I think." He held his hands up to indicate the size of the envelope—about twelve to fourteen inches long—and I tried to figure out if anything that size could carry the amount of money Bill was missing when Grim's foot lashed out and pinned the gun to my chest.

The amazing thing was that he hadn't kicked me. His foot had thrust out like the head of a thick snake and simply pinned my hand, gun, chest, and back to the piling behind me. The move was perfectly timed and perfectly measured. From the moment he had rolled to one side at the shot next to his head, he had changed his position, millimeter by millimeter, imperceptibly closer to me. Now he had me. He bent forward, doubling over his legs with a fluidity only an athlete could achieve, and reached for the barrel of the gun pinioned under my hand. He rolled his foot a bit so that the side of the boot cut into my wrist and numbed my hand. Roger pulled the gun out of my hand and sat back, upright with it. I remained in petrified stillness and silence. He weighed the gun, which looked like a toy in his huge hand, and smiled at me. It was not a reassuring smile. I expected at that moment that he would shoot me and dump me off the pier. Instead, he tossed the gun up in his hand, like the weighing of a bag of coins, and then with a wide sweeping arc of his arm threw it far out into the bay. It twinkled in its flight through the air and disappeared in the water. Roger took his foot off my chest. He stood up, then, and so did I. He had much farther to go up into the air, but he got there first.

The very slight advantage he'd had in shoreside position was monumental now. I was cut off from any escape to the field and the road beyond. I knew, however, that even if I'd been able to run, those incredibly long, educated legs of his would have overtaken me before I was within shouting distance of the street. I backed away in the only direction I had, toward the end of the pier. I thought, then, of jumping off the side of the pier, but my least move in that direction triggered a response in his big curving arm that shut it off. He would have caught me in my leap as a bear spears a salmon with his claws. I concentrated on staying out of the reach of those giant hands that could grip the top of my head more easily than they could a basketball. Very slowly, I threaded my way back down the pier, just beyond the reach of the long, roundhouse, almost lazy blows he aimed at me. He wasn't serious yet. Roger was enjoying himself again. I was terrified of stumbling over the rough timbers of the pier as I made my slow progress backward, crossing from one side of the pier to the other in the hope of getting him to commit himself so I could leap. He didn't have to commit himself. He advanced slowly, and with each step, one of the long arms would sweep out like the blade of a scythe.

At last, out of the corner of my eye, I saw the end of the universe. The pier ended its stretch into the water. Roger grinned at me. He said, "You run out of runnin' room, man." And then so help me, he *wound up*—it was more than just telegraphing a blow—he wound up almost like a baseball pitcher to throw a fist at my more-or-less stationary head. I waited at the absolute end of the pier, tensed in a semi-crouch. He launched the long blow, pivoting on his left foot, but I pivoted, too, on my right, and leaped up into him, catching his looping arm with both of mine, and threw all my weight off the end of the pier. We both went in the water.

The furious clubbing of his other fist exploded in my head as we sank under the surface. The clubbing continued, but with much diminished force in the depths of the water, and, hanging on to the lone, long arm with both of mine, I kicked as powerfully as I could, not at Roger, but to pull us away from the pier and out into the deep freedom of the bay. I kicked again and again, and then releasing one of my arms from his, I began a sidestroke to carry us farther away. All of this was underwater, and I could only estimate how far we had gone from the pier. But I wanted a better hold on Roger, and let him go.

Sheer pinwheel energy thrashed him to the surface, where he swiveled his head to look wildly about. When he saw how far he was from the pier, he opened his mouth in what could only have been a despairing cry. His eyes were full of terror. My guess, an educated guess to be sure, had been quite correct. Like many black men, and some white men, Roger could neither swim nor float. It seems to be a matter of the specific gravity of the individual. It was certainly an immediate test of whether one was suitable for underwater demolition in the Navy, and I had seen many an uncomprehending candidate turned down for this exact reason. Roger's head turned toward me, and with an imploring expression on his face, he cried, "Save me!" The words were barely out when the heavy sea boots, filled with water now, pulled him down beneath the waves. I doubled in the water, pulled the laces to my shoes, and kicked them off.

Roger thrashed again to the surface, and I dived beneath him to catch his weighted ankles and pull him to the bottom. With both my arms clasped around his calves, I held him on the bottom for a full minute. He thrashed his arms insanely and tried to kick, and tried to beat my buried head away with his fists, but there was, of course, no real force in the blows. After thirty seconds he seemed to go limp, but I suspected that this was a trick, if he was still capable of trickery, and I held him there for the full minute. It was much more than a minute for Roger, of course, because he wasn't counting time; *I* was. More seriously, panic was exhausting his oxygen. Finally, I released his ankles and kicked my way to the surface. I regained my breath and waited for Roger. He did not reappear.

I dived down again and found him, inert, in the shape of a fetus, floating a few feet off the murky bottom of the bay. I pulled his sea boots off and he began to rise in the water like a waterlogged galleon freed up by a storm. I took the cuffs out of my back pocket and snapped one over the big powerless wrist. The other I used for a handhold to tow him back with a sidestroke to the end of the pier. What had looked like the distance between life and death to Roger had not really been very far. A huge pad eye was fixed with lug screws to one of the pilings, and I passed the other cuff through this before snapping it on Roger's other wrist. Then I grabbed him by the belt and boosted him up in the water so that his head was clear. I thumped him on the back with my other hand to knock some of the sea water loose and let a little oxygen trickle back. It took a while, but he came around. He snorted powerfully, gagged, and threw up some of the oily contents of the bay. He kicked and struggled blindly with the cuffs that held him to the big steel loop, and, finally, his red eyes looked at me.

"It's all over but a little talking, Roger," I told him. I was supporting myself in the water with one hand lightly on the pad eye where the link of the chain went through. "Who told you to kill Arnold Pelfrey?"

"I don't know," said Roger.

I braced myself against the piling, put one hand on the top of his head and pushed him under the waves. I counted to thirty and released the pressure. It took a count to sixty before he recovered. "Each time I have to push you down, it's going to be longer," I told him, "until it's so long that you'll be dead. Do you understand? I'd rather have you dead than alive anyway. And I'm not going away from here ignorant and you alive too."

"They told me by telephone," said Roger. "I don't know who was on the other end."

"Tell me about it," I instructed him.

"They sent Winey to get me. He said Irish Larry wanted to see me at the hotel, the room behind the desk, and I should get right over there. So, I went over, and Irish Larry told me, 'There's going to be somebody tell you to do something over the telephone, and you're going to do it. You understand?' And I said, yes, I understood.

"So Irish Larry says, 'You stand over here,' and he turns his back like he didn't want me to see who he was calling, you know, what number he was dialing. So finally he got who it was he wanted, and he hands the phone to me, and he says, 'Now listen and listen good.'

"There was a voice I never heard before talking to me. The man said I was supposed to go up and dump this guy Pelfrey, and if I could, make it look like a suicide. He said I wouldn't have any trouble getting in. Pelfrey was waiting for me. He said there'd be good marks for me if I made it look like a suicide. Then he said I was supposed to get a bundle from Pelfrey—actually, I was supposed to get that first, that Pelfrey would hand it over to me without any problem. After I left, I was supposed to give the bundle to Irish Larry. That's all there was."

"Irish Larry waited downstairs while you did it?"

"No. No. He went over to the Coffee Pot, it's on Eighth Avenue, and he waited there in a booth. I took the envelope over to him and told him how it went, you know? And he says, 'Good. Now you stay here for a while.' And then I saw him go out and hand it, the bundle . . . it was an envelope . . . to somebody sitting in a car in front of the place."

"Did he come back into the restaurant?"

"No. I waited about fifteen minutes and then I left."

I asked him, "Are you sure you don't know what number he dialed?"

"No, I don't."

"Was it local or long distance?"

"I don't know."

I looked at him reflectively. "I'd like to kill you, you know," I said conversationally. "What's more, I could get away with it. You sure you haven't got something to tell me?"

"That's all I know," said Roger.

I believed him. Before his startled eyes I swam quickly under the pier and kept going until it was shallow enough to stand. I walked up on to the ragged beach and continued across the field, cursing each time a sharp stone dug into my wet socks on the crooked footpath. Finally, I pulled the socks off and threw them away.

No one on the street seemed to pay any attention to a fully clothed but barefoot, soaking wet man making his way up the business district. They keep them cool in Sheepshead Bay. I got in my car and drove to the nearest precinct house.

They had seen wet pedestrians before. Falling off piers is not unheard of in this end of Brooklyn. But they became more interested when I identified myself and asked them to rescue Roger.

"Before you go down there, though," I told them, "you'd better call Lieutenant Shope. Roger's his pigeon. Also you better take plenty of beef down there with you. Once you get him on dry land, the guy is an army.

"Tell Shope I'll meet him down at his station house. I'll sign the complaint and give him the story. Right now I want to get home and get some dry clothes on, or I'll catch pneumonia."

That seemed to round it out. Except, just before leaving I advised them that they'd better not wait too long to rescue Roger. "Unless I'm mistaken," I said, "there's a tide coming in."

24

Stacked on my desk the next morning were a number of interesting documents, not the least of which was a blank envelope containing a check for a very sizable amount: one of the three that had long been overdue. I waved the check at Edna and said, "Two down, one to go. Edna, you're a genius."

"None to go," said Edna. "It didn't work with the last one."

"Didn't work?" I asked with my usual lancetlike intelligence.

"I had Creative Floorings set up the same way, but when I went over there the Accounts Payable lady said I would have to talk to Mr. Rosenquist, who is a very disagreeable man."

"Rosenquist," I said, "wasn't disagreeable when he hired me."

Rosenquist, in fact, had been fawning. His highly skilled workers had been installing floors by moonlight, using expensive hardwoods extracted from Mr. Rosenquist's warehouse by stealth and guile. The evidence I had provided Mr. Rosenquist with had been so complete as to permit him to be shockingly vindictive. But the evidence had been the result of many hours of long hard work. His vindictiveness should have been the tip-off.

"Well, he was disagreeable to me," Edna sniffed. "He came out of his office—what an ugly man!—so tall, so beautifully dressed, and so ugly! And he said, 'I don't want you coming over here and bothering the help, young lady.' And I said, 'I have no desire to see your help or your horrible office, and I will be happy to leave as soon as you give me our check.' And he said, and he was smiling this very nasty smile when he said it, he said, 'Sue me!"

"Sue me!" I repeated, outraged. "Is he crazy? It costs money to sue people. Sometimes more money than it's worth."

"That," said Edna wisely, "is what I think Mr. Rosenquist had in mind."

"Call Anthony," I told her. "Tell him I want to see him here this afternoon, and there's a hundred bucks a day for him in it until he picks up the check."

Edna regarded me for some time before she acquiesced. She said, "I suppose there's no help for it. But *Anthony!*" She shuddered.

"Right after you call Anthony," I said, "we've got a toughie to chase down. I spent most of yesterday in the station house explaining to Lieutenant Shope how and why I found and caught Roger Grim. I swore out the complaint, and I laid the murder of Pelfrey on him. It took me hours to get loose from Shope. I was supposed to tell him everything.

"Now, one thing I didn't mention to him," I said to Edna, "was Irish Larry Feltzheimer." I stared into space. "In fact, I shouldn't even mention the name to you. You'd do well to forget that I mentioned it. Irish Larry is not a person to have heard of. I want no part of him. And yet," I picked up a pencil and stared at its point, "Irish Larry is the link between Grim and the disappearance of Bill's money."

"You're going to go out and get him? This Irish Larry?" Edna asked, enthralled.

"I most certainly am not," I told her frankly. "Irish Larry has, in his time, supplied half the world's armies and gangs with illegal armament. It would take nearly another army to get hold of him and bring him in. What is more," I lectured her, "is that once you've got hold of him, you've got exactly nothing. You won't get one word of information, and unless you've got him with the gun in his hand, you haven't got anything that sticks.

"What makes him particularly dangerous right now," I added, "is that he's like a rogue animal, a lion or an elephant that's gone past his prime. He's run out the string on gunrunning, and so he does odd jobs to keep his hand in. He is one of the most dangerous men I can think of. Grabbing Irish Larry is out."

Edna looked at me very disapprovingly. She often does that because very often I make good sense when I talk to her. Edna doesn't like good sense. She likes romance.

"What we're going to do," I told her, "is make an end run around Irish Larry, and still find out what the connection is. He had to call a number from the Cardinal Hotel to connect Roger Grim with instructions for the setup—they didn't even trust *him* to relay the instructions. Now, all calls from that hotel business phone are recorded on the bill. So I want you to call the phone company and whine at them that someone is making unauthorized calls from the business phone. You tell them you can't find the bill—maybe it wasn't even sent out yet—but you want the list of numbers that were called on the last week in March and the first week of April. Tell them you need the numbers right this minute. My guess is that they can push a couple of buttons and get a readout on a CRT in five seconds flat. They can read off the numbers to you, and you can copy them down in your flawless shorthand. O.K.? And when that's finished, tell them to send copies of the bill or both bills to this address here, since we are tracking down this dangerous illicit dialer for the management of the Cardinal Hotel."

"Meanwhile, Irish Larry goes free," she said with a frown.

"And long may he wave," I agreed. "If I can get the information without troubling his brow, that is exactly what I'm going to do."

"He's more dangerous than Roger Grim?"

"Infinitely. People like Roger Grim want no part of him."

She sighed and said, "All right," and reached for the phone; but I interrupted her.

"Before you do any of these things with the phone company, I want you to try to get Bill Macready on the phone for me. It's nothing important. Just bat the breeze with him for a few minutes, and tell him I wanted him to know I'm making progress."

"Should I tell him about Roger Grim?"

"Sure. Why not?"

I watched her dial and speak into the phone, and then I saw her lips purse and her nose wrinkle. The obligatory "*thank you*" and "*goodbye*" were snapped out with very ill grace indeed.

"Honestly," said Edna. "That answering service . . ."

"He's not home?" I asked her. "At this hour? He's usually in bed at this hour in the morning. That call should have woken him up."

"They said he is not answering his telephone," said Edna. "Which is something I didn't need some half-wit answering service to tell me."

"I'm going to take a quick trip over there right now," I decided aloud. "I meant to go last night, but I spent last night talking to Shope. I don't like the feel of this. Maybe he *is* shacked up someplace, but I think he'd let us know." I got up from my chair and told her, "I'll be back in an hour or so. Start grinding on the phone company."

It was a beautiful day, and I took the bus uptown so as to stare at the people tromping the sidewalks as in an hypnotic trance. I felt liberated for the hour, since the next move devolved on finding a significant number. My only grain of unease at this moment was wondering where the hell Bill had got to. I comforted myself that he was so irresponsible in everyday matters that the least sinister explanation was probably the correct one.

I got off in midtown and walked the few blocks to Bill's place, which looked even shabbier and more dilapidated in the fresh light of morning. The door, as usual, was swung open, and the simple smell that spilled out over the steps announced that the hallway was not deserted. The morning light did not quite reach to the stairway, and the four bums sitting on the stairs with a fifth of Night Train among them were not very recognizable. They seemed more tattered and degraded than anything I had seen this side of the Bowery. One of them was particularly loathsome, with the filmy stare of idiocy on his face and a smell so rank that I held my breath as I stepped up past him.

The odor faded as I ascended the dimly lighted stairs. At the top, I hammered on the door, pressed the bell, waited, and then leaned on the door bell. Nothing responded. Aware of the state of the old building's wiring, I began to hammer on the door again and shout, "Bill. Bill. It's me, Joe Binney. Open up." By this time I was more concerned with intruding on Bill *in flagrante delicto*. I waited a suitable time to give him a chance to open the door. Again, nothing happened.

I still had the key that Bill had given me as a guest, and I put it in the lock. My heart jumped a little when I tried to turn it because it would not turn. I turned it the other way, and the deadfall lock snapped shut. Then I unlocked it again. It was rare that Bill would leave the lock open, even when he was inside. I eased the door open, prepared for the halt of the chain lock. Nothing impeded the swing of the door. I stood at the threshold warily and called out again, "Bill? Bill? It's me, Joe." I couldn't see that anything had stirred. I stepped in and closed the door behind me.

I went directly to Bill's bedroom to see if he was drunk, asleep, or hopelessly engaged in some sexual entanglement. Niceties had disappeared. I noted only that the bedroom was empty and went quickly to the spare room that I had inhabited. The hospital bed and all the equipment had been removed by the agency. No one was in the kitchen. I went back and stood in the center of the big room, feeling an increasing sense of unease in my bones.

There was none of the classic mysteriousness about the empty place, no half-eaten meals or still-warm coffee pots—no sense of things having been put down hastily and left there, of dramatic interruption. Neither did the place have that neat, barren, untenanted look of a dwelling that has been left for a set period of time, even as vacation cottages are neatened up before the occupants leave to return for the next weekend.

I went into the bedroom again and noted that the bed had not been made up. This was not too unusual for Bill, whose sleeping arrangements were pretty catch-as-catch-can, and whose bed was put to frequent and vigorous use. There were cigarettes of various brands smoked down to the cork tips or down to very short butts snuffed out in the ash trays. The apartment was disordered, but not in disarray. I stood still again, very still, to let the sensations sink in on me. Then I realized what it was had made me uneasy. The smell. It was only a faint echo of the smell down in the hallway, but it was very definitely here. I hadn't noticed it at first, because I had carried part of it up with me in my nostrils. But now, as I sniffed the air again, it was very plain to me that the smell was coming from the apartment itself. In all the time I had stayed here as a guest, the smell had never climbed those stairs to penetrate the metal-clad door.

The disturbing thing about the smell is that it is redolent, reminiscent, of death. It is the smell of living bodies decaying in their own juices, of live men rotting like the dead. I've smelled it in drunk tanks, flop houses, and even in the street, when one bum came to the open window of my car and offered to clean my windshield with a greasy rag. It was not a smell that belonged in Bill's apartment. It unnerved me so much that I went back into the bedroom and looked under the bed to make sure a body wasn't lying there. To make a complete job of it, I checked the few cabinets and closets in the place.

Trying to put it together, I decided that Bill had left in a hurry, probably with a chick, had forgotten to lock up in the full fit of tumescence, and so had left the place open for the bums to wander in. It was, at least, an interpretation I could live with. I locked the door carefully after me and descended the stairs, sinking with each flight of steps more deeply into the odor that haunted the penthouse. When I got to the bottom, I stepped past the four bums and then wheeled suddenly to confront them.

"Listen to me, you bastards," I said. "You've been fucking around in the apartment upstairs. Don't do it again."

Three of them looked dumbfounded, perhaps only that somebody would bother to address them directly. But all three of them, as if by reflex, then stared at the idiotic character, who hung his head.

"You," I said to him. "Look at me. Are you the one who broke in?" He would not raise his head high enough for me to see any answers, and somehow, I could not bring myself to lay my hands on him. "I'm going to be back here, and often," I said. "I'm going to be watching you bastards. If I catch anybody up around there, I'm going to break every fucking bone in his body. Do you understand that? Believe me. I'll do it." All four of them dropped their heads and looked at their puffy shoes.

The futile threatening of that tattered group built up such a frustrated head of steam in me that I decided to walk back to the office and let the waves of adrenaline subside. I slowed my pace so that it took me more than forty-five minutes to get there. When I arrived, I felt reasonably calm and restored.

The first thing I saw coming into my office was a broad back covered with blue serge that could have only one identification. It was Anthony. He had answered the bell like a firehorse. I slapped him on the back and yelled out a greeting. He turned toward me slowly. I suppose the slap on the back had had the same impression as a fly landing on his ear.

Anthony's back is very broad, as I have mentioned, and is also the nicest part of him to look at. The face takes a little preparation. Anthony is an ex-cop who once confronted the mob and for his pains they threw acid in his face, eating out one eye and then clubbed him in the center of the forehead with a short-handled maul. They left him for dead, but Anthony was not dead; he was rather horribly disfigured, not only from the acid, but from the sunken impression on his forehead that is shadowed like a crater on the moon. He was also rather permanently stupefied. Anthony was now good for simple tasks requiring no more than one issue at a time—like bill collecting. The income he got from it added to his very well deserved police pension. I grabbed him by his huge, calloused hand and pulled him into my office. He stood in front of the desk as if on report. I spoke clearly and slowly. I gave him the address of Creative Flooring, and the mission. The mission was to say: "*I've come for Joe Binney's check,*" and to stay in the place until somebody gave him a check with my name on it. "Have you got all that, Anthony?" I asked him.

"I sure do, Joe," the burnt lips said. The flinching and the expression on Edna's face reaffirmed what I had so often been told, but could not, of course, experience for myself. Anthony has a voice like an earthquake. I wrote out a check for a hundred and handed it to him. "That's the retainer," I said. "From here on in, it's a hundred a day and expenses."

"This is plenty," said Anthony. "Thanks, Joe." We shook hands, and he returned my numb limb to me just before turning and leaving.

Edna looked dubious. "Are you sure he won't get into trouble?" she asked me.

"Trouble? Anthony? For what?"

"Well," said Edna, "if they ask him to leave and he won't, can't they call the police and have him put out?"

"There isn't a cop in town who doesn't know Anthony," reassured her. "And the one thing they all know is that whateve he's doing, it's clean. He may be slow, and he may get a littl emotional at times, but Anthony's clean."

Edna set a list of typed figures in front of me. "It worked," she said.

I marveled at her. "You need a raise," I said. "I'm nc kidding. After we get through with this, we'll talk about it." Edna smiled, sat down, and crossed her legs. My computation soared.

She had typed out the numbers almost in a facsimile of phone bill itself. All the dates, times of the call, and charge were arranged in orderly rows. I was getting more from Edn than I had been paying for. We went over the numbers together "I'm surprised that there were so few calls, I mean for a hotel," Edna remarked. I said nothing, but reflected that the Cardina Hotel was hardly a hub of commerce. One local number wa repeated day after day. "That's George's bookie," I told her "Once a day, every day, seven days a week. Like clockwork."

But while I was talking I had already spotted what I wa looking for, and I tried to even out my breathing so my hear wouldn't jump through my nose. "That's it," I said, pointing t the number of a long-distance call. "The date fits. Everythin fits." I sat back and thought about it. "Jesus Christ," I said. "I really does fit." I picked up one of the documents from the pil that Edna had prepared for me. Again, she had done a magnifi cent job. Photocopied articles were set in one stack, type reports in another.

"Call the Sherry-Netherland," I asked her, "and get me meeting as soon as possible with Garson, Cy Garson." Whil she was on the phone, I began to read my way through one o the stacks.

Edna put down the phone. She said, "Mr. Garson checked ou last night."

"All right," I said, still reading, "get me on a plane arrivin in L.A. first thing tomorrow morning. Then call this number an tell them I'm going to see Mr. Garson tomorrow morning. Don' ask. Tell."

"What number?" asked Edna.

I fished in my wallet and took out the scrap of paper tha Garson had scribbled on. "That number," I said. Edna's eye got very round.

"I'm taking this stack home with me while I get ready," I old her. "And I'll finish reading it on the plane. You're much nore than any broken-down gumshoe deserves, and I love you."

Edna sat back, pleased. "But no resting, damn it," I said, at vhich she sat up again. "I want you to start making calls all over the place: Norman—Bill's agent, Vincent Namier, anybody you can think of, and see if you can find out where the hell Bill Macready has got to."

25

The plane dropped me in LAX, rumpled, grumbling, and with a nervous system that seemed to be made mostly of barbed wire. I considered going into the men's room to clean up and shave, but decided against it. If I looked as rough as I felt, I decided, it would be a distinct advantage.

I took my old oversized briefcase, which contained my toilet kit, shirt, underwear, and socks, in the unlikely event that I would be detained for another day, out to the cab rank, where I waited with all the other stunned passengers who were still emerging from this swift transmittal of their flesh. By the contented look on the cab driver's face when I gave him the address, I was confirmed in the suspicion that I would need a sizable amount of cash to navigate the endless wilderness of Los Angeles. I had stopped at the bank on my way home from the office for just such a provision. The ride was a toiling through a series of concrete gullies, which had been, with savage irony, called freeways.

I had expected to be taken to one of the glittering new office buildings, whose peaks I could discern beyond the freeways. Instead, the cab pulled up before a gateway in a mustard-colored wall that seemed to extend for several blocks. I gave my name to the guard. He looked it up on a list and called another guard, who escorted me to a low-slung building with a balcony running around the second floor. There I was turned over to a pert young thing whose shapely behind preceded me up a flight of stairs to a large, well-appointed waiting room. I was then handed over to a less pert, which is to say a much more businesslike, secretar with graying hair and a very stern face, who ushered me into th sanctum sanctorum of Cy Garson himself.

There was no desk in the room. As in the Sherry-Netherlan Garson seemed to confine his surfaces to coffee tables. It was very good, very large coffee table that fronted him from the lo Venetian-looking couch he sat on, and it seemed to support ju as many papers in the way of business as any desk could hold. young man, carefully dressed in sports clothes, stood anxiousl to one side of him staring down at what appeared to be a pile checks. He apparently was waiting for Garson to sign them Garson was staring at them as though they were a nest of p vipers about to sink their fangs in his wrist. Aware of my entry he waved at me without really looking up.

He said to the young man, who had bent close to hear, "Wh are you bringing me all this?"

"These are all due, sir" (or was it Cy?) "and the checks a made out, but they need your signature."

"These people are all screaming? Beating down the doors?" asked Garson.

"No, sir."

"Put this stack to one side," said Garson, "and bring the back one month from today."

The young man's face became quite tense. "It will double th load by then," he said.

"So?"

The young man shrugged then, albeit a very mild, ingratiatin shrug. "It all depends on what kind of credit picture you want t draw," he said.

"Credit picture," Garson repeated. He looked at me, finally and indicated the young man with his eyebrows. "Stanford," h said, "MBA. Do you believe it?" Then he said to the youn man, "There's no way I'm going to turn loose of this kind o money all at once like this. Can't you dance around a little Protect the picture? Keep us looking good?"

"Certainly," said this flower of academe. "I'll draw up memo for short-term credit payment."

"And this will look legit?"

"Certainly, sir." (Cy?)

"Then do it." He handed the young man the stack of check and dismissed him with a glance. The young man vaporize from the room. Garson leaned back on the couch and smiled u at me. "Good to see you, Joe," he said. "What can I do for you?"

I smiled back through my day's growth of beard. "You can knock off the horseshit about the quaint little town in Michigan for starters," I said. "Ecorse is where you come from."

The trouble with his smile is that it didn't change at all. It froze on his face, hung there, and glittered like a ledge of ice. Then he said, "Tell me about it."

"Ecorse is a southeast suburb of Detroit," I recited, "conveniently bordered by the Detroit River, which to this day is paved with man-sized blocks of cement, many of which contain a man, or the remains of one."

Garson's smile broadened. "You're good," he said. "Keep going."

"Ecorse," I said, "was one of the old stamping grounds, or stomping grounds, of the Purple Gang."

"Ancient history," said Garson. "Where do you get these ideas?"

"From sitting up all night reading on airplanes. But you're the one who really gave me the idea." His smile just barely twitched. We seemed to have a war of smiles going on between us.

"The white hats," I said. "I couldn't figure out what you meant by 'the white hats' up there in the hotel. But it finally clicked. The Purple Gang was famous for their white hats, among other things."

He waved me away as if brushing off a fly. "Everybody wore white hats those days. You're not telling me anything."

"The old mob wore white Borsalinos because they were the sign of a well-dressed man with a little money," I said. "But the Purple Gang made a fetish, a badge, almost a mockery out of them."

"It's still ancient history," said Garson. "It's all gone, years and years ago."

"The Purple Gang faded out of Detroit," I said, "but like the Mayfield Road gang out of Cleveland, they drifted out here to the Coast. This is where the action was, and this is what drew the money."

"You flew three-thousand miles to tell me you don't like white hats?"

"I came here to talk about money."

"This crap won't draw you any five-hundred dollars, Joe."

"Specifically," I continued, "about William Macready's money.

When I go back to the airport, I'm going to have it in my briefcase. If, by some mischance, I shouldn't get back to the airport and be smiling at my desk tomorrow morning, there is going to be a lot of interesting material handed over to the New York Police and a number of other agencies."

Garson put his hands on his knees and sat forward. "Is this a heist?" he asked.

"Stop the bullshit, Cy," I said. (I certainly wasn't going to call him sir.) "I picked up Roger Grim." His eyebrows went up. "Who is now a very big man in a very small cell. Through him, I wound up with a lot of interesting numbers and names. Please note that *I've* got them, not the police. Nor are they apt to get them unless I turn over the stuff."

"You've got what," asked Garson. I suppose his voice was as flat as his face.

"I have got, for one thing, your link to the Cardinal Hotel. Pull that string, and the girl falls out of the basket, don't you think?"

"What are you looking for?"

"Not justice," I assured him. "That's not my business. I know how and why Arnold Pelfrey was killed, but he's not my client. Bill Macready is my client. I want Bill Macready's money back. Every fucking dime of it. That's what I was hired for."

"You want to make a deal," said Garson.

"Certainly I want to make a deal," I answered, "I'm deaf, but not crazy."

"But you brought in the big ball player by yourself?"

"Yes," I answered modestly.

"So talk."

"I've stayed alive a long time," I told him, "by being cautious and being lucky and, most of all, by being reasonable. I'm hired to get Macready's money back. I do what I'm paid for. Give me the money, I leave, and you never hear another word about it, and neither does anybody else. Fuck me around and the whole world will hear me scream."

Garson said, "I believe you." He added, "I even like you," but his eyes did not comport with the words. He reached over to the underside of the leg of the coffee table and pushed a button. He looked at me and said, "You've been standing there like a train conductor. Why don't you sit down," he waved toward a chair, "and take a load off your feet?" I sat down cautiously and tried to divide my attention between Garson and the door. I did not, of course, have a gun.

The young man reappeared, and Garson waved him over to the coffee table, where the young man bent over to receive instructions. Garson wrote a number on a slip of paper. Then he took a wallet out of his breast pocket and extracted a key. The young man went off with the key and the slip of paper. I could not see what they had been saying.

Garson sat back and regarded me. "In for a penny, in for a pound," he said. "I suppose you want to know what happened."

"I've got a pretty good idea of what happened," I told him, "or I wouldn't be here."

"Yeah. You know what, but you don't know *why!*" He sat forward suddenly, tense, his face filled with self-righteousness. "You saw me haggling with those clowns in New York," he said. "Do you have any idea what kind of money is involved?"

"I figured a minimum of ten-million dollars."

"That's very good," said Garson. "That was a very good guess, but it is an absolute minimum, and it may go double that. It is a lot of money."

"A lot of money," I agreed.

"To those kids up in the hotel, it's numbers on a piece of paper—abstract," said Garson. "It doesn't really mean much more to them than numbers on a license plate. To me, it's real money."

"And to the people behind you," I added.

He waved it away. "They're realists, I'm a realist," he said. "Real people. Real money. What makes the world go round. So," he sat back, "we're talking about this kind of money, of bringing a huge piece of New York real estate back to life, of launching a deal the size of the QE Two. And what happens? We get told that the star—the *star,*" he spat the word out like a bad oyster, "isn't happy with the deal. He's got the world at his feet, but he isn't happy with the deal. He wants more money? We could hand it to him with a snow shovel. Oh, no. It's not money. It's . . . it's . . ." he groped.

"Integrity," I said.

"Jesus Christ." He sat up. "Can you feature it? Some asshole of an actor doing bits on the soaps is going to cream this whole deal, and the Old Man at the network gets a hard-on every time he looks at him? Am I going to stand still for this? Is anybody going to stand still for this?"

"Cutting his throat wouldn't have helped," I said. I smiled.

"No, no," he agreed. "You're absolutely right. No rough stuff—nothing. We can't even scare him because scaring him maybe spoils him for the work. I'm not stupid. I know that. We don't want a robot in front of the camera. Do this, do that.

"But we find out he lives like a pig. What does this mean? He makes a nice living. No fortune, but a reasonable living—not like the animals hanging around Tomkins Square. He makes enough money to live human, but he's not. How come?

"We find out he keeps his money. He keeps it. I've heard of this before. The 'fuck you' money—enough so that a guy doesn't have to do what he's told."

Garson stared into space for a moment and raised his arms supplicatingly. "If people don't do what they're told," he said, smiling at me, "we're dead.

"So we find out he's got a business manager. Jesus Christ, for peanuts he's got a business manager. And we find out the guy's name. That wasn't hard."

"No," I said. "I think Sally could probably remember a name."

"You know about her, huh?" He smiled. "A nice-looking job, but no score with you, huh?" He beamed at me. "You've got class. I like that. Besides, she's getting a little bit loose in the buns.

"So, we decide the only thing to do is to get his money. Take it away for a while so he won't be so . . ." And here Garson's expression changed because the word he was saying was a curse, ". . .*independent*. He wouldn't be so Goddamned independent with his money gone."

Garson responded to a knock on the door, and the young man came back in. He held before him a large, russet accordion envelope fastened with a string, and handed it to Garson. He also returned the key. I wondered if the young man knew what he was carrying, or if he was one of those who would be very careful all his life to be sure he didn't know what he was carrying.

Garson weighed the envelope for an instant, and then threw it on the table. "Treasury notes," he said with a grimace that suggested nausea. "My grandmother does better than that."

"Mr. Macready," I said primly, "was not trying to make a killing."

"What the fuck *is* he trying to do?" Garson asked me honestly.

"Pursue his career," I answered.

He smote his knee. "This *is* his career."

"But not the way he wants it."

Garson threw his hands up and sighed hugely. "At first we thought that he, Macready, was doing some rat-fucking, you know? And we waited. But no; he was . . ." and the expression that framed the word was again like a curse, " . . . he was *serious*. So we got serious.

"We kept tabs on this Pelfrey guy, and, what do you know? He's one of these types that goes in book joints—Eighth Avenue, Forty-second and Sixth, around in there—and he goes in the kiddie section. He can't keep his hands off the prints. We got some snaps of him with a corner camera. You ought to see the look on his face—you ought to see it—a creep of the first water.

"So we give him a call. We've heard he was Mr. Macready's manager and would he like to discuss some further possible accounts in the industry, blah, blah, blah. And we tell him to come over to a studio—it's not really a studio at all, it's a plant, a prop—that evening.

"So Pelfrey shows up loaded for bear, and he walks right into a set. Cameras, lights, everything, and naturally, he assumes he's right in the middle of business. He's happy. He glows. Everybody is nice to him. 'Presume you'd like to see how it's done, Mr. Pelfrey.' Oh. yes. Oh, yes, he would indeed.

"So what they do, they start to shoot a chicken flick right there. Right in front of him. They bring the kids on, and they start the routine. Pelfrey is free to leave, mind you, any time he wants. But he can't. He's petrified. Sweat breaks out all over him, and it's not from the lights.

"So, get this—the kids break out of the scene. They're all bareass naked, and they come over to Pelfrey, and they open his pants, you know? And he's standing there with his eyes bugging out, but he can't move. He's hypnotized. And they start playing with him and giving him the works, and suddenly he yells—they had the sound going, camera everything—he yells, and he throws up his hands and he pushes them away from him. He yells, 'My God, my God. What am I doing?' And he starts to moan. 'What am I doing?' And he starts to cry. He grabs himself and gets his pants together, and he runs out of the joint like it was on fire. Funniest Goddamned thing you ever saw. We got the whole thing, track and all, on tape. You want to see it?"

"No," I said.

"Funniest Goddamned thing you ever saw in your life," repeated Garson. "And one of the most valuable. That wrapped Arnold for us. We cut out the melodrama at the end, and gave him a preview of the coming attraction for all his clients.

"I'll say this for Arnold," Garson continued. "He wasn't stupid and he wasn't yellow. We had to explain the whole thing to him—that we just wanted to borrow the money. What the hell do I want with Macready's nut? We just wanted to ice it for a while, until Macready saw the light. We were telling him the truth, and he finally understood. It wasn't such a terrible thing he was doing, you know? So we told him to bring the bundle over to the Cardinal."

"Where you killed him," I said.

"Where the big ball player killed him," Garson amended. "We tried to keep the distance from that." His face relaxed into thoughtfulness, and he clasped his hands in front of him. "Look at it from our point of view, Joe; you've been around. Is it reasonable that we're going to let some nickel-and-dime actor fuck up a ten-million dollar deal? No. It's not reasonable. Is it reasonable that we're going to let some asshole with a screw loose and a guilty conscience wander all over town with all this under his hat? No. It's not reasonable. He had to go. Be reasonable."

I put the big envelope in my briefcase and stood up. "I'll be very reasonable," I said, surprised to find myself shaking. "But remember, I'm not Pelfrey. If you decide that I have to go, don't try to send around any big ball players. If you do send anybody around, he'd better be very, very good. Because, if he misses, I'll come back here and kill you and anybody you've got around you. That's a promise."

"Don't be so melodramatic." He spread his arms out and smiled. "Am I threatening you? Who threatened you? I wouldn't fuck around with you, Joe. I respect you. You don't know from people like me, how I operate."

"I know from people like you," I told him. "I put them down in my book with an RBW next to their name."

"RBW? Wait a minute, I'm pretty good at these initials, anagrams, acronyms, whatever the hell. RBW," he repeated, and the smile widened into a kind of likable grin. "I give up. What is it?"

"Raised by Whores," I told him. I picked up my briefcase and left.

But I couldn't stop shaking, not even after I got into the cab. A long day stretched ahead until my return flight was ready, and I couldn't see myself sitting in the airport—shaking. I told the cabby to drop me off at Hollywood and Vine. It seemed fitting. He gave a knowledgeable grin that made me want to flatten his face, but I restrained myself and stared straight ahead.

I walked the fabled boulevard, which has now turned into the tropical version of Times Square: a human sewer. I stared at the famous footprints set in cement in front of Mann's Chinese, and thought about the Purple Gang who used to set whole bodies in cement. I was haunted by the twisting figure of Arnold and his funny photographs. I wondered dully, dumbly, where he had turned his back on time and gone back into the world of children, and where he had finally bounced off the hard shell of the world and attempted to return to dreams and mysteries, only to find he wasn't even prepared for that, but only glossy photographs of some distant land of the heart's desire.

To avoid exhaustion, I went into a movie and sat through a double feature, the contents of which I cannot remember at all, either one.

It was evening when I hailed a cab for the airport. In the airport bar I got drunk, and on the plane back I got drunker until I fell asleep.

When I arrived at La Guardia, I felt like a piece of raw beef that had been ripped out of a living steer. I was hardly aware of the passengers streaming past me as I stumbled along the corridor, but at the newsstand, sheer habit directed my eyes, and a headline in the *Post* screamed at me: STAR BURNS TO DEATH.

I felt that I had read the story before I even picked the newspaper out of its rack.

26

Lieutenant Shope said at me, "Where the hell have you been?" He looked at me more closely and demanded, "What have you been doing?"

"I had to go to the Coast on business," I told him. "Two red-eyes back to back. I saw the paper at the airport."

I was having trouble reading a communication even so direct as Lieutenant Shope's. Although I had told the cab at the airport to go straight to the precinct house, I had made him stop and wait at a couple of bars while I went in and had a drink. On Eighth Avenue, he had waited while I went in and bought a pint of bourbon, the top of which now peeped from the side pocket of my coat. "You're drunk," Shope accused me. I fingered my two day growth of beard.

"I'm drunk," I admitted. "I'm going to get a lot drunker, and then I'm going to get very, very sober." I held the newspaper in my lap. "What happened?" I asked Shope. The newspaper had more sidebar than story. There was a great deal in it about the brilliant past and even more brilliant future of William Macready, but little more factual than that he had burned to death in his bed. The lead story said that the police suspected arson, but in newspapers, the police always suspect arson, otherwise there would be no newspapers. "He was smoking in bed, right?" I asked hopefully.

Shope examined me carefully. "How drunk are you?" he asked. "Drunk enough to look at the pictures?"

"Give me a minute," I asked him. I took the pint out of my pocket, fumbled with the seal until it broke, and took a long pull.

"Don't you want some water?" Shope asked me. I shook my head and dried the corners of my mouth with the back of my hand. He waited for a few seconds and then laid the big print on the desk in front of me.

The large, glossy, black-and-white print was worse than what I had prepared myself for. The image on the rectangle that had been a bed did not quite fit into the pattern that we regard as human. It might have been an ape. The size had been terribly diminished by the heat, and the tendons of the limbs had been constricted so that the legs were pulled back and the arms reached up in an unconscious beseeching. It was entirely black, the deep unreflecting black of charcoal, and featureless. The face was as smooth as a stone, with only the gaping hole of the mouth to indicate a once living being. I stared at the figure and saw that it was a burnt parody, a mannequin-image of a woman prepared to receive a lover. I couldn't take my eyes off it, and I fumbled blindly for the bottle in my pocket. When I had swallowed the drink, I asked Shope, "Is this an extra print? Can I keep it?" He had not looked away from me at all. He nodded.

"What about identification?" I asked bravely. "Do I have to go down and look at it—him?" I fumbled with the snaps on my briefcase and laid the glossy print over the big envelope containing Bill Macready's fortune.

"There's no use anybody looking at it," Shope said. "The M.E. is kind of . . . uh . . . sifting it. There weren't any teeth, you know. Nothing to work with there."

"That's right," I said. "He lost 'em fighting for his country. No teeth. Maybe some bone formation they could work with, but I don't know. I don't even know what kind of name you'd chase down in the Army hospital."

Shope was very patient. I took another drink and said, "So it wasn't just smoking in bed."

"No," said Shope. "If it's any comfort, he probably died of anoxia, suffocation, before he started to burn. The heat went through the place like thermite. Burned up all the air before it got to him.

"It was a torch," said Shope, "but it was a torch so good that only two or three people in town could have done it. We pulled in two of them. They look clean, but you never know."

"There was a bunch of winos hanging out downstairs," I said. "Christ only knows what they did. They could have started a bonfire to heat a can of spaghetti."

"No," said Shope. "The fire was started on the floor in the apartment below, directly under Macready's bed. Somebody broke into the empty apartment and set it. It went through Macready's floor, which is actually a roof full of tarpaper and asphalt, like an acetylene torch. It was a job. Our question is: Who bought the torch?"

"Get hold of your missing third," I answered. "He'll tell you." I discovered that I had gripped the ledge of Shope's desk and was trying to break off small parts of it with the underside pressure of my thumbs. "I can't help you," I told him. "I found the big ball player, but that's as far as it goes.

"Maybe he can help you," I added weakly. "Pull him out of his cage and talk to him." Sensation was beginning to work through the thumbs. They were pretty numb, but I could still feel something in them.

"You're in no condition to talk," Shope said with an unusually gentle expression on his face. "But there's some things that have to be talked about. Somebody has to claim the body . . ."

"I'll claim it . . . I'll claim it," I said quickly. I did not, of course, know what I was talking about. Perhaps I was thinking of keeping it somewhere in my apartment, where I could talk to it and apologize.

Shope was saying, ". . . and arrange for the funeral."

"I'll do it . . . I'll do it . . . I'll do it right away . . . I'll . . ." But my jaw hung open. "I'm the one who ought to do it," I told Shope finally. "He was . . ." A silence gripped me for a while and I stared into space. "He was . . ." I began again. Finally, I got it out: "My friend."

Shope said, "He must have belonged to some organizations, Equity, SAG, AFTRA—wouldn't his agent know? He must have some kind of insurance. It's kind of automatic."

"Yes," I said. "Call his agent. Fix Mendelsohn." I struggled for the phone number, but nothing came up. "My secretary, Edna," I said. "She's got the number. She'll give it to you. Good girl. Smart girl. Call her up."

"We already did that," said Shope. "And Mr. Popper doesn't seem to be around. Anyway, we can't reach him."

"Probably out on the Coast," I muttered. "Probably pulling out of all those commitments."

"Somebody's got to take charge," Shope complained mildly.

I bit down on my lower lip and thought hard about it. "O.K." I said to Shope. "Call Betty Middleton up at the network. She ought to have all this stuff on file. Betty Middleton." I remembered that number, and gave it to him. When I bit down on my lip again, it hurt terribly. I took another swig from the pint for reasons of anesthesia.

Things get a bit hazy after that last burning belt of whiskey. I remember that Shope continued to talk to me, and I must have answered something, although I'm sure I was no longer able to read him after a few minutes. Perhaps what I replied to him was the complete nonsense that follows total misunderstanding between two parties.

I remember then a certain softness, a whiteness and a comforting odor of perfume—not Sally's—a perfume I identified finally as Betty's. Her beautiful, kind face drifted in and out of my vision, and her soft bosom held me upright in a cab ride that ended at my apartment.

Apparently I was not willing, there, to go to bed. Apparently I sat bolt upright at my kitchen table with the pint in front of me, and then another bottle after that. Apparently I could not read what anyone was saying, certainly not Betty, whose soft lips tried to frame condolences, but whose face grew whiter and whiter with shock as I talked and talked or roared and roared, not so much at the face but at the bottle in front of me. I vaguely remember the silent explosion of the empty pint against the sink as I heaved it there, and the wavery figure of Betty rising from the table with horror in her eyes and disappearing from the kitchen and ultimately from the apartment and my consciousness.

In the morning I discovered that I hadn't made it to bed, but had stumbled over the couch in my front room and collapsed for the night. I fixed myself a coffee royal with the remains of the bourbon and tried, with a very shaky hand, to pare down my beard. The result was a countenance that resembled, somewhat, a motheaten rug. I chased down a couple of drink-sized bottles I'd filched from various airline trips, and drank enough of them to fuel my entry into the world outside my apartment. I suppose that I had put on a clean shirt, but I know I gave up on the tie. The suit was the same.

All right. I wanted to see for myself. What kind of satisfaction I expected to get from viewing the remains of the building where Bill had died, I don't know, but a cold, drunken impulse drove me out into the streets where I finally managed to persuade a cab driver—whose cab was parked, I had no chance of flagging one down—to take me up to midtown. On the way, he paused at a liquor store while I picked up another pint.

He dropped me at the corner, and I looked to the roof of the building in the middle of the block expecting to see a smoky ruin on the roof. The crazy cinderblock penthouse had not collapsed, however, and still managed to retain its jaunty perch above the building. Somehow, the sight of it both broke my heart and enraged me. When I entered the vestibule I could not smell as much as I had before because my own odors got in the way—the whiskey fumes, the emetic breath, and the sweat-soaked emanations from my suit. There was, of course, the unmistakable acridness of a burnt-out building: charred wood and tarpaper, burnt plaster, mixed, in this case, with charred flesh and bones. The appearance of the vestibule and stairway had not changed at all. On the fifth floor of the climb, which had me gasping, I saw the open door where the torch had gone in to set his fire. I went through the apartment, looking for the source of the fire. I found it, a blackened section of flooring, but the police and fire departments had removed anything of significance. One thing was very clear. The fire had been set so cleverly that all the flames and heat went skyward. The floor on which it was set was hardly damaged at all. It had whooshed like a rocket straight to the ceiling above. When I looked up, I found myself staring up into the sky through the roof of the penthouse above me.

I climbed the final flight of stairs expecting to go through Bill's apartment to see what I could see. But when I pushed open the useless firedoor, the floor on which I intended to step had disappeared. A few spears of blackened rafters stuck out into the space, and beyond them, the sodden furniture slumped in the final stages of water-soaked dissolution. There was no way I could traverse the floor, and, in truth, I lost all my taste for the idea. I realized that the fire department must have come up on ladders over the parapet. The photographer, too. Indeed, I realized, they must have taken the blackened hulk of Bill out over the parapet in a wire basket and lowered him to the street.

That was the image I carried down the dim stairway with me. When I reached the bottom flight, I was surprised to see the backs of two figures sitting there. I stepped past them, as I had of old, and turned to face them. One of them was the idiot, who shrank back from my stare, and the other was one of the original three.

"I thought you guys had left," I said softly. The nonidiot grinned a weak substitute for a smile and mumbled something that I hadn't a hope in hell of reading. The idiot stared at his shoes. The nonidiot held out a cupped hand. I noticed that for once there was no wine bottle to provide the festive air. It occurred to me, stupidly, that Bill may have pieced them off now and then to support their habit. He had been a very generous miser. I sat down on the step with them and took the pint out of my coat pocket. I took a swig first and then handed it over to them. Each of them took a belt and hande it back. They weren't used to whiskey, and I think it hit them like a club.

"Listen," I said, "you guys have been living here. You must have seen anybody coming in and out." I suddenly realized that they hadn't seen *me* coming in and out. "Did you see anybody . . . uh . . . suspicious?" I bugged my eyes to emphasize the question, "just before the fire? You see anybody coming in or out that night?"

I rubbed the neck of my pint with my palm and took another belt. Following the ritual, I handed it over. Alerted to the power of the stuff, they took much smaller swigs. The nonidiot began to talk earnestly to me, but I was totally incapable of understanding what he was saying or trying to say. The expression on his face was one of earnest and innocent negation. I took it to mean that he had seen nothing suspicious. The idiot seemed to be incapable of speech.

"All right," I said, getting up. If I hadn't been drunk, I wouldn't have done it. In an exercise of sheerest futility, I gave each of them a business card. "If you hear or see anything," I said, "let me know." I stepped out the door with a certain degree of drunken dignity, full of the assurance that I, as yet, was not a drunken bum.

I stepped out into the light and blinked at the huge truck that had pulled up to the curb. It had a lot of pipe-linked equipment in the back that I assumed was scaffolding, since the big curved sign on the door of the cab read, ACME WRECKING CO., INC. I stared at it, absorbing slowly the final meaning of its message. This was really the end of Bill, of all the time he had outwitted them and fought them. I was suddenly galvanized with rage. The driver had dismounted and was talking to a better-dressed man who had arrived in a pickup truck behind him. "Who's the foreman?" I demanded. Both of them were startled. The driver nodded, wonderingly, toward the better-dressed man. "You're not coming in here ripping things up until the police are done," I told him. "Take your truck and get the hell out of here."

"Who the fuck are you?" the foreman asked pleasantly.

I flashed my wallet so quickly that I might have identified myself as the president of the United States, however unlikely my appearance might me. "Let me see your permit," I demanded. The foreman stared derisively at me and answered, "Certainly, sir." He took the permit out of his breast pocket and handed it to me. My first impulse was to rip it up in front of him, but seized with a drunken, formal outrage, I copied down the number on one of my business cards instead and put the card in my wallet. "We'll see about this," I told them as I handed the permit back. I turned away then and staggered down the street. Because I am deaf, I could not hear them laughing.

I took a downtown bus to the vicinity of my office and noted that several people who had sat in the seat next to me got up and moved away. When I arrived at the office, Edna, at her desk in the anteroom, looked up at the clatter and regarded me with—may I use the word?—a sober expression. I collapsed heavily in the chair across from her and fished blindly in my wallet for the card. "I want you to call Fleischer down at the Buildings

Department," I told her. "I want you to verify this demolition permit made out to Acme Wrecking." She reached for the card, but I stayed her hand. "Then I want you to find out who put the buzzer to Acme to get off the dime on this before the smoke has cleared. I want to know who asked for the demolition, the name of the owner, or the corporation, if it is a corporation, and if so, the name of their CEO. O.K.?" I held on to her hand. "And when we find that out, I want you to call up that son-of-a-bitch and tell him I'm coming over there to pull his arms off."

Edna smiled demurely, withdrew her hand, and asked—it took me several readings to get what she was saying—"May I ask what this is all about?"

"They're parked down there ready to tear down Bill's building," I said, aggrieved. "The investigation has hardly started, but the bastards got to City Hall and have moved in for demolition. They'll destroy every possible bit of evidence that might be there." Edna looked at me, and we both realized that this wasn't my real concern. "It's indecent," I said finally. "It's indecent—it's rushing things to the end."

"I'll make the call," said Edna. She flipped through the Rolodex and picked out Fleischer's number. While she was making the very lengthy call, I sat staring at the calender on the wall in a semi-stupor. Edna finally put the phone down and wrote out her information on a memo pad. "The permit is legitimate," she said. Again, it was very difficult for me to understand what she was saying. She gave up, at last, and merely pushed the paper with the information on it across the desk. I stared at it. She then shoved another piece of paper across bearing the question, "Do you want me to call them now?"

I jumped. "No," I said. "Don't call anybody. Don't call anybody." I folded the name and address carefully into four parts and put it in my wallet.

She slid yet one more piece of paper across the desk. "Go home and sleep it off," the note read.

"Yes, Edna, thank you." I stood up and held on to the back of the chair. "That is what I'm going to do. I'm going to go home and sleep it off, and tomorrow I'm going to be very, very sober. I promise you."

Edna held on to my hand, and the shock I'd received enabled me to read her. "Don't do anything stupid," she said. "You're not in shape."

"You're very right," I agreed. "I really am going home."

But going home proved to be a circuitous business: the sort of exercise that children do in the Sunday supplements to connect the dots and get a picture of a camel in the desert. I traveled from bar to bar, two of which proved to be deserts, since they wisely eighty-sixed me. Apparently, they had an easy time of it. In others, I guess, a struggle had ensued. When I got home, my hands were puffy and there was blood on my shirt.

Strangely enough, though, I was totally conscious when I got home. Perhaps it was the long staggering walk, punctuated by pauses in which to be sick in the gutter. I took off my bloody, stained shirt, patched my face up in the mirror, doused my features in cold water, and fell into bed like an honest citizen, pajamas and all.

It is pure miracle that the lights awakened me. Sober, I would have awakened instantly, since I am keyed to flashing lights rather than sound. My doorbell is not a bell or a buzzer, of course, but a circuit that flashes all the lights in the apartment on and off. It is usually sufficient to awaken me almost instantly. That, however, assumes that I am sober. This evening took much longer, but apparently the visitor was leaning on the button. I staggered to my feet, my mind an utter blank and the machinery roaring viciously in my head. I turned the dead bolt back and opened my door. The idiot from Bill's vestibule was standing there. He held my business card in his hand.

27

I don't mean that I instantly recognized who and what he was. Torn out of a drunken sleep, I stood there staring at him until he raised the business card to my face. The smell of the man was overpowering, and I had no desire whatsoever to let him through the door. However, there didn't seem to be any help for it. I stepped back and invited him in with a jerk of my head. After he had entered, I backed away to get my nostrils out of range.

He stood there with the newspaper bindle rolled under his arm and tried to say something which I tried to read. The writhing of that shapeless mouth, which seemed to be nothing more than a hole ripped out of pink, thick flesh, was absolutely unreadable. The closest I could come to what he was saying was, "*Wee-wee. Wee-wee.*" Finally, he shifted the bindle under his arm and made an unmistakable gesture with his forefinger crooked in front of his fly. "Wee-wee," he repeated. "Wee-wee." He began to fumble with the fastening of the fly on his drooping trousers.

"Not here, for Christ's sake!" I shouted. "In there! Come on!" I led him at a half-trot to the bathroom down the hall. I opened the door for him and then shut it hurriedly, promising myself that I'd make him clean up whatever mess he made.

I went on to the kitchen, snapped on the light, and started some coffee. While waiting for the water to boil, I stood guard at the door of the kitchen to make sure he didn't emerge from the bathroom unnoticed and wander around the place. I still wasn't really awake and still hadn't taken it all in. The reasons for his showing up at my door were so wide and improbable that I couldn't even attempt to guess. It was my office address on the business card, not my home. How had he gotten my home address? How had he gotten through the door downstairs? Had he come here only to take a pee? Something, by the smell of him, he ordinarily accomplished in the street?

The water had boiled. I poured it into the filter and went back to the door. The door to the bathroom remained securely shut. He was taking his time, but I also know that urination for some of these people was often a lengthy, painful affair. The whole business of fumbling with his disreputable clothes was probably an elaborate process in itself. Bums have many layers of clothes, both to keep them warm and to carry their worldly goods in the easiest way—by wearing them. It took time; it all took time.

I poured myself a mug of black coffee and carried it into the front room, seating myself so I could look down the hallway and catch him when he came out. The only illumination in the hall was the glancing light from the kitchen at the end, but it was sufficient to see anyone there. I sipped my coffee and waited. Still the time stretched. It stretched unreasonably. I got up and looked around to find a pack of cigarettes and lighted one. Maybe he'd gotten ambitious with the bathroom appointments and decided really to clean up. Who could tell? It certainly wasn't an ambition I would argue with, as long as he cleaned up his messes afterwards. I finished my coffee, went back and poured another cup, and paused helplessly at the bathroom door. I didn't have the stomach for intruding on anything so wretched and horrible at this hour of the night. Whatever his personal maneuvers might be in my bathroom, I really didn't want to know anything about them. I returned to my chair in the front room and lighted another cigarette. The coffee was beginning to get to me, to wake me up, but I was still in a semi-stupor.

He appeared against the light from the kitchen. He had turned off the bathroom light before he stepped out so that no beam of light followed him into the hall. He was almost, but not quite a silhouette against the backlight of the kitchen. But it was not the same silhouette I had ushered down the hall! I froze in my chair, the coffee cup suspended halfway to my lips.

This silhouette was much taller, it seemed to me, very straight, erect, and purposeful. It was wearing gray slacks and polished moccasins that caught the dim light and reflected it. It was wearing a black polo shirt that exposed well-muscled arms and displayed a gold wristwatch at the end of one of them. I couldn't see what was at the end of the other. I was nowhere near any of my guns. I was helpless—a target. The silhouetted figure moved slowly but certainly toward me from the hall, and suddenly, there was something terribly, terribly familiar about it, but terrifying, too. When he stepped into the light of the front room, I cried, *"Bill! Bill! You son-of-a-bitch!"* I rose halfway to my feet and spilled the coffee on the rug.

"Gotcha," said Bill Macready, "huh?"

I had an instant of paralysis, and then I began to curse: a long, long train of curses and obscenities fled out of me. When I had exhausted myself, Bill nodded toward the cup in my hand and asked, "Can I have some of that coffee?"

We went into the kitchen for more coffee and I put on another pot. When that was done, we went back into the front room. We hadn't tried to talk in the kitchen. He was very considerately giving me a chance to absorb what had happened.

"How did you get in downstairs?" I asked him.

"You gave me the keys once, remember?"

I remembered. "Then how come you didn't let yourself into the apartment?"

"I didn't want to get shot at," he said with a significant look.

"You were right," I told him. "In fact, if I'd had a gun, you might have been shot coming out of the bathroom like that. Jesus! What a turn!"

We both sipped our coffee. "What made you go under?" I asked him.

"Well," he began, "it got pretty clear that somebody was trying to knock me over."

"Why didn't you get hold of me?" I demanded. "That's one of the things I'm hired for, what you were paying me for."

"I thought you'd find out more going on as you were," he said. "Besides, it was a kind of challenge, and opportunity. I'd had my eye on the guys downstairs."

"Was it one of them?"

"Oh, no," he said quickly. "I never even thought that. I just wanted to know more about them, and this looked like the chance. Those poor bastards are completely harmless.

"What happened is this," said Bill. "Somebody busted the light outside my door—the one in the cage. At first I thought the bulb was burned out because you never notice these things except when they don't work, and in the dark, you can't tell. I was leaving the place when it didn't go on, and I reminded myself to get a new bulb the next day. But when I came home that night, there was somebody crouched in the corner, and when I got to the door, he stood up and hit me in the middle of the chest with the heel of his hand. It hurt like hell, and it almost stopped my heart. And it knocked me down a flight of stairs.

"I played dead until the guy came down—this was all in the dark, you know—and I sensed that he was right over me and I kicked him in the balls. It was a lucky kick. I heard him moan, and I was going to try to take him, but he got away.

"I thought that this was all one of your everyday kick-ins or muggings, but when I looked at the bulb the next morning, I saw that somebody had broken it by puncturing it with a screwdriver or something through the wire cage.

"The next morning, I was crossing a street on my way to get a new bulb, and a big car missed me by about an inch. It came right up on the curb and I just barely jumped back into a doorway. When it missed, it swerved back into the street and careened around and got the hell out of there. So I thought, maybe a drunken driver or a kid—I didn't know who was in it.

"But that same night when I was coming home again, a couple of guys came out of a doorway after me, just a couple of doors down from my place. I didn't really see them—I kind of sensed them because I was still goosy from the car coming up on me. I jumped out of the way when the one guy swung something, and he hit his hand against a brick wall, and I heard him moan and curse. I heard it while I had already started to run. Well, I know voices. It was the same voice that moaned on the stairway. It's not much to go on, but it's my business. Same voice, same outfit. Besides, they had to be knowing I was coming that way. It wasn't a real mugging."

"Or you'd be dead," I observed.

He looked at it from that direction and nodded wisely, sadly. "I jumped into my hallway, knocked over the bums on the steps and ran up the stairs in the dark," he said. "Which was an advantage for me, because I know them by heart. These two guys tried to come after me, but they got tangled up with the winos, and by the time they reached the top, I'd already opened my door, got inside, slammed it and locked it. They kicked at it for a while, but, of course, they couldn't get through, and there's no other way to get into the place.

"So I sat down and thought," said Bill Macready. "I thought about Arnold. I thought that if they kept trying to get me, they'd sure as hell get me. It's pretty obvious that they wanted to do it without raising a stink—make it look like an accident, a street crime, or a suicide. But they wanted to get me. That's when I decided to disappear, pull a sneak."

"You should have told me." I suppose that the words came out with the normal inflection, but I was suddenly cold and furious. "You should have told me," I repeated, and this time, I'm sure that it didn't sound normal.

"I thought you'd guess," he said with a look of shyness on his face. "After all, I did tell you the story."

"The story?" I sat back, baffled.

"About Macready, William Charles Macready," he prompted.

I was totally blank.

"The Astor Place Riot."

Then I *did* remember—not only the story as Bill had told it, but as I had read it once, too. During the great chauvinistic competition between William Charles Macready, the English actor, and Edwin Forrest, the American actor, a crisis had been reached while Macready was performing *Macbeth* at the Astor Place Opera House in New York. Feeling grew so hot that a riot broke out in front of the opera house, and the riot, whose main ambition seemed to be to lynch Macready, got so violent that the militia had to be called out. Thirty people were killed. But Macready escaped by going backstage to change out of his costume and walking out then as part of the audience. Of course, nobody recognized him. There is no substitute for talent.

"So," said Bill, "I thought I would just disappear for a few days, and the best way to do it was to join the bunch downstairs. I sneaked out of the apartment and purposely left the door open to see if anybody would go in to search the place—whether anybody was looking for something inside, besides me, that is.

"I went to the Salvation Army and got some old clothes, which were way too good for what I wanted. I messed them up some and finally got what I was looking for, but of course," he smiled at me, "my big advantage is my teeth. When I take them out, my whole face collapses. I can look like anything I want. I let my beard grow, and in a couple of days I was ready to join the crew downstairs."

"Who was the man who got burned?"

"That was Benny," Bill answered, and a long sadness stole over his face. "I couldn't tell the guys to stay out of the place without giving myself away, but I made a lot of half-witted noises about it being spooky and dangerous to go there. I didn't really think that any of the guys would get hurt. Hell, none of them looked like me. But Benny just got absolutely fanatical about sleeping in a warm dry bed. There was no stopping him.

"So he died in my place," said Bill. "A terrible thing, and something I'd never thought of. I never thought anything would be that vicious."

He stared into space as if trying to resurrect the adventurous tramp. "You know," Bill said, "I'd always wanted to play *Godot,* Vladimir or Estragon, either one, but now, I don't know if I could do it. On stage, you're a tramp according to Beckett, but sitting on the stairs down there with a bottle of Night Train, I was a tramp according to God. I don't know if I could ever push that back far enough so it wouldn't get in the way of a performance.

"It's all sanitized up on the stage—a couple of tragicomic bums. But when you're sitting there with the real article, watching his legs rot off at the knee—you know, the skin turns red and just cracks open like a rotten melon—when you're sitting there with men whose flesh is turning into some kind of pink fungus, whose brains are being blasted out by wine and misery and hopelessness . . . it's . . . it's different."

"Listen, Bill," I broke in, "we've got to talk. I mean, we're talking now, but we've got to talk about other things, too, and what to do. Then we may have to go up to the precinct house and call Lieutenant Shope. Do you think you could stand a shot of honest whiskey while I get dressed?''

He submitted gracefully. I fixed him a drink and went into the bathroom to wash my face and brush my teeth. In the bedroom I put on old slacks, my old navy sweater, and a pair of moccasins. The fact is that I wanted to return to life and to shrug off the lingering spell of my despair and drunkenness.

He had drunk only a little of his whiskey by the time I came back. I went over to my briefcase, lifted the horrifying photograph off the top of the envelope, and then tossed the envelope in his lap. ''There it is,'' I said. ''Every nickel of it—should be. You've got it all back.''

Somehow, I'd expected that he'd jump into the air and whoop, but he just sat there and fingered idly at the string. He didn't even open it. ''What's the matter,'' I asked him. ''Was there something else?''

''Oh, no.'' He sat up and snapped out of it. ''No. It's wonderful and it's what I hired you for. It's just that—that this cost a guy's life, maybe two guys'. It doesn't seem like so much right now.''

''Arnold was a dead pigeon from the minute they saw him,'' I told Bill. ''He never had a chance. They wanted to borrow your money—*borrow* it—just to keep it away from you so you wouldn't give them any trouble about taking the part.''

''They?'' said Bill. ''They who?''

''Cy Garson.'' Bill's eyes widened. ''I got on to him because Edna, wonderful girl that she is, really dug for the report I wanted and came up with a lot of old articles that all together linked him—oh, so vaguely—with mysterious money out on the Coast. Then we dug a little further into his origins in Detroit, and I strung enough together to make him jump.''

''Has he been arrested?'' asked Bill.

I smiled at the naiveté. ''You don't arrest Cy Garson,'' I said, ''at least not on evidence like this. Shope has got the actual murderer, the same guy that put me in the hospital. Maybe Shope will get some names and addresses out of him that stand up, but I doubt it. The trouble with being Roger Grim,'' I reflected, ''is that you make a very big target. I don't think Grim will tell them anything, not if he wants to stay alive in prison.

''On the other hand,'' I added, ''if we can keep your building standing for a little while, before they tear it down, maybe we can find some evidence there that will link them up. That's why I want to go to the station tonight—to get a hold order on it."

"Evidence," Bill said, sitting up suddenly and shaking his head. "I've got evidence. At least I think it's evidence.

"The night the fire broke out," he said, "this fat guy in a black raincoat went up the stairs. We weren't sitting on the steps then; we were around the corner where the basement door is. I just caught a glimpse of him going up and only by the light of the streetlamp. He was just a big shadow."

"Wait a minute," I stopped him. "Big, meaning how big?"

"Really enormously fat. You could hear him puffing and wheezing going up even the first flight of stairs. And he had, as I said, this black raincoat on, although it wasn't raining or cold. It was unseasonably warm, in fact. He also had a hat, a fedora, that was pulled way down. You couldn't see his face at all."

"You wouldn't have to," I told him. "Any cop in New York would recognize him. That was Flick Ferrara, one of the three best torches in town. They call him Flick because he does it all with his Zippo lighter. He's famous."

"Yeah? Well, he came back down the stairs like a herd of elephants. I didn't know whether Benny was up there or not, or who this guy was. But I thought maybe I could slow him down without blowing my cover. What I really wanted was to hear his voice, to see if he was the same guy that tried to kill me."

"He wouldn't be," I told Bill. "Flick would never stoop to anything that crude."

"So, I put on a crazy act for the benefit of my friends," Bill continued, "I pretended that I was freaked out by the noise, and when this hulk came bouncing down the stairs, I jumped on his back, screaming and babbling. I must have scared the shit out of him. I never heard his voice. He tried to throw me off his back. He's built like a whale, but I hung on to his raincoat, and he just shrugged out of it and ran."

"You've got the raincoat?" My heart bounded.

"Yeah. I kept it and put it in my bindle. It's as big as a tent."

"And as valuable as the Kohinoor diamond," I told him. "Go get it. Let's see it."

While Bill was undoing the complicated structure of his bindle again, I heated myself another cup of coffee. I seemed to have lost my taste for liquor for the time being.

I met Bill back in the living room and took the huge black poplin raincoat from him. "That's Flick," I told him. "He wears it winter and summer, wet or dry. He makes his own weather inside of it.''

I worked it around so that I could feel in the left-hand pocket of the coat. There was nothing there, not even dust or the usual crud. I traversed the enormous back of the coat and felt in the right-hand pocket. The thrill was like a bolt of electricity through my bones. I felt the sharp corner of a business card and then the raised lettering. I took it out and looked at it, noting the hand-written number on the face above the printed number. I looked up at Bill to say, in my best Charlie Chan fashion, ''Ah, so; ah, so.'' But Bill's eyes were riveted on something over my right shoulder in the direction of the door to my apartment.

28

The man at the door was a small gray man wearing a yellow tie that stood out like a searchlight's beacon on his chest. He was holding a complicated-looking automatic pistol with a silencer fixed to its barrel. He held it at Port Arms, the way I'd held mine while talking to Roger Grim, but I had no doubt the long silencer could swing down quickly into an accurate point. The yellow tie stood out brightly because everything else about him except his skin and his shoes was gray: the gray, sharply pressed sharkskin suit, the well-blocked, jauntily set fedora, even the shirt with its button-down collar. The shoes were well-made black oxfords that came to a point just short of qualifying them as bona-fide rat-stabbers. His skin was pink and healthy, and when he moved closer to the light, I saw that he had dark blue eyes. I had a crazy impulse to introduce them: *''Bill Macready, meet Irish Larry Feltzheimer,''* but fear and caution held my tongue. ''Where's the bum who came in here?'' he demanded.

''Out the back and down the fire escape,'' I said quickly, before Bill could utter a damning word.

''He wasn't any bum,'' said Irish Larry wisely.

''He was a cop,'' I lied. ''He knew somebody made him and he wanted out.''

Irish Larry pursed his lips at this. ''I saw him crawl out of that hole Macready was living in,'' he said. ''I watched him go down to the end of the block, and suddenly he straightens up and starts walking like an Olympic champion.'' I saw the disappointment on Bill's face. Irish Larry waved the gun very slightly in Bill's direction. ''Who's this guy?''

''Just a friend of mine, stopped over for a drink.''

''Who *is* he?'' the little gray man insisted.

''His name is John Petty, and, as a matter of fact, he's a bond salesman.'' Bill's face instantly softened in the harmless expression of a bond salesman, half-eager, half-placatory. The dark blue eyes bored into him. Then they turned to me.

''You brought in the big dinge all by yourself, huh?''

''Yes,'' I answered modestly.

''Pretty good,'' Irish Larry admitted. ''But you caused me a peck of trouble.''

''How come you're down here waving a gun around?'' I asked him. ''You run out of school buses to dynamite?''

He smiled. It was a very flinty smile. ''Don't try to rile me, son. I don't enjoy this any more than you do.''

''No kidding,'' I said. ''What happened? Why are you here?''

He stared at me for a moment, and then said, ''Let's get things in order first. We're going to stand here and talk a little bit. If you make any moves at all, your friend gets it first. You understand? Blink wrong and he's dead.''

I nodded my agreement.

''Now,'' he began, ''the trouble you caused me is this. You went out to the Coast, and you laid one on Garson. So they call me direct and they say, 'It's all yours now, pal. Don't hire anybody to do it. You do it.' You think I like that?''

''You're getting old,'' I said. ''There's a lot of white hair under that hat. Nobody used to push you around.''

''Don't hand me any crap,'' said Irish Larry Feltzheimer. ''I do what I have to do.''

''And what is it that you have to do?'' I asked, dreading the reply.

''They gave me a little list over the phone,'' the gunholder said. ''And the last thing on that list was, 'Be sure you bring back the McGuffin.' '' A slow expression of cunning stole over the small pink face. He was obviously waiting for one of us to speak. Neither of us did. The expression stole away again and was replaced by one of crossness. ''The trouble is,'' he said slowly, reluctantly, ''I don't know what they mean, a McGuffin.''

If I had had Mr. Feltzheimer's elaborately silenced automatic in my hands at that moment, I might have shot Bill Macready myself. Like an irrepressible schoolboy raising his hand in class, he lit up like a three-way lamp and almost took a step forward before he bethought himself. *I* had been planning to give Feltzheimer some long-winded, cock-and-bull story that would have sent him to the outer precincts of the Bronx.

"All right, Bright-Eyes," Feltzheimer said to him, "what's the answer?"

It was obvious that Bill realized how stupid he had been. He said reluctantly. "It's a thing that Hitchcock . . ."

"Who's Hitchcock?" asked Feltzheimer, alarmed at another name.

"Alfred Hitchcock, the movie director. What he called the McGuffin is the thing of major significance in the plot of a movie script, the thing that everybody wants."

"Stop talking in riddles," said Feltzheimer. "What kind of thing?"

Bill shrugged, incautiously lifting his hands. "It could be anything: an important clue, evidence, anything like that, or a prize, like the bird in *The Maltese Falcon*, or it could be a will, or a piece of paper, any important piece of paper."

"A piece of paper!" Feltzheimer took him up happily. "That's it. O.K. It's all one and the same thing. They had me stumped there, but I couldn't call back. It's just the same piece of paper they wanted with the phone numbers."

He looked at me. "So where is it?" he asked.

"What were the other things on the list?" I countered him bleakly.

Feltzheimer indicated very slightly that I was a target with the extended muzzle of the gun. "You, of course. You're one of the things. You've got to go. Nobody can hand them the kind of shit you did and walk away. You know that."

The marrow of my bones seemed suddenly refrigerated. My hands and nose suddenly got very cold. The machinery started to roar in my head. Getting a death sentence handed down is very different from fighting for your life. Feltzheimer was even smiling sadly and sympathetically, like a kindly judge. I was terribly frightened. "What else is on the list?" I asked him. I suppose that my voice came out in a strangled squeak, because it took him a moment to understand what I was saying.

He answered, "They want me to find the torch and burn him."

I exclaimed, "Find him! Don't they know who he is? Didn't they hire him?"

"No, they didn't," said Feltzheimer. "As a matter of fact, he screwed up everything for them. They wanted to talk to this guy, Macready, you know? Talk to him like a father. Make a deal. Then this torch comes in and there's no more Macready. No deal. Nobody bothered to clear it with them first, and that is way out of line. So they want the torch and they want who hired him and they want them both dead."

I said very slowly and carefully to him, "What do I buy if I give you the names?"

Feltzheimer looked at me for a long time before he replied. "I could kid you along," he said, "but I won't. You're not going to buy your life with it. There's no way I can let you go."

"What about his life?" I asked, nodding toward Bill. Feltzheimer looked dubious. "Remember," I said, "I've been very careful not to mention your name. This guy doesn't know you from Adam, and there isn't a chance in the world he'll open his mouth or turn state's evidence. He doesn't belong in this kind of game. He has nothing to do with it. There's no reason to hit him."

"I'll think about it," said Feltzheimer. "Who's the torch?"

"Flick Ferrara."

Feltzheimer grimaced. He said, "It had to be him or one of two others. It ain't worth a hell of a lot. Who hired him?"

"That," I said, "is what you find out after Mr. Petty leaves the building vertically."

"I'll think about it," he repeated. "Now," suddenly he was all business, "where's the . . ." and unpredictably, he smiled, ". . . the McGuffin. That piece of paper with the numbers."

"There's a bus station in the Bronx," I began.

"Cut the bullshit."

"No kidding! Do you think I'd keep it here?"

"Yes, I do," said Feltzheimer, "because I've heard all this crap before about the evidence being kept in a safe-deposit vault, or a luggage locker, or under the Great Pyramid of Egypt, but every single time, it shows up right where the guy lives, because the guy doesn't want it out of his sight."

"Not this time," I said.

"It had better be," replied Irish Larry Feltzheimer, "because

I'm going to start shooting little pieces off your boyfriend here, and when there's nothing left, I'm going to start on you."

"You *are* one of those kinky kneecappers," I said. I did not much like my own material being played back to me.

"I do what I come for," he said stolidly. I turned my eyes away from him to glance at Bill. Bill's face was remote, withdrawn. My eyes had been fastened almost hypnotically on the gun whenever I was not reading Irish Larry's lips. But Bill, apparently, could not bear to look at the gun.

"How about it, Deafy?" Feltzheimer prompted me.

"It's in a book-safe," I told him.

"Where?"

I nodded toward the full wall of books that stretched from floor to ceiling and from wall to wall. "It figures," he said. "Whereabouts over there?"

"You should spot it, wise guy," I told him bitterly. "You mean the all-time, great international hot-shot can't spot a book-safe when he sees one?"

Feltzheimer lowered the gun toward Bill, who looked even more remote. "Cut the bullshit," he said. "Where is it?"

"On the top shelf, near the end."

"The very top? You got to get on that little ladder?"

"Yes," I answered. "Or you can get it yourself."

"Not me," said Irish Larry. "Tell you what, though. First of all, you got to remember, I'm pretty good. I can shoot you both before you blink. You're going to go over there and climb up that little ladder and get me the book-safe. And, believe me, there'd better be one, and the paper had better be in it. Your boyfriend is going to stand right here where he is, and if you make any kind of move behind any of those books to pull out a backup gun, your boyfriend is going to get shot first and you second. Even if there's a gunfight, you'll get it. You understand?"

"I understand," I said.

"So move."

I pushed my leaden feet to the small rolling ladder and moved it to the last section of books along the wall. Keeping my hands well in sight, I ascended the few steps and lifted the booksafe out of its row. I carefully climbed down holding the booksafe in both hands, and returned to my position next to Bill. "Do you want me to open it?" I asked Irish Larry.

"I've been to movies too, Sonny," said Irish Larry. "You open the book, take out a gun, and maybe everybody gets killed, huh? Why not? I tell you what. You just hand that thing very carefully over to me. I open it myself, all right? Just hold it with your thumb and fingers hanging down in your hand, and we won't have any surprises."

I did as he directed. He grasped the heavy, steel-backed book-safe with both hands, holding the gun firmly at its side and pointed toward Bill. "I'm sorry about your friend here," he said, "but there's no way I'm going to let him go."

"But you don't know who . . ." I began.

"I know he's William Macready, the young actor," said Irish Larry. "I've seen his photograph, and I made him while you were up on the ladder."

"They don't want him dead," I pointed out.

"They can't have everything," observed Feltzheimer. "There's no way I'm going to leave a live witness running around.

"I'm sorry for all your troubles," he said directly to Bill, "but I'm afraid you die again, Macready."

Bill continued to stare off toward a point in space. Feltzheimer inspected the cover of the book and said, surprised, "There's no lock on this thing."

"Why should there be?" I said. "Anybody who takes it, owns it. All he'd need with a lock is a screwdriver."

"You've got class, Binney," said Irish Larry. "I'll hand you that." He balanced the gun carefully. "Now let's see what we've got here." He put a thumb on either side of the edges of the leather cover and opened the book.

There was a blinding flash of light, and by the distance that Bill jumped in the air and the shock wave that hit me, I could tell that it had been a tremendously loud explosion. Where Irish Larry's pink face had been, there now seemed to be little recognizable under the smoke but a blackened shell.

Although blasted backward, he was still standing, swaying. A few tufts of white hair standing straight up showed where his hat had been. I stepped over to seize him by one arm and take his gun from the other hand. I said into the blackened hole of his ear, "Can you hear me, Larry? Don't try to move your head. Just twitch your hand if you hear me."

The shaking gun hand came up slightly and twitched.

"Don't try to touch your head or it will come away in your hands. You hear me? Your face has turned into jelly. I'm going to take you to a hospital and see if they can glue it back together." His whole body was trembling violently. "Stand still while I get my jacket," I instructed him.

I went to the closet, put on a jacket, and took a wire coat hanger off the rod. I opened the coat hanger and put it over the blackened head. Then I took the gun, with its beautifully carved grip, set the safety, looped the small hook of the clothes hanger through the trigger guard, and bent the wire shut so that his gun was hanging around his neck. I took him by his ice cold hand, then, and led him out the door and down the steps.

We went around the corner and two blocks down, which brought us to the East River. I leaned into Larry's ear and said, "Right now you are standing about twelve feet from the East River, and I hope, that when I leave you here, you fall in and drown." There was a spasmodic jerk in his body. "Now, you little prick," I told him, "you've engineered a lot of bombings in your time, now you know what it feels like to wait around for your brains to seep down through your jaws. You can find your own fucking doctor." I turned around and walked away. Because I am deaf, I could not hear him cry out.

Bill was startled to see me back. He had drunk all his whiskey and was starting on another glass with a shaking hand. I went directly to the phone and wrote a number on the pad. I handed it to Bill. "Call Lieutenant Shope at this number," I commanded him, "and tell him that he can pick up Irish Larry Feltzheimer down by the river two blocks from here. Tell him to hurry, or some bleeding heart will find him and take him to the hospital."

Bill's eyes seemed to revolve in his head with questions. "Do it!" I demanded. "Don't identify yourself. Tell him and hang up."

Bill completed the call—a procedure I watched with great satisfaction. Then he turned to me and said, "You just left him out in the street? A man with his face blown away? Maybe dying?"

"Dying?" I jeered. "There's nothing the matter with that little son-of-a-bitch that an eye-dropper won't cure. He's temporarily blinded by a magnesium flash and some soot that got blown into his eyes. That's all that was, a bag of soot blown out with a shaped charge of black powder and a touch of fulminate of mercury. They'll take him down with that gun around his neck and clean him up and he'll be as good as new."

"A booby trap," said Bill. A smile was beginning to form on his very white face.

"A nonlethal one to discourage people from screwing around when I'm not here," I said.

"It sure discouraged him."

"He's a very lucky man," I told Bill, "because I've got another one of those that's loaded up with old nuts and bolts."

29

They picked up Feltzheimer too late that night for it to make the morning papers, and I was far too busy to check the afternoon editions. It wasn't until the morning after that when Edna and I read the story together in our office, laughing. It turned out to be a day for laughing—and crying.

The item was headed: GUNRUNNER APPREHENDED

> An internationally known dealer in illegal armaments and explosives was arrested in the early hours of the morning as he wandered dazed only a few feet from the edge of the East River.
>
> Following an anonymous tip, police discovered Lawrence (Irish Larry) Feltzheimer pleading for help as he circled, apparently blinded, at the water's edge. An automatic pistol of foreign make was hung around his neck by means of a coat hanger. The gun is being checked for possible association with unsolved murders in the area.
>
> Lieutenant Detective Matthew Shope, who made the arrest, said that no one knew how Feltzheimer came to be in this situation.
>
> "He was wandering around crying, 'Help me, I'm blind; I'm hurt,' " said Lieutenant Shope. "His face was covered with soot, and he didn't seem to know where he was. He begged us to take him to a hospital, which we did."
>
> In the emergency room, said Lieutenant Shope, the doctors washed his face and bathed his eyes. This restored his sight, and it was agreed that he had suffered no serious injury.
>
> "We still haven't been able to get a straight story out of him," said Lieutenant Shope. "After he found out that he could see and wasn't blind or hurt, he became hysterical and had to be restrained."
>
> *Continued on page A33, Column 2*

We both laughed at the story, but when I laughed it hurt my arm.

"This is one for the scrapbook," said Edna, brandishing the scissors.

"Why?" I asked her. "My name isn't in it, spelled right or wrong. No one will know I had anything to do with it."

"*We'll* know," said Edna. She lifted the page and began to snip.

My arm hurt when I laughed because I had it nearly broken the day before. After a few hours of restless sleep I'd gone up to my office, arriving there before Edna did. I had her make a photocopy of the business card I'd taken from Flick Ferrara's raincoat. I told her to treat it with care and stow it in a plastic case for the preservation of fingerprints.

Edna had stared at the card. "Two telephone numbers," she said. "But the printed one is . . ."

I took the folded piece of paper out of my wallet and the information on it matched the card. "Yes," I said. "The same outfit that ordered the demolition." Side by side, they repeated, "DIAMOND ENTERPRISES. Conrad Medellin, President."

"Conrad Medellin," Edna exclaimed, upset. "He was the lawyer you asked me, but I never got a chance . . ."

"Forget it," I said. "Things move too Goddamned fast around here for anybody to keep up."

I took the photocopy along with a photograph from my briefcase, put them both in a manila envelope and went down and hailed a cab. The building the cab dropped me at was a poem in smoky glass and steel. The office I entered reflected the aspirations of the architecture: deep leather outlined with blinding quantities of chromium.

I walked past the girl saying "You can't go in there," opened the door, and was just in time to see Mr. Medellin practicing in slow motion the sacred arc of the serve with a heavy, oversized tennis racquet. "Sorry to interrupt," I announced, "but I have something of the utmost importance to show you, Mr. Medellin." His expression was about the same, I imagine, as I would have seen interrupting a lady in a toilet booth. He was sputtering things like, "What the hell do you think . . ." when I put the glossy photograph on his rosewood and chromium desk.

"You don't know this man," I said. "His name is Benny. He's the man you had burned to death."

He recoiled from the caricature of death in the photograph and began to say, "This is outrageous." I put the photocopy of his business card next to the photograph. Somehow, centered in a piece of 8½ x 11 photocopy paper, "DIAMOND ENTERPRISES. Conrad Medellin President," did not look quite so imposing. Of course, the lettering was not raised.

I said to him, "This is a photocopy of a card we took from the pocket of Flick Ferrara, the well-known arsonist. Mr. Ferrara was seen leaving the building you own, or manage, just after the fire was set. He is now in custody."

"Anybody can have my business card," said Medellin. "What is this?"

"This is evidence that you hired Flick Ferrara to burn the building while William Macready was in it," I told him. "You wrote a special number on the face of it, which is apparently a phone drop for you. This is your writing, and the number is neither that of your office nor your home."

"You'll have a hell of a time proving that those printed numbers are my handwriting," said the lawyer.

"But not that the fingerprint on the back of the card is yours," I said. "Everything has been carefully preserved as evidence. The fact that Diamond Enterprises owns the building that was burned will come as a thrilling revelation during the trial."

"You think a Grand Jury is going to touch something as flimsy as this? You think they'd indict a man like me on something like this?" I noticed that the tennis racquet was revolving slowly in his hand.

"Yes, I do," I answered. "Not so much on this evidence as the fact that Vincent Namier is at this moment spilling his guts all over the precinct floor."

"That son-of-a-bitch," said Medellin. "He was the one who wanted . . ."

"Macready dead?"

"Certainly. All I wanted was the building the hell out of there so we could move. Namier's the one who begged me for the contacts. All I did was call a few numbers and see a few guys."

"And produced this." I nodded toward the photograph.

I should not have been so foolish as to take my eyes off him for a fraction of a second. He had a terribly powerful forehand, and had he connected with my skull, at which he was aiming, he would have left a crease in my head the depth of an Alpine crevasse. However, I sensed it and twisted so that the edge of the racquet came down on my forearm, numbing it completely. I looped my other hand around the back of Medellin's neck and butted him in the face.

It had a startling effect on him. He was a big, strong, youngster, in excellent shape, and had, no doubt, endured a great deal of pain in stretching and refitting his muscles. But this was a different kind of pain; it had the shock of destruction to it. He tasted the blood on his chin and became aware that it was cascading down on his sober tie and his light blue custom-made shirt. While he was pondering this turn of events with widely staring eyes I hit him with a right hand on the point of his chin in the pure spirit of revenge for my left hand. Mr. Medellin collapsed. I punched a number of buttons on his beautifully appointed desk, and when the girl came running in, I ordered her to call Lieutenant Shope, whose number I now had by heart.

Watching Edna turn the pages of the newspaper to find the jump to our story, I flexed my left hand reminiscently. It would be quite a few days before all was well with that wing again. At first I thought that Edna had found the other end of the story. Her eyes lighted up, but then they widened with incredulity, and her face took on the expression of someone who has been stabbed—shock, disbelief, and pain. She began to cry, and her twisted mouth said, "Oh, no!" She got up hurriedly, pushing the chair back to the wall, and ran into the bathroom.

The item had nothing to do with my story. It was centered neatly on columns two and three of another page, and stated,

> Mr. and Mrs. John J. Askew of Rye, New York have announced the engagement of their daughter, Nancy, to David Sartin, M.D., ...

There was a fine-looking, professional portrait of Dr. Sartin on the left, and an equally fine representation of Nancy Askew on the right. Dr. Sartin looked, as always, handsome and incredibly blue-sky innocent. Miss Askew looked busty, toothy, dull, and determined. I took up the scissors, found the jump to my story myself, and cut it out.

I became aware of the doorway to the hall opening, and in strode one of those young women with a messenger's pouch slung over her shoulder. She fished an envelope out of her pouch, handed it over and made me sign for it. Inside was a letterhead envelope from Creative Flooring, clipped to a note from Anthony. The laborious handwriting said "Dear Joe! Sorry this is a day late. Forgot to send it yesterday. Very truly yours, Anthony."

Inside the letterhead envelope was a check made out to me for the proper amount to the last penny.

Edna's eyes were still red when she came back to her desk. I waved the check at her and said, "Anthony." She tried to produce a grim little smile, but somehow the thought of Anthony was too much for her, and she started to cry again. I put the check on the desk and reached over to pat her on the shoulder, but she pulled away from me. It was all certainly not my fault, but on the other hand, I was the only man in the office. Edna began turning the pages of the newspaper again to locate the damnatory item. She had the look of one who expects to find a toad in her shoe.

Apparently, the phone had rung, for she reached blindly across the desk, with her eyes still fastened on the fatal article. She spoke listlessly into the mouthpiece, but her eyes refocused with interest at whatever was coming through the receiver. I raised my eyebrows in the tacit question of whether this was an emergency, but she shook her head and then, unaccountably, smiled. I had long ago given up trying to follow this kind of conversation, although I saw Edna say several times, "He did? He did?" with an expression of awe on her face. The conversation took quite a while and was punctuated with smiles, expressions of surprise and/or awe, and then suddenly, little squalls of suppressed tears. Finally, she hung up the phone after a protracted farewell to the caller, looked at me and said, "That was Miriam Hennessy."

This drew an absolute blank on my mental references.

"She's the accounts payable lady at Creative Flooring," Edna informed me.

"Oh," I marveled. "*That* Miriam Hennessy." For some reason or other, this statement made Edna start to cry. However, it was brief. She used another Kleenex from the rapidly sinking box.

"It's about Anthony."

"Is he in trouble?" I was alarmed. Trouble concerning Anthony could be real trouble, in comparison with which the Haymarket Riots would be a bagatelle.

"No," said Edna, blowing her nose. "It's about what happened yesterday when he came for the check."

She began to laugh wildly.

"He didn't," I asked cautiously, "er, destroy anything, did he?" In my mind's eye, the check took wings to pay for the destruction of property.

"I guess not," answered Edna. "Miriam didn't mention it anyway. But he sure shook that place up. Mr. Rosenquist didn't come in today. That's why she was able to make the call to us, that is, a long telephone call like that."

The fear of property damage evaporated, to be replaced with a more chilling apprehension. "Mr. Rosenquist is . . . uh . . . all right? Anthony did not . . . I hope to God . . . lay hands on him?"

"Not that Miriam mentioned."

"She would have," I said, sighing with gratitude. "Believe me."

"Miriam said that when Anthony came into the office, his head was turned so that she and the girls only saw the nice side of his face, which is very sweet, though big." There was something in the words *nice, face,* and *sweet* that caused Edna to burst into tears again. I waited sympathetically.

"And then," she continued, having dried her eyes, "he boomed out, 'I've come for Mr. Binney's check!' and she said that she'd never heard a voice like that, a voice you could feel in your chair, the way an organ makes a church shake. It was so loud, she said, that Mr. Rosenquist heard it through the door of his office."

Edna began to laugh.

"So, Miriam says, they all heard Mr. Rosenquist's very nasty voice when he opened his door, before he really looked out, and he was saying, 'I thought I told you people to stay out of this office.' And he came charging out with his head down, you know, and then he got a look at Anthony, and the other side of Anthony's face, and he went 'Eek,' like a girl that's seen a mouse.

"So, back inside his office, he calls Beatrice, the girl at the desk, and he says 'Beatrice, I want you to call the police immediately.'

" 'And what shall I tell them, sir?' asks Beatrice.

"And he says—it took him a minute to think it up, I guess, 'Tell them we have an intruder. And tell them to hurry!' And he slams down the telephone on poor Beatrice."

The thought of poor Beatrice caused Edna to cry again.

Recovered, she said, "Everybody in the office was very nice

to Anthony. They asked him to sit down, and all, but he said no thanks, and he smiled on the good side. Mr. Rosenquist would open his door a crack and see Anthony there and then slam it shut. And he kept calling poor Beatrice and asking where the police were and had she called them and all.

"Finally, two of them came in a squad car, patrolmen, I guess, in uniforms, and everybody in the office was very surprised, because when they came in they said, 'Hi, Anthony. Where's the intruder?' "

We both laughed at this.

"So Miriam said, then, Anthony was like a big kid. He put his arms around these guys and hugged them, and said how glad he was to see them. He knew their names, and all about them, and asked about their wives and kids. And when he hugged them, you know, he picked them right up off the floor, holding them up in the air.

"So when Mr. Rosenquist heard all the voices, he opened the door and stepped out and saw this man Anthony standing there holding a policeman up in the air with each arm. And she said Mr. Rosenquist—it's not very nice what she said—she said Mr. Rosenquist almost crapped himself.

"They had to coax him back out of the office, and when he saw it was all right he started jumping up and down and swearing and saying weren't they going to do something and make a report.

"And they said, sure, they'd make a report, but they'd also have to report all the fire code violations in the office, and the zoning violation with the sign sticking out over the sidewalk, and that they noticed there was a cornice that looked loose on the roof of the building that could fall into the street and kill people, and they guessed they'd have to put a police barricade around the building and get everybody out until the corrections were made.

"And finally, one of them said, 'Look, you. If you want this guy out of here and to go away, why don't you just give him what he came for?'

"And Mr. Rosenquist went back into his office, and he did. And that's how Anthony got the check, Miriam says." Edna began to cry again.

"And then Anthony went out and spent the hundred dollars I gave him buying drinks for policemen. And that's why he didn't send the check in yesterday," I concluded. "It figures."

She was still crying. "Edna," I said to her earnestly, "please don't cry. Let me tell you about the raise you're getting as of this week . . . and . . . and the bonus for all the good work you've done," I added helplessly.

"I feel like such a fool," she said. "Such a fool."

"Don't feel that way," I said with utterly hopeless advice. I took her hand and held it.

She had to withdraw her hand because the phone had rung again. She composed herself sufficiently to speak into it, and her expression suddenly became very alert and sober. She covered the mouthpiece with her hand and said, "It's Betty Middleton. She wants you to come and get her right away."

"Where is she?"

"At the network."

"Tell her, right away," I said.

Edna spoke into the phone while I was getting up from the chair. When she'd put it down, I said, "What happened?"

"*Mr.* Namier is dead," said Edna.

I reached over and took her hand again. "Please, Edna," I asked her, "hook up the answering machine and come along with me, will you? I don't know what we're going to find."

30

We found Betty sitting on the couch of her ante-office. The door to Vincent Namier's office was open, and several policemen and their entourage were wandering back and forth across the thick carpeting. The big window looking out over the flinty landscape of Sixth Avenue had a jagged and gigantic hole in it. The Nakian bronze lay upended on top of the desk.

Our cab had snaked around the police barricade and the crowd surrounding the shrouded figure in the street.

Betty's face had the blankness of shock. I identified myself to the officer in charge (not Shope) and asked if I could take Miss Middleton away with me. He said yes, but required that she make a statement later. Edna had seated herself on the couch with Betty and put her arm around her. We went out a side door of the building to avoid the spectacle in the street, and took a cab to Jimmy Ray's on Eighth Avenue. I had agreed much earlier to meet Bill Macready there for a drink, and I felt, instinctively, that Betty needed people around her at this moment. None of us said anything in the cab ride over.

We took a table in the back, and I ordered a double martini for Betty, a scotch sour for Edna, and a bourbon and soda for myself. Mundane facts in a mundane world. Betty drank half of her martini before she spoke.

"I heard the crashing," she said. "Four sharp crashes close together, so fast they almost seemed like one. I ran to his door and opened it, and he tossed the Nakian back on the desk. He'd been holding it by one wing, like a hammer. He never turned around, and then he was gone. I didn't see his face." She closed her eyes, "Thank God," she said. "I couldn't go up to the window where he'd been. I couldn't look."

She finished her martini while I was signaling the waiter for another. When it was set in front of her, she looked at me and asked very simply, "What happened?"

I was about to try to tell her when, in the mirror behind the bar, I saw the image of Bill Macready and Sally entering. I held up my arm and waved to them. When they came over, Bill gave his order to the waiter and pulled up another chair to the table. He and Sally sat down gently, quietly. They had heard.

"What happened," I said to Betty, "is this. Mr. Namier went in with Conrad Medellin in Diamond Enterprises—remember the card he showed me by mistake?—and you know all that." Betty nodded. "Well, Diamond Enterprises is a kind of scavenger real-estate operation." Betty's mouth hardened. "That is to say, the point of the business was to operate without very much capital, but to move in on strategic properties wherever they could and extract the most money from them possible. It was mostly Medellin's show, but Mr. Namier went along for the ride and was an officer of the firm."

"He was so proud of himself," said Betty. She began to cry. "He told me that this was real business—hardball—that he was playing. He thought he was a tycoon, and then he laughed about it, about what Harold Ross of *The New Yorker* had called Henry Luce—'a baby tycoon.' " She sipped her drink.

"All right," I said. "It was mostly Medellin's operation, and I think he was leaning on Namier for more leads. You know, opportunities—association.

"And then Namier did come up with something. He knew that

Bill, here, was slated for the lead in a big production—that Bill would wind up with maybe millions, and there was no way that Bill was going to stay in that crumbling building. The building itself was the keystone to a big deal. The people who owned it were stumped. They had no inkling that Bill would not be there forever. Medellin made a special deal on the place, leaving those people the financial benefits of the entire package, but reserving a very nice piece of change for Diamond Enterprises if they could complete the deal. It took every dime that either Medellin or Namier could scrape up in the past, present, or future to get hold of the building. But they did. And then Bill began to back away from the part."

Both Sally and Betty looked accusingly at Bill. Bill, however, was looking at Edna.

"Medellin was in a spot," I continued, "but Namier was in hell. If Bill didn't go the way he was slated to, then Namier's real estate deal went down the drain, but what was worse, his job and his career went down with it.

"All that Medellin wanted was for the building to burn. But that would still not save Namier. Namier had to have Bill go down too. He went to Medellin to explain the situation: that the only way he could keep going was for Macready to die. If Macready died, then the whole deal would be off, because the Old Man was hooked on Macready, and saw the whole deal in terms of Macready."

Macready suddenly piped up, "The Old Man has resigned, you know. He did it yesterday. It was all planned. The show was supposed to be his signature. But nobody knew until just now. I mean, right now it's just going over the wires. Only two or three people in the network knew about it. Kite told me just before I came down here. He's at the airport right now on his way back to the Coast."

"All right," I said. "Medellin went out and hired some thugs to try to knock over Bill in some way that wouldn't raise too much of a stink. But Bill got wise and went underground. Medellin then decided, the hell with it, and got hold of Flick Ferrara. The results made both him and Mr. Namier happy because Benny the bum didn't have any more teeth than Bill does, so identification was impossible.

"After I brought in Medellin, Shope called Namier and said he wanted to talk to him. However, Medellin's lawyer got hold of Namier and tried to tell him what he should say. I had conned

Medellin into thinking that Namier had already spilled the beans. Medellin wanted to flatten me and make a rush to Brazil. Medellin is not as bright as his clothes.

"So that," I said to Betty, "is why Mr. Namier jumped."

"He needed money," said Betty.

"They don't pay him at the network?" I asked her.

"He has a house in Montclair, a wife, and three dim-witted children he's trying to put through college," said Betty. "He has an apartment in New York so that he doesn't lose his mind, and he has many, many commitments.

"Nobody can live on a salary, any salary. It doesn't work that way. The government takes it away from you, and unless you're a pirate, you go down."

"He was going to have Bill Macready murdered," I said, "in order to put his kids through school. Is that it?"

"You don't understand," said Betty. She began to cry again. Edna put her arm around Betty again, and she began to cry too. Bill Macready reached out his hand and touched Edna on the shoulder.

"Please don't cry," he said. She stopped instantly.

While Bill Macready was talking to Edna, I put my arm around Betty and tried to comfort her. We were a sad-looking little circle, but then, Jimmy Ray's has seen a lot of sadness as well as gaiety. I was flagging down the waiter for another round of drinks, based on the validity of my newly delivered check, when I noticed that Edna and Bill were standing up together. I queried Edna with my eyebrows.

"Bill has to go to a rehearsal," she said. "He invited me to come along and tell him what I think."

"Oh, Edna," I said despairingly. "Edna." But they were gone.

Sally watched them go. Her little Tom Sawyer face was very unhappy, and the freckles stood out on the pale skin. "And what," she asked of me, "am I supposed to do?"

"Try Wackenhut," I suggested, "or there's Pinkerton or Burns. A lot of outfits use labor spies. I'll be happy to give you a reference. It's a hard life, and the money isn't much, but you'll always have the emotional satisfaction of betraying your friends."

Sally got up and went over to the bar. She sat well away from the other customers and ordered a drink for herself.

Bety said to me almost challengingly, "You always thought I was sleeping with Vincent, didn't you?"

I answered, "I didn't permit myself to think about that."

"Well, I wasn't," said Betty. "I never did. The Paisley robe
vas a joke, and he would put it on when he came over to have a
rink. He didn't want to sleep with me. He just wanted to talk
nd be nice. He was a very lonely man, and now I'm a very
onely woman."

"Don't say that, Betty. I'm here. I'll be around."

"No . . . no." She shook her head. "I've thought about
ou." She touched my face. "I thought, 'Maybe this is it.' But
isn't. I couldn't live like that."

"You could live in a house in Montclair?" I suggested.

"Don't be dense," she instructed me. "That's not what I
nean. I thought I was tough. I've lived alone, earned my own
vay, stood on my own feet, and met the world. I'm proud of
nyself. I always thought I was—solid." She slapped her flank
vith her palm. "But that morning when I saw you put on the
un, and after, when I saw you—when you thought Bill was
ead—what you were like when you were dealing with the world
ut there. I couldn't live like that. I could never live like that.
hat's a different kind of toughness. It's crazy, ugly, illogical,
rutal, awful. I could never live like that."

I did not say anything about the smashed window.

"I'm so alone!" she cried.

I took her hand across the table. "Not for a while, Betty," I
aid. "Not for a while."

About the Author

JACK LIVINGSTON is an ex-merchant seaman who works as a medical editor and lives in upstate New York. His first mystery, *A Piece of the Silence,* was nominated as the best hardcover private eye novel of 1982 by the Private Eye Writers of America.